# MAYBE SHE WILL

## GINA ANDREW

*For L. and M., my greatest teachers*

# CHAPTER 1

*From: Gavin Steinberg <gsteinberg@psd41.org>*
*To: Josephine Palladino <momof2masterofnone@hmail.com>*
*Date: Wednesday, September 26, 1:02 p.m.*
*Subject: Special Education Meeting*

*Mrs. Palladino,*

*I'm writing to confirm our meeting for Friday at 8:15 a.m. We will be discussing Jackson's academic progress and goals that morning in room 109. Since you're new to the school, just remember to check in at the front office first by giving your child's full name, showing a valid photo id, and getting a nametag to wear at all times while you're in the building. Room 109 will be through the sliding doors, down the hall, and on your left.*

*The team and I are looking forward to meeting you there, Mrs. Palladino!*

*Make sure your photo identification is a valid, government-issued form. For a list of approved forms of such identification, see the school district website below.*

*Gavin Steinberg*

~

*J*osephine Palladino quickly scrolled through Gavin Steinberg's email, mentally noting the location of the meeting and the depressing level of modern school security before tossing her phone on the bed and scrambling to a nearby pile of laundry.

"I'm sorry, Mr. Steinberg," she said as she sifted through the clothes for something to replace her sheep pajama pants and oversized yellow nightshirt. "*Mrs.* Palladino won't be there today." She extracted a pair of black yoga pants. "But *Ms.* Palladino might make it, if she can manage to at least find a bra..."

Since all her shirts seemed to be missing in action, Jo was considering leaving the house in the yellow pajama shirt. Sure, she'd slept in it, but it didn't look like something you couldn't wear in the daytime. Technically.

"Are you talking to yourself again?"

Jo looked over to see her sixteen-year-old daughter, Kayla, standing in the threshold to the bedroom. Kayla was shaking her head, those dark curls she'd inherited from Jo bouncing—though with coiled streaks of dyed blue hair on each side.

As Jo blinked the sleep from her eyes, it also became clear Kayla had on what she recognized as her own *what the hell* face, an expression reserved for when one of her kids did something so beyond the pale, every muscle in her face had to get involved.

"We're going to be late," Kayla said. "Like really, really late."

Jo exhaled hard. "I know." She had woken four minutes ago in a panic, having slept through her alarm after falling asleep

2

late the night before reading her son Jackson's educational paperwork—all those indecipherable test results, legalistic academic goals, and cryptic teachers' notes—in prep for the morning's meeting. She'd even met the day with a page stuck to her face, affixed with drool. If that wasn't a metaphor for something, she didn't know what was.

"Two minutes," Jo said. "I'm treasure-hunting for a bra right now."

Kayla didn't care much about getting to school on time, but from growing up with an autistic brother, she knew that showing up tardy to a special education meeting wasn't good. Especially a meeting like this morning's.

"Okay." Kayla tossed an object in her direction, the item landing softly on the bed. "Anyway, I brought you breakfast."

Jo looked to see a small candy bar nestled in her comforter. She shook her head at Kayla, but snatched the chocolate up. "If we keep breaking into our Halloween stash, what are we going to hand out to the kids?"

"Those baby carrots we never eat," Kayla said, ripping open her own fun-sized bar.

"Good point." Jo added, "Is Jackson—"

"He's up. He's eating cereal." Kayla turned around, strolling away as she munched on her bar.

"Okay. Okay..." Jo inhaled the chocolate while stumbling into the yoga pants, then she returned to rummaging through the clothing pile, quicker this time, violently shoving items to the ground—a nightgown, a pair of jeans, one of Jackson's shirts, and half a dozen socks that they could normally never find. Finally, she discovered a cherry-colored bra at the bottom of the pile, hiding out for a more special opportunity.

She wouldn't normally wear a bright red bra on the day of a parent-teacher conference, but sometimes the universe had other ideas.

"Aha! You'll do." Jo plucked it up and fastened it underneath her shirt. It was well over a decade old—probably some bachelorette gift she'd forgotten to throw out—but desperate times called for inappropriate lingerie. No one would notice it under her giant yellow shirt, anyway.

Grabbing the stack of papers she'd fallen asleep in and shoving them under her arm, she ran to the bathroom to run a toothbrush over her teeth and fasten her curls back with a clip, then darted to the kitchen where she could hear the *pings* of the game Jackson was playing on his iPad.

Kayla stood by the stove, eating cereal from the box by the handful and scrolling through her phone.

Shoving the pages into her bag on the table, Jo reached over and ruffled her son's soft brown hair.

"Morning, Jax." She feathered a quick kiss on his head before bending down, checking if his shoes were on. They weren't. "Bud, we need to get your socks and shoes on. Like right now."

His eyes still focused on his game, he let out a low grunt— her younger, nearly nonverbal child's way of telling his mother he didn't want to deal with her.

"C'mon, Jax."

A soft hacking noise came from the other side of the kitchen. She and Kayla both turned to see their old black cat, Chuck, coughing up a hairball.

"Gross," Kayla said.

"We don't have time to deal with that," Jo said, running over to the door and grabbing Jackson's shoes. "Jackson, shoes on. Now."

Setting the device down and pushing his chair back, Jax walked over and grabbed the sneakers, sitting on the floor and putting them on.

While Jo shoved her own feet into sneakers, she watched over her shoulder to make sure Jax was putting the right shoe on the right foot. It was times like these that she wished there was another adult in the house. But it'd been just the three of them for eight and a half years. If only Neil hadn't—

"Mom!"

Jo's heart skipped a beat. She whipped around to see Kayla staring at her phone, her brown eyes large.

"What? *What?*"

"The Fisticuffs broke up."

"The *who?*"

"The Fisticuffs. That band I love."

"Okay." Jo released a shaky breath. "This morning's rule: if it doesn't have to do with us all leaving this house in one piece in the next two minutes, I don't want to know about it."

"But it's really sad."

"I'm sure it is." She grabbed her bag and headed for the front. "Okay, let's go."

Jax stood up from the floor. "Fish," he said.

"Jackson," Jo said. "We're late. Pickles and Prometheus can wait."

"Seriously," Kayla said, stowing her phone in the pocket of her skinny jeans. "They're getting really fat. We've got fat fish."

"Kayla, don't fat-shame the fish. Jackson, we're super late, buddy. Later?"

"*Fish,*" Jackson repeated, his voice cracking in the way it had been more lately—yet another sign he was entering puberty, but they were late and there was the meeting, so Jo stowed that away to freak out about later in the day.

Jackson's green eyes—also from her—were resolute, and Jo guessed they weren't going to make it out of the house without their fat fish getting breakfast.

She sighed. "Okay."

Jackson strode over to the fish tank and took down the container of fish food, rocking on his feet. The fish swam to the glass as Jackson pushed the lid away, their eyes wide and adoring at their master. He sprinkled a few flakes from the container on the surface of the water, slowly and carefully.

"Nice job, Jax," Jo said as he closed the container and slid the aquarium lid back, his eyes on the fish as they nibbled the flakes from the water's surface.

Exhaling, Jo turned to open the front door when Kayla yelled, "Jax!"

Jo's heart stuttered. She whirled around.

*"What?"*

"Chuck's hairball," Kayla said, her pretty face scrunched into a look of disgust. "Jackson just stepped into it."

Jo threw up her hands. "Well, don't just stand there!"

Kayla darted over to keep Jackson from tracking the cat's vomit around while Jo ran over to the kitchen and grabbed the roll of paper towels. Jackson stood in place, rocking, his eyes down as his sneaker squished against the floor.

Well, it probably did make an interesting sensation.

Jo kneeled in front of him with a wad of paper towels. "Okay, Jax, lift your foot."

He did—a gangly boy in flamingo pose—as she wiped the vomit off his shoe and the floor.

"Our cat's too fat too," Kayla whispered, and Jo snorted in response.

The adrenaline pounding in her veins, Jo threw the towels in the trash and declared, "Okay, *now* we're going."

They trudged out of the house and into the car, where the rays of late summer sunlight made Jackson sneeze and reminded Jo of how very late they were going to be.

She started the car and turned on the music. "Okay, Jackson: *1989* or *Folkore?*"

"*1989!*"

"Not again," Kayla said. "I should've ridden with Misty." She crossed her legs and slouched down in the seat.

A music snob, Kayla had taken to only listening to bands

whose names sounded like a bunch of Old West rabble-rousers. Yet as Jo pulled out of the driveway with a pop tune of Taylor Swift's cartwheeling out of the speakers, her daughter's leg bounced in time with the music.

Jackson was in the backseat clutching a white plastic clothing hanger, his favorite comfort object of late. He watched its movements as he twisted it back and forth like a dial. "Music," he called without looking at them.

"Taylor Swift," Jo said automatically. This was a thing they did; in the past year, Jax liked them to identify the artist of whatever song was playing, even if he already knew the answer.

"Music," he called a minute later.

Kayla sighed. "Still Taylor Swift."

Jackson laughed and rocked happily in the backseat.

Jo pushed down the gas pedal, only her heartbeat dancing. The meeting this morning was important—one she couldn't afford to not bring her A game to. And after the hectic start to the day, she felt barely in C minus territory. She needed to pull it together—for Jackson.

Her son had started junior high several weeks ago, and he was struggling.

Back in elementary school, Jo had worried about him less. They'd been past those early, hard years after his diagnoses— first autism, then later intellectual disability. She knew some things, and then elementary school had lasted six years, plenty of time to acclimate to the culture and staff. Jackson had always had nice, pathologically positive teachers there—usually women in their twenties or early thirties who always exclaimed how much they loved her son at every opportunity. Their coordinator, who ran special education meetings and completed the related paperwork, had been a woman named Marian who wore hand-knit sweaters and always started and ended each meeting with, "Isn't Jackson a joy? An absolute joy." Jo had had to hold herself back from mouthing the words along with the woman—not that she didn't agree.

Now she realized she didn't appreciate Marian while she was in their lives. Because junior high was a whole different beast. Despite Jackson being in a separate special education classroom housed in a regular school, there were different schedules and particular rules, and his teacher had been calling and emailing her a few times a week with "concerns" about her son's behavior. Not to mention that the school district coordinator—their main point of contact—was this Gavin Steinberg, who wrote boilerplate emails to her like he was her bank loan officer. Every time she read his emails, she could almost hear the ping of him checking it off on some daily tasks app. The *Mrs.* was just the icing on the cake.

From the passenger seat, Kayla started laughing.

"What?" Jo braked at a stoplight.

"You've got a word on your face."

"What?"

"On your cheek. It's in red and, like, in reverse. Did you fall asleep reading paperwork again?"

"Shoot." Jo slapped down her driver's side mirror and turned her face. Sure enough, there on her right cheek in faded red ink was a single word, *Functioning*. She could read it in the mirror, but probably to anyone who saw her, it looked backwards.

If that wasn't also a metaphor for her life...

"Ugh." It was just another thing—like her hastily-put-together outfit and late arrival—that was going to make this meeting that much harder.

"I'll wipe it off after I drop off Jackson," she said, after rubbing the smudge to no success. The light turned green and a car honked behind her. "I'm going, I'm going."

"I'm going, I'm going," Jackson repeated in the back seat.

"That's right, Jax," Jo said. "You tell them."

She hadn't met Gavin Steinberg in person yet, but she could

already tell he wasn't the type to wear hand-knit sweaters—he nor any of his band of educational executioners who would be at the meeting. Because, based on the calls from his teacher— her voice hesitant over the phone, her many "concerns"—she guessed that they were going to take a hatchet to Jackson's academic goals at this very meeting, cutting down what they thought he could achieve, hacking away at all the progress they'd made.

Jo wasn't going to let them.

She dropped Kayla off at the high school before speeding to the nearby junior high, hitting the brakes hard right before the school zone sign and coasting into the lot. The school, which was mostly full of typically-developing students, looked like many in the Philadelphia suburbs where they lived: two stories of dark red brick sitting on a lot of green grass, with newer wings growing from the older heart of the building.

One of the assistants in Jackson's class was waiting around the circular drop-off area for special education students, her arms crossed and her mouth in a firm line. Jo pulled into a parking spot and sighed. After unbuckling her seatbelt and walking around to Jackson's door to let him out, they walked up to the assistant.

"School," Jackson said. "School, school, school."

"Yeah, school."

A few feet before the assistant, Jo turned and caught him in a big hug, squeezing him tight. He patted her back rhythmically, probably in tune to some Taylor Swift song in his head. He was already almost her height; in a few years, he'd have half a head on her.

"Don't worry, Jax," she whispered. "Mama's going to go in there and fight like hell for you."

The assistant cleared her throat, and Jo reluctantly released her son. She watched him walk away a beat, blinking back the tears that'd suddenly filled her eyes. Then she entered the building to sign in at the front desk with her government-issued identification.

"They've all been waiting for you," the brunette woman at the front desk said, handing her a nametag and hitting a buzzer to unlock the sliding glass doors to the classrooms. "You can go ahead and walk down. Room 109."

Jo took a deep breath and strode towards the room.

She would fight. Her son deserved it. He was *an absolute joy*, dammit.

At the door marked 109, she stopped. Collected herself. Raised her knuckles to the door.

She'd barely knocked when the door opened to a younger white man with tousled brown hair offering her a polite smile and an outstretched hand.

So this must be Gavin Steinberg.

Her shoulders slumped. God, it was worse than she thought.

He was wearing a tie.

# CHAPTER 2

*G*avin held out his hand as Josephine Palladino walked into the room.

"Mrs. Palladino," he said. "It's nice to finally meet you."

The woman smiled slightly and held out her hand to shake.

"Hello," she said, her voice tight. She nodded to the others around the rectangular conference table—her son's teacher, the speech therapist, an occupational therapist, and a regular education teacher—but mostly she looked like she was walking into a room full of centipedes.

Gavin stifled a groan. Some days, he missed his old job in sales. Despite the twelve-hour days and frequent travel, at least he'd kept happy customers.

Smiling wider to make her more comfortable, he grasped her palm and gave her a friendly shake.

"So glad you could join us," he said. "We're just getting started."

"Sorry I'm late," she said, pulling out a chair to his right, one close to the door. "We had a rough start today."

"No worries at all," he said, walking back to his spot before sliding an attendance sheet and folder across the table. "We'll just have you sign in and look over some of the usual procedural safeguards—I'm sure you're familiar with those—before we dive in."

"Sure." She nodded, her attention focused on the pages he passed to her.

Gavin leaned back and gave her a few minutes.

Ah, the dreaded special education IEP meeting. Technically it stood for individual education plan, but, in his head, he liked to make up alternatives. *Inconvenient enigmatic paperwork* was one of the latest ones, or, when it got heated, itty-bitty earsplitting party. Not that they were all bad, or all the parents as tense as this one, but a meeting was a meeting, and he'd had some uncomfortable ones since he'd started this position last spring.

This one had the potential to be uncomfortable.

Mrs. Palladino's gaze met his, one eyebrow raised, as he realized—too late—that he'd been softly humming a song that he'd heard on the radio on the way over.

"Sorry," he said quickly, and they both looked away.

The junior high meeting room was freshly vacuumed and had a stash of colorful electronic toys on one end of the table—necessary distractions for parents who needed to come to these meetings with younger kids. Gavin was half-tempted to tap on the rainbow-hued keyboard himself some days.

"It's really nice out today," Jackson Palladino's teacher, Jeannie, said from down the table. "Great weather for late September."

They all nodded and murmured agreement, waiting for the mom to finish the paperwork. Though she'd probably been to a dozen or more of these meetings, Josephine Palladino slowly and carefully read over the paperwork explaining her rights and options as a parent—she was one of those. Which probably meant she was well-educated, smart, and ready to go to bat for her kid. A wave of apprehension moved down his spine.

Her look was what Gavin had come to think of as momwear: yoga pants, bright sneakers, and a ponytail. It varied across a range: some of the more appearance-conscious moms had sleek ponytails, name-brand pants, and rings on each finger as they clutched a trendy latte across the table. Mrs. Palladino was on the other end of the range. Her yellow shirt was big and wrinkled, like she'd slept in it, and her ponytail was fighting a losing battle with the curly dark brown hair it was intended to hold back, a chunk having found its way out, if it was even in to begin with. She had a smattering of light freckles across her nose and definitely hadn't bothered with makeup.

But she had a smudge on her cheekbone. As she bowed down to sign her name at the bottom of a form, Gavin squinted at what looked like letters on her pale skin. They were in red ink—some kind of word. Except it was backwards. He peered closer, trying to decipher the letters. *F-u-n...*

*Functioning?*

A grin tugged at the corners of his mouth. If he was a betting man, he'd guess she'd face-planted in some paperwork last night.

Josephine Palladino looked up and he straightened, averting his eyes. Probably best not to mention it and embarrass her. She pushed the paperwork towards him.

"Great." He smiled, taking the pages and sliding them into a folder. "Let's get started. Jeannie, do you want to start by going over Jackson's current progress?"

"Sure." The teacher tucked her blonde, iron-straight hair behind each ear and looked down at her notes. "Well, Jackson started in my class five weeks ago. I've been taking data on all of his goals since he started."

She passed the mom a sheet of paper, then handed a copy to Gavin for his records.

"As we've talked about," Jeannie continued. "We've been seeing a lot of regression—in all areas."

Mrs. Palladino's mouth fell open as she scanned the data sheet.

Gavin glanced at the page. It held several line graphs. All of them looked like ski slopes he'd be too chicken to go down.

"For instance," Jeannie said, "in the area of communication, Jackson has been using less language than his former school reported he used last spring. And he seems to be using his words less and less, especially two- and three-word phrases."

"Even when using his speech device?" Mrs. Palladino asked.

"He doesn't seem to like to use it," Jeannie said.

Mrs. Palladino frowned.

"We're seeing similar data across all goals," the teacher continued. "He's gone from identifying 50 sight words to less than 30. He is still able to count to 100 and label his numbers, but he's not progressing, and he seems unable or unwilling to trace numbers or his name like he had previously. He does seem to like to trace the hands of certain preferred staff members, but sometimes that can interfere with his need to do other work." She turned a page. "Greeting peers or staff, even with prompting, is a struggle. We've also seen his frustration levels increase, to the point we've seen him try to strike some of the staff."

"Obviously what you're doing isn't working," the mom said to Jeannie.

Everyone in the room froze. No one else spoke, but eyes darted between the teacher and Mrs. Palladino.

"Well," Jeannie began, "something *is* off, in the sense that he hasn't been progressing. Have there been any changes at home?"

"No," Mrs. Palladino said.

"Any deaths in the family, separations…"

"No," Mrs. Palladino said. "Just this school."

She stared hard at Jeannie. The room was steeped in silence, and the tension made the back of Gavin's neck itch.

He put up a hand. "Mrs. Palladino, I think we're all in agreement that given this data, we need to look at changing our approach with Jackson." He looked around the table at the other women, who all nodded.

Mrs. Palladino turned to him. Her posture was stiff, her gestures hard. "Look, I know Jackson's been struggling some, but this has been a big change for us—for him. It's normal for kids to regress once they've started a new school, right?" She exhaled. "I know he can meet these goals, we just have to—"

"Mrs. Palladino—" he started.

"—give him more time," she continued. "Maybe by October, November he'll be—"

"We're not suggesting a change to Jackson's goals," Gavin said, his stomach twisting in the anticipation of delivering the news, "although that might be more realistic. We're suggesting he be moved to a different classroom."

Josephine Palladino stopped and stared at him, her voice low. "What?"

"The team feels Jackson would be better served in an alternate classroom," he said smoothly, keeping his voice as professional and reasonable as possible. "As you're aware, he's just not making progress in Jeannie's class. We understand that when students enter new classrooms, there will be a period of regression. But it's been over a month and we're—"

"Which classroom?" Her eyes narrowed.

"When we suggest a possible shift in classes, we of course take all factors into consideration," he said, padding the news to come with logic.

"*Which* classroom?"

He clasped his fingers on the table and leaned forward. "Jackson's currently in a class of eight students, and maybe that's not the best fit. We think he'd do better with a smaller class size and more individual attention. The other students in Jackson's room now are—well, they are working on tasks Jackson is still struggling with. And, as a result, we're seeing behaviors that have become difficult to manage—"

Mrs. Palladino slapped her hand on the table and leaned in. "Which classroom do you want to put my son in?"

Gavin cleared his throat. "There's a spot that's opened up in another classroom at Rydell Junior High, and we think that would be the most appropriate placement for Jackson at this time."

Her green eyes widened. "You mean you want to move him somewhere so he can learn *fewer* skills. You mean that my kid couldn't hack it in his current class, so he's being demoted. You're giving up on him."

"That's not the case," Gavin said quickly, but she ignored him.

"Jackson doesn't do well with change. We just started here, and yet another change is going to make him regress even more. He needs more time. The answer is *no*."

"Mrs. Palladino, the team here thinks this would be the most appropriate fit. Maybe if you could tour the class…"

"No."

Gavin glanced around the room, but the others looked away. He got it. When the situation got this heated, it was his job to be the peacemaker. He fought the urge to yank the tie away from his throat.

"And, anyway," Josephine Palladino said, her eyes lit with a fire Gavin couldn't seem to extinguish, "who's this 'we' you're always talking about? Am I a part of this 'we'?"

"Of course," he said. "We're a team here."

"Really," she said, and it wasn't a question. She lifted her hands in the air to finger-quote. "Because it seems like 'the team' already made this decision before I got to the room."

"Mrs. Palladino…"

"No." She shook her head. "He needs a fair shake in his current class before you write him off. He's not going into yet another new class."

Gavin exhaled and opened up the folder in front of him. He

hated to be a Numbers Guy, but it was time to break out the big guns. He had to do his job.

"This is a big position," Charlene, the Director of Special Ed, had told him when he interviewed for the job last spring. "You need to keep in mind what's best for the entire district. That means considering the kids as a whole. Appropriate placements, yes, but also which classrooms have space and which are overcrowded, how many kids will be transitioning in and out in a given year—and of course budget constraints." Her eyes were half a shade deeper than her dark skin, and she rolled them heavenward and put her hands palm up. "Would that we had an unlimited sum of money in education. But that's not the case."

"I get it," he'd said. "There's a certain amount of money to work with. We have to allocate it wisely."

"Hmm, yes." She clasped her hands together and leaned forward. "I'm going to be honest: this job is like doing one of those 500-piece puzzles. But about thirty times more frustrating, especially if you're sitting in a room with a parent who wants their child to have everything. I need to know if you can handle it."

"I can handle it." At his last job, he'd been the top salesman for years, selling millions of dollars of software. He could be friendly, he could be calm, he could be funny. He could convince executives and startups that the educational software he sold was what they needed.

When he'd turned thirty, he'd realized his soul was slowly leaking out of him, and what he'd always thought he wanted wasn't what he wanted after all. Not selling software for a successful Philadelphia company, not dating the nice Jewish girl his mother adored, not doing the thing all his friends were doing, which was proposing marriage, throwing a big splashy wedding, and starting a family. He didn't know what he really wanted, but it wasn't that.

His bachelor's degree had been in education before he'd

gotten sucked into sales, so he'd switched positions by returning to his roots, but in an administrative capacity. But he hadn't counted on mothers like Josephine Palladino.

Gavin cleared his throat. The problem was, there'd been steep budget cuts in the district. For the livelihood of the entire special education department, they needed to close some classes and consolidate others to save money, especially with new kids entering the program all the time. Jackson Palladino's class was first on the chopping block—not that they were announcing that publicly and stirring up panic, as Charlene made clear. They just needed to move the students there to the next most appropriate placement. Sending a new kid struggling in the class to a half-full class at Rydell just made sense.

He started speaking, looking between his records and the mom. "At Jackson's former school, he was in a classroom of four to six students, where he made steady progress. It was also less academically rigorous, more play-centered. It's possible Jeannie's classroom wasn't the best fit, but he had been meeting his goals, and we like to see if we can challenge our students."

"You think my son's not up for a challenge?" she snapped.

"I didn't say that." He coughed, trying a different tactic. "Don't you want Jackson to succeed?"

Her eyes hardened into a glare. "Of course I do." With a huff, Mrs. Palladino reached down to dig in her bag. "I've got my own data," she said. "Yours is wrong. His elementary class was seven students at some points, and he did fine. And he used his device regularly."

Jeannie and the staff looked away, clearly uncomfortable.

"Okay." Gavin folded his hands on the table and kept his voice even. "If you have any records you can share, we'd of course find that helpful."

"I know I have it here somewhere..." Shuffling pages, Josephine Palladino leaned forward further, and, as she did, her yellow top gaped open, revealing what looked like a—*red bra?*

"Um, that's...okay..." Startled by her lingerie, Gavin's thoughts didn't so much derail as smash into an oncoming train. The garment was bright red and lacy, and fetching as hell on her.

And he couldn't seem to look away.

She was still digging in her bag. "Shoot. I thought I had it..."

Straightening up, the bra disappeared from view, Mrs. Palladino's shirt fell back in place, and Gavin managed to avert his eyes. Somewhere in there he remembered to breathe.

He darted a quick glance around. The others were all either studying their notes or staring at the table. He let out a breath. At least no one had noticed him unintentionally ogling this mom. *She* was certainly oblivious in her ire.

What had he been saying? *Was it even his turn to talk?*

"Mrs. Palladino," he began, going back a few thoughts, "I—I think we can all agree we want Jackson to s-succeed."

She met his gaze. "Yes, but we certainly don't agree how we can get there, do we?"

"No?" He didn't know what he was saying.

"No," she answered, raising her eyebrows.

"Oh."

Gavin stared at her, his mind blank. All he could think was *red bra red bra red bra.*

She shook her head at him, like she couldn't even. Which was fair.

She stood up. "I think we're done here."

"Wait!" Gavin reached out a hand. "Mrs.—if you could just sit down a moment and we can talk about this calmly—"

"Calmly? *Calmly?*" She shook her head again, and another curl sprung from her ponytail. "You realize we're talking about my kid here, don't you? The one you're supposed to be looking out for."

"We are looking out for Jackson, Mrs. Palladino." Gavin was starting to get a headache and he sure as hell needed another coffee. Maybe spiked with vodka. "I think we'll be able to find him the most appropriate placement—"

"Enough with your 'most appropriate placement' crap!" Her irises held twin flames. "What are you, twenty-eight? Do you even have kids?"

"No, I—"

She huffed. "I don't need some jerk in a suit to tell me what's appropriate for my kid."

"Mrs. Palladino..."

Gavin wasn't sure the precise moment he'd lost total control of the meeting, but it was probably when he'd caught sight of that red bra. Were they teaching parents in support groups this as a diversionary tactic?

"No." She pressed her lips together. "This meeting is over." In anger, she pushed her stack of paper toward him—then, reconsidering, snatched them up and headed for the door. As she turned, her ponytail of curls swung to the side, like an axe at an execution.

He stumbled up to half-standing, leaning on the table for moral support. "Let's... We—Mrs. Palladino—"

She wheeled around. "And it's *Ms.*, not *Mrs.* Jackson's father bailed before we even had our first one of these meetings."

She walked out the door and slammed it behind her.

# CHAPTER 3

*A*fter the meeting, Jo found the idea of finalizing the details of a retired couple's trip to a nudist beach resort nearly impossible.

She'd work on it later, when she calmed down. Her job as a travel agent afforded her the flexibility to work from home, and she usually used the time wisely while the kids were at school to contact clients and hotels, research trips, and take care of the minutiae that traveling entailed. And her job was interesting, especially since she'd acquired a reputation for serving clients who wanted unusual travel destinations.

But right now she was too furious to sit still, wringing her hands and pacing the house and trying not to trip over Chuck when he wound his furry black form through her legs.

The nerve of the district to suggest Jackson should move to another classroom at a totally new school—especially after he had already been through one transition this fall. Had they never met an autistic kid? Did they not know how difficult even small changes could be?

In third grade, Jackson's teacher had left on maternity leave. Although the long-term sub was good, the change alone had caused Jackson to lose six months of progress. To a lesser degree, the same thing had happened last year when school construction meant he'd had to switch to another location in the building. If he went to yet another new class, Jo feared, he would have even more issues.

"Uhh!" She ran her hands through her curls as she paced the living room again. She'd wanted to tear that tie off Gavin Steinberg at the meeting, then push it down his throat. What she would've given to have Marian with her sweaters and cloying phrases still be their coordinator.

Could she fight it? If so, how? A lawyer was out of the question—too expensive—and Jo wasn't sure she could afford a special education advocate, either. Honestly, she'd never looked into advocates, because she'd never needed to. The staff at Jackson's elementary school had always seemed to have his best interests in mind—unlike Gavin Steinberg and his "team."

In the meantime, would the school move forward with its plans to relocate her son?

An hour after the meeting, she'd received an email from the jerk himself.

*Ms. Palladino*, it began, not *Mrs.*, and Jo rolled her eyes because at least he'd listened to something, *I'm sorry this morning's meeting became so heated. I know these conversations can be difficult. We would like to reschedule a meeting to discuss Jackson's placement further. I'll contact you later today with times the team can meet next week. If you do not wish to hold another meeting, I've attached an outline of your rights as a parent to this email...*

She'd been so annoyed to see his name pop up on her phone that she hadn't opened the attachment. She would later, of course. One thing she knew for sure: she'd probably be falling asleep in paperwork again the next couple nights, until she could figure this out. At least the weekend allowed her a few days to plan a strategy.

Maybe ripping that tie off Gavin Steinberg's neck and shoving it down his throat could be part of that strategy...

The ringing of her phone startled her out of her revenge fantasies.

"Hello?" Jo answered, not recognizing the number.

"Is this... Josephine Palladino?" a woman asked. "The travel agent?"

Jo took a deep breath, focusing her mind. "It sure is."

The woman on the line wanted her to plan a honeymoon to London. Grabbing a pen and pad as she jotted down notes in the kitchen, Jo launched into describing how great the city was, the must-see sights, and the best places for a couple to stay. She welcomed the distraction, waxing rhapsodically about Britain and how much they'd love it.

Truth be told, Jo had never been to England—never been to most of the places her clients traveled, in fact—but thanks to the internet, she didn't have to experience these vacations herself to know what they were like. She could tell clients the exact hues of a sunset on the Florida coast or how nice that Colorado bed and breakfast owner really was without leaving her suburban Pennsylvania home. Which suited her tremendously, since she wasn't a fan of travel—although she did admit to sparks of envy at how excited some clients sounded at the prospect of relaxing for a week or more. The last time she felt relaxed had been in the waiting room at her gynecologist, a space devoid of her children and reminders of work, with a stack of magazines and a lengthy wait time Jo, and Jo alone, had been grateful for. In every other context, she usually had things she should be wiping or researching or fretting about.

As the woman told Jo about her fiancé and what he was interested in doing on the honeymoon, Jo's mind briefly wandered to Neil. They'd honeymooned by taking a simple camping trip out west. They'd planned to hike, but it'd rained most of the trip, so they'd huddled inside the tent and gotten their energy out another way—a way that brought them Kayla nine months later.

Looking back, the rain had been an omen. They had been happy enough together, but when Jackson came along, he'd proved there were weaknesses in the foundation of their marriage. Or maybe that was just Neil. He began gradually pulling away as Jackson had neared his second birthday and gone from singing a few nursery rhymes to barely speaking. They didn't understand why—or felt inklings that they buried under the busyness of parenthood and a rich layer of denial. Their son would be fine. He was just a late bloomer. Her dentist's niece didn't talk until she was five, and now she was a college professor. Jackson was constantly rocking or moving, but he was an active kid and that was great, wasn't it? Everything would be fine. Kayla hadn't been like that as a baby, but then again she was a girl, and boys were a completely different species, weren't they?

Then came doctor's visits and early intervention therapies and moments where she wondered if everything wouldn't be fine. If there was something different about Jackson, something that would make it harder for him to move through the world. Sometimes she felt tears spring to her eyes, but she'd bury her face on top of the soft brown hair on Jackson's head, whispering how much she loved him.

But Neil—Neil pulled away. From all of them.

Though he now lived two time zones away, he still kept in touch with his daughter, calling her on her birthday and Christmas—conversations that didn't last long, probably because Kayla gave her father one-word replies to almost everything. Jo's heart ached when she thought of what Kayla must've experienced. It might've been a big change for Jackson too, but he didn't remember Neil. Kayla remembered. Two years ago, she'd sneered and shown Jo a picture up on social media of Neil on his honeymoon with his new wife. They were at the Grand

Canyon and it was sunny—blindingly so, from their squinty smiles as they wrapped their arms around each other.

Well, let him have the Grand Canyon. They had something better. Not easy. Better.

As she ended the call with the client, assuring her that she just had to see Big Ben, there was nothing like it, a car rumbled to a stop outside. Jo walked over to peek out the window.

Kayla was in the passenger seat of a car pulled in front of the house, but instead of Misty's ride—her usual way home—it was a dark sedan Jo didn't recognize.

A car with a boy in it.

"Who's that?" she whispered to the window.

It was hard to see through the tinted car windows. She could make out the shape of what looked like a guitar case in the backseat, and stickers for unfamiliar bands adorned the car's bumper. The boy in front had dirty blond hair that fell into his eyes, and, as he cut off the engine, he leaned across the seat and kissed Kayla on the mouth.

Jo inhaled sharply and stepped away from the window, racing towards the kitchen so her daughter didn't notice her snooping.

*A boy.* This was new. This was—Jo didn't know what this was.

She busied herself in the kitchen, pouring herself a cup of cold coffee from the pot, as the front door slammed a few minutes later and Kayla walked in.

"I'm home!" the girl shouted, her backpack thudding on the floor.

"Hi, I'm in here." Jo bit her lip. "Do you want something to eat?"

Kayla appeared in the threshold to the kitchen in jeans and a tight purple shirt. Her cheeks were flushed, and she was doing a funny thing with her mouth, like she was trying not to grin.

Jo gave up trying to play cool. "Okay. Who's the boy?"

Kayla's mouth flew open. "You were spying on me!"

"Give me a break, I've had a bad day." Jo grabbed her mug and took a sip of cold coffee. "I just heard the car pull up and checked to see who it was. Was Misty sick today? Or is she just not as good of a goodbye kisser?"

"Oh my God." Kayla opened the fridge, kneeling on the floor to rummage in its contents and blocking herself from view. "He's just a guy who gave me a ride home."

"I got that much." Jo bit back a smile. "Does he have a name? Does he play that guitar or just use it to get girls?"

Kayla ignored her. "Do we have any peanut butter?" she said behind the door.

"Probably. Check in the plastic bag underneath the pears. I'm hiding it from Jackson right now. He ate half the jar yesterday."

"Why'd you have a bad day?" Kayla mumbled as crinkling sounds emanated from the fridge.

"Uggghh…" The details of the meeting came raining down on Jo like a garbage spill. She took a moment to gulp down more coffee. Jackson would be home on the bus in half an hour, and she had a feeling she'd be downing brew 24/7 with all the work she had in front of her.

"The meeting?" Kayla asked.

"Yup."

Her daughter emerged from the fridge, a loaf of bread in one hand and peanut butter under her arm, and kicked the door shut with her foot. She weaved around Jo to grab a knife from the silverware drawer. "They try to change his goals?"

"Worse." Jo folded her arms. "They want to switch him to another classroom."

"Why?"

"They said he's not making progress."

"Is he making progress?"

"I don't know…" Jo uncrossed her arms and looked away. "No. But it's a new school. To be honest, I don't know if it *is* the right classroom for him, but the hell if I'm going to let them move him to yet another classroom and make everything worse."

Kayla unwrapped the bread, pulling out two slices which she spread with copious amounts of peanut butter. "That sucks." She put her sandwich together and moved towards the kitchen table, taking a big bite along the way.

"Yeah, it does."

Kayla sat at the table, glancing at some school paperwork Jo had left there. "*Present levels of functioning*," she read off the top sheet. "Huh. Sounds like a band name." She pulled out a thick, shiny piece of cardstock that peeked out from underneath her brother's records. "We got another college thing?"

"Yeah, I just hadn't gotten a chance to put it in the box yet." A junior, Kayla had started getting brochures and flyers in the mail from schools around the country. Jo found it irritatingly early—they'd figure that out next year, when it was more on the horizon—so they'd just been stacking the mail in a big cardboard box to sift through at a later date. The box had originally been beside the dining room table, until Jo had found it made her increasingly depressed and had stashed it in one of the kitchen cabinets, out of sight and usually out of mind.

Kayla sighed and took a bite of her sandwich.

Jo walked around the counter to sit across from her daughter. "Listen, I'm going to need you to watch Jackson some this weekend. I've got to go over his paperwork and make some calls, see how I can present an argument to the school district to stop this from happening."

Kayla put down her sandwich. "I've got another idea. Maybe you can get a life."

Jo flinched. "What?"

Kayla rolled her eyes. "You do this stuff all the time. Paperwork, goals, all those books… even when he doesn't have an IEP meeting."

Jo crossed her arms. "It's important, Kayla."

"I know, but... don't you ever get sick of it?"

"I'm sick of it all the time," Jo said. "That doesn't mean I don't do it. That's adulthood, kid."

Kayla peeled off a piece of crust and set it aside. "No, it's not. I mean, Misty's mom at least goes out with friends once in a while. She has this group of other moms, and Misty says they go have margaritas at Applebee's every Friday, and she comes home tipsy and tells Misty stories about the guys she dated in high school."

"Well, that's great for Fiona." God, she'd kill for a margarita about right now. "I go out too, you know. I went out with some friends the other week, remember?"

"Those aren't your friends," Kayla said. "That was your special needs parent support group. It's not the same."

"Says someone who's never needed a support group."

Kayla peeled off the rest of her crust, forming a neat pile before taking a bite of her sandwich. "I mean you don't have normal friends," she said. "Friends who don't have special needs kids, or work with special needs kids... friends you can get buzzed with and talk about your old boyfriends with."

"I've repressed all those memories." Jo frowned. "And I do have other friends."

Kayla met her gaze. "Name one."

"Holly and I talk about normal things."

"Bzz! *No*," Kayla said, like Jo had lost on a game show. "She used to work as Jackson's therapist. She's your friend because you used to pay her."

"I don't pay her now," Jo said. "And we exchanged Christmas gifts."

"Doesn't count." Kayla polished off her sandwich and wiped her hands on her jeans while Jo pressed her lips together and thought furiously. She was friendly with the lady who worked the counter at the pharmacy. Did that count? Would she be able to ask her out for margaritas and swap high school dating horror stories?

Kayla raised an eyebrow. "That's what I thought."

"Don't look at me like that!" Jo said.

"Like what?"

"Like I'm your mother and I'm uncool."

Kayla went to the fridge and pulled out a carton of milk. "You said it, not me."

Jo set her elbows on the table and slumped her chin in her hands. "Man, this day keeps getting better and better."

Six months ago, she couldn't have imagined Kayla saying these things to her. Her daughter had had friends back then, sure, but she'd spent a lot of nights curled up in Jo's bed watching crime shows with her. They'd both gasped and sighed at the same parts, felt a similar satisfaction when the perp was caught. Real life was rarely so cut-and-dried. But since she turned sixteen, she was home less often—off with friends who had driver's licenses, putting weird colors in her hair, apparently meeting boys.

Kayla looked over as she poured a tall glass of milk. "His name is Austin."

Jo dropped her hands and turned in her seat. She failed again at being nonchalant; she couldn't keep the smile off her face. "Is he in a band?"

"Shut up," Kayla said.

Jo's phone pinged. She made the mistake of glancing at it.

It was another email from Gavin Steinberg, something about his free times to reschedule a meeting.

She groaned, but then her gut twisted.

If she was going to be preparing all weekend for their next meeting, would he be doing the same?

# CHAPTER 4

$\mathcal{H}$is muscles tensing, Gavin grabbed the barbell over his head and pushed it into the air.

"So how's it going?" Angelo asked from the bench beside him.

Gavin exhaled hard as he set the weight back down. "Okay. Well, I had an IEP meeting yesterday, so that was a blast." He gripped the barbell and lifted it again, grimacing as he remembered the scorn on Josephine Palladino's face as she'd walked out of the meeting.

Angelo chuckled. "IEP season, man." He pushed his own barbell up, almost effortlessly from Gavin's side glance.

A thickly-muscled man with close-cropped blond hair and gray eyes, Angelo was a personal trainer, but he also worked part-time as a speech therapist in the school district—it was how they'd met last spring, when they'd gotten into a conversation that transitioned from wheelchairs to biceps, with Angelo offering to give him some tips at the gym. They'd met up one Saturday morning, and it'd just turned into a habit from there. The mix of lifting weights and talking about their lives had turned into an almost necessary thing, especially on mornings like these.

After setting down his barbell, Angelo stood, adding another ring of weight to his bench—and then more weight to Gavin's, because he was a good trainer and a terrible friend. His biceps gleamed with sweat under the oppressive lighting of the gym, and Gavin could tell by the way his own hair clung to his forehead that he wasn't faring any better. The air was the familiar burnt-rubber odor of overworked exercise machines diffused with the peppery tang of perspiration. Anywhere else it would have been unpleasant, but here it signaled a certain productivity or accomplishment—something that'd been sorely lacking in Gavin's workday yesterday.

Over the metallic clanks of barbells and the sound of dozens of feet pounding on treadmills, Angelo sat back down and chuckled again. "I tell you, I don't envy you having to lead all those meetings," he said. "The few IEPs I go to—they're enough for me."

Gavin lowered his barbell and wiped sweat off his forehead with the back of his hand. "This one yesterday was brutal. Mom with a kid new to the school. She was really pissed at what we were offering her." He sometimes told Angelo vague details about the situations he had, making sure to leave out identifying information.

"That's nothing new," Angelo said. "I'm sure you have moms pissed at you all the time."

"Sometimes. But they don't usually storm out calling me a twenty-eight-year-old 'jerk in a suit.'"

"Ha!" Angelo snatched a towel to wipe his face. "Aren't you like thirty-one or something?"

"Thirty-two."

"So she took a few years off. Most people over thirty would be flattered."

Gavin sat up, grabbing his own towel to rub his eyes, which

stung from perspiration. "Yeah, well. Did I mention the 'jerk in a suit' part?" What was wrong with wearing a suit to work, anyway?

"Duke up, baby. This is your life now."

Gavin lowered the towel and stared at him, the corner of his mouth lifting. "Did you just call me 'baby'?"

Angelo stood, gesturing widely. "I mean, this comes with the territory, right? It's an IEP, everybody shows up all tense. These moms and dads are just trying to do right by their kids—and they're pissed if they feel like you're not on the same page." He slung his towel around his neck. "Did you hear about the mom who spat at the IEP meeting last year?"

Gavin stood too, but did a double-take as Angelo's words hit him. "*Spat?*"

"Yeah." Angelo grinned. "Now I wasn't there, so I can't say for sure, but apparently this mother was upset at what the teacher was saying about her son, and she just... spat at him."

"Man."

"Yeah."

They started walking towards the locker room.

Shaking his head, Gavin asked, "You don't think that's some kind of suburban legend?"

Angelo shrugged, fist-bumping a friend who passed by them.

Gavin exhaled. "Okay, maybe I'll be a jerk in a suit."

They reached the door to the locker room and Angelo flung it open, giving him a wide grin. "There's the spirit."

After they both showered and dressed, he said goodbye to Angelo, who was loudly telling stories to another guy. Leaving the gym, Gavin was glad he'd brought a fleece. It was almost October, and the weather was finally falling in line, the temperature having dropped overnight. A chill coursed through him as a cool breeze ruffled his still-damp hair. He strode quickly to his car, climbing in and revving up the heater.

He was headed home, but, on an impulse, he pulled into the

grocery store lot to grab a six-pack of beer on his way. Usually he'd avoid shopping on a Saturday—way too many people—but a football game was on later, and he had big plans to ignore his work email and crash on the couch.

As he strolled to the entrance, he spied a bin of holiday wreaths next to the overflowing boxes of pumpkins that decorated the store's front. Giant yellow-orange pumpkins for carving spilled out next to the smaller, perfectly-round sugar pumpkins and dainty white ones. But the winter holidays—at least, the consumer aspect of it—found a way to nudge in as early as possible.

Gavin's mind couldn't help drifting to the previous winter as he came closer and noticed the bright red bows on the wreaths. Less than a year ago, his life had been so different. He'd been living in the city and working like crazy, like he had for years, with calls and deals and traveling. On a Saturday in December blissfully free of work, he and Ellie had grabbed brunch in downtown Philly and then strolled the cold streets, bundled up in wool coats and scarves. Lights were wound around trees and strewn across the snow-dusted streets, the bright touches of red in the decorative ribbon and ornaments hung all around making the sight pop with cheer.

They'd paused in front of a small department store front, where a miniature electronic Christmas village was set up. Being raised Jewish, he hadn't grown up celebrating Christmas, but it was as unavoidable as oxygen—especially in December, where you couldn't help but breathe in tinsel. Ellie exclaimed at the village, all those tiny figures and buildings and train tracks. A train chugged around the circumference of the miniature town, and inside, parts and people moved to an invisible timer: Figures skated around an ice rink. Santa moved across a roof with his reindeer. And the doors of a small Victorian home opened every minute to reveal a tiny boy whose painted-on expression of excitement seemed almost manic to Gavin.

"Oh my God, it's so cute! Isn't it so cute?" Ellie pressed her palms to her cold-flushed cheeks. They'd been dating a year and a half, and he knew it was probably time he got a ring, that she might be expecting it. His mother was certainly expecting it. They were both Jewish, had similar taste in movies, and he was over 30; he knew how these things went.

"Sure, it's cute," Gavin said, but really wasn't there something creepy about this Christmas village, the way the figures moved by invisible strings on a timeline that wasn't their own? Did Santa really want to stay on one roof for the rest of his life? Wasn't that train conductor tired? Were the tiny ice skaters slowly dying of hypothermia?

His gut twisted as he realized why it bothered him. These past few years, he'd fared only slightly better than these figures. Pushed and pulled by the demands of his job until there was little joy left in it. And now with Ellie—twenty-nine-year-old Ellie who also worked at his company and was smart and accomplished and classically beautiful, whose mother knew his mother, who was ready to settle down and start a family like he'd said he was. Ellie who, he realized with a flinch, he couldn't discuss his anxiety with, because in the mechanics of their own relationship, it wasn't one of the things that happened. It was the most ridiculous thing, but in front of that damn Christmas village he unspooled. All the hemming and hawing over *when* he should propose—or travel back to Chicago to nab that potential client—had distracted him from the question of *if* he wanted to do those things. And he didn't. Not anymore.

He wanted off that ride.

There in front of the grocery display, Gavin shook off the memories and the cool fall wind and entered the store. After the breakup with Ellie and leaving his job, he'd pivoted, searching for a job in the nonprofit sector, something he could feel good about. He'd found the position with the school district, then he'd moved out to the suburbs to be near his new workplace—and closer to his parents' home.

The chaos of suburban grocery stores had taken some getting used to, especially on the weekends. Today the lanes were crowded with people, so he made a beeline straight for the liquor aisle. He wove through the throngs in the cereal aisle, dodging a young dad and his cart, which was full of so many little kids it looked like he was pushing a basket of monkeys. Gavin stifled a laugh, grateful that he wasn't pushing a cart in these crowds.

He reached the empty end of the aisle, about to turn the corner and enter the booze section, when he stopped cold.

Josephine Palladino was there.

Not in the liquor aisle—but at the end, in the dairy section around the store's circumference.

Gavin pressed his back against some bagels, hiding himself from view. He was no shrinking violet, but running into her like this, after the meeting they had, would be awkwardness on steroids. He'd sent Mrs. Palladino—*Ms.* Palladino—those two emails after their aborted meeting yesterday, to smooth things over and reschedule a time to talk. He'd felt comfortable doing so—he was just doing his job. But emailing her a standard response and encountering her face-to-face out in public—when he was wearing joggers and headed towards the beer—was another thing entirely.

What if she saw him, and they had a conversation? What would she say—what would *he* say? What if she brought up something in Jackson's record here, when he didn't have his notes with him? What if she called him a jerk in a suit again?

It was also Saturday. Since he'd left sales, he'd grown accustomed to the weekends being work-free, and he just wasn't in the mood. It would be waiting for him Monday.

Gavin inwardly groaned, willing her to move further down the aisle so he could get his beer and get out of there.

Her grocery cart was loaded with a rainbow of items, and next to her was a boy, almost her height and with light brown hair and freckles which resembled her own. She had her hand on his arm and was speaking to him in low tones as he reached over and grabbed a four-pack of yogurt off the shelf. Josephine nodded and he thudded it into the cart so unceremoniously it tugged a smile from Gavin's lips.

He guessed the kid was Jackson; he looked the right age, and from the boy's rocking movements as he stood by the dairy, he could tell he was likely autistic.

Ms. Palladino's hair was down. She had the kind of curls that if you tugged on one, it would spring back with a *boing*. She wore faded jeans and a long-sleeved, fitted striped top with a cardigan sweater. Gavin briefly wondered what color of bra she had on underneath her shirt before shaking his head to clear the thought. He didn't fit in with this Saturday morning crowd of families, and his thoughts weren't exactly Saturday morning, either.

Their cart hadn't budged, and as she leaned over, grabbing another four-pack of yogurt, it didn't seem like they would any time soon. They obviously didn't keep casein-free like some of the other autistic students at school. Besides the yogurt, he saw a pint of ice cream in the pile in her cart, a couple packs of shredded cheese, and some coffee creamer.

As they dawdled by the dairy, Gavin noticed he wasn't the only one waiting for them to move. An older woman was behind them, staring at the yogurts and looking impatient. Two carts were headed in their direction, too: one with the dad and kids Gavin had passed earlier, and another with a young woman with a screaming toddler.

Jackson Palladino slapped his hands over his ears as the wailing child drew closer, the rocking of his body growing more erratic. Gavin couldn't blame him. Jackson's mom turned around at the sound and was grabbing her son's arm in one hand and the cart's handle in the other to move them away from the noise when two things happened: The guy with the cart full of kids, who was too distracted to watch where he was going, rammed his cart into theirs, sending one of his kids on his own wailing spree. Then the woman behind the Palladinos, assuming they were moving away, pushed her cart forward, trapping Jackson and his mom in a small, triangular space.

Gavin wasn't sure what was going to happen next, but, like witnessing a car accident, time slowed down as all hell broke loose.

# CHAPTER 5

*J*o felt the walls of the grocery store close around her so quickly, it was like a hand squeezing her throat.

"Sorry," she said, trying to wrench her cart free from the tangle. A family had hit their cart from the side, a little boy wailing loudly—too loudly—and in the back someone had pushed a cart far too close to them. "Excuse us."

Jo tried to keep her voice polite, but there was an urgency to her tone she couldn't hide. She and Jackson usually did their weekly grocery ritual on early Saturday mornings, but today they'd gotten a late start, and the crowd was much thicker this time of day. As they'd filled their basket, they'd increasingly needed to bob and weave through the aisles, or flat-out stop to let someone roll past or choose their own mustard.

Jo might've been aware of it even without Jackson, but she'd sensed his growing discomfort as strangers pressed closer to them, their loud voices laughing on phones or chiding their kids, forcing them this way or that with big carts. The press of bodies, all the accompanying smells and squeaky shoes and reaching hands—it would've been overwhelming for anybody, but it was especially so for Jax. All the details clamored for his attention, overloading his sensory system.

Not to mention he was already struggling from the challenges he'd been having at school. He'd come home Friday and had a meltdown like Jo hadn't seen in years, screaming and punching his fist into the wall hard enough to dent the plaster. Jo had eventually coaxed him into a warm bath to calm him down, but his unhappiness at school was palpable, and it was bleeding into other areas of their life.

After throwing the yogurt in the basket, she'd made the decision to head straight to the checkout. They hadn't finished the shopping, but they'd at least done two-thirds, and she had the necessities: Jackson's yogurt, tampons for her period that'd just started, and a pint of ice cream.

But she was too late.

His hands over his ears, Jackson moaned loudly and started rocking back and forth on his feet. Not happy rocking—agitated rocking. Jo's gut twisted.

"Sorry," the father in front of her mumbled with an embarrassed half-smile, pulling his cart away to soothe his screaming child—but not far enough; no, not nearly.

Jo stepped in front of Jackson, putting her hands on his arms and staring into his green eyes so like her own. "Shh, it's okay, Jax. It was an accident."

"Accident!" Jackson shouted. "No, no, no!" His face contorted, and before Jo could stop him, he reached out to the cart behind them and shoved it away.

A woman gasped.

Jo whirled to see an older woman stumble back before righting herself.

"He almost knocked me over!" the woman exclaimed, gripping her cart handle for dear life and glaring at them.

"I'm so sorry," Jo said quickly, her arm wrapping around Jackson to keep him in place. "He's having a hard time today."

"That's no excuse," the woman said, her face pinched. "He almost knocked me over!"

Another woman, a brunette carrying a basket of produce, stopped and put her hand on the older woman's arm. "Oh my God, are you alright?"

The boy in the cart in front screamed louder, and Jo knew they had to get out of there—immediately.

"Come on, Jackson," she said, placing his hands on the cart handle and moving behind him, attempting to create a bubble around his body so they could make a safe, speedy escape to the checkout.

But Jackson pulled away.

"Jackson," she muttered. "This isn't the time to start being a teenager."

His moaning grew louder, and he stomped his foot loud on the ground twice. It wasn't a good sign. It was like a bull about to charge. They were in deep shit.

"Aren't you going to punish him?" the woman behind her called. "He almost knocked me over!"

"I know." Jo gritted her teeth. "We're sorry. He's autistic and—"

"So?" the woman shouted. "That doesn't mean you shouldn't punish him. What's wrong is wrong. He needs to learn that." Now it wasn't just this lady glaring. The face of the woman beside her, who was touching her arm in comfort, was creased with consternation.

"Do you need some help?" the brunette whispered in a low voice to the older woman, as if Jo was too incapable or inhuman to sense that, and Jackson was beyond assistance.

Jo glanced around the store. *Normies*, she thought, recalling Kayla's name for people who existed outside the special needs world. They varied across a spectrum, too. In response to Jackson's unusual vocalizations and movements, some deliberately avoided them, looking uncomfortable, even fearful, of Jackson's unpredictability. Some gave them understanding smiles, room to move, kind words. Still others averted their eyes, trying to have no reaction whatsoever.

Then there were the assholes.

"What I *need*," the older woman said, "is an *apology*." She glared at Jo. "Don't you know how to raise your child?"

The man picked up his screaming kid, trying to comfort him, and Jo tried to ignore them all and push forward with Jackson and the cart. But Jackson wouldn't budge.

"Come on, buddy," Jo whispered. "We've outstayed our welcome."

Jackson wrung his hands. Shouting "Come on, come on!" he grabbed a container of yogurt and smashed it on the ground.

Jo gasped as the yogurt slopped and splattered in a three-foot radius all around. *"Jackson!"*

A big mountain of it was piled around their shoes, and splashes of it covered their jeans and their cart. Of course it was a thirty-two ounce container. *Of course.* Strawberry-flavored, from the scent and the clumps of bright pink Jo spotted on her jeans.

And it had sprayed both the young family and the older woman, who all stared at her wide-eyed in shock.

"Look, everybody," Jo snapped. "He's got special needs. Like real special. Like he's going to throw another yogurt if you don't get out of here right away special. Got it?"

All around them, a space was growing, though the store was still crowded. An invisible fence of discomfort separated them from the rest of the shoppers. People still wove through the aisles, but they avoided the chaos with their eyes—and their feet, Jo noted, as she glanced down at the yogurt spill to assess the damage, her eyes stinging from unshed tears.

But then a pair of man's sneakers stepped into that space.

"How can I help?" a deep voice asked.

Jo sighed and lifted her chin, assuming he was the manager or some store employee with a mop.

Instead she looked into the blue eyes of Gavin Steinberg.

Jo's mouth fell open.

The old woman stirred to life behind him, her voice raising so everyone could hear, "I cannot believe this—"

Gavin Steinberg turned sharply and cut her off. "I'm sorry, ma'am, but this boy reacts strongly to negative personalities. I'm going to ask everyone to move away in case there are any negative personalities in the store right now."

Baffled, the woman closed her mouth and scurried away with her cart, the woman helping her casting appalled glances back at them. The father with the kids split, too.

Without thinking, Jo whipped off her cardigan and knelt on the floor, trying to sop up the yogurt with her sweater, because what else could she do? She swallowed, willing the tears that smarted her eyes to dry up. This wasn't the first time something like this had happened, but it had been a while. She'd forgotten how ignorant people could be.

She also needed a moment before she could look at Gavin Steinberg again. Why was he here?

From her vantage point, she took in his exercise pants and sneakers. It was like he'd been out running. Part of her wished he hadn't stopped.

"Sorry, I should've stepped in sooner," he said in a low voice. "That woman was a jerk."

"It's fine," she mumbled without thinking. "We're fine. Thanks for your help." She glanced around at her agitated son and the strawberry yogurt soaking into the knees of her jeans. A fresh wave of horror rocked through her.

This was the man from the school district. The one trying to move Jackson to a new class because he thought her son couldn't hack his current environment.

And there they were, in a strawberry-scented, fermented dairy hell of their own making.

"You can go," Jo said quickly, meeting his gaze. "We're fine. Just an accident, that's all."

But she could tell by his expression that he knew it wasn't, that he'd seen everything—seen and maybe was going to jot it down on Jackson's records or file it in the back of his head as yet another reason why her son shouldn't be in his current classroom.

"Here," he said, taking two steps back and fishing something out of her cart. A roll of paper towels.

He ripped it open and unrolled a wad of the towels, kneeling down beside her. "Let me do that." He balled up her sweater, set it aside, then proceeded to wipe up the mess.

Jo still hadn't moved, but as Jackson let out a loud cry, she jumped to her feet.

"Shh, Jackson, it's okay," she said—as much to him as to herself. "We'll just clean up and get out of here."

She might have to leave the entire cart, but she wanted out of there while she still had a shred or two of dignity. Though as Gavin passed her paper towels to wipe herself and her son, she felt even that slipping away. In its place came anger. Was he doing this to help her? She didn't understand why he was here. She didn't need his pity and didn't want his charity.

In abrupt strokes, she quickly wiped Jackson's hands and legs, then her own, but her son still wasn't fine. He reached his hand out to the yogurt again, and Jo stopped him—barely.

"No, Jackson," she said, her hands on his shoulders. "*Home soon.*"

"Home," he repeated.

"Yes, home."

She was worried how they'd make it out of the store, but they couldn't stay there, could they? Jackson twisted out of her grasp and shook his arms.

"Jackson, for the love of God…"

Gavin Steinberg got to his feet and held his phone out to her. "Here," he said. "Maybe it'll help him calm down?"

She lowered her eyebrows at him. "What?"

"I don't know, I thought maybe there's an app for this?"

"There's no app for this," Jo scoffed. But she grabbed the phone from him, scrolling until she found YouTube. With trembling fingers, she typed in *Taylor Swift* and found one of Jackson's favorite videos. Then she cranked the phone volume all the way up.

"Jackson," Jo said. "Listen. *'Shake It Off.'*"

She had her own phone with her, of course, but it was buried in the vast caverns of her purse and would've taken too long to find.

Jackson kept rocking, pulling his fingers back with his opposite hand like he did when he was agitated, but at the chorus of one of his favorite songs, his movements slowed.

A teenage boy with a mop and bucket showed up then, looking faintly terrified.

Gavin wiped his hands on a paper towel and grabbed her cart. "Here, I'll push this thing, and you take care of Jackson."

"That's not necessary," Jo said. "We're fine."

"I'm headed that way anyway," he said, though Jo didn't see that he had any groceries. "Let me."

Pressing her lips together, she followed Gavin with Jackson in one hand and the phone playing music with the other. This time, Jackson let her guide him. The power of Taylor Swift was strong.

Embarrassment came, heating her face and neck. She went shopping with Jackson each week, and though he usually was fine, and helpful even, he did things that often brought them stares: made noises or moved his body in unusual ways, sat on the floor, sometimes took off his shoes. Usually Jo was immune to the public reaction, but with this recent incident and Gavin

Steinberg's presence, she felt vulnerable, her soft, tender side exposed.

He was a tall man, probably an inch over six feet, and Jo had to move briskly to keep up with his long strides in those track pants. His brown hair was flatter than it'd been Friday, damp around the roots. He'd probably come from some gym. Jo guessed she'd been right about him being child-free. His appearance and long, loose movements spoke of leisure, of unhurried weekend sessions at a health club followed by casual brunches and maybe Saturday night dates. He probably never had to wipe yogurt off his knees.

If she was in the habit of noticing such things, she'd probably think he was cute. Well, his ears stuck out a little.

Passing by a big display of Halloween candy, they reached an open checkout counter. Jo hit replay on the Taylor song as Gavin turned and held out his hand.

"I can play DJ while you get these," he said.

"It's okay," Jo said, mentally praying he'd now leave. "I got him."

But just then Jackson flapped his hands, underscoring the lie in Jo's words. If Gavin Steinberg hadn't been here to push her cart—if she hadn't had help—she might very well have abandoned these groceries for fear of not being able to make it through the checkout aisle.

Gavin raised an eyebrow.

Her lips pressed together, she passed the phone to him and turned, swiftly unloading the groceries onto the conveyor belt.

"Come on, Jackson," Gavin said, "let's go over here to supervise your mom."

Still holding up his phone, Gavin nodded his head toward the end of the checkout and held out his hand to him. Jo almost snorted, because no way was Jackson going to take some strange man's hand, especially in his current mood.

But then Jackson did.

Jo clamped her mouth shut, putting the rest of the groceries on the belt while she darted quick glances at her son holding the hand of their enemy, then walking with him through a deserted checkout lane to where a bag boy filled their cart. Jackson was nodding his head to Taylor Swift, and after a moment Gavin Steinberg did too, smiling at the boy.

It was all so bizarre and embarrassing and not a little infuriating, because he was acting like a nice guy, but really, Jo had seen him at a special education meeting and the man did not have her son's best interests in mind, even if he was now humming along to Taylor and tapping his toes like he was actually enjoying this.

Sure, she'd be grateful—later, when she was home with her tampons and ice cream and frozen pizza and didn't have to look this man in the face.

After she paid the cashier, she pushed the cart full of groceries forward until she reached where her son waited with Gavin.

"Thank you," she said, attempting a small smile at Gavin while she simultaneously reached for Jackson with her free hand. "Come on, Jax, let's go to the car and get a snack."

Head bobbing, Jax took her hand as they began walking—but didn't let go of Gavin's hand on his other side.

"I'll make sure you get to the car okay," he said, walking with them and smiling at her over Jackson's head as he slid his phone back in his pocket.

What did he think she was, completely helpless? Her son was calm now, and yet he was still here. Did he not realize she did this every week? Did he moonlight as some kind of grocery store meltdown superhero?

The three of them rolled over the exit and out into the parking lot, the sun making her eyes squint. As cold as it had suddenly become—and she was missing her cardigan now, as it was covered in yogurt and balled in a corner of the cart—the sunlight still shone brightly.

He was probably just doing this because she'd called him a jerk in a suit. Because he was. In that setting, at least.

She tried again. "I think we've got it now. Thank you for your help."

"No problem," he said, though he still didn't release Jackson's hand. "It's the least a twenty-eight-year-old jerk can do."

*Oh my God.* She looked away as her face heated and her eyes widened.

"Just so you know," he added, his voice laced with humor. "I'm not *that* young."

"Uh, okay."

They reached the car. She popped open the trunk, released Jackson's hand, and started loading groceries into it at lightning speed.

"We probably listened to the same bands growing up," he added from behind her.

She wedged a jumbo pack of toilet paper in the side of the trunk, resisting the urge to shake her head. "Okay."

She turned around.

He was standing there, holding Jackson's hand, the corner of his mouth upturned in a smile. "I mean, I don't know how old you are, but I'm assuming..."

His eyes twinkled. Well, she was glad he was amused by the situation.

Gavin Steinberg had eyes the dark blue of river rocks. It was a nice color. Calming. They were nice eyes.

He was still a jerk.

"*Jackson,*" Jo said. She grabbed her son's free hand and pulled him toward the car. "Come get in the backseat."

The groceries weren't all unloaded yet, but maybe if her son let go of Gavin Steinberg's hand, that would be enough to make him leave.

Jackson trudged over to the backseat, yanked open the door, and climbed in, humming the exact way Gavin had sounded humming the same song two minutes ago.

After prompting Jackson to fasten his seatbelt, she faced the man and plastered a polite smile on her face. "Thank you."

Then she lifted the last few plastic bags into her trunk—but one of the bags split open.

Gavin rushed forward, grabbing a bottle of shampoo and a couple of other cartons before they spilled out.

"They always forget to double-bag," he said. "Good thing I've got sharp reflexes, huh?"

But not sharp enough. A box of tampons tumbled to the ground.

Gavin's eyes popped open, and *God, could this day get any worse?*

*Yes, yes it could.*

Because before Jo could grab it, Gavin reached down to pick up the box of tampons, too.

With a sheepish smile on his face, he offered her the shampoo, a box of tissues, and the tampons. "Here you go."

*God.* She could guess what was running through his mind. Her behavior at the meeting. The fact that she was now on her period. That her behavior was probably premenstrual and not logical or completely justified.

"Just so you know," Jo said quickly. "The reason I acted the way I did Friday wasn't because I had PMS or anything. I mean, it was probably only thirty-six percent that. Or less. Probably less." She straightened. "I stand by what I said."

Though horrified at herself, she felt worse when she noticed his lips bunch up, like he was completely uncomfortable too.

Or, wait…Was he *trying not to laugh?*

She snatched the items from his hands, turning and practically throwing them into her trunk.

"Anyway, you can go now," she called.

He started laughing. "Sorry," he said. "It's not a big deal. I grew up with sisters. Are you sure it was thirty-six percent though? Not thirty-four or thirty-seven?"

She turned and rolled her eyes. "Why are you here?"

His smile dimmed. "I needed beer. And then you needed help."

"Well, we're... helped." She crossed her arms over her chest and softened her voice. "Thank you. Again."

"You're welcome." He smiled again and started walking backwards, nodding his head toward the backseat of her car. "That's a good kid you've got there."

# CHAPTER 6

*G*avin was still thinking about Josephine Palladino and her son when he pulled up to his parents' house Sunday afternoon.

The previous morning, he'd been almost all the way home before he realized he'd never gotten the beer—his entire reason for going to the store. All thoughts of alcohol—and avoiding any awkwardness—had fled once he'd seen Jackson start to lose it. Gavin had seen kids with special needs having breakdowns in school hallways, and he knew it could be a challenge. The idea of that happening in a crowded grocery store—especially with that mean woman giving them a hard time... He couldn't in good conscience turn his back on them at that moment—not as special education staff, but not as a person either.

He only wished he'd jumped in sooner.

Gavin was no trained therapist, so he'd had no idea exactly how he was going to help them. Being a closet neat freak, he'd gone to clean up the spilled yogurt first. Pushing the cart to the checkout next was easy enough. But then he was surprised that Jackson had let him hold his hand while his mom paid for their groceries, the kid's large green eyes in his freckled face darting curious glances at him as they both bopped to Taylor.

Even after Josephine had paid and was ready to leave, Gavin hadn't wanted to let go of the boy's hand. It'd seemed almost superstitious, like he was holding the situation together, and he didn't intend to drop it—even when it seemed like Josephine Palladino was trying to shoo him away.

He grinned as he turned off the car in his parents' driveway. He thought of her expression when she'd first seen him. He didn't need her to say a word to know that he was the last person she wanted to see. She was embarrassed and uncomfortable, and, when they'd gotten to her car to load the groceries, even a little annoyed. It hadn't been Gavin's intention, but he'd be lying if he didn't admit to being amused at the look on her face when he had picked up that box of tampons. Her green eyes wide, her mouth a small o.

It was definitely going to make for an interesting second meeting—if she ever got back to him, that is.

After strolling to his parents' door and giving a quick knock, he flung it open. The Steinbergs didn't stand for ceremony, especially with their youngest child.

An older man with thinning brown hair sat in the recliner in the living room.

"Whatever you're selling, we don't want to buy," the man called out in a jovial tone, standing and spreading his arms.

"Whatever you want to buy, I'm not selling," Gavin said, hugging him and slapping him on the back. "Hi, Dad."

Ray Steinberg pulled away, gripping his son's arms and looking him up and down. "You look like you're having a good weekend."

"Yeah, pretty good."

Both his parents were born and raised nearby in New Jersey, and it showed in their accents—especially when they bickered or raised their voices to be heard, like his mom was doing now from the other room.

"You two," she called from the kitchen. "I'm putting out the takeout. Come in the kitchen and let's eat."

Since moving closer, Gavin had never once skipped coming to see his parents on the weekends. He almost always made Friday night Shabbat dinner, and often came around later if he was in the neighborhood, like today. Last year, he'd missed them most weekends, because he'd been traveling or catching up on paperwork or, God forbid, sitting in on conference calls. His mom hadn't been crazy about him leaving a stable job, not to mention leaving Ellie, but she'd warmed to this aspect at least.

He walked into the kitchen, his father trailing him, to find his mother opening up cartons of Chinese food on the table from a local place. The warm, salty smell of General Tso's, spring rolls, and chow mein reached his nose.

"We thought we'd keep it simple," Dina Steinberg explained. "Your father didn't feel like cooking."

"Game was on," Ray explained. "Good one, too. You see that?"

"Caught one yesterday," Gavin said. "Today I was cleaning and doing laundry."

"A shame," his mother said. "Eagles won 24 to 7."

Her dark hair pulled back in a bun, Dina wore a pale yellow sweater with matching cardigan over navy slacks—a crisp, almost professional outfit that she could've worn to her job at the local university where she served as an administrative assistant to the dean. Gavin had gotten his humor from his dad, his cleanliness and professionalism from his mom.

They sat down at the table and Gavin spooned some beef and broccoli onto his plate, the rich smell making his stomach growl. "This looks good, Mom."

"Mmm-hmm." She passed him a water bottle and they spoke

a few minutes before Dina switched to her current favorite subject. "So have you met anybody?"

"You mean since you asked me the same question Friday night?" Gavin speared a piece of broccoli.

"I take it that's a *no*," his dad said, winking at him across the table.

"I meet people all the time," Gavin said. "But, yeah, the answer is no."

"I don't understand, an attractive man like you..."

Gavin inwardly groaned as he broke an egg roll in half. "Mom, I'm a big boy now. I'm thirty-two. I've been finding my own girlfriends since I was twenty-nine."

Dina waved her fork. "I just wanted to tell you the Scotts' youngest daughter just moved back to the area."

"Okay." He braced himself. Dina had seemed as shocked as Ellie at the breakup last year, especially when it was quickly followed by a big career change. *I just want my kids to be happy* was a constant refrain of hers, especially when it came to him, her youngest child. And he couldn't hide the fact that he'd been a little lost, a little directionless, since leaving his job and girlfriend.

In his mother's eyes, a good woman could fix all that. So she had taken it upon herself to help the process along.

"Their youngest daughter," Dina repeated, stirring her chow mein. "The one who used to dance. Do you remember her?"

He considered. "Was she the redhead?"

"No."

"I only remember the redhead."

"This is the blond."

"The redhead was really lively," Ray said.

"Well, this is the *blond*," Dina said. "The dancer. Anyway, she's not dating anyone now. That's what her mother told me. Just, you know, in case you were interested..."

"In this blond woman I don't remember?" His mom was the most extroverted person he knew, and it showed. They didn't know who she was talking about half the time.

"Well, if you met up with her, you might remember. I asked for her number." Dina took a small bite of noodles as if to punctuate her thoughts.

"She was a dancer," his dad said, wiggling his eyebrows at Gavin.

Gavin had to laugh. "Seriously?"

Dina poked her fork in his direction, squinting one eye like she was about to take aim at him. "Seriously. I'm serious about this. I'm serious about how you're my son, and you deserve to find someone that will make you happy, and there'll be a big wedding and I'll wear that burgundy dress I've been saving and there'll be grandbabies I'll get to squish—"

"She loves squishing babies," Ray said.

"I know," Gavin said. "I've seen it." He had two older sisters. Emily had split for grad school across the country and had stayed there, happily single and child-free. The middle kid, Liz, married Gavin's high school friend Ben, who joined the military. They were currently stationed in England, where Liz and sometimes Ben texted Gavin at odd hours of the night as they were up feeding the baby. They had two very squishable kids, but they were an ocean away. You couldn't squish baby pictures, especially digital ones.

Dina was on a roll. "And I can take them sometimes for the weekends—because you'll need a break; children may look cute, but they can be a handful, and you'll be tired, trust me."

He was already composing the text he'd send to Liz later. *Mom just offered to babysit my hypothetical kids. Should I take her up on it?*

Gavin exhaled and shook his head. As usual, she was about three steps ahead of him. After what happened with Ellie, he wasn't sure he wanted to be married or have kids. Sure, once he'd hit his thirties and friends started posting photos on social media with their chubby babies at the park, it certainly didn't seem like a bad idea. Even with his sister Liz's frequent complaints of sleeping four hours a night, it still seemed like fun, like some more adult version of a college all-nighter.

Yet he'd been on the brink of that with someone perfect for him, and he'd shied away. There had to be a reason for that, didn't there?

With all the changes of the past year, he wasn't actively looking for someone to have hypothetical kids with so his mom could hypothetically babysit. He was pausing. Regrouping. Meanwhile, maybe because she sensed his ambivalence, his mother's attempts to reel in women on his behalf were growing more and more aggressive. Which left him with few defenses. Mainly humor.

"So you've got this all mapped out," Gavin said. "Great. Just point me in the direction of this woman I'm supposed to breed with, and we'll be all set."

"I'm your mother, and—"

"A mother's job is to make sure her kids are happy," Gavin finished.

Dina stood. "I need another water. Ray, tell your son he needs to find a woman."

With a sly smile on his face, Ray turned toward Gavin and gave him his best serious face, which wasn't serious at all. "Son, you need to find a woman."

"So I've been hearing."

Ray glanced around, and seeing his wife's head stuck in the fridge, he leaned closer and whispered in his son's ear. "I'm a happily married man, so I wouldn't notice such things," he said. "But if I did, I'd notice that the youngest Scott daughter has a pretty pert little body."

"Really?" Gavin whispered back. "Okay, I'll investigate."

His dad would've been happy either way. That was the Steinbergs in a nutshell: Gavin was close to his dad because he didn't care, and close to his mom because she did. Usually too much.

Dina walked back to the table, water in one hand and a bottle of soy sauce in the other. "And I'd like to have another grandbaby someday," she said, returning to her original point. "Two is not enough, especially when they're an ocean away. You may think you have all the time in the world, and I know a lot of people wait until they're older nowadays, but really, you try raising a toddler when you're over forty."

Gavin laughed and grabbed the soy sauce from her. "I hope I'm not too old now. Maybe my sperm have already shriveled up."

"Don't say 'sperm' while we're eating." Dina looked at her husband. "Where are all the egg rolls?"

"I don't know," Ray said. "I only had two."

Dina's mouth fell open. "There were only three!"

"Oh."

She closed her mouth and shook her head. "You're lucky you're cute, Ray Steinberg."

Gavin's phone pinged with an incoming message, and though he didn't have to keep on top of his phone like he did at his sales job, he pulled it out of his pocket and glanced down. It was an email to his work account.

From Josephine Palladino.

*Mr. Steinberg*, the message began, *I have tomorrow afternoon free if we could have another meeting about Jackson's progress. Let me know what time works for you. I'm flexible.*

He put his phone away to see his mom staring at him, her eyes narrowed.

"You're seeing somebody," she accused. "And you didn't think to tell me?"

"I'm not seeing anybody, Mom."

"Why are you smiling?"

"It's just a work thing." He picked up his fork again. "Somebody got back to me about something. Somebody I wasn't sure I'd hear from."

"See," Ray gestured, nodding at his wife. "He's happy at his job."

# CHAPTER 7

*A*t support group Sunday afternoon, Jo was on her third coffee and out of ideas.

A group of special needs parents had been meeting in the basement of a local church for the past couple years. It'd slowly become a lifeline to Jo, especially at times like these, when she sorely needed advice. Though the group waxed and waned, today half a dozen were gathered, seated in metal chairs around a circular table in the room. The ubiquitous coffee pot was softly humming, and a plate of brownies nearby was siren-calling Jo to come stress-eat.

As embarrassed as she'd been after the grocery incident, in retrospect Jo had to admit that Gavin Steinberg's helpfulness at the store made her feel warmer towards him. Or not as cold. Tepid, maybe. There was a chance he was maybe human after all —or at least someone who drank beer, which was basically the same thing. Anyway, he was just a man, and he probably meant well. He even seemed to like kids, if the way he'd held Jackson's hand was any indication. She still didn't agree with the district's assessment of her son—and she intended to keep fighting like hell against their plans—but she wanted to try a different approach.

Earlier she'd sent off an email to him to reschedule. In the meantime, she decided to go into the next meeting slightly less mama bear, and slightly more... she didn't know what.

"We're going to talk about self-care today," Holly, the group's leader, said. "I know that term is often overused, but it's something important—and something we should revisit from time-to-time."

Holly looked around the group, catching Jo's eye and smiling warmly. A special needs mom herself—her fourteen-year-old daughter, Abby, had Down Syndrome—Holly had been in their lives for years. She'd first met them as Jackson's at-home speech therapist when he was young, often bringing along her older son, Sean, who'd played games with Kayla. They lived in the neighborhood, and they'd grown to be friends ever since. Everything about Holly was comforting: her way with kids, her slight southern accent and strawberry blond hair, her Rubenesque figure.

"Anyone want to talk about what they've been doing for themselves lately?" Holly asked.

Everyone was silent for a few seconds, then Jackie snorted. "Does peeing with the door shut count?"

They all laughed. A tanned white woman in her fifties, Jackie had a beautiful thirty-year-old daughter with cerebral palsy at home and a wisecracking personality that helped put the rest of them at ease.

A few moments later, Sadie and Tom exchanged a glance, and Sadie's eyes filled with tears. The couple had a seventeen-year-old autistic son, Toby, who'd been struggling with aggression lately. Having two younger kids at home made it all the more complicated, and everybody was hurting, including Toby. Jo could tell by the Yateses' pale, drawn faces that things remained difficult.

Holly gentled her voice. "Sadie and Tom, have either of you been able to attend to your own needs with everything going on at home?"

"Barely," Sadie whispered. Her husband wrapped an arm around her and shook his head, his eyes downcast.

Dirk, a slim Black man whose energetic seven-year-old daughter Deenie had autism and intellectual disability like Jackson, stood up, walked over to the brownies, plopped two on a napkin, and brought them back to the Yateses.

"Here," he said. "Start with this."

"Thank you," Sadie whispered, a tear rolling down her cheek.

Dirk cleared his throat. "We had a cookout last weekend, when it was still warm. Invited some friends and their kids."

"Oh?" Holly said. "How was that?"

"It was pretty good." He shrugged. "Stood around with some old buddies, drinking beer and remembering old times. So that was good. But sometimes it's hard, you know, with people who've got kids who aren't like Deenie. Like it's hard to relate."

"I think several of us can understand that," Holly said, and Jackie murmured, "Mm-hm."

"My daughter, Kayla, says I need to get a life," Jo said. "She says I don't hang out with anyone or do anything that's not related to Jackson's needs." She laughed, waving a hand dismissively, trying to pretend like Kayla's words hadn't grated on her.

Jackie rolled her eyes. "She's a teenager. Her job is to do homework, date inappropriate boys, and criticize you."

"She's working on the inappropriate boys thing, too," Jo added, thinking about Austin and his guitar and his lips on her daughter's.

"Huh," Jackie said, "so she's at least two for three."

Kayla was home now watching Jackson, like she usually did when Jo went to support group Sunday afternoons. She'd even suggested Jo go out with her best friend Misty's mom and her friends that Friday—though Jo wondered if there was a hidden agenda there, one involving inviting over her new boyfriend once Jackson went to bed. She'd declined. What would she talk about to those women at Applebee's? Jackson's meltdown at the store? The fiasco with the school district? Which sight words he could and could not read? Would they even get it, or just look at her with confusion or pity?

"It's not like I don't have friends with typical kids," Jo said. "It's just…"

"I know," Holly said, shifting in her chair. "Trust me, I get it. Since Abby was young, I don't think I've hung out much with parents who don't have special needs kids, either. We just live in such different realities sometimes." She chuckled. "It's like they're worrying about whether their kid's elementary school offers Mandarin Chinese as a second language, and we're over here just trying to work on English."

"Yeah, exactly," Jo said. Before Jackson's diagnosis, there'd been playgroups and library story times, plenty of opportunities to hang around other moms, commiserating about lack of sleep and munching on Goldfish crackers while their toddlers swung or played in the sand. But then the other kids had started speaking more, and Jackson less. He had done things the other kids didn't—laying on the ground at strange times or looking at the same book over and over for long stretches. Jo already felt their path diverging by the time the official diagnosis came. They were different—Jackson, and her by extension—and though she loved her son, not fitting in hurt more than she would have guessed.

"Speaking of self-care," Holly said. "Paul and I tried to go out last week. Emphasis on *tried*."

"Yeah?" Jackie said.

Holly smirked. "Guess what we did?"

Seeing that Sadie had eaten her brownie, Jo stood and

grabbed the plate, bringing it back to pass around the room. "What?"

"Nothing." Holly laughed. "Sean was home to watch Abby—he left for the semester. Anyway, that's a story for another time." She waved her hand. "So Paul and I went out to a restaurant, but we didn't make any reservations ahead and it was Friday night, so there were long waits at all the good places. And when we finally found a place and got seated, we just looked at each other like, 'What do we talk about?' All this time you spend dreaming of having an evening without kids, and when you finally get there, you can't remember what you like to do for fun."

Jackie laughed. "I hear that."

Holly leaned on the nearby table, resting her chin in her hands. "What did you all do for fun—I mean, before kids?"

"My wife and I used to watch a whole season of a Netflix show on Saturdays," Dirk said. "Just crash on the couch, without interruption." He chuckled. "I can't imagine that now, unless we're talking about *Yo Gabba Gabba.*"

"I used to write poetry," Jackie said, and added, "Believe it or not, there's a soulful woman under all this makeup."

Sadie let out a giggle, wiping her face with the heel of her hand.

Jo nimbled a brownie. "Back in college, I used to go vintage shopping with friends a lot."

"That's fun," Holly said.

"Yeah. We'd find fancy dresses and try them on. We also used to just drive around, listening to music."

Dating was another thing she'd done for fun. Those first couple years after the divorce had been consumed with adjusting to single parenthood and Jackson's diagnosis, but after she'd tried to meet someone—because it seemed like she should, and occasionally she wanted adult interaction. She just hadn't met any men she wanted to see more of. The last straw had been the guy who'd ordered French fries and left a nub on each fry uneaten, like they were shrimp, and kept steering their dinner conversation to his IQ.

"My IQ is 142."

"Oh?" Jo took a sip of water at the restaurant where they were, her thoughts wandering to the meeting she'd had about Jackson earlier that week, where she learned his own IQ level had qualified him as intellectually disabled. "Sorry, that doesn't mean much to me."

"It means it's really high," the man had said, misunderstanding her meaning.

"Okay."

She'd politely listened, but what she'd really wanted to say was, "Who cares?" Not that she thought high IQs weren't a good thing. Certainly the world needed Einsteins and DaVincis. But the world also needed people like her son.

She could do without romance. Time and energy—those were what she needed more of. And her son being in a place where he could thrive.

Her stomach flopped as she remembered what she wanted to ask the group. "Not to switch the conversation off self-care, but can I ask for some advice?"

"Sure," Holly said.

"I had Jackson's IEP on Friday. Let's just say it didn't go well."

"How bad are we talking?" Dirk asked.

"Like I called the coordinator a jerk and stormed out of the room."

He let out a low whistle.

"I need a new strategy," Jo said. "I've had a chance to calm down, and even though I know what's best for Jackson, I want to start off the meeting on a better foot." She gave them a quick summary of the meeting before looking around the room. "Any suggestions on how I can do that?"

Holly snapped her fingers. "Bake them cookies."

"What?"

Jackie nodded. "Yeah, I've heard of moms doing that. It's supposed to sweeten them up at the meeting. I know a mom who bakes something for every IEP."

"*Every* meeting?" Jo said.

"It's a way of saying, 'Thanks for all you do for my kid'," Holly said. "Anyway, it'll help start this next meeting on a more positive, pleasant foot, so it's easier for everyone to see eye to eye."

Jo sighed. "Well, I guess it's harder to scream at them with a cookie in your mouth." The trouble was, she wasn't much use in the kitchen. She had almost never baked—unless toast counted, and even that was iffy sometimes.

Holly knowingly caught her eye. "Don't worry, I'll bring you a recipe and ingredients after the meeting."

Jo smiled in gratitude as Jackie added, "If the cookie thing doesn't work, there's another strategy I used to employ from time to time, back when my daughter was in school."

"What's that?"

A slow smile spread across Jackie's face. "Take a shot of rum before you walk into the meeting."

AN HOUR after Jo returned home from support group, Holly arrived at the door. Brushing past Jo, she walked into her kitchen and set a brown paper bag on the counter.

"This has everything you need to make a batch of oatmeal raisin cookies," Holly explained, brushing her straight strawberry blonde bangs out of her eyes. "I figured by your frightened look this afternoon that you didn't have many baking supplies."

"You figured that out, huh?" Jo squinted at the bag of ingredients, wrinkling her nose. "You sure this will help? I'm not sure Gavin Steinberg is the cookie type. I think he's more like the salad-for-lunch, baked-chicken-breast-for-dinner type."

"He's a man," Holly said. "He'll eat your cookies."

Holly leaned a generous hip against Jo's kitchen counter. "So besides telling you you have no life, how's Kayla?"

"Fine. A little snarky." At the thought of her eldest, Jo's ears tuned into the sound of loud music coming from the teenager's room. It was clashing with the pop tunes and squeaks from the living room where Jackson jumped on their small trampoline. Underneath the sounds, she swore she heard Kayla giggling.

Jo lowered her voice. "I think she's got a boyfriend. The inappropriate boy I mentioned."

Holly leaned forward, her own voice dropping to a conspiratorial whisper. "Really?"

"His name is Austin. He's in a *band*."

"Uh-oh."

"Yeah." Jo smirked. "I suppose it had to happen sooner or later."

Holly grinned.

Inappropriate or not, she was coming around to the idea—Kayla was sixteen, after all, and Jo had been far wilder at that age.

Holly turned and started unpacking the bag of ingredients she brought. "You know, I'm happy to come here and stay with Jackson if you ever wanted to go out and have some fun one night. Or on a date or, you know, whatever."

"Date?" Jo said. "I don't date."

"But, you know, if you ever did." Holly pulled out a bag of flour and set it on the counter. "Trust me, I wouldn't mind the break from home. Especially since Sean is home for the semester."

Remembering Holly's mention of this at support group, Jo

leaned her elbows on the counter. "What happened there?" Holly's son was a sophomore at the state university two hours away. Or had been.

"He quit. Says he needs some time off to figure out what he wants. Paul and I aren't happy about it, but we gave him until the New Year."

"That was generous of you."

"I know his childhood was different, with Abby coming along. I thought going away would do him some good, but I think he missed her. Maybe us, too." She shrugged. "Anyway, he's gotten Paul and Abby hooked on this game that plays the most annoying song. So, believe me, I'd welcome the chance to come over here and get a break from it."

"Oh. Okay." Jo appreciated the offer. Kayla watched Jackson some of the time, but Jo didn't want to rely on her so much, especially since she, unlike her mom, was starting to have a life. Plus, Jo wondered where she'd even go, if she had a couple hours to herself.

"What about that playground thing?" Holly asked.

"What thing?"

"The fundraiser. The one for the sensory playground at Jackson's old elementary school?"

"Oh." She vaguely remembered a yellow flier coming home in her son's bag the previous week. "I don't know. I assumed I wouldn't be going."

"I can stay here with Jackson if you want to go," Holly offered. "Word among my clients is that there's going to be live music. Like sort of classy. I guess they're going after some big donors."

Jo tilted her head, considering. It'd been years since she'd gone anywhere that required formal wear. But then she started laughing. "A sensory playground fundraiser. God, Kayla is right. These are my options for social outings. I really don't have a life."

Holly laughed too. "Well, at least it's something. Sometimes you just need to get out. Do something different."

Jo pressed her lips together. Maybe she'd think about something like that months from now, when the situation with Jackson's school was more settled.

She sighed and picked up the heavy bag of flour from the counter, examining it in her hands. "Maybe I should just tour this new class. See if it is a better fit."

"No, I think you should stick to your guns," Holly said. "Rumor has it that the class at Rydell is a special ed weigh station. Lots of kids go in and out pretty frequently."

Jo looked up. "Really?"

"Really."

"Well, screw that. I'm not letting them toss him somewhere just because they don't know where else to put him." She dropped the flour and shook her head. "But what if the cookies don't work?"

"Then you'll get an advocate," Holly said. "I know someone— she's the best. You can get more affordable advocates through some agencies, but you should go straight to this woman. She's a force to be reckoned with."

"How much does she charge?"

Holly smiled grimly. "How much do you have in your savings?"

LATER THAT NIGHT, Jo squinted at Holly's cookie recipe, trying to decipher the correct amount of flour, sugar, and oats from a page smeared with a dark purple substance that she was too afraid to sniff. But she had a big metal bowl on the kitchen counter, and she was going to do this, dammit.

"What are you doing?" Kayla asked. Both she and Jackson, and even the cat, had drifted into the kitchen, drawn by the unfamiliar scent of the oven preheating. Chuck circled the room, his little nose quivering high in the air.

"I'm making cookies," Jo said.

"Really?"

"Really." The recipe called for a cup of flour, so Jo opened up a bottom drawer to dig for a measuring cup. She had one of those, didn't she? It sounded like something an adult woman should have.

"Why?" Kayla asked.

"Why what?" Jo located a plastic half-cup behind an orange casserole dish she didn't remember owning. "Aha!"

"Why are you making cookies?"

Returning to the bowl, Jo scooped out two half-cups of flour and plopped them in. "Holly suggested it," she said. "To bring to the meeting tomorrow. To sweeten them up or something, make them more willing to hear what I have to say... I don't know, it made sense how she said it." Granted, it seemed to make less sense now, as Jo realized how woefully unused to baking she was, and how much the recipe she was using resembled hieroglyphs. Did it say one teaspoon or one tablespoon of cinnamon?

Kayla sat on a dining room chair cross-legged, her brother sitting next to her. Jackson at first traced his sister's hand on a loose piece of paper on the table—his new favorite hobby—before he walked up to Jo's bowl, grabbing the spoon and stirring the concoction around.

"Thanks, bud," Jo said, adding somewhere between a teaspoon and tablespoon of cinnamon, the spicy scent reaching her nose.

"Can't you just *buy* the cookies?" Kayla asked.

Jo walked over to the fridge and grabbed a cube of butter. "No, because I want it to seem like I'm making a gesture." She unwrapped the butter and dumped it into the bowl, letting loose a cloud of flour, much to Jackson's appreciation. He made a loud noise as he watched with fascination the miniscule white particles momentarily suspended in the air.

"Why don't you buy the cookies, take them out of the package, put them on a plate, and pretend you made them?" Kayla asked.

"I can't do that!" Jo turned to grab a salt shaker, adding a quick flourish to the bowl, then another, feeling almost domestic. "I only did that for your elementary school bake sales."

"Hmm, yeah," Kayla said, laughing. "And I guess you didn't convince anybody then. Carry on." She pulled out her phone as Jo consulted her recipe again and pulled out a baking tray.

"Cookies!" Jackson shouted, his green eyes wide and bright.

"Not tonight. If there are any leftovers, I'll bring them home tomorrow." Jo added a cup of oats, Jackson helpfully stirring the mixture with wonder. Since he was young, he enjoyed what little cooking had gone on in their kitchen, watching ingredients mix and blend to form something new. Jo sometimes wondered if they were truly related, despite sharing the same eye color. Neither she nor Neil was ever adept in the kitchen.

It was time to add some baking powder, but the purple smear on the recipe hid the exact amount. Half something... half a cup? Half a tablespoon?

She raised the measuring cup over the bowl, intending to add an amount between the two measurements, when a big clump of baking powder broke loose and fell into the bowl.

"Oh, sh—*shoot*," Jo said, reaching in and trying to scoop out some excess with the measuring cup—though Jackson was already stirring it all together. "Kayla..."

"What?"

"How much baking powder is usually in oatmeal raisin cookies?"

"Do I look like I cook? You're the one who's over forty." At

Jo's look, she put down her phone and sighed dramatically. "I don't know, not much. Like maybe half a cup?"

"Half a cup…" Jo examined the bowl. In that case, maybe she hadn't added enough. She picked up the canister and added a liberal amount of powder to the bowl.

Gavin Steinberg had better be the cookie type.

# CHAPTER 8

*G*avin found a seat in the conference room ten minutes before the meeting was scheduled to begin, using the extra time to catch up on text messages as the others arrived. There was a response from Liz about their mom's latest attempts to get him breeding (*Trust me, ANY kind of babysitting is good, even the hypothetical kind. Get it in writing.*) and another from his former co-worker Tanner, who wanted to grab drinks Wednesday night. Though he and Ellie no longer spoke, he still heard about her—and his old company, which Tanner told him numerous times would be happy to have him back.

It was the first day of October. Though chilly enough for a jacket, inside the school they'd cranked up the heat too high, so he'd taken off his suit jacket to cool off. Rolling up the shirt-sleeves of his white shirt as Jackson's teacher and the others strolled in, he felt confident this meeting would go more smoothly than the first with Josephine. Since their encounter at the grocery store, he had more sense of where she was coming from. She was struggling, and she just wanted what was best for her son.

Putting himself in her shoes, he could see how she could be

alarmed at the idea of moving Jackson to a new class—one she knew nothing about. He'd sprung the idea on her without showing her what that new room would be like.

So he'd ease her worries. As he nodded to the others as they took their seats, he gave an especially grateful smile to Tina, the teacher in the class they wanted to place Jackson in. With her ponytail of straight dark hair and ready smile, Tina was personable and professional, and, from what he'd seen, great with the kids.

"I think this is going to put her more at ease and make this transition smoother," he said to Tina.

Everyone nodded, murmuring their agreement.

A few minutes later, there was a knock on the door.

Gavin stood to open it, and there was Josephine Palladino, five minutes early and with nary a word on her face. In fact, she looked considerably more put together than the previous meeting. She wore a knee-length navy skirt and flats, with an off-white blouse on top. Her dark curls were down around her shoulders, freshly washed. Gavin was close enough to catch a whiff of something earthy-sweet like amber. It smelled so good, he almost took a step closer before he caught himself and thrust out his hand.

"Ms. Palladino," he said. "It's good to see you again."

She had a canvas bag slung over one shoulder and a plastic container in both hands, which she shifted to shake his palm.

As her warm palm touched his, Gavin flashed back to that red bra before banishing the reptilian part of his brain to the corner.

*Jesus, Steinberg.*

"Hello," she said.

"Hi," he said, giving her hand a squeeze before releasing it.

She didn't echo his sentiment, the *good to see you* part, but her face looked a smidge more welcoming than he remembered it, though wary—like people greeted their well-meaning yet opinionated uncles at holiday dinners. She glanced around the room with a slight smile on her face.

"I made cookies," she said, raising the container in her hand. "Oatmeal raisin. I thought it would show... how much we appreciate what you've all done for Jackson." She walked over to the table and tentatively set the bounty down in the middle.

Gavin's errant thoughts aside, this meeting was off to a hell of a good start.

"Wow, thanks," Gavin said, pulling out a chair for her. "I never turn down cookies."

Her smile turned brighter and she took her seat, pulling a notebook out of her canvas bag.

As Gavin sat in his own chair, he noticed her notebook had little color-coded tabs throughout.

It was then that he felt the first tingles of apprehension.

He reached to open the container and take a cookie before passing it around the room.

"Oatmeal raisin is really the king of cookies," he said. "Give me one of these over chocolate chip any day."

Remembering where he was, he set his cookie down for a moment and cleared his throat. "Ms. Palladino, as we discussed at the last meeting, we believe Jackson would be most suited for the class at Rydell. But," he held up a hand, "I know you were surprised by that, which I understand. So I brought the teacher of that class, Tina, here today, so you could meet her and she can answer any questions you might have."

Josephine flicked a quick glance at Tina, but then addressed him. "Excuse me, Mr. Steinberg, but I'd like to correct some things that were said at the last meeting."

"Okay." Gavin picked up his cookie. "Sure."

She opened her notebook to one of the tabs. "At the last meeting, you suggested that Jackson would be a better fit in a different classroom because of how far he's regressed. But..." She pointed to a document in front of her. "Jackson historically

73

has shown periods of regression after school breaks in which it takes him up to six weeks to recoup lost skills. I have it right here."

"Oh?"

"You can make a copy of this if you'd like."

"Oh—yeah, of course."

She held the document out to him, and Gavin fumbled to take it. He realized then that he hadn't prepared for this meeting in all the ways he should have. He'd wondered if she'd get back to him and then, after the store, he'd thought about her possible feelings. But he hadn't done all his homework.

Josephine Palladino had done her homework.

Stalling, Gavin turned to the teacher of Jackson's potential class. "Tina, why don't you tell Ms. Palladino about your classroom while I look this over?"

Josephine took a deep breath and looked at the woman.

Tina had just taken a bite of a cookie and was chewing carefully, a strange look on her face. "Sure," she said, swallowing it down. Jackson's current teacher and therapists had cookies in front of them as well, but beyond a nibble or two, they hadn't been touched. Maybe they were all too nervous to eat; Gavin could understand that.

"I think you'll be pleased with the classroom," Tina said to Josephine. "It's only four students right now. Jackson would be the fifth. And—"

"Forgive me," Josephine interrupted. "You seem like a nice person. I don't mean to be rude, but I'm not sure I need to hear about this classroom yet when we haven't determined when—or *if*—my son should be moved from his current room."

She turned back to Gavin. Her eyes sparked, but unlike the first meeting, she was controlled, prepared. Determined. Gavin felt a bloom of sweat underneath his arms. Even with the vulnerability he'd seen in her face at the grocery store, here was a woman who knew what she was doing—who maybe knew things he didn't.

He didn't know what to say, so he bit into his cookie to stall, and everything got so much worse. The cookie had a faint hint of cinnamon and sweetness, but mostly it tasted—and felt—like biting into a piece of the moon. Trying to keep his face blank, he crunched over the bite in his mouth. He was sure they could hear him at the other end of the building. What the hell had she put in this thing?

Josephine was still looking at him, waiting for him to speak. He couldn't do what he desperately wanted to do, which was spit out the cookie into his hand, run out of the room, and rinse out his mouth with a gallon of water. Plaster had better texture.

Had she done this to test him? To retaliate? Or was she just a violently bad cook? Whatever the reason, he couldn't show that it was affecting him. He took another bite.

When she noticed he wasn't speaking, Josephine turned to another little colored tab in her notebook. "I'd also like to clarify what you said about class size at the last meeting," she told him. "At his elementary school, Jackson was in classes ranging from six to eight students. I have all the class lists here."

Gavin swallowed the plaster in his mouth. "That may have been appropriate for Jackson at the elementary level—they usually have more staff in those classrooms—but the staff configuration is different at the junior high level. It's like apples to oranges."

She tilted her head at him. "I doubt it's *that* different."

Before this meeting, he'd assured his boss Charlene that he'd handle this. Josephine Palladino had just been caught off guard on Friday, he'd told Charlene, same as he'd told himself. She'd had a few days to adjust, and he'd give her more information about the new classroom to make her comfortable with the transition. But instead, she was digging her heels in.

"You know why I got this job?" Charlene said to him during

that same phone call. "Because I believe in education. But I've kept this job because I know how to handle money." He could hear her tapping her pen over the phone, almost see her with her suit and dark tights, her dark hair in a neat twist, looking almost regal in her office chair. "A lot of people think money is in endless supply, you know. Like we've hidden it from them. It's not. We've got to help everybody."

He'd understood, and he'd come to this second meeting with the same purpose as the first: to facilitate Jackson's transition into that new classroom for the betterment of the entire special education program. But it was proving trickier than he expected.

"Ms. Palladino," Jeannie, Jackson's teacher, broke in. "Jackson is really struggling in the classroom. Really struggling. He struck a peer this morning."

Josephine's expression slipped a little. "He did? About what?"

"He's frustrated," Jeannie said. "We're not sure why. We were working on math skills, and he ripped up his sheet and then turned to a peer and hit him."

"Why didn't you call me?" Josephine said.

"I knew we could talk about it at the meeting," Jeannie said. "But this is what we're trying to tell you: this environment is not working. We don't have the staff to give him the one-on-one support he needs."

Josephine paused. "Then give him the one-on-one support he needs."

"What?" Jeannie said.

Josephine turned to him, a defiant look on her face. "It sounds like the team is saying Jackson needs one-on-one support in his current environment."

Gavin held up his palm. "Um—I'm not sure…"

She raised her eyebrows at him. He ate the last of the cookie in his other hand, hoping it didn't bust any of his dental work. Swallowing, he darted an uncomfortable glance at Jeannie before saying, "That's certainly something we can discuss. Though our preference is for the kids to be in the least restrictive environment, and having a one-on-one would be more restrictive than—"

"But the new class would be more restrictive," Josephine interrupted. "And you seem to be okay with that."

"That classroom is specifically designed for kids who need a more intense level of support," Gavin said. "If you'd listen to what Tina has to say, I'm sure you'd understand better what we have in mind."

This time, it was Josephine that paused, her lips pressing together as they considered each other. They might've been two people when they ran into each other at the grocery store, but here at the IEP table, they were on opposing sides; nothing had changed.

Gavin had run track in high school and college, and some of that competitive spirit still flowed through him. One of the primary rules of competition? Don't let the enemy see when they're getting to you. He reached across the table to the container of cookies—which was still full; no one had taken seconds—and took another disc of oatmeal plaster.

"Thanks for the cookies," he said, looking her right into the eye as he took a big bite.

"You're welcome," she snapped.

He broke the heated look between them long enough to notice the others gaping at him with expressions ranging from shock to a newfound respect. No one else had even braved taking a second *bite* of those cookies.

"I'd like to formally request Jackson be evaluated for a one-on-one aide," Josephine said. "In his *current* classroom. And I'd like to know what other classrooms would be available."

"That's going to require another meeting," Gavin said.

"Then let's have another meeting."

Gavin rubbed the back of his neck, closing his notebook.

"Ms. Palladino," he tried, "can't you hear that Jackson isn't doing well in his current class?"

"I hear that, Mr. Steinberg," she said. "But do you think it'll solve the problem to move him to an entirely different class, with different staff and classmates? Different rules and structure?" She shook her head. "My son isn't in a game of hot potato where you just toss him to a different room and hope for the best. You can't just say it's not working in his current class, but we aren't sure why, so let's just throw him somewhere else and see if that works."

Gavin exhaled, the fight leaving him. In its place would probably come indigestion from those cookies. She was right. He'd brought the wrong tools to this fight. He was thinking feelings, but she needed data—proof that this new class was where Jackson belonged.

"The two of us can meet again," he said, "after I discuss this with my supervisor. I don't think we need the rest of the team here until we're ready to make a decision about the class." He nodded at Jeannie, Tina, and the rest of the staff, and they got up, excusing themselves from the table.

As the others walked out of the room, Gavin pushed his notebook away and pulled up the calendar on his phone. "When are you free?"

She broke her gaze. "I'm not sure yet. I'll have to check my calendar at home."

"Okay. Just let me know."

They were alone in the room now, and he tapped his pencil on the table, studying her. Her expression was still set, but he saw her shoulders relax.

"I'm sorry this wasn't..." he started, casting a quick glance at the doorway. They were still alone. "...resolved," he finished.

"It's fine," she said quickly. "I mean, it's... well." She stood, looking away as she put her canvas bag over her shoulder and grabbed her container of cookies. "I guess it's special education," she said under her breath.

She wasn't any warmer to him, but Gavin felt something coming from her he'd sensed in the store. A sense of the person she really was away from the IEP table, someone with pains and disappointments and vulnerability and a slightly dark sense of humor. He wondered what she'd be muttering about on her way home. He wondered a lot of things about her, actually.

He stood. "I'll walk you out."

"Oh. Okay." Josephine looked surprised, and again, he saw that hidden side of her.

They walked in silence down the hall and out of the building. Even once she'd donned her sunglasses, he could sense her looking at him out of the corner of her eye. He could hardly blame her. He never usually walked parents to their cars after meetings. He didn't know why he was doing it now. Maybe he was still trying to prove he wasn't a jerk. Maybe it was because the meeting ended too soon. Maybe it was because out here in the parking lot, it was almost like they were just two people again.

As they reached her car, she was the first to break the silence. She faced him and held the container of cookies out. "Look, do you want to take the rest of these home? I saw you eat two at the meeting. If I take them home, Jackson will eat them all in one sitting, and then he'll be up until one in the morning."

"Um." Gavin shuffled his feet against the asphalt.

She tilted her head at him, her dark curls shifting and catching the sunlight in red glints. "Sorry, is that weird to ask? It's an old container, I don't need it back."

"No, it's not that." He narrowed his eyes at her, considering. Was she the type of woman to value her own pride over the truth?

No, he thought. Honesty was the way to go.

"They're terrible," he said. "Your cookies. I'm not sure I've had anything that bad in a while. It tasted like a construction crew was working in my mouth."

"What?" Her eyebrows raised over the sunglasses, and he thought he'd made a mistake, so he quickly took the container from her arms, his fingers brushing her wrists.

"Here." He popped open the lid, grabbed a cookie, and held it out to her.

She looked at him for a moment, and he realized it was a weirdly intimate gesture, but then she stepped forward and took a bite from the disc in his hand.

He slowly counted in his head as she chewed and her face puckered in disgust.

"Oh my God, that's terrible!"

"Yup." He laughed, fishing a napkin out of his pocket and holding it out to her.

She grabbed it, spitting out the remains of her cookie. "You ate two of those?" she exclaimed as she wadded the napkin. "For the love of God, why?"

"I don't know," he admitted. "Politeness? To prove I was man enough?"

"No one's man enough for that."

They still stood less than arm's length apart—closer than most acquaintances would—but Gavin didn't step away. Neither did she.

Instead she covered her face with her hands and made a small noise.

Was she about to break down? "Ms. Palladino, I didn't—"

She started snickering.

"I'm not a great cook," she said between giggles. "On account of never cooking."

He started laughing, too. "Yeah, I sort of got that."

She dropped her hands, and her voice, when it came, was warmer than he'd ever heard her address him. "I'm so sorry. I mean, about the jerk thing a little, but mostly about those cookies."

There was something that stirred inside him that was beyond relief, something almost giddy. "It's okay."

"No, really." She hiccupped back a laugh, the corners of her mouth still turned up in a smile. "My friend said it might make the meeting start off on a better note."

He shrugged. "It was memorable at least."

She sniffed. "You can call me Josephine or just Jo," she said. "The whole *Ms.* thing makes it seem like you're bagging my groceries and makes me feel ancient."

"Okay," he said. "And you're not. Ancient, I mean. Like I said, we probably grew up listening to the same bands..." He didn't know why he'd said that, why it mattered, but for some reason it did. He wanted to keep talking to her.

"Right." She straightened up, gently taking the container back and stepping away like she remembered where she was. "Well, I'd better..."

"So what bands did you listen to growing up?" he blurted.

She stopped and paused, her mouth open in surprise before she managed to answer. "Um. In high school, it was Alanis, Ani DiFranco..." she started tentatively, then added with some conviction, "Also a little Tori Amos. And a *lot* of Liz Phair."

He realized he was pushing their conversation into uncharted territory. Personal territory. But though she was only two steps away from her car, she didn't move to pull out her keys. She simply stared at him through her sunglasses—maybe because, like Gavin, she wanted to see what would happen next.

He grinned. "So Alanis and Ani, huh? What was it like being an angry young woman?"

"A lot more fun than being an angry middle-aged woman."

His smile faltered, but once he caught the teasing note in her voice he braved on. He hooked a thumb at his chest. "Tom Petty."

"Hmm?"

"My first concert."

"Oh, right." She dug her keychain out of her bag then, and hit the button to make her SUV unlock. But then she glanced back at him and her arm dropped as he heard her playing with the button. *Lock. Unlock. Lock.* "So if your first concert was Tom Petty, that means you're either seven years old or seventy."

"Try thirty-two."

"Thirty-two..." She took off her sunglasses, propped them on her forehead. "What, no Justin Timberlake?"

For a minute, Gavin was stunned by the sight of her eyes. Out here in the daylight, the green in them was incandescent. Then, the words catching up to his consciousness, he grinned. "Ha, please. Justin Timberlake? That was my second show."

"You seem like a Justin Timberlake guy." Was she teasing him? Was that what that tone in her voice meant?

"Is that an insult?"

"It's not anything. Just an observation." She was definitely teasing him.

"My third concert was Counting Crows," he said. "What do you think about me now?"

Her eyes sparkled. "That you have a better memory of your teenage years than I do."

He squinted at her. "You do a lot of drugs back then?"

Her eyes widened and flicked around the parking lot as she shook her head, incredulous. "No. And do you think I'd tell you if I had? In the parking lot of my *son's school?*"

He took a step closer to her, lowering his voice. "I'm not casting any judgments about you. Not like you seem to be casting about me and my love for Justin Timberlake."

She stared at him for a moment. And then she laughed.

For all her seriousness inside the conference room, Josephine Palladino could laugh. She scrunched her shoulders and threw her head back, dark curls bouncing. The sound was like mirth skipping. He couldn't help but smile.

She glanced back at him, biting back another giggle. "I get it. *You're funny.*"

His eyes widened. "Looking? Acting?"

"No, just... funny." She twisted her lips to the side. "I didn't realize it at first."

He smacked a hand over his heart. "Ouch." But it didn't hurt to hear, not even a little. In fact, it felt like something had shifted between them, that Josephine had decided, definitively, that he wasn't a jerk after all.

"It makes sense now why you were saying weird things at the store," she continued.

"Double ouch." His hand was still over his chest. Under his palm, he felt his breath deepen. He was enjoying this. Probably too much.

Her eyes sparkling, she gave him a devilish grin. "I think the suit threw me off."

"Again with the suit." He smiled and shook his head.

He caught her lips curling into another smile before she could help it. But then she bit her lip. "I should go," she said, jangling her keys. "I've got some work..."

"Got it." He nodded and reluctantly took a step back. "Well, it was nice talking to you... Josephine."

She looked startled for a moment, and he wondered whether he'd miscalculated. She had told him he could call her by her first name, hadn't she?

Her face smoothed and she did something with her lips that passed for a shy smile. "Okay, thanks, uh, thanks." She turned around, opening her car door.

"Okay." He couldn't help but notice she didn't call him his first name back—didn't call him anything, in fact. Maybe he'd misspoken.

Before she sat in the driver's seat, she turned. "I bet Tom Petty put on an amazing show."

His face melted into a wide grin. "He did. He really did."

She turned to sit in her car and grabbed the door handle as he shuffled his feet and started to speak. "Call me—"

Not hearing him, she pulled the door shut a second before the words came out, so they were unfortunately cut off.

"...Gavin," he finished, then swallowed with embarrassment.

LATER THAT DAY, Gavin was finishing paperwork in the conference room after another IEP when a familiar face appeared.

Jackson Palladino bounded into the room, bouncing on his toes, an occupational therapist chasing behind him.

"Jackson, wait!" she called, but Gavin held up his hand.

"It's fine," he said, closing his laptop. "Hey there, Jackson."

"Hey there," Jackson repeated, climbing into the chair by Gavin, his long legs bent towards his body. Unexpectedly, he reached out and grabbed Gavin's hand and slapped it atop some papers on the table. Then the kid grabbed his pen.

"What..." Gavin started.

"*Jackson.*" The therapist walked over, tugging on his arm and flushing madly. "I don't think he—"

"No, it's okay," Gavin said, curious about what he was going to do. "We're buddies, right Jackson?"

He watched as Jackson took his pen, bit off the cap, and put it back to the paper right besides Gavin's thumb. Then he began tracing the shape of Gavin's hand on the paper, his head bent low over his work.

Gavin chuckled. The pen tickled as it whooshed up each digit before diving back down into the sensitive webbing between his fingers.

"Sorry, he's been doing this lately," the therapist explained. "He likes to trace hands. He usually just does it with me and another therapist, though. I've never seen him run up to someone like this."

"It's fine," Gavin said, watching as Jackson lifted his hand, removed the sheet of paper, and grabbed another. He then proceeded to trace his hand again, like he hadn't gotten it quite right the first time.

"It's kind of cool, actually." He smiled up at the therapist. It was oddly soothing, the feeling of the pen against his fingers. Gavin sometimes forgot how nice it felt to remember he had skin and wasn't just made of emails and data charts.

The therapist shrugged and plopped herself down in a chair, returning his smile. "I guess it *is* good for his fine motor skills."

"True." He laughed. "Is this billable time?"

"I suppose it could be."

Jackson traced his hand a few more times—five more, actually—before he satisfied himself and, without ceremony, jumped out of his seat, grabbed three of the sheets, and bounded out of the room.

Gavin laughed as he rotated his hand to view the blue slash marks on the edges of his fingers.

He wondered about Jackson's father. Clearly he wasn't in the picture—Josephine hadn't even added his name to any of the school forms. Yet he wasn't dead. What was it she'd said at the end of that first IEP? *Jackson's father bailed before we even had our first one of these meetings.*

So he'd left them. Gavin clenched his hand into a fist, popping the knuckles on each finger. What kind of man left his family like that? A cute, interesting kid like Jackson? A woman like Josephine? Sure, she was tough and couldn't bake a cookie to save her life, but she had other things to worry about, especially if she'd been left to raise an autistic child on her own. She was also smart as a whip and loved her son, and she had decent taste in music and curls that were probably as soft as they looked. What kind of asshole did you have to be not to appreciate that—to walk away when you already had that locked down?

Gavin's hand suddenly relaxed. It dropped to the table. He leaned back in his chair and stared at the ceiling.

"Oh, no," he said into the empty conference room.

He was starting to get a crush on Josephine Palladino.

# CHAPTER 9

Jo was still working late that night, her laptop cracked open on a dining room table strewn with brochures, a few about all-inclusive resorts in the Dominican Republic and one for Carrie Stiepler, special education advocate. The IEP meeting had made her behind. The meeting that made her realize there were going to be more meetings, less friendly ones—certainly ones where Gavin Steinberg didn't walk her to her car afterward.

She sighed and took a big gulp of warm decaf coffee with extra cream and sugar. The district was still singing the same tune. She hadn't been in the meeting that afternoon long before she realized she needed an advocate immediately. She'd gone to the office of the person Holly recommended straight from the school.

"Ms. Stiepler will review your information and call you as soon as possible," the receptionist had said.

"How long will it be?" Jo asked. She knew she'd have to put off scheduling another meeting with Gavin Steinberg for however long it took to get the advocate on the phone. She wasn't about to go into another face-to-face without a bulldog by her side.

"She'll get back to you in a few days," the receptionist said, smiling politely.

"Is she worth it?" Jo asked.

The receptionist nodded, her sleek ponytail bouncing. "Oh, believe me, she's worth it."

Now Jo was playing the waiting game. She pushed away the brochures, stood, and stretched her arms over her head. She strolled by the fish tank, tapping hello to Pickles and Prometheus, before she grabbed Jackson's backpack to check for any notes from his teacher—a nightly ritual she'd come to face with stomach-clenching dread. Sure enough, in a folder next to his lunch sack was his daily progress note saying there'd been another "incident" that afternoon.

Maybe the school staff was right. Maybe her son did need another class. But what kind? Jo knew in her heart he hadn't lost those skills he'd gained during the past couple years. Could he be bored? Could he just be unhappy? What did he need?

She exhaled again, noticing another couple pages behind the progress note. She fished them out. They were all tracings of the same hand in a blue pen. Jo smiled. At least Jackson had done something he enjoyed that day. She read a pink post-it on the corner of one page in his therapist's handwriting.

*Jackson visited Mr. Steinberg today*, the note said. *He seems to really like him, or his hand at least.*

"Hmm." Jo set the page down on the kitchen counter, musing. Jackson liked to draw hands lately, but usually only hers or Kayla's or one of his favorite therapists—familiar people, and all women. She thought back to Jackson holding Gavin's hand in the grocery store. What was it about him Jax liked? His job aside, she had to admit he was nice and even funny—if strange; she was still processing the things he'd said to her after the meeting. She couldn't believe he'd told her the cookies she'd baked were terrible, but it'd made her laugh like she hadn't in months. And his questions about music... Maybe Jackson sensed him as a fellow music lover.

Flattening the page against the counter, she put her hand inside the tracing and spread her fingers. Since Jackson usually traced women's hands, they were almost always smaller. Gavin's hand was so large hers fit easily inside, his fingers at least a couple inches longer, his palm encapsulating her own. It was comforting in an odd way, and thinking about that—and the way he'd stood close to her in the parking lot, asking her questions and making her laugh—made her stomach flutter in a way she hadn't felt in years. That look in his blue eyes... Was it possible that—

"Mom, can I talk to you about something?"

Jo whirled around.

Kayla stood in the dining room, her arms crossed.

"Oh, sure." Suddenly flustered, Jo pushed the tracings of Gavin's hand under the school folder before turning around again to face Kayla.

If Kayla suspected something was up, she didn't say so. She might've been wearing SpongeBob pajamas, but her face was serious.

Jo felt a tickle of apprehension under her ribs. She walked over and sat down at the table, glancing briefly at the time. Jackson had gone to bed an hour ago. It wasn't strange Kayla was still up—she was a night owl like Jo—but she usually kept to her room at this hour. Earphones on, lights low, and texting Austin if the giggles were any indication. "What's up, honey?"

Kayla took a seat on the other end of the table and paused, tucking her dark curls behind each ear.

She finally spoke. "I want an IUD."

"What?" Jo blinked. "I mean... *what?*"

"An IUD." A pink flush colored Kayla's cheeks. "So I can be protected. When I have sex."

Jo's stomach dropped. "Sex? Are you—"

"No." Kayla shook her head. "Not yet. But... maybe soon?"

She'd phrased the statement like a question, and it gave Jo enough of a wedge to try to put a stop to it.

"I don't think that's a good idea," she said quickly. "You and... sex."

Kayla's eyebrows lowered. "Why not?"

"You're only sixteen."

It'd only been last week she'd gotten her first period, hadn't it? And the week before, she'd been in the third grade laughing at fart jokes. They weren't really here already, were they?

"Some of my friends are having it," Kayla said. "I'm a *junior*."

"Look," Jo said, shifting in her seat and trying to sound reasonable when she felt anything but, "I know you and this Austin have been hanging out, but it hasn't been that long. You can wait. You can tell him he needs to wait. If he's a good guy, he'll respect that."

She frowned. "What if *I* don't want to wait?"

"What if you..." Jo's words caught in her throat. Her eyes fell on the brochures scattered around the table, landing on the one for the advocate. "Kayla, do we need to do this now? Can we table this discussion for, I don't know, three months from now when I'm not in this big battle with the school district and our lives are a little calmer?"

"No." Her daughter crossed her arms. "Because it'll be something else. There's always something else. You can't just put this in a box and shove it in the kitchen cabinet like you do with those college brochures."

Jo flinched.

"Jackson will be starting a new school or needing a different kind of therapy or in one of his moods," Kayla continued. "If I have to wait for our lives to be calm, my lady parts are going to shrivel up and die." She threw up her hands.

Jo sighed and ran a hand across her eyes. "You're not a lady. You're a *girl*."

"I'm a young woman." Kayla straightened up in the seat. "I'm old enough. And I know what I'm doing."

"I don't think you've thought this through." Jo herself had never even had an IUD. Those were for people who were having sex. The last time she'd had to worry about that, IUDs were still something that seemed out of a science fiction movie. She'd been comfortable with condoms and the Pill. Not that she wanted Kayla asking her for either of those, either.

Kayla's chair scraped hard against the floor as she stood up, her voice rising. "How do you know I haven't thought this through? Are you a mind reader?" Her brown eyes were hard, the lines of her face taut. "You know, this is bullshit. You act like I can come to you about anything. But I try to talk to you about this openly, and you just shut me down."

Jo groaned. "You can talk to me about this stuff, Kayla. But I'm your mom, and I'm allowed to give you advice to protect you. You can't just ask me for an IUD like you're asking for twenty dollars or a new pair of jeans." She stood up, holding out her hands. "Look, let's go sit on the couch and talk about this rationally."

Kayla didn't budge. "You're the one who's not talking about this rationally. You're acting like I'm some little girl. How old were *you* when you first had sex?"

Jo squeezed her eyes shut. She'd been sixteen—and barely sixteen, even. Her boyfriend at the time was a part-time jerk, but she'd been full-time in love with him. He'd been in a band, too. Those damn musical boys.

She opened her eyes. For a few seconds, she considered lying to her daughter, but that'd never been part of their deal. Plus, Kayla would've seen straight through her.

She sighed. "I was sixteen."

"See!" Kayla shouted.

"Sixteen then was different than now," Jo said quickly. "The '90s were a different time. Sixteen then is like, I don't know, maybe nineteen now."

Kayla's mouth opened in indignation. "Your age reasoning is completely invalid. You totally know it." She put a hand on her hip. "And I've thought this through. I *have*, Mom," she said at Jo's look. "So give me one good reason I shouldn't have sex."

"Because *I'm* not having sex!"

Jo bit her tongue as soon as the words left her mouth.

Mother and daughter stared at each other, startled. The silence that followed sounded like an avalanche to Jo, a pileup of realizations that thundered in her ears. Her daughter wanted to have sex. Her daughter was probably going to have sex. She was old enough to have a daughter who was old enough (maybe) to have sex. She herself wasn't having sex. She herself would probably never have sex again, because who in their right mind…

"Okay," Kayla finally said in a small voice.

They both knew it wasn't Kayla agreeing to not do the thing. More like an agreement that they needed to end this conversation immediately, because it'd taken them to a place neither wanted to go.

"We'll talk about this later," Jo whispered, but Kayla was already sprinting to her room.

At the slamming of her daughter's door, Jo collapsed back into the kitchen chair and put her head in her arms on the table.

"Shit," she mumbled.

# CHAPTER 10

*From: Gavin Steinberg <gsteinberg@psd41.org>*
*To: Josephine Palladino <momof2masterofnone@hmail.com>*
*Date: Tuesday, October 2, 8:08 a.m.*
*Subject: Time to meet*

*Ms. Palladino,*

*We discussed yesterday holding another meeting with just the two of us
with regards to Jackson's placement. I've consulted my calendar and it
looks like Thursday afternoon my calendar is wide open. Would this be
a good time for you to meet?*

*I look forward to hearing from you.*

*Best,*

*Gavin Steinberg*

*From: Josephine Palladino <momof2masterofnone@hmail.com>*
*To: Gavin Steinberg <gsteinberg@psd41.org>*
*Date: Tuesday, October 2, 8:32 a.m.*
*Subject: Re: Time to meet*

Mr. Steinberg,

*Unfortunately Thursday afternoon is busy for me with work. In fact, the rest of this week is pretty booked. How about we touch base next week to schedule a meeting?*

*Thanks,*

*Josephine*

∾

*From: Gavin Steinberg <gsteinberg@psd41.org>*
*To: Josephine Palladino <momof2masterofnone@hmail.com>*
*Date: Tuesday, October 2, 8:37 a.m.*
*Subject: Re: Time to meet*

*Josephine,*

*Thanks for getting back to me so promptly. Sounds like this week is full for you. Perhaps we can tentatively schedule a meeting for next week, to get it on the calendar? Let me know your thoughts—I believe we can come to an agreement on Jackson's placement.*

*Gavin*

∾

*From: Josephine Palladino <momof2masterofnone@hmail.com>*
*To: Gavin Steinberg <gsteinberg@psd41.org>*
*Date: Tuesday, October 2, 8:44 a.m.*
*Subject: Re: Time to meet*

*Gavin,*

*Unfortunately, I'm not really sure of my schedule next week at all, so I'd rather we hold off scheduling anything for now. (It's like when you shake a Magic-8 Ball and it says, "Reply hazy, Try again later.") I hope you understand. I will make a note to contact you next week when things are more clear.*

*Josephine*

≈

*From: Gavin Steinberg <gsteinberg@psd41.org>*
*To: Josephine Palladino <momof2masterofnone@hmail.com>*
*Date: Tuesday, October 2, 8:48 a.m.*
*Subject: Re: Time to meet*

*It's funny, I always get "Outlook Not So Good" when I shake a Magic-8 Ball, but I guess that's the trouble with asking a hunk of plastic for dating advice.*

≈

*From: Gavin Steinberg <gsteinberg@psd41.org>*
*To: Josephine Palladino <momof2masterofnone@hmail.com>*
*Date: Tuesday, October 2, 8:49 a.m.*
*Subject: Re: Time to meet*

*Josephine,*

*Anyway, jokes aside, I'll look forward to your email next week so we can arrange the next meeting.*

*I'm also happy to discuss any of the district's concerns with you over the phone ahead of the meeting. I believe you already have my number, but, in case not, it's in my email signature below. Please don't hesitate to call me.*

*Gavin*

≈

*From: Josephine Palladino <momof2masterofnone@hmail.com>*
*To: Gavin Steinberg <gsteinberg@psd41.org>*
*Date: Tuesday, October 2, 8:52 a.m.*
*Subject: Re: Time to meet*

*It's really a shame more girls don't appreciate a guy who likes Justin Timberlake. ☺*

≈

*From: Gavin Steinberg <gsteinberg@psd41.org>*
*To: Josephine Palladino <momof2masterofnone@hmail.com>*
*Date: Tuesday, October 2, 8:53 a.m.*
*Subject: Re: Time to meet*

*You're really starting to give me a complex here. I'm not sure a woman who used to listen to so many angry female singer-songwriters should be casting stones.*

≈

*From: Gavin Steinberg <gsteinberg@psd41.org>*
*To: Josephine Palladino <momof2masterofnone@hmail.com>*
*Date: Tuesday, October 2, 8:54 a.m.*
*Subject: Re: Time to meet*

*And what did you mean by, "You seem like a Justin Timberlake guy"
anyway?*

*(In my book, it means I'm incredibly cool.)*

∾

*From: Josephine Palladino <momof2masterofnone@hmail.com>*
*To: Gavin Steinberg <gsteinberg@psd41.org>*
*Date: Tuesday, October 2, 8:57 a.m.*
*Subject: Re: Time to meet*

*I didn't mean anything that bad by it. His songs are very catchy.*

*(Here's where I admit I used to listen to Justin Timberlake, too.)*

∾

*From: Gavin Steinberg <gsteinberg@psd41.org>*
*To: Josephine Palladino <momof2masterofnone@hmail.com>*
*Date: Tuesday, October 2, 8:58 a.m.*
*Subject: Re: Time to meet*

*Ha! The secret's out.*

∾

*From: Josephine Palladino <momof2masterofnone@hmail.com>*
*To: Gavin Steinberg <gsteinberg@psd41.org>*
*Date: Tuesday, October 2, 9:00 a.m.*
*Subject: Re: Time to meet*

*Don't tell me you never listened to Alanis.*

≈

*From: Gavin Steinberg <gsteinberg@psd41.org>*
*To: Josephine Palladino <momof2masterofnone@hmail.com>*
*Date: Tuesday, October 2, 9:04 a.m.*
*Subject: Re: Time to meet*

*I did. I missed some of the subtext in "You Oughta Know," though, considering I was a preschooler at the time.*

≈

*From: Josephine Palladino <momof2masterofnone@hmail.com>*
*To: Gavin Steinberg <gsteinberg@psd41.org>*
*Date: Tuesday, October 2, 9:05 a.m.*
*Subject: Re: Time to meet*

*OMG. Thank you for making me feel incredibly old.*

≈

*From: Gavin Steinberg <gsteinberg@psd41.org>*
*To: Josephine Palladino <momof2masterofnone@hmail.com>*
*Date: Tuesday, October 2, 9:06 a.m.*
*Subject: Re: Time to meet*

*You're not. I was hanging out at the playground watching those high school girls drive by blasting Alanis and Ani and thinking how I'd never be that cool.*

*At least we'll always have Tom Petty to make us both feel timeless.*

～

*From: Josephine Palladino <momof2masterofnone@hmail.com>*
*To: Gavin Steinberg <gsteinberg@psd41.org>*
*Date: Tuesday, October 2, 9:11 a.m.*
*Subject: Re: Time to meet*

*That's true.*

～

*From: Gavin Steinberg <gsteinberg@psd41.org>*
*To: Josephine Palladino <momof2masterofnone@hmail.com>*
*Date: Tuesday, October 2, 9:20 a.m.*
*Subject: Re: Time to meet*

*Anyway, I know you're busy with work. Which is where I'm at now too, so... Again, please let me know if you have any questions before our next meeting. I'll look for your email next week. If I haven't said it before, I think we can come to an agreement we're all satisfied with.*

*Into the Great Wide Open,*
*Gavin*

# CHAPTER 11

*a*fter a school tour on Wednesday, Gavin holed up in his car and called his sister Liz.

It was five hours ahead in England, around dinnertime. But he knew she'd pick up; they usually only texted, so calling would catch her off-guard.

Sure enough, she answered on the second ring. "Ok, who died?"

"Nobody," he said. "But I need you to talk me down from a ledge."

"A ledge?"

"Yeah." He grimaced in embarrassment. "A romantic ledge."

She paused, probably recalling his breakup with Ellie. "Seems like you're pretty good at getting off those ledges yourself."

He exhaled and leaned back in his driver's seat. A couple teachers walked by in the lot of the school where he was parked, casting glances at him through the windshield. He waved awkwardly.

He knew his vehicle was soundproof, but still he lowered his voice to answer Liz. "This is someone new. Someone I shouldn't be developing feelings for. But I am. I need you to talk me out of it."

Liz sighed, and he heard the sounds of her adjusting her position in the background. "Okay, but Bea's here nursing and she's had a low-grade fever all day and a mood to match. So you're going to have to tell me the good parts first."

"The good parts?"

"Why you like her. What she's like. You know, the good stuff."

"Okay." Gavin took a deep breath. "Okay, so she's really smart and fights for what she believes in. And she's genuine, like her attitude is very much here-I-am-and-everything's-a-mess-but-deal-with-it. It's refreshing. I should mention too that she's got curly dark hair and these green eyes that are, like, I don't know. I've never seen eyes like this."

Liz's tone was singsong with humor. "Uh-huh."

"She's got decent taste in music, which we both know is important. And she smells really good… Gah!" He rubbed a hand down his face. "This is counterproductive. Tell me to get over it."

"Get over it?" Liz said, and dammit if she didn't say it like a question.

He made a frustrated sound. "Say it like you mean it."

Liz laughed. "I'm sorry, but this is too much fun. You've never asked me to talk you out of liking a woman before."

"She—she's the mother of one of my students," he said, putting his forehead on the steering wheel.

"Oh, boy," Liz said. "Hold on, I need to switch boobs."

"I didn't need to know that," Gavin murmured at the rustling sounds in the background.

"Oh, I'm sorry, was that too TMI for you?" Liz said once she'd gotten back on. "You want to tell me more about how this woman you like smells?"

He straightened up and exhaled, trying to smooth down his

hair. He would have to go back to work eventually. "I'm in trouble, Liz. I walked her out to her car the other day and we ended up talking about which bands we loved growing up. And then yesterday I emailed back and forth with her. I'm trying not to email her again today, just to check in and say hi."

"Sounds tawdry," Liz said, but cleared her throat. "Okay, let's be logical about this: how many women have you dated since Ellie?"

"Two. Maybe three. Nothing that lasted very long. A couple drink dates here and there."

"So maybe she's a rebound," Liz said thoughtfully.

"This doesn't feel like a rebound," he said. "It just feels like a... bound."

After a pause, they both started laughing.

As their laughter died down, he added, "The situation is just really complex. I'm actually negotiating with her over where the school district wants to place her son versus where she thinks he needs to be. Or doesn't need to be. It's complicated and frustrating." He sighed. "And dammit if I can't wait to see her again."

A deep voice rumbled on Liz's end, then at her response, the voice raised.

"Gavin? On the phone? Did someone die?"

"No," Liz said, and Gavin could tell she was smiling an ocean away. "He's got *woman issues*."

More rustling came before Ben, his high school buddy-turned-brother-in-law, popped on the phone. "Gavin! Hey there, man."

"Hey, Ben."

"So you found someone else, huh? I knew it'd happen. I told your mom at Passover that you'd find someone and fall in love and get married and all that sh-stuff eventually."

"So you're the one who started that rumor," Gavin said. "Thanks a lot."

Liz's voice came back, like she'd wrenched the phone from

her husband. "If you really don't want this to happen, Gavin—if it's really that complicated of a situation—I have a suggestion."

"I'm all ears."

"Be honest with her. Try to give her more perspective on the district's side of the things, why they want to do what they're doing, as much as you can. Then maybe you can reach an agreement quicker, so that—"

"—we can get everything resolved and stop having meetings," Gavin finished. "You know, that might actually work." He'd have to be careful, not reveal too much of the district's plans, but maybe a little hint of the future of Jackson's current classroom would let Josephine know that her son couldn't stay there forever. They could work much quicker to find a solution and finalize the paperwork. And that would likely mean no more meetings until next year.

He tried to ignore the way the disappointment of not seeing her for so many months sat heavy in his chest.

LATER, he met his friend Tanner for a drink on his way home from work. Still with Gavin's old sales company, Tanner and his wife lived in University City, a neighborhood bordering the western Philadelphia suburbs and close enough for Gavin to come meet him without being stuck in traffic for an eternity. Their local bar reflected the neighborhood: clean mahogany booths and warm lighting, a mix of grad students and city professionals with a smattering of suburban tradesmen who appreciated good craft beer. The steady hum of conversation flowed over the buzz of the television screen at the bar broadcasting a football game.

As Gavin walked in, Tanner stood and clapped him on the back. Sporting trim brown hair and a beard, Tanner still had on his button-down dress shirt from work, but he'd loosened the green tie around his neck.

"I started without you," Tanner said. "Sorry not sorry."

"I see how it is." Gavin slid into the booth across from him, a tall dark beer already waiting at his spot. Feeling that old competitiveness from sales, he grabbed the beer and took a long, deep swallow, catching up to whatever lead Tanner may have had in the drinking department. He needed it. It wasn't that it'd been a hard week, but it'd been a complicated one, that was for sure. His body hummed with a dozen emotions, most he shouldn't be feeling. After his conversation with Liz, he had a plan to gain some distance from Josephine while giving them both what they needed, but damned if he didn't already feel rebellious against it. Would it be possible for the two of them to argue for just two more meetings? Three? Long enough to determine how strong his feelings were?

Setting his beer down, Gavin looked at Tanner, eager to focus on anything else. "So how's everyone back at the company?"

"They're all pretty good," Tanner said. "Jack's wife is pregnant with twins. Scooter got transferred up to New York. So there's an open spot if, you know, anyone was interested. Oh, and Ellie says hi."

Gavin paused. "She does?"

Tanner watched his face carefully. "Yeah. She does."

"Oh." Gavin tried to smooth over his surprise. "Well, tell her I said hi back."

He hadn't seen his ex since a week after they broke up, when they'd met to exchange items they'd left at each other's places. She hadn't wanted to, and he respected that.

He thought of Ellie's devastated face as they'd gone back to her apartment after that holiday walk downtown. He'd fumbled through the breakup, his usual charm and organized planning replaced with a quick decision spurred by the panicky realization that he didn't want the life he had. He said that watching that mechanized Christmas village had made him think of how he was just going through the motions, and did she know what he meant? She didn't. He said he was sorry, and that this was coming out wrong, and that she was such a catch, plenty of guys would want her, but he needed a break because he no longer knew what he wanted. She was crying then, and he added she could put a mob hit on him, that he would understand that, and that he'd like to remain friends but he'd leave it up to her, it was totally in her court.

He'd told his mother much the same, minus the mob hit part, because with all her connections in their community, he didn't want to take that chance. She'd barely spoken to him all through Hanukkah.

"You know," Tanner said in the bar. "You still hold the sales record. Nobody's touched it yet."

"Huh." Gavin took another drink. This wasn't the first time Tanner had mentioned this.

Tanner picked up his glass of beer. "So how's your new job?"

"Pretty good," he answered. "I like knowing I'm helping these kids. I mean, of course there are frustrations, just like any job." Truth be told, he didn't know if working for the district was what he truly wanted, either. He felt good about making a difference in the kids' lives. Yet even after six months, there were still some days when going to work felt like pulling on a sock that'd shrunk in the dryer.

Tanner took a sip and eyed him over his beer. "You like the people you're working with?"

"Sure. They're fine." Gavin guessed, based on the way they'd trash-talked people who'd left the company when he was still there, that his old friends probably thought he hung around old ladies and Mr. Rogers types. But then his mind, like a lighthouse beacon, swung to Josephine once again.

Gavin put his elbows on the table and leaned toward Tanner. "Hey, man, can I ask you something?"

Tanner raised his eyebrows. "Sure."

"What would you do if, say, you started developing feelings for a client at work? Feelings that would put you in a hard spot ethically. What would you do?"

"I'd go out with someone else," Tanner said automatically.

"To distract yourself? To prove you can do it?"

"Yeah. All that." Tanner nodded, eyeing him suspiciously. "You okay, Gavin?"

"Yeah. Sure." Gavin gave an uneasy smile. He didn't want to say more about Josephine, recalling how much the people at his old job gossiped. He sat back and tried to appear relaxed, glancing at the screen over the bar, where the Philadelphia Eagles had just tackled Dallas, both teams clearly revved to break the tied score. Appearing unaffected had been his usual demeanor in sales, one that had seeped into other areas of his life. Pretend that everything's fine, everything's cool, it's all water off a duck's back. Seemed a good strategy until you realized that real life was messy and unpredictable and you didn't always know what you were doing.

As they watched the game, Dallas pulled ahead, a player spiking the football on the ground and throwing his hands into the air.

Now it was Tanner's turn to lean forward. "Listen, Gavin, I just want to say that, what happened between you and Ellie? I get it."

Gavin's smile fell. "You do?"

"Yeah." Tanner put his left elbow on the table and held the back of his hand up, pointing to his wedding band. "Before this happened, I was freaked out. I thought, ok, we'll get married, but then she'll expect us to wear matching pajamas over the holidays and then we'll get a dog and he'll have to get a pair to match and then kids and I'll never be able to sleep in and I'll be living in some cheesy holiday card..." He shuddered. "But it's not that bad. Really. And even if it was, it's like, this is what it means to be a man. You know?"

"Yeah," Gavin said, even though he didn't.

Tanner leaned back and drummed his fingers against the table. "Just think about it."

# CHAPTER 12

*J*o was waiting for advocate Carrie Stiepler's call Thursday afternoon when Kayla got home.

The teen collapsed on the couch with a textbook to study for a test. She mumbled only a quick hello to her mom. Neither of them had said more than a handful of words to each other since what Jo had come to mentally refer to as *that God-awful sex talk*. As difficult as it seemed to figure out how to meet Jackson's needs, parenting a teenage daughter was fraught with perils she hadn't properly prepared herself for. In the place of her sweet, crime-watching companion was now this adult-sized young woman who wanted sex and independence and was quick to point out all the places her mother was lacking.

Jo was trying to ignore the deafening silence that stretched between them and working on a few travel itineraries when her friend Holly's son, Sean, showed up.

The nineteen-year-old was brawnier than Jo remembered, tall and growing a red-gold beard to match the hair he'd inherited from his mother.

He stepped over the threshold, putting his hands into his

pockets. "Um, my mom wanted me to pick up the cookie supplies?"

"Sure, Sean."

As she gathered the sack of ingredients Holly had brought her, she heard him speaking to Kayla in a deep voice.

"You studying or something?"

"Yeah. American History."

"Any good?"

"No."

The kids had known each for years, but as Jo came back carrying the bag, she noticed Sean giving her daughter a distinctly extra-friendly look as she studied.

Was Kayla dipping herself in pheromones each morning? Jo couldn't even with these boys. And she wasn't ready for her daughter to be involved with anyone college-age, as sweet as Sean was.

Jo cleared her throat. "She's studying for a high school exam," she said pointedly. "Because she's still in high school."

Kayla glanced up to give her a brief confused look, but Sean got her message, turning a deep red as he took the sack awkwardly from her hands.

"Th-thanks," he said, stumbling back towards the door.

"Tell your mother thank you."

As Sean left, Jo's phone rang. It was Carrie Stiepler. *Thank God.*

The advocate cut right to the chase. "I've reviewed Jackson's paperwork," she said. "I think it's unacceptable, what the district is doing."

"Right?" Jo flushed with righteous anger at the advocate's words, and not a little gratitude.

"They can't do this," Carrie said. Her tone was sure enough to brook no disagreement. Jo could already tell why she was the best. "They may want to, and I'm guessing there's some other reason why they're wanting to shuffle him. But Jackson's almost up for evaluation. We can demand he be evaluated first. We should."

"We should? But won't that just delay—"

"Yes," Carrie said. "But that will give us time to explore options. I don't trust the district. Any of them. Really. And you shouldn't, either."

"Okay." Jo paused, thinking of her email exchange the other day with Gavin Steinberg and feeling guilty—although for what, she wasn't sure. "I told our coordinator that I'd meet with him, one-on-one, to discuss other options. Can you come with me? I can tell him you'll—"

"Yes. Every meeting you go to, I'm at. If you're hiring me, at least," the advocate added, though the confidence in her voice made it seem like it would be impossible for Jo not to. "You don't need to tell the coordinator I'm coming. It's your right to have anyone you want at that meeting. Let us have the element of surprise."

"Oh. Okay." Jo wondered what Gavin's face would look like when she arrived with Carrie. Would it be better or worse than his reaction to those terrible cookies? She shook her head. Why was she worrying about it? She was doing this for her son—*he* was what mattered, not the feelings of some grown man who was supposed to be helping them.

Carrie's tone softened. "Look, I know I sound like a hard ass. I *am* a hard ass. It's how I get them to do what they should be doing." She paused. "My sister has special needs like your son. She has Down Syndrome. But when we were growing up, there were almost no resources. I'm fighting for what she never got a chance to have." She cleared her throat. "Anyway, I'll fight like hell if you hire me."

Jo took a deep breath. "Of course I want to hire you. When can you meet?"

They settled on a few free days and times within the next week, and by the end of the day Jo fired off an email to Gavin

Steinberg, saying her schedule had opened up and could he meet Monday? She didn't mention that Carrie Stiepler would be attending as well.

IN THE CONFERENCE room at Jackson's school on Monday, she was seated at a table with Gavin once again. Except this time, they were alone—until Carrie showed up.

The advocate had sent Jo a text earlier, saying she was stuck in traffic and would be a few minutes late, and not to make any decisions until she arrived. Jo thought of dawdling in her car, but she was already outside the reception area of the school, and Gavin had spotted her through the clear glass front.

"Hi," she said, clutching her bag against her body nervously. She had on a black dress that she normally only wore to meet clients in person. It was nice and suitable—at least, that's what she told herself.

"Hi." His grin was warm, easy. He had no idea that she was bringing reinforcements. "Let's get you signed in and we can head back to the room."

He gestured with his hand as she walked past him, and Jo thought for one second he was going to touch her shoulder and guide her to the desk. He didn't, of course, but the feeling lingered. The dynamic had shifted between them since the last meeting, certainly since they'd emailed but probably even earlier, when he'd walked her to her car and fed her one of her own terrible cookies.

When they'd emailed back and forth the other day, things had turned friendly... even flirtatious? Maybe she'd started it when she'd made the weird offhand comment about the Magic-8 Ball, but then he'd said the thing about dating and they'd gone back and forth, teasing each other.

It had felt like flirting—at least, how she'd remembered it

felt. Like drinking too much espresso too fast. Later that afternoon, she'd had the urge to send him a link to a Justin Timberlake music video but had held off, shaking her head to herself. They weren't friends. They probably were never going to be friends.

After she signed in at the front desk, she followed Gavin down a school hallway to the conference room. He held the door for her. Today he wore a light blue dress shirt that made his eyes look less like the hue of river rocks and more like the ocean. His brown hair was also messy, like he'd run his fingers through it one too many times.

"So you had a busy week?" he asked as she took a seat.

"Yeah, pretty busy," she said lightly, feeling awkward at the half-lie she'd fed him while waiting to hear back from Carrie.

"Things have calmed down?" He took a seat at the table, but this time it was near her. He dropped a folder on the table and swiveled to face her, studying her face attentively.

"Things never calm down," she said.

"Never?"

"Not when you have kids and a job and a cat that vomits every twenty minutes."

The corner of his mouth quirked up. "You're right, that doesn't sound calm."

Jo shrugged. Then, realizing she should probably keep up the small talk until Carrie arrived, she turned her seat to face him and asked a question. "So is your life... calm?"

He glanced away a moment, straightening his folder on the table. "Not at the moment." He met her eyes. "Maybe calm is overrated. Maybe it's just another word for boring."

Jo gave a short laugh. "I wouldn't mind a few boring months."

"Yeah?"

"Yeah."

Gavin glanced away briefly before leaning forward to rest

112

his elbows on his knees and lowering his voice. "Listen," he began, "these placement decisions, like in Jackson's situation, I know they can be complicated. There are many factors involved —things we don't always discuss with, um, parents." He paused, then rolled his chair close enough to her that their knees touched.

Jo's nerves tingled. It was such a light touch, it was nothing, he probably didn't even realize he'd done it. Still she remained absolutely still, her attention riveted by that inch of contact where his pant leg brushed her bare skin.

"Josephine..." he started.

Carrie Stiepler opened the door and walked into the room.

"Sorry I'm late," she said, her tone brisk. "Traffic."

Josephine stood quickly, her heart hammering—both from the advocate's arrival and Gavin's nearness to her, not to mention their knocking knees. He'd been about to say something. What had he been about to say?

"No problem," Jo said, her voice quaking on account of not feeling like she had the breath to speak. "Um, Mr. Steinberg, this is—"

"Carrie Stiepler," he finished, standing up himself. "Good to see you again, Ms. Stiepler. What's it been, two months?"

His voice was as calm and professional as ever, but Jo knew a lie when she heard one. Nobody at the district was ever glad to see this woman.

Gavin cast a quick glance at her—it wasn't unfriendly, but she detected a trace of *Et tu, Bruté?* there.

Well, so, he should've seen this coming. She was fighting for her son and if the district didn't do what was right for him, she'd call in the troops.

His face smoothed and he reached out to shake the advocate's hand. "So you're working with Ms. Palladino, I assume?"

"Correct." Giving him a tight smile, Carrie found a seat at the table—the head of the table—and opened up a manila folder covered in notes. She wore a royal blue pantsuit, her dark blond hair pulled back in an elegant knot and a pair of thick-framed glasses over her eyes. "I think we can go ahead and get started," she said, like she'd been the one waiting for them.

"Sure." Gavin dropped a pen on the table and sat down heavily while Jo took her own seat, resisting the urge to apologize. She didn't have anything to be sorry about, did she?

No, she didn't.

"Word to the wise, Mr. Steinberg," Carrie began. "You always need to have a plan in place, *especially* with special needs kids. 'It isn't working in classroom A, so let's toss him in classroom B' is *not* a plan. You don't have any clear data to show why this would be a good idea. Next time, bring your receipts."

"We've been—" Gavin began, but Carrie raised her voice.

"You haven't got the data. And that's the problem, isn't it?" Carrie glanced down at her notes. "This child is due for reevaluation in December. We're requesting the district reevaluate him now. *Then* we'll talk. In the meantime, we would also like to request that he has a one-on-one aide assigned to him."

Jo sensed him looking at her from the corner of her eye. Not looking at him, she nodded her assent.

"Excuse me," Gavin said. "I've got to make a quick call."

He slipped out of the room.

Jo let out the breath she'd been holding.

"He's got to go call the director of special ed," Carrie said. "Charlene Matthews is the one who makes the big decisions around here. He's going to confer with her, but she knows she has to grant this request. Especially once he tells her I'm involved."

"So what happens now?" Jo asked.

"The district has forty-five days to evaluate him," Carrie said. "And believe you me, they'll take that whole time. In the meantime, they'll be trying to see if they have enough data to place him where they want."

"And if they do?"

Carrie shrugged. "They might still give us what we want. Especially if we're causing too much hassle—and too much of the district's money—to make taking the situation further not worth it. They don't like squeaky wheels." She pushed her glasses up her nose and flashed Jo a grin. "I'm a very loud wheel."

Jo didn't doubt it. She recalled Gavin's words before Carrie had arrived. *There are many factors involved—things we don't always discuss with, um, parents.* Whatever he'd been about to say, she knew it was something he shouldn't, something off the record. The other thing she knew was that she wasn't going to tell Carrie what he'd said. It would add more ammunition to their arsenal, sure, but she felt that odd warmth to him, some secret loyalty she couldn't pull out like a weed.

She took a deep breath. It didn't matter. The evaluation would help show what Jackson really needed—or at least a clearer picture of where he was at. "What options should we explore?"

"*All* the classrooms that the district has for special ed," Carrie said. "And private placement."

"Private school?" Jo said. "Isn't that—"

"The district would pay for it," Carrie said, "if we can prove that's the most suitable placement."

"I know," Jo said. "But it's just that Jackson did well in the district elementary school. I'm not sure we need something *that* different." She'd never considered private school before—to pay out-of-pocket would cost her nearly as much as a college tuition. "I've always supported the public school system."

"This isn't about making a political statement," Carrie said. "It's about what's best for your son. Some school districts are large and specialized enough to accommodate a wide variety of kids with special needs. Some are too tiny. We're in the middle here. You should consider private placement," she repeated.

Jo pressed her lips together and nodded. "Okay." She added, "Thank you for being here."

"My pleasure."

Gavin returned to the room, slipping his cell back into his pocket. "We're going to reevaluate Jackson," he said—but to Jo only. "I can tell you a bit more about the process, but it will last up to forty-five days and include assessing him across all areas of functioning."

Jo met his gaze. "Good," she said, and then because she still felt a flutter of guilt, she added, "Thank you."

His smile was slight and carried a hint of wistfulness she felt in her gut.

"I'm going to need some additional information," Carrie said, rummaging through the pages in front of her. "There is some data missing from Jackson's file."

"Okay." Gavin turned to her, his voice resigned.

Carrie started listing the information they needed as Jo's mind wandered. Had he been flirting with her the other day? Maybe he was just being friendly. He was probably one of those nice, funny men who seemed like they were flirting with everyone. Maybe he was even doing it to butter her up between meetings.

Maybe he was married, even.

As he jotted down some notes while Carrie spoke, Jo's glance slipped to his fingers.

No ring.

So he wasn't married. Not that it mattered. It mattered not at all. Zero. Especially now. She didn't know why she'd even looked. He probably had a girlfriend. Maybe a couple. And even if he didn't, he was a decade younger than she was. And even if that didn't matter, he was still the man across the table. Grocery heroics aside, at the end of the day he was a gatekeeper, and she meant to burn down the fence.

The advocate still reading him the riot act, Gavin leaned back in his chair and noticed her staring at him.

She glanced away, flushing in a mixture of embarrassment and guilt. When she looked over again, he was still staring at her. His gaze looked down at his hand, then back up at her. His eyebrow raised.

He'd caught her.

# CHAPTER 13

*O*ver the past week, Gavin had tried to reconstruct when he first started developing feelings for Josephine Palladino. Initially, he assumed it was when he'd caught sight of her red bra that first meeting. It'd certainly been a point when he'd gone from viewing her as a mom to seeing her as a woman. But he wasn't in the habit of trawling for women at work. Sure, he noticed when he was in the room with an attractive woman —he wasn't blind—but he never considered romantic potential there. At this job especially, he assumed most of them were married, and they were almost always older, with lives more settled and complicated than his own.

Granted, Josephine was older and had a more complicated life than his own, but something else had made him see her as more than just a mom at the table.

No, the red bra wasn't the whole story. There'd been that run-in at the grocery store, and the conversation after the second IEP, and their email exchanges. Somewhere in there he'd begun seeing her as a person he wanted to learn more about. He could name qualities about her he liked, like he'd done for his sister—she was smart and funny and fought like hell for her son

—but mostly there was this: he wanted to get to know her better. He wanted to know what she thought and felt, how she ended up where she was, where she wanted to be in five years, what her curls felt like in his hands. He wanted to unwrap her like a Matryoshka doll. He wanted to *know* her.

But it was an impossible situation. She was still a parent, and he was the guy on the other side of the table—a guy she'd called a jerk, even—and approaching her as anything but her son's coordinator was not only tricky, it was unwise. And now it would be impossible.

She knew it, too. Which was why he was surprised to see her looking at his hand.

He would've thought nothing of it had he not been the recipient of a ring check before or been in the habit himself. It was a thing that people did.

But he didn't know people included Josephine Palladino.

She looked away again, tucking a lock of dark curl behind her ear, and Gavin second-guessed himself. Maybe she hadn't been doing what he'd suspected. After all, she was playing hardball now. She had an advocate, and not just any advocate but Carrie Stiepler. The woman practically had a wanted poster in the main special education offices. She was the Annie Oakley of advocates. Gavin had been warned about her when he'd first started at the job, and it'd hardly done her justice.

"Carrie Stiepler's involved," he'd told Charlene over the phone when he'd stepped out of the meeting.

"Oh, Lord," she muttered. "What are they asking for?"

"A reevaluation," Gavin said, adding, "He is due for another in the winter. It could be helpful. For everybody."

"Fine," Charlene said. "Give it to them. I'll call the lawyer."

This is where they were now. This is why anything starting between them would be impossible. It ended here. It would no longer be he and Josephine at the table, but her advocate and the district lawyer hashing out the gory details over the phone. As much as he'd tried to take Liz's advice to bring the situation to a close quicker, he was frustrated it'd come to this, and they couldn't work out a speedy solution for Jackson's best interest— not to mention her not telling him earlier, which he guessed was Carrie's suggestion. But in a moment of clarity, he realized not seeing Josephine again was a disappointment he almost couldn't stand, a fist of remorse he didn't know how to work around.

He really, really wanted to see her again.

All that time he'd spent in sales flirting with flight attendants and professional women in tight skirts, and here he was falling for a woman who wore words on her face and had aggressively bad baking skills.

"I think we're done here," Carrie said after she'd finished dictating to him the paperwork she needed. He got that she meant *done* in more than one sense of the word, and that *we* meant him only.

Josephine stood up, thanking Carrie swiftly before excusing herself to the bathroom and studiously avoiding his gaze.

He gave Carrie a polite handshake on her way out, then packed up his own paperwork. It was the end of the day, and he was vacillating between hitting the gym and grabbing a six-pack on the way home. Either way, his tense muscles needed a release from work, his heavy spirits a lift out of this frustration. Yet he dawdled in the hallway, wanting one last word with Josephine.

When she walked out of the restroom, he was leaning over getting a drink at the water fountain.

She stopped. "Hi." She had on a black dress that was too nice for any IEP meeting. He liked the way it narrowed at her waist. He imagined his own hands at that very spot.

He'd already straightened up, but his finger still pressed the water fountain button like a trigger, the stream of water arcing up.

"Hi," he finally said, releasing the water. Was this how boxers greeted each other after a fight? A sort of awkward politeness, an uncertainty about where you each stood outside the ring?

"I was just leaving for the day," Gavin said. "Walk you to your car?"

After a hesitation, she nodded and adjusted the bag slung over her shoulder. "Sure."

They walked out into the lot in silence. Even though Gavin's car was parked on the other side, he walked beside her, as if by some unspoken agreement.

Beside her car, she turned to him and her lips parted. Nothing came out.

So Gavin rushed to fill the silence with the thing he wanted most to know.

"So," he started, "how are you?"

Her lips pressed together, and he became aware of it, that wall she'd put up between them for the meeting, before he saw it slip down, piece by piece. Then he saw what he'd seen before —at the store, in this same lot: a woman who used to rock out to Alanis Morissette and was just trying to do her best. *This* is what he'd been missing with Ellie, this awareness of life's difficulties and dead-ends, messy realities and impossible choices. An aching vulnerability that still got up in the morning and brushed its teeth. For all Tanner's talk about being a man, Gavin realized with a jolt that his former co-workers often acted like kids playing dress-up—swapping designer outfits, posing, doing the very next thing in the collective storyline they had all decided to follow.

She swallowed, her gaze holding his. "I'm okay."

"Good."

They stood two feet apart, right on that slim boundary between polite distance and intimacy. But she wasn't moving to her car and neither was he, so he threw another question at her. "So what do you do for work?"

"I'm a travel agent."

"Oh." He jiggled the keys in his pocket, wanting to lighten the mood. "Any deals on getaways coming up? Because I'm feeling the need for a vacation right now."

He caught the start of her smile before she managed to hide it. "There's a discounted cruise out of Galveston leaving in two days," she said. "If you drive fast, you might be able to make it."

"I can drive fast."

"It's a cruise for two, though," she added.

"Damn," he said. "It is really rough being single sometimes."

Her eyes twinkled then, with something like curiosity or interest. Something Gavin wanted to see more.

He remembered her looking at his hand earlier. Was it possible the attraction he felt for her wasn't one-sided?

"It's a pirate cruise," she said softly, rocking back and forth on her feet. "You'd need to be in pirate garb the whole time. And bring a wench."

"I'm fresh out of wenches."

Through Gavin's veins came a flush of excitement like he was about to jump into something he'd never before experienced.

As his heart skipped a beat, he did something foolish.

"Are you going to that formal fundraiser later this week?" he asked in a rush.

# CHAPTER 14

*J*o's heart started hammering in her chest, but at first she didn't know why.

"The thing to raise money for the elementary school playground?" Gavin continued, taking a step closer to her. "It's supposed to be a pretty nice event."

"Oh," she said. "I don't know…" Jo stared at him. This close, she had to crane her neck to meet his gaze. His blue eyes were wide, almost beseeching. She added, "Maybe. I mean, it was Jackson's former school, so I probably should."

"You should," he said quickly.

She paused. "I should?"

He held her eyes a beat. "Yeah."

"Well. Okay then."

They both took a deep breath—she felt her lungs expand at the same time his chest rose—and when they exhaled, they shared a smile that made Jo's stomach flip.

"Good," he finally said. "So I guess I'll see you there?"

She blinked, but then nodded. "Yes, I guess I'll see you there."

She turned and opened her car door, a desperate need to flee filling her veins. Something between her and Gavin had gotten intense—and quickly. She needed room to breathe—and time to think about what had just happened.

After starting the car, she pulled out of the lot, giving him a quick wave as butterflies banged on the walls of her stomach.

Gavin's words echoed in her head.

*Are you going to that formal fundraiser later this week?*

Had that been... him asking her out on a *date*?

"No." She said the word out loud to herself and shook her head while stopped at a traffic light. God, she was completely ridiculous and pathetic. Her dry spell was really showing. Gavin hadn't asked her anything of the sort—certainly not if she'd go with him. He'd just asked, out of polite curiosity, to see if she was attending a school event.

But then what had his *Good* meant when she'd said she'd be there?

She rehashed the conversation in her head, but it was fruitless. It hadn't been anything he said, but the way he'd spoken. The way things had felt between them. The way he glanced around... Like his behavior with her wasn't because of his job—maybe it was even in spite of it.

Then there was the way he was standing so close to her, and the look in his eyes, and the way his voice had gone low when she said she'd be there. The way her heart had been beating—softly, but audibly—while they'd exchanged words. The way it was still beating now, her breath coming quicker and her body flushing.

She made a turn and drove down a street that had a cute little vintage clothing shop. She'd passed by it countless times, but had never stopped. When she was in high school and college, she loved shopping for antique and secondhand clothes with her friends—funky and offbeat outfits, dresses with delicate beading or soft fabric that she could never wear now for fear of mustard stains.

Now, on a whim, she pulled into the small parking lot in

front of the store. *Vintage Frocks*, it was called. She turned the car off and stepped out, her body guided by the thrummings of her heart more than any sense.

The door to Vintage Frocks had a little bell overhead, and it dinged as Jo entered a low-ceiling room with a smell that reminded her of those long-ago secondhand shopping days: an almost sweet scent of fabric underneath the fresh aroma of detergent—clothing worn and washed and waiting to be worn again.

A circular rack of gowns was directly in front of her—a rainbow of fabric from soft peaches to beaded blacks to bright emerald satin—and along the front window of the shop, tiny jeweled shoes paraded.

Jo knelt down to check the tag on a shiny pair of heeled sandals when her eyes popped open at the price. *That* had changed since she'd been in school, for sure. Now vintage was trendy, and certain items were considered more valuable.

*What was she doing here?*

"Can I help you?" an older woman called, walking up from a room in the back.

"Oh, no—thanks," Jo stammered. "I'm just looking." *Looking at dresses I can never afford*, she added in her head, because if she wasn't able to pay the equivalent of the water bill on a pair of shiny pumps, she had her doubts about being able to purchase anything else in this store.

"Are you looking for anything in particular?" the woman asked. She had dyed auburn hair styled in careful waves, a pantsuit, and a kind smile on her face. "Something for a special occasion?"

"Um, do you have anything discounted?" Jo said. "There's just this thing at my son's old school in a couple days. He's special needs, and there's this fundraiser..."

The woman's smile widened. "Sure."

She walked to the far end of the store and Jo followed,

admiring several flared '50s-style dresses they passed on the way to a rack against the wall.

"There are some lovely affordable dresses here," the woman said. "What color are you thinking?"

"Black, maybe?"

"Of course. It's classic." The woman ran her hand along the rack and started pulling out a number of dresses—two black gowns, and a long, slinky red one as well. "Just in case we want something for contrast," she said, looking back at Jo and winking.

Jo marveled at the woman's ability to guess her size as she led her to a single small changing room at the back.

She lifted a heavy maroon curtain aside for Jo to enter the space. "I'll just be right outside here," she said, "if you need anything or want to get my opinion—though I think they'll all be lovely on you."

"Thanks," Jo said, stepping inside as the curtain whooshed behind her.

She hung up the dresses one by one on a high hook on the wall and exhaled a shaky breath. In this place of gorgeous, expensive dresses, she felt gangly and weird—a preteen trying on her mother's wedding dress. Except in her case, she had stretch marks and baby weight to hide, and breasts that required extra lifting and tucking as she put on the first dress, a simple, elegant black dress with a v-shaped neckline.

Jo smoothed a hand down the front of the dress and twisted from side to side in the mirror. It wasn't bad. She had a couple black dresses at home, but this one felt fresh and stylish. Her mind drifted to walking into the fundraiser wearing just this thing—maybe with that pair of silver and turquoise earrings she saved for special occasions—and running into Gavin. Would he find her attractive in this?

Jo dropped her hands and sighed. "What am I doing?" she muttered into the mirror.

"Do you have the first dress on?" the shop lady called from the other side of the curtain.

"Yes, but—"

With a whoosh, the woman pulled aside the curtain.

"Oh, that fits well," the woman exclaimed.

"Yes, thanks," Jo said, casting another glance in the mirror before shaking her head. "It's just... I'm just realizing I already have a couple black dresses, including the one I wore today, so I probably don't need to buy another."

"Hush," the woman said. "You can always have another dress."

"It's not even really a special occasion, this thing I'm going to," Jo continued. "It's just a fundraiser for this special ed playground they're trying to build at a local school. Parents and school staff, that sort of thing." She reached up her back to unzip the dress. "So, you see, not so special."

The shop woman's hand grabbed her forearm, catching her eye. "Just because the event's not special doesn't mean you shouldn't *feel* special."

Jo stopped unzipping. Moisture stung her eyes.

She opened her mouth to speak, but then, over the woman's shoulder, she caught sight of something in brilliant blue.

A strapless chiffon dress hung from a side rack. A deep twilight hue that seemed both dark and bold at once, it gathered at the waist before flaring out like a princess gown.

The woman followed her gaze. "It's beautiful, isn't it? Just came in earlier today."

"Mmm-hmm," Jo murmured, her eyes dazzled by the color and lines of the garment.

"You're right," she said, though Jo hadn't said anything. "It would look perfect on you."

She opened her mouth to respond, but the shop lady briskly strode towards the dress, plucking it off the display and gingerly carrying it back to her.

"Oh," Jo said quickly, "I was just looking—I didn't mean..."

"Well, you should at least try it on," the woman said, offering it to her. "It would be a shame to let it just hang there all day."

Nodding, Jo stepped back and pulled the curtain, enclosing herself alone with the dress.

After peeling off the black number and hanging it up, she slid the blue garment off its hanger and put it over head, the chiffon whispering to her as it slid over her shoulders, breasts, and hips until the length tickled her legs. She reached back and zipped it up, then felt it instantly—that sense of rightness when an item of clothing fits you to a T, like its proportions were designed with yours in mind.

Jo looked in the mirror to see her eyes shining before her gaze dropped to note the way the gown accentuated her breasts and waist, the womanly curve of her hips, before falling in a gentle, almost royal line down her legs.

And she did feel like royalty—granted, a single-mother-with-too-high-a-mortgage version, but still.

"Well?" the woman said on the other side.

Jo parted the curtain, unable to keep the smile off her face.

The woman's mouth fell open and she pressed her hands to her cheeks. "You're ravishing."

"No, it's just..." Jo laughed and turned back to her reflection as she twisted in place, the swish of chiffon echoing her movement. "It *is* a very pretty dress."

"It was meant for you," the woman breathed, and Jo laughed again.

"I'm not sure I believe in clothing destiny," Jo said, "or the other kind either."

The sentiment reminding her who she was, Jo bit back her smile. Trying on expensive dresses was as bittersweet as a vacation: it was wonderful while it lasted, but sooner or later, you had to put it back on the rack and return to normal life. But, maybe because she hadn't done either in a long time, she took just a minute more… She gathered her curls up with one hand and turned around in the mirror, admiring the way the dress exposed her upper back and rounded shoulders. They were not bad shoulders—maybe good even, at least in this dress.

"It's yours," the woman decreed.

"Oh." Jo dropped her hair. "I'm not sure I can afford…" She glanced down to find the price tag hanging from one side and gingerly turned it over—*hoping, hoping*—and finding it not only the price of her water bill, but the electric, internet, and home-owners' fees as well. Her shoulders slumped.

Especially with what she owed the advocate, she couldn't buy this dress. And she wasn't about to throw away Jackson's chances for her opportunity to feel like a princess for an hour on a weeknight.

"I'm sorry," she said, dropping the price tag and looking at the woman. "It's beautiful, but it's out of my price range. I should've thought of that before I put it on. I'm sorry to have wasted your time."

Her face serious, the woman stepped closer to her and took the price tag. Then, with a quick motion of her hands, she ripped off the first number of the three-digit price.

"Oh, look," the woman said. "It looks like this dress has gone on sale. Does twenty-five dollars fit your budget?"

# CHAPTER 15

*A fool is born every second* was one of those phrases that his mother was fond of saying, and after his last meeting with Josephine, Gavin knew he numbered among them.

What was he doing? Was he trying to lose his job? Hitting on a mom after an IEP meeting, in the school parking lot no less. Sure, he hadn't directly asked Josephine out, but he'd hinted like crazy he'd like to see her again, and when and where that could happen. He was in deep caca.

Worst of all, he couldn't manage to fully regret it. Because if Josephine did show up to that fundraiser...and he had a moment alone with her...

"Damn." He gripped the steering wheel of his car and pulled in the parking lot of Gwen's apartment complex.

"Gwen. Your date. Remember?" he muttered as he put the car in park and tried to rally.

Desperate times called for taking not only Tanner's advice, but his mother's. Specifically taking down the number of their neighbors' daughter—the blonde, not the redhead—and calling to ask her out.

"I'd go out with someone else," Tanner had said, when Gavin had asked what he'd do if he fell for a client. And after his sister's advice had combusted—the arrival of Jo's advocate rendering it moot—he had to do something. This was all too complicated.

Dina had answered his request for Gwen's number reluctantly, like it'd been all his idea. He could smell the reverse psychology a mile away.

"Sure," she'd said slowly over the phone, "if that's what you want."

"Yes," he said, closing his laptop, where he'd been rereading the email exchange he and Josephine had had the other day, the one where he'd sworn they'd almost been flirting. "That's what I want."

Maybe going out with Gwen would save him from making a bigger mistake when he ran into Josephine at the fundraiser Thursday night.

He stepped out of the car, walked across the lot, and climbed up a flight of steps to the door with Gwen's apartment number.

"Hi," she said as she opened the door. "Gavin, right?"

"Yes," he said. "And I assume you're Gwen."

"You assumed right." She smiled, and Gavin had to admit she was attractive. She wore a red sweater that looked fuzzy to the touch, and pale hair framed her face. He then remembered her, vaguely, from growing up in the neighborhood, though she was a few years younger, so they hadn't swum in exactly the same ponds.

"You were a dancer, right?" he asked as she slung a small black leather purse over her shoulder and stepped out, locking her door.

She laughed. "Let me guess: my mom said that. I danced for a few years in school, yeah. But my mom treats it like it's this essential part of who I am."

He laughed and followed her as she gestured him down the steps. "What would we do without our mothers?"

"Probably be set up a lot less," she called over her shoulder.

"True."

As they climbed in his car, Gavin exhaled in relief. Maybe this wouldn't be so bad. Gwen was nice, and funny, and knew this was a setup as much as he did. As he drove to the frozen yogurt place she suggested, the conversation flowed between their memories of the neighborhood, their moms, and Gwen's work before she asked him about his job.

"So my mom said you have a temporary position at the school district, helping kids with special needs?" she asked.

Gavin shook his head and parked at the frozen yogurt place. "Yes. But it's not temporary. I worked in sales before, before I decided it wasn't for me. My mom's still in the denial stage of her grief process."

Gwen nodded and rolled her eyes in solidarity as they walked into the froyo place. "That's really great you do that, though. Work with those kids."

Her eyes shined with admiration. Gavin knew that to the outside world, his work made him some kind of Hallmark hero. The inside story was a bit messier.

"Thanks," he said. "I'm trying to help."

"It must be really rewarding," she continued.

"It can be." He thought of the flash of anger in Josephine's eyes as she walked out of that first meeting.

He truly wanted to be a champion for the kids. And he had, placing some in classes where they would thrive, helping shape goals that would aid learning. But with so many competing demands and constraints, Gavin too often felt like, as Josephine had put it, a jerk in a suit.

Gwen smiled, satisfied he must be some kind of saint, before grabbing a small cardboard cup and walking over to the chocolate frozen yogurt dispenser.

Gavin grabbed his own cup, but then dropped it on the floor, his fingers fumbling to grasp it. He felt agitated. He walked over to the vanilla frozen yogurt dispenser, not feeling experimental in the least. He'd get the vanilla, maybe a few chocolate sprinkles on the top, and then steer the conversation from his job. With it, memories of Josephine poured out, like in the prior fifteen minutes he hadn't thought about her, thoughts had built up like water behind a flimsy dam that would break at the merest mention.

He pulled the yogurt dispenser, swirling the vanilla down into this cup. He remembered the ice cream carton in Josephine's cart when he'd seen her and Jackson at the store. Which flavor had it been? He tried to recall. Was she the vanilla type? Maybe not. It was too plain, and she was the farthest thing from that. Unbidden, his mind started to draw comparisons between her and Gwen. Obviously Gwen had to be the better cook. Gwen was closer to his age, of course, and at the same stage of life he was—the go-on-awkward-setups, try-to-find-someone-to-breed-with stage. On the surface, she was a bit more pleasant, a bit more polished, than Josephine's mama bear demeanor.

The problem was that he didn't really know Josephine as much as he'd liked. He'd only spoken with her a handful of times, and although he remembered all he'd gleaned, he mostly had questions about her. Somehow that was even more frustrating. Which ice cream *did* she eat? Would she even go to a place like this? Did she understand what he was trying to do when he'd asked if she was going to the fundraiser? If she did—if she came—would she yell at him or tease him? Or both?

And, either way, would he be able to stop her by pressing his mouth to hers?

"Gavin."

"Huh?" He jumped and realized his cup of froyo was overflowing, vanilla dripping down his hand.

"Oh, crap." As Gwen laughed, he grabbed a stack of napkins to wipe off.

"I guess you really like frozen yogurt."

He attempted a smile. "I think I was hungrier than I realized."

They sat down and ate their dessert. Their conversation was fine, it was better than fine, but for all his inward emotional response, Gavin might as well be exchanging pleasantries with a cardboard cutout of an attractive woman. Not that Gwen noticed. He was good at conversation, good at faking it—thanks to his experience in sales and his personality. *Natural charm* was what his mom called it, claiming it was how his father had wooed her when he'd worked maintenance at the university and she'd been the well-dressed young admin in the dean's office.

He wondered if Josephine Palladino was immune.

It was the car ride home that cinched it for Gavin. As the conversation with Gwen lapsed into silence, he felt himself growing more excited for the fundraiser in two nights than the date he was currently on.

He pulled into Gwen's lot and cut the engine. They sat still in the dark for a minute, the heat seeping from the vehicle.

"Well, this was really fun," Gwen finally said.

"Yeah…" Gavin dropped his hands from the wheel and turned to her. "Look, Gwen, you're really awesome. I had a good time tonight. But I have feelings for someone else right now."

Gwen exhaled and threw her head back. "Oh, thank God. I do, too."

"You do?"

She nodded. "I've been having an affair with my married boss for the past two years."

"Whoa."

"Yeah."

He ran a hand through his hair. "Okay, how can we let our

mothers down easy? Maybe we can say there's just no chemistry... or that we discovered in genealogical research that we're actually related? You're Jewish, right?"

"Yeah, but my mom has done a bunch of family research. She'd ask for proof." She scrunched up her face, deep in thought. "There's got to be something."

"I'll let you decide," Gavin said. "Just nothing too wild or creepy. I still want to be able to show up in the neighborhood." He joked, "You can tell them you think I'm hideous."

Gwen shrugged and laughed. Then she glanced at him out of the side of her eyes. "Are you having an affair too?"

"Naw," Gavin said. "I mean, the woman I'm... Well, it's a sticky situation. She's someone related to... one of my students."

"Ah, that's sweet. A single mom?"

She had that naïve, admiring look on her face again, and this time Gavin had to correct her. "Actually, it's not that sweet. It's kind of inappropriate, to be honest. Job-wise. God..." He rubbed a hand down his face. "I shouldn't even be saying this out loud. I just can't stop thinking about her. I don't even know her, other than she used to listen to Tori Amos when she was younger and she's got really incredible hair and she's this weird mix of needy and take-no-prisoners..."

Gwen raised her eyebrows and smiled. "You should tell her."

"I don't know." Gavin shook his head but couldn't keep the smile off his face. "Life, right?"

"Yeah."

Gavin twisted the key in the ignition and the car roared back to life, the vents blowing warm air at them. "Anyway, you should probably tell your boss to leave his wife or break it off. You seem like a person who deserves better."

Gwen laughed harshly and grabbed the door handle, opening it to the night. "Yeah, that's probably what my mom would say, too."

She shut the door and walked off, but Gavin didn't start driving yet, thinking of Gwen's advice.

"Okay," he said into the empty car. "I'll tell her."

# CHAPTER 16

Jo walked up to the fundraiser Thursday evening with a pretty dress on her body and her heart in her throat.

Though she strolled behind a couple in formal wear, she felt overdressed in the beautiful dark blue gown and not a little silly. She didn't even have a date—all she had was the suggestion that Gavin Steinberg would be there. If it wasn't for the shopkeeper's encouragement, and the dress purchase, she might not have had the guts to come. What if he never showed? What if he was sick? What if his asking if she'd come was more casual than it seemed?

Maybe she'd read him all wrong. It'd seemed like years since she'd been flirted with, and much longer since she'd been interested in anyone else. And she could no longer deny that she was. She had a gorgeous dress on that said she was anything but disinterested.

She paused at the door to the school. At least she'd had Holly come over so she could go out at night for once—and not to a support group, either. At least she was dressed up, and her gown whispered with the promise of something exciting, even if she

137

suspected she'd end the evening like she always did, sweeping cereal off her kitchen floor and then collapsing into bed with *Law and Order* on.

Yet the fall twilight air smelled like something new, fresh and cool with a hint of woodsmoke. She took a deep breath, tightened her jacket around her, and pushed open the doors.

The room, already half full of mingling guests, had been transformed. Housed in a district building with administrative offices and meeting spaces, this large room was usually reserved for major events. Jo had been here before but she'd never seen it like this. A bar was stationed against one wall with a tuxedoed bartender pouring drinks. Other tables held auction baskets, displays of fruit, and even a chocolate fondue fountain. The sound of adult conversation between men in suits and women in cocktail dresses filled the room. Two-thirds of the women's dresses were black, and Jo felt self-conscious again, like she'd come to a community fundraiser dressed for prom.

"Jo? Jo Palladino?"

Jackson's third grade teacher walked towards her, a big smile on her face.

"Hi, Kim," she said, grateful to see a friendly face. She leaned in and they gave each other a big hug.

"Oh my God, Jo, you look incredible," the short, auburn-haired white woman said. She pulled away but held onto Jo's hands. "Look at you."

Jo giggled nervously, shrugging out of her jacket and putting it over her arm. She wore simple navy pumps to match the dress, but Holly had pinned her curls in a sophisticated twist and fastened it with a jeweled barrette. Jo didn't mention Gavin, but her friend was thrilled she was finally going out.

Kayla had left to hang out with friends by the time Jo was getting ready, and it was just as well; she wasn't ready to field questions from her daughter about where she was going, and especially why she was taking such pains with her appearance.

Jackson himself was confused: he had hovered in the hallway beside the bathroom where Jo and Holly were, his clothing hanger in one hand as he watched them.

"Halloween," he'd said. "Trick or treat."

"Not yet, buddy." She turned her head to let Holly fix the other side of her hair. "Less than three weeks."

"Mama. Halloween."

Jo grinned wryly, thinking his assumption that she was playing make-believe wasn't so far off. "Three more weeks until Halloween for Mama, too. It'll be here soon."

Holly had left a few tendrils loose around her face, even though Jo had protested she looked like her client who had attended the Jane Austen Ball. It was one of these strands that Kim now touched. "Just gorgeous," she said, shaking her head in awe.

"Thanks," she told Kim. "Just trying to get out."

"Well, you're putting us all to shame." Kim squeezed her hands. "We should catch up sometime. How are you? How is Jackson?" She followed Jo over to the nearby coat closet, where she hung up her jacket and smoothed down her dress.

"Jackson is… well, he's okay." Jo was about to bend Kim's ear about what was going on. They'd gotten along before, and Kim had been in special education for years. Jo felt as if she could trust her. Yet at the thought of launching into the drama with the district, exhaustion washed over her.

*No, not tonight,* she decided. Let me just pretend that for tonight, everything *is* okay.

Make-believe.

It wouldn't penetrate every level of her consciousness. After all, anxiety about her kids, especially Jackson, was the background radiation to her life. But just for tonight, she had the wild urge to play dress up, in all senses of the word. Put on a pretty dress and pretend to be, if not someone else, then some easier version of herself. A version that could go out, have a glass of wine, and worry about less than three things at once.

"We're doing well." Jo smiled at Kim. "We're all doing really well."

"Good."

They caught up for a few more minutes on Kim's life and some gossip about elementary special ed staff they both knew before Jo excused herself to grab a glass of wine.

Turning, she caught sight of Gavin Steinberg.

He'd already seen her. Was staring at her, in fact. Dressed in a sharp navy suit, he looked so terribly attractive Jo felt like she'd already drunk half a glass of Merlot. He was easily one of the youngest people in this room of parents and local business-people. And with his brown hair smoothed down and his blue eyes staring wide at her, Jo also felt sure that he was the very best-looking.

And they were still staring at each other across the room. Not speaking. It'd been half a minute, probably too long—embarrassingly long—and Jo had to do something, so she gave him a small wave and a smile.

He waved back. Then they both, as if steered by some hidden pulley, started moving toward each other.

There was a band set up in the corner, and as she walked to him, the band started playing some instrumental version of a Michael Bolton song from the '80s.

Gavin's face had been so serious, but the corner of his mouth turned up then, and Jo felt an odd sense of rightness—as in, everything would be all right here. She wasn't used to the sensation. It was a pleasant, warm, pervasive thing, and she had to search her feelings to see from whence it came. The sudden assurance that this was the right thing—not just her wearing this dress and coming tonight, but walking towards him now—was lovely, if fleeting.

Because before she reached Gavin, a woman stepped in front

of her.

"Josephine Palladino?" She wore a classy red gown that emphasized her tall, statuesque frame. Her pumps matched her dress perfectly. Josephine had a feeling that this woman's shoes always matched her dress.

"Yes?" she asked.

The woman reached her hand out. "I'm Charlene Matthews. The Director of Special Instruction. I've been wanting to meet you."

Jo instinctively knew Charlene Matthews wanting to meet her was not for the usual reasons, but she put her hand out to shake. "It's good to meet you, too."

"I know you've been working with Gavin Steinberg," Charlene said. "We all hope we can give your son what he needs."

Her words were confident and not impolite, but Jo felt a flicker of annoyance. Did this woman really want to give Jackson what he needed? Or did she simply want to stop Josephine from getting on the district's case?

"Yes," Jo said. "I hope you can, too."

The two women stared at each other, sizing up the other's mettle.

"Ms. Palladino."

A deep voice interrupted the standoff, and Josephine turned to see Gavin with a pasted-on, polite-but-nervous smile on his face. He stood between her and Charlene, but off to the side, adding another point to their triangle. Jo couldn't help but notice he stood slightly closer to Charlene.

He was holding out his hand. "It's great you were able to attend tonight."

"Thanks, it's good to see you," Jo said automatically, touching his palm to hers.

At the contact, Gavin's smile faltered and his eyes glowed. "It's good to see you, too." He cleared his throat and took a step back from her. "I hear they're about to start the bidding."

As the fundraising raffle began, they turned towards the front as others joined their cluster: another coordinator, a physical therapist Jo knew, and a fellow parent who stood to Jo's side. They exchanged pleasantries between bids for the auction items, which seemed to be raising money at an impressive pace. Jo bid on a basket as a courtesy, but with the prices going so high and her budget so low, she was swiftly outbid. Twice, she caught Gavin staring at her. Someone handed her a glass of wine, and she drank it too quickly.

Jo marveled at the strangeness of the situation they were all in. They were all here—the parents and teachers and support staff—because they liked kids and wanted to help them. But underneath their suits and cocktail dresses, they all wore a fine layer of chainmail. It came down to money. There wasn't enough of it. Not in the world and certainly not in special education. The law could state that every child had a right to a free and appropriate education, but with so many kids with so many needs—and more every day—it was complicated.

That feeling of rightness frayed along the edges. Her coming tonight, the dress—it didn't matter. She and Gavin were only a few feet away, but it could've been a giant chasm.

At a break in the auction, she turned to the group. "Excuse me," she said, giving a tight smile as she swiveled and strode toward a side door of the room. There was a restroom in the hall out there, and she needed it—needed a break from this pretending. She slipped into the dimly-lit hall.

In the bathroom, she looked at her face in the mirror, those tendrils framing her cheeks and the soft pink lipstick she dabbed on, the fine lines around her eyes and hiding under her freckles. The vertical wrinkle forming on her forehead. She almost laughed. She was here because she felt flirty with her son's special education coordinator. His much younger, totally inappropriate for her, special education coordinator. She could've been his—well, his sister, but much older sister.

Wiping her hands on a towel, she exhaled and left the restroom, stepping back into the dim hallway.

She took her time walking back, glancing at the pictures of students on the walls. Most of the images hung there were high schoolers—the winning track team, the dance troupe smiling at a competition, the chess club. Jackson would be in high school some day. Would his picture be on this wall? Would he be among these young, smiling faces with science team trophies or pom-poms, or would he be stuck in some back room somewhere?

A door squeaked open further down the hall.

She glanced to see a man in a suit walking towards her, and as he came closer, she realized it was Gavin. Her breath caught.

"Hi," he said, stopping ten feet away. "I wondered where you'd gone."

"Bathroom," she said.

"Oh." He shoved his hands in his pockets, jiggling some change. "The fundraiser is going well. They think they're about to surpass the playground goal."

She managed to find her voice. "That's great."

Music filtered into the hallway, some instrumental cover of Patsy Cline's "Crazy." The distance between her and Gavin hung odd and heavy. They were farther apart than most casual conversation dictated, further than before, but there was something about it—or something about the way it was just the two of them in the dark hallway—that felt filled with meaning. Like there would be an invisible magnetic pull if they got too close. Already she was aware of him in ways she hadn't been aware of men standing half as far away.

"Are you okay?" Gavin asked, catching her eye.

"Yes." She drew a shaky breath.

"Then do you want to dance?"

Her lips parted, but for a few seconds she couldn't speak. "You're asking me to *dance*?"

143

"Yes," he said. "It's what you do when music is playing and there's a pretty woman nearby."

She blinked. "Here? In this hallway?"

"Yes."

"But they're not dancing in there. It doesn't seem like a dancing thing."

Gavin ventured a few steps closer to her. "Just because they're standing around awkwardly doesn't mean we have to."

She couldn't muster a good reply to that. "Okay."

He was standing in front of her now, and there *was* a magnetic field—Jo could feel it pulling from a place deep within her solar plexus. It was sending tingles to her extremities, a push/pull of sensation that gave her simultaneous and opposite urges to both run away and collapse against him.

"Okay then," he said, taking her hand and leading her to a small alcove by a trophy display case.

As the music reached them, he put his arms around her waist and guided her smoothly to him as her hands nervously flew up to his shoulders. This new contact with his body, his torso brushing against hers, made her almost shiver. Even in her heels, he had half a head on her.

She was not yet comfortable enough to clasp her fingers behind his neck, because what if she did need to push him away after all?

He started swaying her gently to the music—nothing fancy, more your standard clutch-and-spin—as Jo furiously thought back to the last time she'd done this. Neil had never liked to dance, and it's not like adulthood was filled with proms. It was probably her wedding day: she and Neil with their arms locked around each other, posing under bright lights for the photographer. It was nothing like this.

But all thoughts of her ex evaporated as Gavin pressed his hand against her lower back and guided her closer. His arms

held her gently, but firmly, and in them she felt small and...
*adored?*

Thus far, she'd avoided eye contact with him, but being this close meant it was impossible to avoid his scent. He smelled soapy and clean, finished with a complex scent of sandalwood and spice—some cologne, she guessed, that was making her mouth water.

"Is this okay?" he asked, and she couldn't ignore his eyes any longer.

Her gaze rose to his face. Straight nose, barest hint of five o'clock shadow, wide open blue eyes that looked more serious than she'd seen, perfectly unlined skin. God, she was way too old for him.

She realized she hadn't answered him. "Oh. Yes. It's okay," she said softly.

"You sure?"

"Mmm-hmm." She was looking at him full-on now, locked onto those blue eyes. She should've mumbled her answer into his suit. He really was an attractive man.

Then she saw something she didn't expect. Below his jawline, his Adam's apple bobbed as he swallowed once, twice.

He was nervous.

She half-laughed in relief.

And here she thought it was just her.

"Something funny?" he said.

Maybe it was the alcohol hitting her system, or the dreamy, hazy atmosphere of the hallway. Maybe it was the pull of Gavin, or the knowledge that he was just as nervous as she. Whatever the reason, she simply smiled, and, with a resigned sigh, relaxed her arms around his neck and laid the side of her cheek against his chest.

His heartbeat was drumming fast through the fabric of his suit —further proof of his nerves—but as she settled against him, he breathed out and held her close. His jacket was smooth against her cheek, his body warm against hers, the hall calm and shadowy as the music played on. That fresh, manly scent of his enveloped her.

He started to speak, then stopped. Started and stopped again.

Jo waited him out.

"Josephine…" he finally said.

"Yes?"

"I want to get to know you," he said in a rush. "Outside of least restrictive environments and—and—and present levels of functioning. Outside of all this."

"Is there a world outside of all of this?" she mumbled dreamily against his jacket.

"Yeah," he said. "I think so. And if not, we can create it together."

She moved her head off his chest then. Tilted it up to look at him.

"Why?" she asked.

His eyes were wide. "Why…?"

"Why do you want to get to know me?"

He took a deep breath and she felt his torso push against hers.

"Whenever I think about you," he started. "I hear The Cars playing in my head."

Her lips parted.

"And you're smart and funny and you're real and you're just…" His eyes widened and looked at her face then, all over, and she felt a blush creep in. "You're exceptionally beautiful."

She looked down, unable to think of a response to this, let alone a witty one. She took a deep breath, trying to center herself, but when she tilted her face back up to him again, he was beholding her like he was about to kiss her.

She froze. The music was still playing—a new song now—but they were just standing there in the dim hallway, their bodies flush against one another. Only Gavin's hands moved. His palm rubbed against her lower back slowly, pressing her body to his.

Slumbering nerve endings were waking up. No one had touched her in that spot, not for a long time. Who knew the back could be so sensitive? The gesture was sweet—and not a little sexy. As his thumb brushed over a tender spot at the base of her spine, she couldn't hold back a shiver of pleasure.

He made a low noise in the back of his throat, and the fingers of his free hand reached up to touch one of her curls.

"These," he said, and, though his face was intense, he pulled on one of her ringlets and released it, watching it spring back into a curl, "are something else."

She laughed. "You're a strange man."

"What do you hear," he started, "when you—when you think of me?"

"My own inner critic." She swallowed. "And sometimes Wilson Phillips."

"I'll take it."

He cupped her face and kissed her.

It was a solid kiss—too considerate to be rough, but too hungry to be gentle. A whole new constellation of nerves exploded across her body. Her eyes closed as her mouth opened, and though he didn't do anything fancy, pressing his lips to hers and holding her the way he did was enough.

After a minute, they parted, their bodies still against one another.

Jo's eyes fluttered open to see Gavin watching her face, a dazed look in his eyes. His hand was still cupping her jaw.

"Oh," she breathed.

"Oh?" he asked.

She swallowed and nodded. "Oh."

"Is that a good *oh*?"

"Give me a minute here."

# CHAPTER 17

*G*avin took a deep breath and waited. His mind still reeled from that kiss; his body was suggesting he take another stab at it. But he couldn't remember feeling this strongly for a woman as quickly as he had for Josephine, and if she asked him to give her a minute, he sure as hell was going to do that.

She looked as dazed as he felt—and that was good, wasn't it? There in the hallway, she stood warm in his arms, dressed in that exquisite blue dress.

If he hadn't already realized on the date with Gwen that Josephine was slowly ruining him for other women, he would've known the minute she stepped inside the fundraiser wearing that dress. It reminded him of a summertime evening sky when he was a teenager, when he'd hopped into his car with carefree, wild thoughts and knew he had the whole night in front of him.

He shouldn't have felt so careless—should've been more professional—but the color of that dress and the way it showed off her body... Well, thank goodness for darkened hallways.

They were still holding each other, still staring, and she drew a deep breath he felt over his body. They were that close.

Her lips parted to speak—*finally*—but she was interrupted by a loud burst of conversation at the other end of the hall as a door opened and a trio of people tumbled out.

He and Josephine sprang apart, smoothing down their clothes. Thank God they were tucked away next to the trophies and not in full view.

"Here, Ms. Palladino," he said quickly, and too loudly, "the entrance back to the fundraiser is this way. This place really is a labyrinth."

He laughed nervously. She arched an eyebrow but started walking to the door alongside him.

Not that their ruse mattered, since the group of what looked like moms enjoying a night out were absorbed by their own uproarious, wine-fueled conversation as they strolled past them and toward the ladies' room.

"Clever lie," she whispered dryly to him as they reached the doorway.

"You still haven't answered my question," he whispered back. "Either of them."

She opened the door, and there was a clutch of people close to the entrance—including Charlene.

His boss glanced over as Gavin followed Josephine back into the room, but her expression was, as always, impossible to read.

He felt a bloom of sweat break out on his body for entirely different reasons than it had two minutes ago.

*What was he doing?*

But then, as Josephine strode to the bar, he couldn't help but follow her movements in that beautiful blue dress. His dad would've called her a *vision*, and Gavin would have agreed. Her eyes, after that kiss, had looked almost aquamarine.

"Hey, man."

Gavin turned to see Angelo a few steps away, holding up an

amber bottle of beer to salute him. His blond hair was shaved close to his head, his suit jacket straining against his thick arms.

"Hey, Angelo."

"You okay?"

"Yeah." Making sure Charlene had turned away, Gavin's eyes sought Josephine again—she was at the bar, getting a glass of water—before glancing away. "Yeah."

"You hear they raised the money?" Angelo continued.

"Yes." He nodded. "That's great."

Angelo, never one to miss details, followed the path of Gavin's gaze. "Who's that?"

"Just this parent," he said quickly. "Do you mind if I—can you give me a minute?"

Angelo waved his free hand. "Do your thing." His mouth opened like he was about to say something else, maybe *She's cute*, but he wisely shut it at the expression on Gavin's face. Gavin hadn't thought to talk to him about his dilemma before. As a district employee, he'd assumed it would be too risky to do so. Now Gavin briefly wondered what Angelo would have said before his attention moved to the beautiful woman at the bar and his feet followed.

Josephine stood there, sipping a glass of water. She looked calm as a cucumber, but Gavin detected a slight flush on her neck and chest as he sidled up next to her, leaving a generous space between them for propriety. He leaned his forearms on the bar, like he was about to order a drink, not make a blatant pass at one of his students' mothers within shouting distance of his boss.

The tuxedoed bartender was turned away, filling a glass, so Gavin spoke low and quick.

"Like I was saying, I think we should get to know each other better. Go on a date."

Her eyes cut to him, then away. "Isn't that a conflict of interest for you?"

"Yes."

She paused. "Is there anything you want to add to that?"

"Not really."

He waited for the moral indignation to creep in. They were on opposing sides of the table. As part of the school district, he couldn't advocate for her individual son's needs, and she couldn't do anything but. A personal relationship between them would muddy those waters—and he, the professional out of the two of them, was aware of that more than anyone.

But it never came—certainly not for him, and not for her either, from the looks of it. He watched as Josephine Palladino flushed a pretty pink and glanced at his mouth, biting her lip in a way that made him want to taste its sweetness. The need to see her again, and alone, overwhelmed him.

The bartender turned. "Oh, I'm sorry, sir, I didn't see you there. What can I get you?"

Gavin straightened. "Just a beer, thanks."

The young man nodded and turned away.

"So if we go on a date," Josephine started in a whisper, "couldn't we be seen if we're out in public? By a teacher or something?"

Gavin looked casually over his shoulder, making sure no one was the wiser. "I've thought of that."

"Please don't say something skeevy like, 'Let's just hang out at my place.'"

He put a hand over his heart to feign insult. "I'd never."

"Right."

Setting his beer down, the bartender said, "Here you go, sir," and Gavin pulled some money out of his wallet to pay for the drink.

A couple came up to order a round of gin and tonics. Gavin nodded his hellos but was counting the seconds until they left. Josephine sipped her water and stared straight ahead, a study in blankness.

When they were finally gone, he whispered, "I think we should go cruising."

Josephine turned fully to him. "What?"

"Like they did in the '50s." Gavin couldn't keep the smile off his face. "I pick you up in my car—after dark, of course—and we just drive around."

"And that's not skeevy?"

"We can talk, see the city lights. I promise I'll keep both hands on the wheel. Ten and two." He put out his hands to demonstrate.

She stared at him, her eyebrows raised.

*Just say yes.*

But before she could, Angelo walked up to the other side of the bar, ordering another beer and throwing a curious glance their way. Gavin nodded but mostly ignored him; he didn't know what his friend was thinking, but the fewer people from the district that knew the details, the better. He pulled out his phone, faking the need to check important emails.

"I'm out of practice," Josephine whispered. "With this stuff."

"I'm an excellent teacher," he whispered back to his phone. "Okay, that sounded a little skeevy."

She started to speak, but then stopped abruptly.

He set his phone down and looked up. There was no one at the bar now, and the bartender was cleaning up at the other end. She still hadn't given him an answer—about the cruising or what she'd thought of that kiss. She may have been out of practice, but she was well-versed in the art of teasing a guy.

"You're killing me here," he said, unable to resist staring at her.

She studied the bar. "It's hard to get someone to watch Jackson," she said. "I'd have to see."

"But if you can..."

She looked at him and drew a breath. Her eyes were shining. "Yes."

A smile broke out across his face.

"How do we…" he started, but she was pulling her cell out of her purse. She slid it across the bar to him.

Understanding, he quickly programmed his personal cell number into her phone, saving it in her contacts as "Gavin, Not Skeevy."

She stifled a laugh and deposited the phone in her bag. "I need to go."

"Okay," he said.

She was turning as she said it, and whispering so softly it took a few seconds to reach Gavin's ears, and a few more to realize she was answering his question about the kiss.

"It was perfect."

# CHAPTER 18

*J*osephine was still thinking about that kiss the next afternoon. Or, not thinking—*feeling* it.

Between emailing clients and booking airlines, she'd find her fingers reaching up to her mouth. What sensitive things lips were. She used her mouth all the time—to speak, to inhale food while standing at the kitchen counter, to kiss her children's foreheads, to let out breath at the end of a long day. And yet after the previous night, it seemed her lips had been asleep this whole time. Now they tingled after she took a long drink, felt warm and full when her teeth grazed them. Last night, as she'd walked out of the fundraiser, they'd felt almost swollen, flushed and wanting.

How could a little kiss have done that?

She didn't know, and she'd practically run out of the event to figure it out. She couldn't think about it in the same room as Gavin, his blue eyes wide and questioning, that all-too-attractive cut of suit and *that mouth*.

She was trying to ignore her lips' insistence that she text him now to arrange another meetup—just two mouths, four lips, who would know?—as she picked up Jackson from school early to get a flu shot and a new pair of shoes.

"Another hard day," his teacher said. It wasn't hard to guess the subtext: *he's not fit for this classroom and you won't let us move him.*

"I think his shoes are too tight," Jo said. "Maybe that's why he's been so moody. I'm going to get him new ones."

It was a game they all liked to play, the caregivers and teachers and therapists. Jackson was, for all intents and purposes, nonverbal. He could say some words and short phrases aloud or on his speech device—*apple* or *outside* or *stop* or even, when properly motivated, *I'm mad.* Yet the reasons for his mood swings were often unfathomable things. Was he upset because they'd gone to the playground at a different time at school? Because the music was too loud? Because a full moon was coming? Because of something biochemical in his head? So much of the time, they didn't know, and all they had were guesses—things that they clutched like talismans. Maybe if they got back on schedule or turned down the music or the moon waned, he would feel better.

So maybe it was just the shoes. And because Jo felt helpless to do anything else, they went to the shoe store.

"Hey there," the salesman said as they walked through the entrance and the bell above them dinged.

"Hi," Jo said, Jackson trailing behind, scuffing his sneakers.

"The usual?" The salesman, Alim, was a lanky man with salt-and-pepper hair. He was friendly with Jackson and knew just what they needed: the same navy and white sneakers her son had been wearing since he was seven.

Jo smiled. "Yup, the usual." She had learned the hard way years ago not to try out something new. Jackson wanted a certain sensation on his feet, the velcro straps, the particular colors. And Jo wanted as little drama in her life as possible.

"Jax, have a seat," she said. "It's shoe time."

"Shoe time, shoe time." Jackson dragged his feet over to one of the low benches. He peeled off his sneakers and Alim knelt beside him to measure his feet.

"He's grown!" Alim said. "One full size bigger."

"I knew it," Jo said. "He's been so off at school lately."

"He's at that age," Alim said. "He's so tall now. Maybe next time, he'll be a new size in just one month."

"Ugh." Jo didn't want the reminder that her son was growing up so fast. "Either you're a good salesman or that's the most depressing truth I've heard all day."

"Not depressing." Alim laughed, opening up a shoebox and pulling out a pair of identical sneakers two sizes bigger. "Let's see how this fits, my man."

He held out the first sneaker to Jackson, but the boy leaned back and turned his head.

"No?" Alim tilted his head.

"Jax, it's the same shoe," Jo said. "Here." She picked up his old sneaker and held it next to the new one, showing him they were nearly identical.

But Jackson grunted and dodged away, standing and walking in his socks around the corner.

"Shoe time," came his voice one aisle over.

"Jax," Jo called. "C'mon, we need to make sure these shoes fit and get home before your sister throws a party at the house and invites half the high school." Or a certain somebody over, Jo thought. She'd taken Jackson out while Kayla had the place to herself many times before, but those times weren't when she had a boyfriend. And a precocious urge to get an IUD. She and Kayla still hadn't cleared the air from that God-awful sex talk, and the tension between them still hung thick with unsaid things. Not that Jo saw much of her these days; she was always out with Misty, though Jo was suspicious that sometimes "Misty" was actually a boy with a guitar.

Jackson came padding back, but in his hand were a pair of Converse Chucks. Bright orange Converse Chucks.

"Shoe time," he said.

"Jackson, those aren't the shoes we get. We get these shoes." She held up their standby sneakers.

"Shoe time."

"They don't have velcro. See." She reached over and jiggled one of the laces on his Chucks.

"*Shoe.*"

Jo sighed while Alim laughed, stood, and rounded the corner before bringing back a couple boxes of the orange Chucks. "He's becoming his own man," the salesman said.

"He's not a man," Jo retorted. "He's thirteen. They're going to feel different on your feet," she warned her son as Alim fitted the sneaker on him.

But Jackson stood, stomped his feet, and then hopped up and down three times. He stared at the Converse as if they were encrusted with diamonds. "Ooh!" he shouted.

"He wants a new shoe!" Alim exclaimed. "They look nice, right?"

"They look orange." Jo watched her son. "He never wants a new shoe."

"He does today."

"But they have laces." She held the usual sneakers up to her son, but he pushed them away, making a noise of protest at her.

"Maybe we'll try these new shoes," she finally said. "But get the usual pair too, just in case."

But as Alim tried to ring up both pairs, Jackson kept grabbing the non-orange shoes and putting them back on the shelf. He was getting more agitated too, his movements growing erratic and his sounds louder.

"Jackson, don't act like I'm one of your teachers at school," Jo retorted, then realized—too late—she probably sounded like one.

After he growled in frustration when he couldn't fit a shoebox back on the shelf, his fists clenching, Jo relented. They left the store two minutes later, the new orange shoes on Jackson's feet and no other. Maybe later she'd kick herself, when Jax realized he couldn't go back to his familiar way of moving through the world.

*Or maybe he's growing up and wanting to try new things.*

After she'd gotten him into the car, she collapsed into the driver's seat, and Gavin's words came back to her, unbidden.

*I want to get to know you. Outside of least restrictive environments and—and—and present levels of functioning. Outside of all this.*

Her fingers found her lips, which tingled again with the memory.

She'd said yes to a date, but they hadn't made any plans. It wasn't too late to back out. To just not call him. She shouldn't call him. It was messy and she was too old and tired. Everything was changing, and so fast.

The phone rang.

Startled, she swiped to answer without seeing who was calling.

"Hello?"

"Hi, Jo."

"Hello…" It was a familiar male voice, but one she didn't immediately place.

She blinked a few times, and then it came to her.

"Oh. Hi, Neil." Her ex-husband didn't usually call her, unless there'd been a mistake with a child support payment or something needed a signature. "What's going on?"

"Is Kayla okay?"

"Yes," Jo said slowly. "Why?"

"She hasn't returned any of my calls," Neil said. "I called her months ago on her birthday, and she never called me back. She didn't even text. And I've called three times since then."

Jo shifted. "She's a teenager. She's just busy." Busy with a new boyfriend, she added silently, but she wasn't about to tell Neil that. It wasn't hers to tell.

"Too busy to send me a *text?*"

"I don't know, Neil." Jo sighed. Jackson made a noise and pushed his foot against the back of her seat, a sign he was growing impatient or maybe just wanted to observe the powers of his new orange shoes.

She'd started the car and the volume of the radio was on low. Jo didn't have time to turn it off before Jackson said, "Music."

"Rihanna," she said, reaching to turn down the dial—but Jackson pressed the toe of his shoe into the middle of her back until she winced.

"Buddy," Jo said, "I'll leave it on. But please be nice." Jo wondered if Jackson could hear his father's voice over Rihanna's singing. Being so young when he left, it was unlikely he remembered Neil living with them and being the present father he no longer was. But sometimes Jo suspected that Neil's voice scraped at some empty place deep within Jackson, the sound triggering the knowledge that Neil spoke to him fewer times than he should, and was far less a father than he deserved.

"Look," Jo said to her ex, "I'm in my car. Jackson and I are out running errands. I'll tell her to call you." She paused. "Is everything okay?"

"Yeah, everything's fine. Just that my daughter won't call me back." He cleared his throat. "Everything okay with Jackson?"

"Mostly," Jo said. "Some trouble in school. I'll figure it out."

"Okay."

Jo rolled her eyes. Neil had never figured out how to ask after his son, and he knew how to communicate with him less. After a few attempts to put Jackson on the phone so his dad could wish him happy holidays—times when Neil was clearly uncomfortable and Jackson didn't respond to the voice on the other end of the line—they'd sort of all let it drop by unspoken agreement. Now he usually only called Kayla, but apparently

Kayla was resisting even that small gesture. Why hadn't she responded?

Jackson pushed his foot against her seat again. "I've got to go, Neil. I'll talk to Kayla."

After she ended the call, she turned up the radio, gave Jackson a half-empty container of Tic-Tacs from her purse to tide him over, and called her daughter as she drove home.

"Hi, Mom. What's up?" It had taken until the fourth ring for Kayla to answer. Jo's eyes narrowed at the distinctly breathless quality to her daughter's voice.

"Just checking in. Your dad called."

"What?" There were noises in the background. Shuffling, a door squeaking open and closed.

"*Kayla.*"

"Hmm?"

"Is someone over?"

"What? No. I mean…" Her voice came in and out, like she'd switched ears. "Austin was over for a while, but we were just hanging out."

"I don't want him over when I'm not there, Kayla. Okay?"

From the backseat, Jackson's voice repeated, in a pitch-perfect imitation of Jo's sternness, "Kay-la, Kay-la, Kay-la."

"*Okay,*" Kayla said peevishly. "Jesus, it sounds like a Greek chorus is lecturing me. What did dad want?"

"I should ask you." Jo flipped on her signal and turned a corner. "He said you haven't been responding to his messages."

"Whatever. I was getting around to it."

"You're certainly taking your time about it. Did something happen? Something to upset you?"

Kayla huffed. "He should know."

"Know what?"

Her daughter breathed heavily into the phone. "He missed Jackson's birthday. He didn't even call. Not even to check in."

Jo stopped at a red light. Which was more depressing, the

fact that her son's father hadn't bothered to call him on his birthday, or that they'd been so unused to hearing from him that she hadn't realized?

But Kayla had.

Jo sighed. "Your dad…"

"Is an asshole," Kayla finished.

"He's not, Kayla. He's just… how he is." Not really in the picture, was how he was. But like pretending she knew the whys of Jackson's behavior, going through the motions of those regular calls to their eldest at least made it seem less broken. And though distant, Kayla had never seemed that bothered by it before.

"It never bugged me that much before," the girl said, echoing Jo's thoughts. "Then, it's like, I'm realizing how he just left you, left us. My friend Corey's dad did the same thing. This is what men do. And that's messed up."

Jo couldn't deny that. "I'm sorry he's like this." She straightened in her seat as the light turned green and she drove forward. "This is between you and your dad; I'll let you handle it."

"Okay."

"Can you put some frozen meal in the oven for us to eat? We'll be home in twenty minutes."

"Which one?"

"I don't care. Something that takes less than twenty minutes and that your brother will eat. Oh, and Kayla, I'm going to go out this weekend. I have a… a thing. Probably. But I'll ask Holly to come over to watch Jax."

"I was going to stay over at Misty's one night anyway. Can I do that the night you're out?"

"Sure." It would probably be easier that way. Jo wasn't ready to have her daughter asking questions about what she was doing if the answer was a date. *If* Jo contacted him.

They ended the call as Jo pulled onto the freeway, her thoughts blowing past her as the car accelerated towards home.

At the last support group, Holly had brought up self-care. They talked about that a lot at support groups. When you were a caregiver, you had to put on your own oxygen mask before helping someone else put on theirs. Though as far as Jo was concerned, if a plane was going down—and sometimes it felt like it was—she was more likely to scream a Nine Inch Nails song than try to make sure she had more oxygen to hyperventilate with.

But, no, she was supposed to get out, and shower, and do hobbies, and not be all autism, all the time. But Gavin asking her out was the first time in a long time she'd felt like she was invited to something so far afield from the reality she swirled in —the diagnoses and snarky teenager and frozen pizzas and absent ex-husband. It would be something for herself, and no other.

She bit her bottom lip, the blood rushing to the skin's surface in memory. Going out on a date with him felt less like some pastel, pamphlet-prescribed version of self-care than sticking a middle finger up at the world. And she liked that.

She liked it a lot.

# CHAPTER 19

*Does this Saturday night, around eight, work for you? Or Sunday night? Sorry I can't do tonight—too late to get a babysitter.*
*Oh, this is Josephine Palladino texting. Sorry, I should've led with that.*

*Thanks for the clarification. I thought at first you were the cable guy.*

*You text all your cable guys?*

*Only the hot ones.*
*And Saturday is perfect. I usually do Shabbat dinner with my parents tonight anyway.*

*Oh. Sorry. I should've asked.*

*You should've asked if I was Jewish?*

*No, I mean... yes?*

*Ha! I'm guessing you're not. Which is a shame, because you're missing out on challah. Which is amazing, especially when my dad bakes it.*

*But anyway... Saturday at eight o'clock. I've uploaded it into the hardware of my brain.*

*That sounds painful. So do you want to meet... somewhere?*

*Sure. What about the convenience store across from the fire station?*

*Um, no.*

*I could buy you a Slurpee.*

*No. Let's meet in the lot of the county library. Nothing skeevy ever happened by a library.*

*Oh, so this is going to be a classy car date.*

*It better be. This is the first date I've had in a looonnggg time. I probably shouldn't have admitted that.*

*When's the last time you went on a date?*

*When was "Uptown Funk" on the radio?*

*Wow. So it's been a while.*

*Yeah.*

*Wait.*
*So you're telling me that, since the last time you've dated anyone, we've... had one president... and then elected a new one...*

*YES.*

*And Taylor Swift has had, like, half a dozen albums released...*

*YES. Way to rub it in.*

*...and you've probably walked past, I don't know, hundreds and maybe thousands of guys and NONE of them asked you out? I don't believe it.*

*A few did. I said no.*

*Were they not as attractive as me? I have to admit, I set a pretty high bar.*

*I barely remember. I wasn't interested. It just seemed easier to spend my nights eating ice cream in my pajamas and watching* Law and Order *and not paying a small fortune in babysitting.*

*I've got bad news for you.*

*What?*

*We're not going to be able to watch* Law and Order *in my car.*

*Bummer.*

*We can get the ice cream, though.*

*Thank God for small miracles.*

*You're welcome to wear your pajamas. Victoria's Secret, right?*

*!!!!*

*What, too soon?*

*I just... I don't think there's an emoji for this.*

*I promise from here on out to only make you feel things that you can express with a smiley face on your phone. You know that face with the heart eyes? Yeah, get ready to use that one a lot.*

*This is already the weirdest date I've been on.*

*I'm chalking that one up as a compliment. I'll see you Saturday night at eight o'clock in the parking lot of the library where nothing bad happens.*

*Okay. Eight. Okay.*

*Thank you for texting, Josephine. I could say I wasn't waiting to hear from you, but I'm a terrible liar. Ask anyone.*

# CHAPTER 20

*H*e needed to nail this.

A car date required a unique set of worries, Gavin was realizing. It wasn't just about choosing the right place to drive to. There were the same anxieties about wearing or saying the wrong thing, but along with that he had to make sure his car wasn't full of paper cups and strange, mildewy smells. Josephine Palladino hadn't dated since "Uptown Funk"; it was the least he could do.

But he was running out of time. It'd taken longer than expected for the auto place to detail the interior of his car. By the time he raced home to grab a shower and shave, there wasn't time to run his sedan through the car wash. He hoped she didn't judge a guy for his car not being as dark and shiny as a grand piano.

*Would she judge him for it?* He was overthinking this.

When Josephine pulled into the library parking lot, he was already there, fiddling with the heat, nudging it colder and hotter and colder again, trying to find the perfect temperature— warm enough so she was comfortable, cool enough so maybe she'd want to have him close for warmth.

He'd worn a pair of slacks and a plaid button-down under a navy jacket. As he climbed out of the driver's side, he smoothed down his shirt and grabbed a bouquet of pink roses off the passenger seat.

She climbed out of her own car, shut the door, and leaned against her vehicle, staring at him across two parking lot spaces. Her curls were down around her shoulders. She had on a brown skirt, brown tights, and ankle boots, and a flowy white blouse that stirred in the breeze of the autumn evening.

It was too soon to kiss her, he reminded himself.

"Hi," he said.

"Hi."

He traversed the two spaces with the bouquet. As he reached her, he held out the flowers with his right hand. "These are for you."

She took them and smiled, leaning her face into them and inhaling the exact way he wanted to smell her hair.

"This is very... date-y," she finally said.

"Hey, it's the least I can do," he said, "since we're not going to a fancy restaurant."

They just smiled at each other a beat, before he shook to life.

"Okay, come get in my car."

"Okay..."

Her voice wavered slightly, but she followed him back to his Prius, where he held the passenger door open as she climbed inside. She sat there staring straight ahead and gripping the flowers awkwardly until he entered the driver's side, reached across her to take them, and stuck the stems in the cup holder as a makeshift vase. He hadn't needed to add any air freshener. The interior was filled with the scent of roses, and now that Josephine was inside, the fragrance underneath was amber and lilies, still floral but sexy as hell.

His body humming with excitement, he started the ignition and pulled out of the lot.

"Before we go anywhere," Josephine blurted, "there's something you should know."

Startled, he glanced over at her before turning his attention to the road. "Okay."

"I'm forty-one. And some change. I'll be forty-two in February." She was nervously shaking one of those little ankle boots. "You might've thought I was younger or something. But I'm not."

Suppressing a grin, Gavin said, "There's something you should know too." He paused for effect. "I'm a Taurus. We're a reliable bunch and very loyal. But I've got to warn you: we can be stubborn to a fault."

"You're thirty-two," she continued, her voice growing more emphatic. "I've got almost a decade on you. Shouldn't you be dating girls your own age?"

"My generation calls them women. Wait," he started, "when's your birthday?"

"February thirteenth."

"Shoot." Glancing quickly at his rear view mirror, Gavin pulled over to the side and stopped the car. He should put her at ease, but this was much too fun. He turned to face her. "You're an Aquarius. I don't think this is going to work."

She just shook her head and sighed.

"You might be too emotional and independent for my stable nature." He shook his own head sadly. "You're right. I don't think this is going to work at all."

"I'm being serious about the age thing!" Jo cried. "Think about it."

He grinned wickedly. "I'm serious, too. I mean, not about the horoscope stuff, but about the not-caring stuff. Which I guess I didn't say, but it was heavily implied in the subtext to our conversation." He lifted his foot off the brake and pulled back onto the road. "Anything else I should know about that I didn't already learn from Jackson's paperwork?" he said, glancing over his shoulder to check his blind spot.

"Oh, God." She let her head fall back. "They ask for *everything* on those forms."

"I know." He didn't add that in this case, he was part of the *they*. "I'm glad your pregnancy with Jackson was uneventful, by the way."

Jo started laughing. "This is the weirdest date ever."

Laughing in response, he turned on his signal and merged onto the highway. "So you said it's been a while since you've done this."

"Yeah." Some of the tension released from her muscles, but then she asked, "Do you do this a lot?"

"Car dates?" He looked to the side as he switched lanes. "No, this is my first."

"No. Date older women."

Taken aback, he glanced at her swiftly before focusing on the road. Maybe she didn't realize it, but almost everything about her was new to him. "No. Whatever you're thinking, no. And you're not that much older. We're both over eighteen, we both remember Alanis Morissette…"

"I just had to ask."

"I get it." He tapped the steering wheel with his forefinger. "So, 'Uptown Funk' was really the last time you've done this?"

"Really." She relaxed back in her seat. "Jackson was obsessed with that song. I still hear it in my head sometimes when I'm trying to fall asleep. I probably remember it better than any of those dates."

"Ouch."

"Yeah." She turned in her seat. "When's the last time you've done this?"

He slowed as he exited the highway. "It's been a few months since there's been anybody I've gone out with," Gavin said. "And anybody serious? Not since last December." Not since Ellie, who, he realized, would have probably never let him take her on a car date.

"Wow. An eternity," Jo said drily.

Suddenly the other night came back to him. Gwen and the frozen yogurt. "Wait, that's not entirely true."

She raised an eyebrow.

"Earlier this week, there was this thing... My mom tried to set me up with this daughter of her friend. So we went out for dessert one night, no big deal. Neither of us was interested." He glanced back at her, keeping his voice casual. "Obviously."

"I'm not your first date *this week?*" she asked.

He shrugged. "You're the only one I want to count." He didn't want to admit he'd gone out with Gwen as a last-ditch attempt to avoid his attraction to her. It could seem either flattering or insulting, and he didn't know which ball she'd run with.

He turned into a shopping center.

"Where are we going, by the way?" Josephine asked.

"To dinner," he said, pulling up to a local drive-in. "I hope you like burgers and shakes."

"I have a pulse, don't I?"

They parked alongside the menu, and Jo ordered a regular cheeseburger with sautéed mushrooms. Gavin chose one of those fake beef burgers, no cheese, extra napkins. They both ordered fries and chocolate shakes. He didn't keep as kosher as his parents—he still ate meat occasionally at restaurants—but that didn't mean he wouldn't hear the voice of his mother lecturing him if he'd gone and ordered a cheeseburger.

When the cashier told them the cost, Jo reached for her purse. He waved her away. "Driver pays."

She bit her lip. "At least let me give you gas money."

"Nope."

"Next time then."

His smile was instantaneous, and as he caught her glance,

her eyes widened slightly like she couldn't believe she'd said it, either. His heart kicked up a few beats in his chest.

*Next time* implied a second date.

While they waited for their food, he lowered his voice and got the awkward part over with. "Just so you know," he said, "the stuff with the district—with Jackson's placement—it's above my pay grade now. So it won't really be between us, exactly."

Her face was hard to read. "Okay."

"Charlene—the director—gets involved when it gets to this point. And the lawyer. I'm sure your advocate mentioned this." He struggled to keep his voice from sliding into professional-speak. He felt glad that he hadn't managed to follow Liz's advice of telling her of the district's plans to shuffle classes. It would've made the lines he needed to draw too blurry. There was work Gavin and date Gavin, and with Josephine, he wanted to shrug off the former.

"Yeah." She nodded slightly.

"I'll still be sending you emails, like when the evaluation is complete. But it won't be such a conflict with… this. I mean, I'll still technically be your coordinator, but we won't be at meetings together like we've been. Or, if we are, I'll have a lawyer next to me."

She let out a short laugh. "It'll make me nostalgic for my divorce."

He was surprised at how well she was taking this. She seemed calm, even accepting, of the situation. He didn't know what would happen in forty-five days when Jackson's evaluation was complete and another meeting was held, but she seemed okay with keeping this personal thing between them separate from whatever was happening at school. Maybe she understood that it wouldn't be him in her way anymore. He hoped she got that, at least.

Their food came and they sat back in their seats and dug in, biting into the burgers and munching on hot, salty fries.

"You know, I eat at these fast food places all the time," Josephine said between bites.

"I'm sorry." He dropped his burger and looked over at her. "We really need to get fancier drive-thrus in this area."

"No." She held up a free hand. "I wasn't criticizing. We grab food at these places when I'm taking Jackson to therapy or doctor's appointments or home from school. But I'm usually trying to eat while I drive or scarfing down something before a meeting. I barely taste it." She nibbled on the end of a fry and smiled shyly at him. "I like this. Eating without having to rush, tasting instead of treating my stomach like a gas tank I just need to refill between errands."

"Slow food," he said. "It's a thing." Watching her mouth, he took a long swallow of his chocolate shake, the cold richness complementing the salty fries. He wondered if when he kissed her later, she'd still taste like chocolate. He wondered if she'd let him kiss her later.

"What the..." Jo started loudly.

Startled, Gavin raised his eyes to see her staring into the passenger side rear view mirror, her face tense. Her green eyes narrowed. "What?" Gavin asked, craning his neck to look at what she was glowering at behind them in the restaurant parking lot.

A group of teenagers stood there clumped together, laughing and smoking.

"Excuse me a minute," she said, opening the car door and climbing out. She didn't slam the door behind her, but she shut it firm enough he could tell her slow food mindset had dissipated into the night.

There Gavin sat on his car date. Alone.

"What just happened?" he asked the dashboard.

The dashboard didn't know, either.

# CHAPTER 21

*J*o hadn't gone out on her first date in years—literally *years*—and worn clothing that reminded her she was a woman and spritzed something expensive over her curls so they weren't as frazzled as her nerves and skipped over some ethical issues dating her son's much younger school coordinator only to have her daughter ruin it.

Across the parking lot, Kayla stood under the neon drive-in lights with a group of three boys—*all boys*—who were smoking and laughing. Austin had his arm around her. Kayla didn't have a cigarette hanging from her lips, but she'd lied to her mother about where she'd be that night, and as far as Jo was concerned, she could do no greater sin with her mouth.

Jo strode over to the group, but they were laughing so hard that they didn't notice her until she'd reached them.

Kayla's head was thrown back in laughter, curls bouncing, before she caught sight of Jo and jumped. The smile slipped from her face and she stepped away from the group, Austin's arm falling off her shoulders. "M-mom?"

"Hi, Kayla." Jo folded her arms. "So you're at Misty's tonight, huh?"

Exchanging a quick glance with her boyfriend, she scurried towards her mother. "We just went out for a minute. To get something to eat."

"Oh? And where is Misty now?"

Kayla shrunk into her jacket.

"Yeah, that's what I thought." Jo rolled her shoulders back. The boys watched them, their cigarette smoke sending cirrus clouds up into the dark night. "I'm instituting a new policy in the house. An honesty policy. I thought it was already in effect, but apparently I was wrong. I'll draw up a contract and you can sign in blood when you get home."

Kayla darted a glance at Austin before taking Jo by the arm and walking her a few feet away. "You're being weird and embarrassing me," she whispered. "And who is that guy?"

Jo looked over her shoulder to where Gavin stood leaning against his car. As the sound of him slurping up the last of his milkshake reached their ears, he gave them a little wave.

Jo turned back around. "He's someone from my… support group." Boy, was she bad at this dating thing. She wouldn't blame Gavin if he took her straight back to her car after this and never called. But Kayla, out here alone at night, with a group of guys? No way.

"You're going home," she told her daughter. "Holly's there watching Jackson."

"Can't I just—"

"No." Jo fixed her with a stare. "You lied. You get that, right?"

Kayla pressed her lips together, pissed at her mother but unwilling to make a scene.

"You can say goodbye to Austin first," Jo added. "As long as it takes less than two minutes." She took out her phone and started pushing buttons on it. "I'm texting Misty to come pick you up. And her mom."

*"Mom."*

"Save it." She'd spoken with Misty's mom, Fiona, a few times before. They were friendly when they saw each other, but not friends—though Fiona had started texting her invites to Friday night happy hour, probably after Kayla shared how pathetic she was. Jo hadn't gone. Still, her feelings towards the woman warmed at Fiona's swift reply, which said that they'd be right there, along with an angry face at the teens' deception.

*Thanks,* Jo wrote back. *I'd drive her, but I'm actually on a date.* It sounded so strange, it almost felt like an excuse. She hastily added, *Kayla doesn't know it's a date. If you could not mention it?*

*Sure.*

Jo shifted her weight and looked back up at her daughter. "By the way, you can tell Austin I'll be the one picking you up after school on Monday."

Some of Kayla's control slipped. Stomping her foot, she hissed, "Wait, am I *grounded* now?"

"No." Jo lowered her voice and took a step closer to the teen. "Well, yes. But also I made you an appointment. With Dr. Murphy." Her gynecologist.

Awareness dawned in Kayla's eyes. She nodded and walked back to Austin.

"I'm waiting here until I see Misty and her mom get here," Jo said, adding in a tart voice, "Nice to meet you, Austin."

She knew that Kayla would probably be bitching about her to him later. She didn't care; Kayla knew better than to lie to her. A cold breeze blew around Jo, ruffling her shirt. Luckily, her anger kept her nice and toasty.

Though she regretted doing this while she was out with Gavin. She inwardly groaned, turning around to give him an apologetic wave. He was still leaning against the car, and he waved back. What was he thinking? But she couldn't worry about that now.

*God.* She had a teenage girl. An honest-to-God, lying-to-her-mother, dating-a-boy-in-a-band-who-smoked, asking-for-birth-control teenager. Maybe Gavin could take her by the bar before he dumped her back at the library.

She waited until Fiona's car pulled up, exchanging a few words with the other mom as Kayla got in. Then she walked back to Gavin's car.

Without saying a word, he tossed his drink in the nearby trashcan and moved to get back in the driver's seat.

"I'm sorry," Jo whispered, walking around to the passenger seat and climbing back in. She shut the door.

The car was silent.

"So you've got a guerrilla parenting style," Gavin finally said. "I think I like it."

Jo sighed. "That was my daughter. Her name's Kayla. She's sixteen going on... sixteen."

"Yeah, I figured you were related. If I hadn't seen the look she gave you behind your back, the hair and the attitude would've been a dead giveaway."

Jo slumped back in her seat, but turned her head to gauge his expression, her cheek resting against the upholstery. In the dark, neon-backlit car, his eyes twinkled with mirth. She gave an apologetic smile, but then the expression fell as she looked back at the boys through the rear view mirror.

"She said she was over at a friend's tonight," Jo explained, "but she was out with this new boyfriend. He's the one in the olive jacket."

"Ah."

"Yup."

Jo exhaled. "If he's going to take her virginity," she mumbled, "I'm at least letting the guy know her mother's not going to be taking it lying down. Wait, that came out wrong." Flustered, she shook her head and turned to Gavin. "Doesn't he look like bad news to you?"

"Oh, yeah." Gavin nodded, narrowing his eyes as he watched

Austin in the mirror. "That guy's got *regrettable first time* written all over him."

Jo threw up her hands. "Exactly. Thank you!"

Gavin tilted his head, his gaze still on the teen. "I think it's that thing he's doing with his hair."

"He's in a band," Jo said, gesturing even broader. "She's been playing his music in her room, and from all over the house I can tell his guitar is out of tune on half the songs. I don't know how she can't hear it. She *must* know."

"She's blinded by the hair." Gavin glanced at her. "Just so you know, when your back was turned, I glared at him. It just felt like the right thing to do."

She started to smile at him—he was too sweet—before shaking her head. "I'm sorry, that was probably inappropriate. I mean, not me ambushing the kids—who cares about them?—but interrupting our date."

His eyes held hers. "Don't worry about it. This isn't exactly the typical date. We don't have to abide by any rules. Except for the one I'm making up right now that says we're not playing 'Uptown Funk.' I'm superstitious about that now."

"That's a fine rule."

"But let's throw the rest of the rules out of the window. Got any other teenagers you want to stop and harass?"

She threw her head back and laughed—harder than she had in days, longer than was probably necessary. The tension from everything—Jackson's school to this date to realizing Kayla had lied to her—sputtered out in great gulps. Gavin joined in, throwing her frequent glances as he started the car and drove away from the restaurant.

"You've got a great laugh," he said.

"Thanks." She wiped her eyes and sniffed back another giggle. "Where are we going?"

"I have no idea."

At that, she laughed hard again, squirming in her seat.

"Oh, I almost forgot." Gavin pushed play on his stereo system and the sounds of a female pop singer tumbled out. "I thought you'd be more comfortable if I put some Liz Phair on. But it's 2005 Liz Phair, not '90s Liz Phair."

"I like 2005 Liz Phair."

For half an hour, he drove at a leisurely pace, turning on roads at random, as they talked. Jo liked how he drove. Neil had often been too speedy and reckless behind the wheel and prone to fits of anger. Gavin handled the car by-the-book, but with an ease she envied—and that was somehow making him more attractive. That and the way his shirt fit over his broad shoulders.

So he knew her age. Knew her age and didn't mind.

"So your parents live around here?" she asked.

"Yeah," he said as he drove. "I was born and raised here. My parents met when they both worked at one of the universities. My mom had the better job, and my dad's more patient and a better cook, so he stayed home to raise me and my sisters."

"What does your mom do?"

"Set me up on dates," he said. "But professionally? Works for the dean." He looked at her. "How about you? Is your family local?"

"No," she said. "My parents live far away, and they're getting older, so it's hard for them to visit. And traveling with Jackson is tricky. But my brother lives near them. And my mom has a cousin who's autistic, so they understand." She swallowed back the guilt she often felt when thinking of her family. If circumstances were different—if she had more time and energy, if it were easier to travel... Changing the focus to him, she asked, "So you have sisters?"

He held up his fingers. "Two. They both live far away, too. Liz and I are the closest. She's in England."

"That is far." She paused. "Have you ever been married?"

"Nope."

"Okay then." She'd guessed as much, but it never hurt to ask. Still, the question hung awkwardly in the air a moment, reminding them both of how different their lives had been—and maybe still were.

He cleared his throat. "So," he said finally, turning a corner, "what were you like when you were young?"

"Like…"

"Like eight or fifteen or Jackson's age."

"Oh. Well." She glanced out the passenger side window, as if through the image of the dark, leaf-strewn street behind them she could look back in time. "I liked to bike. And stay out too late. I might've been a bit of a smart ass."

He smirked. "You don't say."

"It's true. When I was home, I'd shut the door and play music all night—four, five hours at a time. It drove my parents crazy." How much freedom she'd had then—to think and feel and daydream, to let the world blow past her without assuming she had to keep all the parts moving lest it all come crashing down.

"I'm picturing it," Gavin said. "Was your hair long or short?"

"Long." She put fingers up to her forearm. "This long. It was a pain in the butt to comb."

He smiled and pulled into the empty lot of a gas station. "Let's park for a while. Take it easy on the environment."

"Okay," she said, but her stomach fluttered. If he wasn't driving, they could touch. If he didn't need to focus, they could kiss. Her body was of two minds whether she was ready for that, a delicious war of fight or flight twisting her insides.

He shifted the car into park, removing his hands from the wheel. "That reminds me," he said, pointing to a glowing green car wash sign, "I meant to wash the car before I picked you up. I hope it's okay that it's a little dirty."

"Of course it's okay." She added, "But you can get it washed now if you'd like."

"Attendant not available at night," he said, reading a large sign by the car wash entrance. "Enter at your own risk."

"Let's live dangerously," Jo said for the first time in two decades.

He looked over at her and raised an eyebrow. "I'm game if you are."

Driving over the leaf-spattered lot, they pulled up to an automated machine, where Gavin paid with his card and the gate lifted so they could drive into the car wash tunnel.

"This looks kind of long," he said. "I hope it's not actually a way into another dimension."

Jo laughed. "Car wash time machine." A frisson of excitement ran up her spine. It was just a silly car wash, but it was rare for her to be so spontaneous—especially with another adult.

Smiling like he was enjoying this too, Gavin steered the Prius onto a track, then popped the car in neutral and eased his foot off the brake.

"Keep your hands on the wheel," Jo chided, pointing to a rule on the sign at the entrance.

He gave her a faux injured expression. "Do I look like the kind of guy who wouldn't drive responsibly in a car wash?"

She giggled and leaned back in her seat as the car caught on the track and moved forward, trembling like an old carnival ride.

They entered the dark tunnel. The cleaning machines whirred to life, sounding far too loud and grating for a calm autumn night. Yet paradoxically, the darkness and noises, the lack of control, comforted Jo, like they really were driving into another dimension. Soon enough the loudness drowned out the worries and errant thoughts that ran on a constant ticker-tape in her head. The track assured her that there was no getting off this ride until they'd rode it through. She sat there and let it happen.

All was dark except for the silhouette of Gavin beside her and the alien lights of the machine. Sprays of foam began to hit the car.

She felt inexplicably free.

It had been much, much longer since that had happened—way before "Uptown Funk." She imagined that this is what her clients experienced when they took pirate cruises or lay out on the sunny beaches of Florida. A buoyancy of peace.

Liz Phair's album *Somebody's Miracle* was playing, and the track switched to her upbeat, sexy "Got My Own Thing." She'd loved this song years ago when she'd first heard it, the singer so sure of her own allure, her ability to drive a man stupid. Now, along with the freedom, she felt the rush of blood in her body sync with the flow of the song.

Despite her nerves–despite catching Kayla out–she was having such a good time.

And she wanted to kiss Gavin Steinberg.

She wanted to kiss him *now*.

She unbuckled her seatbelt and moved to him, so quick he barely had a chance to see it coming.

"What—"

But in the darkness Jo overshot the movement—way overshot. Instead of landing in his arms, she somehow ended up half in his lap, her butt against his firm thigh and her hands scrambling for something to grip and finding his shoulders. The pink roses squished beneath her knees; she'd forgotten about them. But she'd committed to kissing him—and even if she hadn't, because she'd launched herself on him so thoroughly, she didn't so much put her lips to his as fall onto his mouth.

His body jerked, startled.

She moved to pull away, completely embarrassed, but then his fingers were in her hair and he was pulling her close and kissing her back.

His hands had left the steering wheel.

He pulled her fully onto his lap as the machines rumbled like waking beasts outside the car. She held his shoulders for support, a shiver of warm pleasure coursing through her as a giant rotating sponge pounded against the sides of the car, sheets of foam cascading down the windows. As they broke the kiss to breathe, she was grateful the noise overpowered her gasp. Was she too into this? It had been so long.

But Gavin's hands roamed to her waist and then up to her hair again, gripping her like he'd been wanting to do this all night. His eyes were lidded, his gaze focused on her mouth as he took it again.

A small noise escaped her, almost a whimper, a *this-is-good-and-please-don't-stop*.

As water cascaded down the windows, they kept kissing, enclosed in their own safe, separate world from the tempest outside. His mouth was warm and tasted like chocolate. He smelled like spice and dark nights. It was sexy. *He* was sexy.

The machines roared like a jet engine as the dryer came on.

Were they at this part already?

The car shuddered, pummeled by air on all sides, but that was nothing compared to the small, private sensations of Gavin's hands on her. His fingers tucking a curl behind her ear as it fell between their faces. His thumb rubbing her scalp. His mouth nipping at her bottom lip in a teasing, taunting way so that she almost pulled away to give him what-for until she remembered she'd never been kissed so well.

The car lurched. Jo started and pushed away.

They were on the other side. The end of the track. The night, the empty lot, the scattered leaves all around.

Gavin's face was illuminated by the garish gold gas station sign.

"Okay," he said, his face full of wonder. "So this is a great date." He pulled back gently, then leaned forward again to kiss her, almost chastely, on the lips, then jaw, then neck.

Jo's life came back to her in a rush. "Oh, crap. What time is it?"

"I don't know. Do you have a curfew?"

"No, I have a babysitter."

"Right." He fumbled for his cell in his pocket and checked it. "It's almost eleven."

*Shoot.* "I should get home." Blowing her hair out of her face, Jo extricated herself and moved back to her own seat, gathering the pink roses she'd disrupted on her way. Placing them back in the console, she ran her fingers through her hair.

"Okay," Gavin said, then, "Okay." He started shaking out his hands in front of the wheel.

She paused. "What are you doing?"

"I'm trying to get the blood back in my fingers so I can drive you home."

She closed her eyes and slid down the seat, pulling her top up to cover her face. "Oh my God."

He laughed. "I'm starting to think it's been longer than 'Uptown Funk' since… other stuff."

"Is it obvious?" she mumbled.

As he started the car again and made his way to the library, she emerged from her shirt to send Holly a quick text to let her know she'd be late.

"You know, that car wash is open twenty-four hours," Gavin said. "Any time you'd like to go again, just let me know."

"Is that suggestive?" she asked. "Because it sounded suggestive."

"It was suggestive. And I'm hoping inspirational."

She bit back a laugh, but grew silent as he pulled into the lot of the library next to her car. She didn't know how to do this. They'd kissed, but what did he expect now? What did it mean?

And where could this go if they had to keep it a secret?

"I had a nice time," she said stupidly, because that's what you said on dates, even she remembered that. "I like your car."

"Thanks," he said. "I like your legs."

She laughed.

His blue eyes, light when he wore certain shirts, were dark to match the night, and the humorous twinkle usually in their depths had gone serious. He leaned forward like he meant to kiss her again, but Jo reached behind her to the door handle, fumbling to open it.

"Thanks for tonight," she said, nearly falling backwards out of the vehicle.

# CHAPTER 22

*T*hat kiss had really been something, Gavin mused as he lazed around his apartment Sunday morning. His body was still electrified from the way Josephine had jumped on him and kissed him the night before—the warm weight of her on his lap, her mouth mingling with his, the loud and shuddering sounds from the car wash as he'd run his fingers through her soft curls.

He'd enjoyed their kiss at the fundraiser, too. It'd been sweet and simple, a confirmation of their feelings and a promise of things to come. But that kiss last night had wheels. It was going places.

Was it too soon to text or call and ask when he could see her again? She'd seemed as eager as he had been in the car wash, but she'd also practically run out of his car at the end of the date. He didn't want to scare her off.

He reclined on his couch, reliving the night, until it was time to meet Tanner for lunch. He and his old sales buddy usually just met for happy hour every few weeks, so Gavin had been surprised by last week's invitation to get together on the weekend.

They met at a local bistro, where they both ordered the truffle mac and cheese to warm them up from the increasingly frigid weather. After the late summer, the fall was coming on with a vengeance, chilling the temperatures and coloring the trees in a bouquet of russets and golds to rival the New England autumn Gavin remembered from business trips.

Cold as it was outside, the bright trees against a brilliant blue sky made for an incredible fall day, and the memories of Josephine had Gavin feeling as light and carefree as the leaves.

As he sat across from him, Tanner noticed.

"You look like you're having a good weekend," the man remarked.

"Pretty good," Gavin said, aiming for nonchalance but falling off the mark as a goofy grin tried to erupt on his face. He took a large bite of hot, gooey mac and cheese to cover it.

Tanner picked up his fork. "So, hey, what are you doing after this?"

"A few errands," Gavin said. "Nothing too exciting. Why?"

Tanner twirled the fork between his fingers. "We're having a few people over to watch the game, and we thought you'd like to come. A lot of people from the company."

Gavin chewed carefully over his pasta. "Oh?"

"Yeah." Tanner started stirring his dish, studiously avoiding Gavin's gaze. "Bryce, Jones, Cartwright, Lyndsay of course… I think Ellie may stop by, too."

"Oh, uh…" He swallowed. "I'm not sure. I'll think about it." He didn't have any hard feelings for Ellie, but socializing with his ex, especially around all their old friends, didn't seem all that appealing. It would feel too much like old times. It might even be tempting to slip into those old patterns of going through the motions. After his sudden feelings for Josephine, and especially after last night, he felt like he was starting to want something, really want something, for the first time in what felt like ages.

Tanner frowned and speared some of his macaroni. "I thought you said you weren't doing anything."

"Yeah. It's just..." Gavin shrugged.

Tanner's eyes narrowed. "Are you seeing somebody new?"

Gavin had intended to keep it a secret, but his mouth was doing that goofy-smile thing again. "Sort of," he admitted. "It's new. Not really at the divulging point yet."

Tanner's eyebrows knit together. "What does that mean?"

The bistro hummed with the pleasant background sounds of conversation and clicks of utensils on dishes, but part of Gavin wished they were at the bar with a game blaring on the TV. With no loud noise to shout over, it was too tempting to talk.

Gavin wasn't trying to be coy. After all, he remembered that Tanner had been the first one he'd talked to when he and Ellie got together. They'd been friends for a few years. He deserved to know at least the gist of it.

Gavin decided to share some details—because he didn't want to be a jerk, and he also couldn't help himself. "We've only been out once," he admitted. "Last night. I'm not ready to announce it to the world, for several reasons. But I really like her a lot, and I'm hoping I get to see her again."

"Huh," Tanner said flatly. "How'd you meet her?"

"At the grocery store." It wasn't quite the truth, but it wasn't all lie, either. "She's just... really different from any woman I've dated. So I'm trying not to screw it up." He laughed, remembering her practically falling out of his car at the end. Would texting her today make her want to run away, too?

"How?" Tanner asked.

"What?"

"How's she different?"

"Oh." Gavin sat back, feeling a warmth fill his veins as he thought of Josephine. "She's, um, a few years older. And she's got kids. Divorced," he added, lest Tanner think anything else.

"Kids?" Tanner let out a low whistle and ran his hands through his short, scrubby hair. "You sure about that, man?"

"Yeah, I'm sure," he joked. "I've seen the kids myself."

Tanner didn't crack a smile. "That's not what I meant."

"Yeah, I know," Gavin said. "Look, I know it's a little different, but that doesn't mean it's bad, you know?"

"Maybe not." Keeping his eyes on him, Tanner took a drink of his beer, put it down, and then leaned forward, lowering his voice like he was giving away insider trading info. "I was interested in a single mom once, a few years back, but I didn't go for it. You know why?"

*She said no*, Gavin wanted to respond, but instead said, "Why?"

"Because a woman with kids is a package deal," Tanner said, leaning back in his seat and grabbing his napkin to wipe his hands. Throwing the napkin on the table, he gestured, his palms wide. "It's like buying a stereo system. Could you buy the entire system at once, maybe save yourself time and some cost? Sure. But is it a good idea?"

Gavin's stomach tensed.

"If it were me," Tanner continued, "I'd rather get it all piece by piece, so you can see what you like, if you need to exchange something, what you want next. You know?"

"Just so we're clear," Gavin said, "are you comparing people to parts of a stereo system right now?"

"Think about it," Tanner said, ignoring the question. "Think about whether you're ready for all that, all at once."

Gavin's fingers clenched. He was pretty sure that if he and Ellie had gotten engaged last winter, they'd be about to get married, and maybe with a baby on the way soon, if Ellie and his mother had had their way. He doubted if Tanner would chide him for suddenly having *all that, all at once* like he was now.

He wondered if Tanner had always been like this, and he was

just starting to notice. He knew Tanner wanted him back at the company—he said so, frequently—but under his chummy bravado, Gavin was starting to detect a resentment from Tanner that he had chosen to leave sales and Ellie to have a different life.

Still, he didn't want to ruin their friendship—or their meal. Forcing his muscles to relax, he switched the topic to football, and Tanner relented.

But his words stayed in Gavin's head through the rest of lunch and as he drove home. As crude as Tanner's analogy had been—stereo system; what the hell?—was there some truth that Gavin was jumping into something too big, too quickly?

As he parked and went back inside his apartment, he collapsed on his couch and scrubbed a hand over his face. Then he pulled his phone out of his pocket and held it in the air, staring at it.

"Text her. Don't text her. Text her." The various arguments were duking it out in his head: He should text her because she was amazing and also jumped him in a car wash. He shouldn't text her because he'd scare her off. He shouldn't text her because he'd scare *himself* off. So he messaged someone else instead.

Instead of writing him back, Liz called him from England.

*"No one's dead, but can you call me back tonight?"* she said, repeating the text he'd sent her. "I'm guessing our plan didn't work?"

"No." He grimaced at the memory. "She brought an advocate to the meeting. And Tanner's idea didn't work, either."

"What was Tanner's idea?"

"Go on a date with someone else to distract myself."

"That's a stupid idea." Liz's tone was amused. "So where are you in the stages of this crush?"

"I blew right through denial," he said. "And then through the stage where I kissed her and admitted my feelings at a community event. And then asked her out. And then went out and made out some more. Which brings us to today."

"Wow," Liz said. "And you're just telling me now?"

He smiled. "I didn't want to hear any more sensible advice that would steer me away. Because… making out."

Liz laughed. "Yeah. I'm getting that."

"I'm trying to decide if it's too soon or even a good idea to contact her about going out again," Gavin said in a rush.

"Well—"

"She has kids and is forty-one. I should mention that."

"Wow, is—"

"So I'm not sure what my plan should be."

"I guess there's a first time for everything." Liz paused. "What does your gut tell you?"

Gavin fell into silence, surprised his sister wasn't raising some of the same concerns Tanner had earlier. He was also unsure what his gut was saying. To stall, he joked, "Shouldn't you be asking what my heart is telling me?"

"No," she said automatically. "Too high. And before you ask, not any lower parts, either. The gut. Right in the middle. There's your answer."

"There's my answer?" Gavin echoed. But then it came to him.

RIGHT AFTER ENDING the call with Liz, he wrote the text.

*I don't want to text you this soon because I don't want to scare you off—I think you left nail marks on my passenger door, by the way—but if I did, I'd say how much I can't stop thinking about you or last night or you (did I mention you?). And then I'd probably ask you when we could do that again, because in addition to being an incredibly attractive guy, I'm also really practical.*

HER REPLY CAME twenty minutes later.

*I could do Wednesday night.*

Then:

*I keep writing and deleting a response to what you said, which is making me smile so much the kids are starting to get suspicious. But it isn't coming out as good as yours, so let me just say: thank you for taking the risk of scaring me off.*

# CHAPTER 23

*A*t Dr. Murphy's office Monday, Jo sat next to her daughter, pretending to read a health magazine.

The room was decorated in rose and beige tones, and a vase of melon-colored roses sat on the front counter. The flowers and pastels couldn't quite mask the sight or scents of medical personnel in scrubs and rubber gloves. Still, Jo found it calming, even today. So little in her life was sterile.

Kayla's leg bounced up and down, a telltale sign she was nervous. They'd barely spoken since Saturday night—beyond a lecture from Jo on honesty, trust, and safety—yet at her daughter's discomfort came Jo's maternal instinct to soothe.

"It'll be fine," Jo said in a low voice, leaning close to her. "I've been going to Dr. Murphy for years now. She's nice and she knows what she's doing."

"Okay." Kayla stared straight ahead.

"I know you're getting older," Jo said. "And I know you're mature for your age. All the times you've helped me with Jackson…"

"*Okay,*" Kayla said, a little peevishly, like even though they were there to get birth control, she didn't want to get into it, which Jo took as confirmation she was nervous. The girl had her dark hair braided back, the streaks of blue winding in and out of the braid, and she kept tugging at a thin strand that had sprung loose.

"Okay," Jo said. "Well, if you have any questions…"

"Just one." Kayla looked over at her. "Who was that guy you were with the other night?"

Ugh. She'd walked right into that one. Her insides fluttered at the thought of him, but she instantly regretted her new insistence on honesty. She took a deep breath. "He was my date. His name is Gavin."

"*Gavin?* What kind of name is Gavin?"

"The name of the guy I went out with Saturday night." Jo tossed the magazine on a nearby table. "I'm trying to get a life, per your request." She hadn't gone out for Kayla, of course, but she couldn't resist reminding her daughter that she maybe, sort of, had done something that wasn't related to Jackson or his needs.

Sort of.

"He looked way younger than you." Kayla narrowed her eyes. "Where'd you meet him?"

Jo shifted in her seat, her muscles tensing. "Um, at a meeting."

"You're dating someone from your support group?"

"No. He's not a dad." Her cell pinged, and Jo looked down to see a message from Gavin.

They'd been texting back and forth since he'd asked her out again last night. She was enjoying it—probably too much. She opened this latest message to see a link to a video of Rose Royce's 70s disco hit "Car Wash."

She couldn't bite back the smile in time.

Looking up, she caught Kayla staring between her and her phone with the same face she'd used when they'd found a spider in the bathtub.

Jo glanced quickly around the room, but the only other woman there was reading a novel. She might as well get it over with. "He works for the school district, actually. As Jackson's coordinator. It's new and we're not sure where it's going yet." As strange as Saturday night was, and as embarrassed as she'd been later at how she'd attacked Gavin in the car wash, he wanted to see her again. He'd kept texting her, even though their date on Wednesday was just around the corner. His texts had included some smiley faces. A lot of smiley faces.

Kayla's mouth dropped open. "You're dating someone from the *district?*"

"He's a nice man, Kayla. It just happens to be his job."

"His job sucks."

Jo sighed. "It's a complicated situation. You'll find there are a lot of those when you get older." She shifted, feeling a quiver of annoyance. "Why are you being so weird about this? I thought you wanted me to have a life."

Kayla looked away, a sour expression on her face. "I meant like go get margaritas with Misty's mom and her friends at Applebee's. Not this."

"This? You mean me dating?"

"Yes. It's weird. And it's... weird." Kayla shook her head. "And he probably doesn't get our lives at all."

"No one gets our lives. But he wants to try."

She looked back at Jo, her eyes narrowed. "Is this an IEP negotiation tactic?"

"What? No!" Jo was shocked she'd asked, before remembering that she too had suspected Gavin of being flirtatious for his job. She hardly suspected that of him now, given that he'd gone and made out with her in a car wash. But maybe she'd passed down a mistrust of men to her daughter—genetically or through her own attitude.

A nurse appeared in pink scrubs in a doorway to the waiting room. "Kayla Palladino?"

*Could it have killed you to show up five minutes before now?* Jo wanted to ask. But at the panicked look on Kayla's face, she realized harassing her mom about her date had at least distracted her from her first gynecologist visit.

Jo set her hand on Kayla's knee. "Do you want me to come in with you?"

"No," Kayla said. "I got this." She stood up and walked away with the nurse.

But ten minutes later, the nurse appeared in the waiting room, smiling slightly. "She's asking for you."

Jo sprung up and followed the nurse to the exam room, where her daughter was already laying on the table, a pink drape over her knees. Jo was nervous about this, too. In fact, she'd almost accepted Misty's mother's invitation to last Friday's happy hour to discuss the terrors of having teenage girls. But despite having that in common, they still came from two different worlds, and Jo had decided against it.

Dr. Murphy was getting her equipment together, but paused to smile at Jo as she slipped into the room.

"Jo, good to see you. It's only been a month, right?"

"Yeah," Jo said. "Do we get a punch card for frequent visits?"

Kayla groaned. "Mom."

"Just trying to lighten the mood." Jo walked over to her daughter and rubbed her shoulder. "This goes really quick, Kayla. I promise. It's like before you know it, they're done. And Dr. Murphy is really gentle."

Dr. Murphy sat down on a stool and rolled to the end of the exam table. "Thank you for bringing her in today. Kayla, you're just going to feel a little pinch now, but your mom is right: this will be over before you know it."

Kayla's body tensed and she clasped and squeezed Jo's hand.

"Good," the doctor said. "You're doing fine. Just relax your knees."

"What do you want for dinner tonight?" Jo asked Kayla,

trying to distract her. "We could do Indian, sandwiches, Chinese, sushi."

"Sushi," Kayla said, a little breathlessly as her eyes locked on her mother's. "That sounds good."

"It does." Jo nodded. "What about dessert? I feel like we need dessert."

"Just another minute, Kayla," the doctor said. "You're doing great."

Kayla's face was strained, and she squeezed Jo's hand a little harder before saying, "Cake. Maybe carrot?"

"Carrot cake it is." Jo laced her fingers with Kayla's, squeezing back. She blinked, and at the sudden rush of moisture to her eyes, she bit down on her tongue. It was never easy to see either of her kids uncomfortable, even if it was for something as necessary as a medical exam. And here was further proof that Kayla was entering womanhood: her first OBGYN visit, her first birth control, probably soon her first time. There'd be more boyfriends after this, and breakups, and maybe eventually marriage and mortgages and kids. Jo looked at Kayla now, with her pretty face and woman's body, and could still remember holding her in her trembling arms at the hospital, those first frightened cries and her grapefruit-sized head.

"Okay. We're all done." The doctor pulled away, and Jo felt her daughter's body relax all the way down to her fingertips. She herself let out a long breath, feeling surprised and shaky by the emotions the exam had stirred up.

Standing up and taking off her gloves, the doctor smiled and looked between Kayla and Jo. "Why don't you get dressed, and then we'll talk a little?"

After Kayla had put back on her clothes and Jo found a chair against the wall, Dr. Murphy entered the room.

"So I see you're a junior," she said conversationally, looking down at Kayla's form. "Have you started looking at colleges?"

"Uh, not really," Kayla said, perching at the end of the exam table.

"We're working on it," Jo said quickly, her stomach twisting in knots. Kayla raised an eyebrow. "We are?"

"Yes." Jo gave a tight smile. "We are." *Soon*, she thought. *In the winter—or maybe spring. Whenever this stuff with Jackson is resolved.*

The doctor cleared her throat and sat down on a stool by the counter. "So your mom tells me you want to talk about birth control options."

Kayla glanced at Jo again, but then nodded. "Yeah."

"I'm glad you told your mom." She winked at Jo. "Sometimes that can be hard for moms to hear, but it's a responsible thing to do."

Jo didn't trust herself to speak. She wanted to ask Kayla if she was sure, like really sure, and then show the gynecologist Kayla's baby picture and ask if *she* was sure her daughter was ready. Also, crying was not out of the question yet.

Dr. Murphy reached behind her and grabbed two colorful pamphlets, which she handed over to Kayla along with a small square of paper. "I've given you a prescription for birth control pills, but I know you're interested in an IUD. Of course, with either of these, you also need to make sure you're using condoms to protect yourself. Do you have any questions about those?"

Kayla colored. "Nope."

"Okay." The doctor smiled. "Anyway, this brochure tells you more about the IUD and what to expect. If you'd like to have one inserted, you can call the office here and make another appointment. It's a simple procedure. I'm also happy to answer any questions in the meantime."

"Thank you," Kayla said softly.

Jo eyed the brochure. Maybe she'd have a peek when Kayla was at school tomorrow. Those young women on the covers of the pamphlets sure looked happy to be sexually active.

She shook herself. "Thank you, Dr. Murphy." She stood and turned to her daughter. "Kayla, can you wait out front a second while I talk to the doctor?"

The girl looked between them. "You're not going to, like, talk about how my vagina is weird or something, are you?"

Dr. Murphy laughed.

"Of course not," Jo said. "I just had a question for the doctor about"—she thought quickly—"insurance."

"Oh. Okay." Like most sentient beings, the word *insurance* summoned enough confusion and vague unease to make Kayla skedaddle. She slid her butt off the exam table and moved towards the door.

Dr. Murphy gave Jo a wide smile as the door shut. "You did a good thing, Jo."

"I know." She crossed her arms and sighed. "You know I would've preferred she waited until she were forty."

The doctor laughed. "Don't we all. But everything looked fine. We'll call if anything strange comes up on the pap results." She reached out and squeezed Jo's arm. "No need to worry."

"That's not why I wanted to talk to you," Jo said. "I mean, not entirely."

"Oh?"

Jo looked down at her shoes, wondering who was more shy about this, teenage girls or divorced single mothers who had dry spells as long as the Mojave Desert. "I just started seeing a man. And it's, it's been good. Like we're going to be seeing more of each other, I think."

She met the doctor's eyes, which were bright with curiosity.

"And you want to discuss birth control options," Dr. Murphy finished.

"Yes." Jo held up a hand. "I mean, I don't want anything too high-tech. Maybe just a prescription for birth control pills. I used to take those."

"Sure." The doctor swiveled her chair around and grabbed

her prescription pad. "You've just been in for your yearly exam, so this will be quick. I assume I don't need to remind you to use condoms?"

"Nope." Jo's face turned as pink as Kayla's probably had two minutes ago. "And thanks." She took a deep breath, but on the exhale a torrent of words flooded out. "Do you have any idea nowadays when two dating adults are expected to, you know, seal the deal?"

The doctor looked up. "Have sex for the first time?"

"Yes. I mean, what's usually standard? Do you know much about dating nowadays? Are you married or single? I'm sorry, I feel like I should know that. I've been coming here for like six years…"

Dr. Murphy smiled. "It's fine, Jo. I've been married for a decade."

She'd been wondering all this since she'd gotten home from the date Saturday night. Was there something about three dates? Would they even make it that far? *Should* they? She'd been at support group yesterday afternoon and had wanted to ask or confess something about Gavin, but she couldn't. First, it was a secret. She hadn't even told Holly yet whom she'd been out with the other night. Second, most of them were either married or solidly single and not looking. Of course, *she* hadn't been looking, either. But she knew what she would fear if any of the other support group parents had announced they were dating someone new: That the relationship would come with an expiration date. That they would bolt when they discovered how hard it could sometimes be to raise a special needs child in a misunderstanding world. Because certainly Neil had bolted.

Jo tried to focus back on the doctor, hoping for rational, research-based, confidential advice. "But do you have any sense of when sex is supposed to happen? Like as a medical professional."

"Hmm." The doctor pursed her lips and tilted her head. "I

imagine it's somewhere between four minutes after meeting and four years, if you have certain beliefs, some patience, and a lot of jigsaw puzzles."

"Oh."

"Probably closer to four minutes."

"Oh." Jo's breath grew shallow. It'd been way longer than four minutes. Maybe he would expect it when they went out again Wednesday. She didn't know how she could both yearn for and fear something so strongly at the same time.

The doctor held her gaze. "The important thing is that you're comfortable and enjoying yourself."

"Yeah, but…" Jo twisted her hands together. "Do you think a thirty-two-year-old man has any clue what a forty-one-year-old woman who's had two kids might look like naked? I saw an article a year or so ago about how men viewing porn has changed what they think women should look like, like we're all supposed to shave ourselves so we look like hairless dogs or something. Do you think he watches porn? Do you think he thinks that? Do I need to shave like…all the places?"

"I'm not privy to the thoughts of many thirty-two-year-old men," the woman admitted. "But I imagine most men would just think, 'Hey, I'm with a naked woman right now,' and that'd be that." She smiled. "Based on what I know about men."

Jo exhaled shakily. "I hope you're right."

The doctor laughed. "Trust me, I'm right." She ripped the prescription off her pad and handed it over. "One last thing, Jo."

"Hmm?"

"Have fun."

# CHAPTER 24

*T*hey met at the library lot again Wednesday night. It was raining, so Gavin grabbed the umbrella under his seat and rushed outside to meet her. At the same time, she was darting towards his car, a bright green raincoat pulled over her head. Before he knew what was happening, they collided into each other, the umbrella tumbling to the pavement.

"Sorry!" Gavin shouted over the rain, one hand reaching out to steady her by the waist.

"It's okay." A lock of wet curl was stuck to Jo's cheek, but Gavin chose to open up the passenger door with his free hand and usher her inside.

As she dove in, he picked up the umbrella and raced back to the driver's seat.

Inside the vehicle, they were both breathing heavily from the sprint, condensation clouding the windows.

"I guess a picnic is out of the question," Gavin joked as he shook water off his hands.

She laughed and smirked at him, her fingers smoothing her wet hair. "Was a picnic really in the cards? A *night* picnic?"

"Sure. Why not?" He inhaled her perfume as rain battered

the windshield, the wipers softly swiping across the glass every few seconds. He was remembering the car wash. He wondered if she was, too.

"So," he started, "how have you been?" The engine was on and the heater was making quick work out of drying their wet hair and clothes, but he didn't put the car into gear. He didn't know where she wanted to go, and he just wanted to look at her for a while.

"Fine," she said softly. Under her green raincoat, which she was shrugging off, she wore a thin black sweater that hugged her curves, with a maroon scarf draped around her neck. Her dark curly hair hung longer than normal in its wetness, and as she turned away to disrobe, a lock caught in the jacket.

Instinctively he reached over and freed the hair.

Startled, she turned towards him, her green eyes wide.

"Your hair…" he started.

"Oh. Okay."

He smiled, trying to put her at ease. "Hi."

"Hi." Her chest rose and fell through that thin sweater. Yeah, she was nervous. He was trying not to notice. But.

"You okay?" he asked.

"Yes. Sure." She cleared her throat. "I mean. *Yes.*"

"Do you want to play some Boggle or something?"

That earned him a grin. "Do you keep Boggle in your car?"

"No, actually." He smiled back. "Unfortunately."

They both paused, looking at each other. He was aware of each breath she took. It was their second date, and they both should have been *less* nervous. But now they knew what was simmering under all this small talk.

Trying to put her at ease, he attempted another joke. "We can just start with the making out part, if you want," he said. "I mean, just to get it out of the way. Not that we'd enjoy it."

Her eyes flew open, bigger than before, terrified, and he realized his mistake.

"Or not," he said quickly. "We don't have to do that, now or… later. It's totally cool either way." Fumbling, he buckled his seatbelt and put his hands on the wheel. Responsibly. Not lecherously. "Forget I said anything. Maybe we can just go get tacos?"

She swallowed and turned to look out the windshield. "Tacos. Okay."

Damn, he was coming on way too strong.

He put the car into reverse and started backing out into the lot. "So what have you—"

"Do you watch porn?" she blurted.

He slammed on the brakes. *"What?"*

Her voice was insistent. "Porn. Do you watch it?"

The rain tapped on the car's roof and the wipers swung across the windshield as they sat in silence.

"Umm…" He cut a glance her way, laughing nervously. "Is this a trick question?" *Porn?* Were they going to talk about this in a library parking lot?

"Are there certain expectations about this—" She stopped. "I mean about when we…"

He turned to see her motioning with her hand in a circle. Her tone was slightly louder, with an emotional edge—not unlike it had been at the IEP meetings, actually—and he realized that as nervous as he was, she was far worse.

"No," he said carefully. "I don't have any expectations." He risked reaching a hand out to one of hers, turning it over and clasping her palm. He waited until he caught her eye, and then he squeezed her hand once. "Okay?"

She took a deep breath. "Okay."

"Okay." He released her hand. "Do you like tacos?"

"I do."

"Good."

He felt them both relax as he drove to the nearest taco joint, where they both ordered two tacos, chips, and drinks. After getting food from the drive-thru window, he pulled into a parking spot to divide it up. The rain had lifted momentarily, the streets and lots slick and shiny in the dark. His fingers grazed hers as he passed her a drink, the small touch giving him a thrill. Even worse, when she leaned forward at the same time he was passing her a taco, the back of his hand brushed her chest.

"Sorry," he said, hurriedly moving his hand away.

"It's fine." She bit her lip and shifted in her seat. "This is great. Thank you for the tacos."

The meal sat warm in his lap, but he didn't make a move to open up the foil. Neither did Jo. Instead she turned her head towards him, her gaze slowly dragging to his. As their eyes made contact, her lips parted and a shot of adrenaline raced through him.

He wasn't sure who moved first, but suddenly they were kissing, the tacos forgotten in their laps—the tacos *falling* off their laps. Her hands were cupping his jawline and his mouth was swallowing her whole, her warm, damp, amber-scented self. She murmured and tilted her head, their kisses growing more passionate. Fingertips trailed up his arms and his hands rubbed down her back.

She was the first to break away. "Is there somewhere we can—"

He nodded for a full ten seconds before his words caught up. "My apartment's only five minutes away. Is that what you—"

"*Yes.*"

He shoved the car in reverse and backed out of the spot in a wide arc, generously pressing the gas pedal as he zoomed home.

Neither of them said anything, maybe out of nerves or not wanting to break the spell. But when he slowed as he reached his apartment complex, Josephine yelped and slouched down in her seat.

Startled, he looked over. "What?"

"Jeannie," she hissed.

"What?"

*"Jackson's teacher."*

He'd just found a spot, but he looked over to the entrance to the apartment complex to see Jeannie getting mail out of the mailboxes there.

"I had no idea she lived here," he murmured. "What are the chances…"

"Probably less than the chances of you getting fired if word gets out we're spending time together," Josephine said.

Jeannie cast a glance their way and Jo yelped again, clicking the button to release her seatbelt and crouching down low. She reached over and flicked off his headlights.

Realizing what was about to happen—or not happen—he groaned. "Let's just wait a few minutes until she goes inside. And then—"

And then Josephine's phone rang. Still crouched down, she dug in her purse to extricate it.

"Kayla?" she whispered, then, "Oh, no. And still coughing?" A pause. "Give him some Tylenol from the cabinet. And a popsicle. I'll be home in a few minutes." With a sigh, she ended the call.

"That doesn't sound good," Gavin said, trying not to sound as disappointed as he felt.

"Jackson's sick. He's got a fever." She sighed again, her eyes apologetic. "I've got to head back."

As if on cue, the rain began again in earnest, with a few fat, errant drops that soon turned into sheets of water cascading down his windshield.

"No problem," he said smoothly. "We can reschedule. Maybe for this weekend?"

She started to nod, but then she held out an index finger, her face scrunching up. A moment later, she sneezed into her elbow.

"Maybe we should push that back a few days," she said.

# CHAPTER 25

$\mathcal{I}$t was a full seven days before Gavin got a chance to go out with Josephine again, but they exchanged texts around the clock. Despite a week passing when they couldn't see each other—when Jackson was sick, and then she was, and then *he* was—it was becoming a thing—*they* were becoming a thing. At work and at home, he thought of her often. Had wild urges to go over to her place or ask her over to his that he knew he couldn't act on. As much as he wanted to tell everyone now—his friends, therapists at work, Angelo, his mailman—he knew it couldn't be public yet. And he wanted to protect what was growing between them. Especially after Tanner's reaction.

At least Liz knew. But he hadn't told his parents. Well, not exactly.

That Friday after their second date, he'd come to Shabbat bearing a basket of flowers for his mother, because he was happier than he'd been in months.

His mom, however, was not.

"She's in a mood," Ray whispered as Gavin walked in with the bouquet. "She had a talk with the neighbors."

"Huh?"

From the kitchen came the squeaks and thuds of cabinets slamming shut, the dishwasher opening, mugs being angrily placed in their rightful places. Either his mother was putting away the dishes or building a high-powered weapon. And she wasn't the domestic type.

He strolled into the kitchen. "Mom?"

Dina spared him a glance before clanging a plate onto its pile in the cupboard. "That girl. I never…"

He set the flowers down on the table, like one might offer raw meat to a large carnivore. "Did something happen?"

"She said you were—she said—oh, I won't repeat it." She stared at Gavin, and the look of fierceness in her eyes momentarily reminded him of Jo's face at those IEP meetings. "That yutz wouldn't know a handsome man if he planted a kiss on her."

"Why are you talking like grandma? And who's a yutz?"

"That Gwen," his father said behind him. He rested a hand on his son's shoulder. "You best let that one back into the sea."

"She said you were unattractive!" Dina broke out. "You! My handsome son."

They fell silent, waiting for Gavin's heart to quietly break.

He started laughing.

"What?" Dina said. "It's true. And I told her mother maybe it's best if we didn't take any more morning walks together. If she could raise a daughter *so foolish*…"

"Wait." Gavin held up his hand, still laughing. "Did she happen to say I was 'hideous'? Because I told her to say that."

His mother's jaw dropped.

"We just weren't attracted to each other," he continued. "Neither of us. We wanted to let you two down easy. Apparently that backfired."

Dina closed her mouth. "Was it because she wasn't the redhead? Maybe I can ask if her sister—"

"No. It's not that." Gavin cleared his throat. "I've been seeing somebody. Somebody else."

"Who?"

His mother was frozen, a porcelain bowl in one hand.

His stomach contracted. He hadn't intended to tell them this soon. "It's not exactly... well, public. It's new, and we're just enjoying each other's company right now. We're not ready to tell the world yet. For a variety of reasons."

"Enjoying each other's company?" his mother echoed. "She's not married, is she?"

"No." Gavin stuck his hands in his pockets and looked between his parents. "I'd love to tell you about her, but it's too soon."

"I don't understand," his mother said. "This doesn't make any sense."

"Dina," his dad said, a rare stern note entering his voice, "no more questions. Can't you tell the man has taken a lover?"

Gavin opened his mouth to protest, but closed it again. He and Jo hadn't even got to second base, but he didn't know how to explain to his parents what was happening. They might take issue with any number of things: the ethical dilemma with his job, the fact she wasn't Jewish, her previous marriage, possibly her age. He didn't want to put it up to the parental microscope yet. He just wanted to live it.

THAT FOLLOWING WEDNESDAY NIGHT, their third date, he'd gotten sushi for them to eat in his car and they'd made out like two teenagers.

After they'd polished off their food, he'd taken her carton and pushed it into the brown paper bag the takeout had come in. Then he'd interlaced his fingers with hers.

"Hey," he said.

She bit her lip and smiled at him. "Hey back."

He could've said something romantic then, or at least funny, but his brain was wont to short-circuit around her, and all he could think of was how pretty she looked sitting there in the passenger seat, the yellow street lights singing her curls with gold, her green eyes glistening with warmth. He put his hand on the back of her head and pulled her mouth to his.

Her lips tasted salty at first from soy sauce, but underneath was the sweetness he'd come to expect—come to crave—from kissing Josephine.

That week he'd thought a lot about how she was different from the women he'd dated before. He'd never dated a woman this much older than him, it was true, and definitely none with kids. He liked that she was older and had that experience. There was something more real about her than anyone he'd known. A confidence radiated from her, even in moments of self-doubt. A certain flexible but steely backbone.

As their kiss deepened, she made a small noise of pleasure. These past few dates, they'd done a lot of kissing, but they'd kept their clothes on and their hands had steered clear of places of no return. Not that he didn't want to go to those places. His body and his brain were of the same mind there.

But she'd said it'd been a long time. Plus, she seemed to vacillate between attacking him and pulling away, like she wasn't sure what she wanted, or if she wanted to want what she did. He wanted her to be comfortable and not feel pushed anywhere she wasn't ready to go. If Josephine wanted to wait, he was damn well going to take his time.

But he wondered where it was going. He wanted to see her outside the confines of his vehicle. And after the Jeannie sighting, his place no longer seemed like a safe possibility. How he wished they could spend the weekend together—stay the night wrapped in each other's arms, spend a leisurely weekend morning walking down the street holding hands, grabbing brunch, going back to bed again.

THURSDAY EVENING, as he and Angelo ran next to each other on treadmills at the gym, his questions spilled out.

"Hey," he said between breaths as his feet pounded the conveyor belt, "have you ever, you know, dated an older woman?" His stomach clenched in anticipation of Angelo reacting like Tanner had, but he needed some advice.

"Like that mom from the fundraiser?" The muscled speech therapist grinned at him, his face gleaming with sweat. "The brunette in the blue dress who seemed like she was playing hard to get?"

"Yeah," Gavin said. "Like that."

"I've dated older women, sure." Angelo waggled his eyebrows. "They know things."

Gavin waved the comment aside. "Yeah, but have you ever dated a woman with *kids*?" It wasn't as if he were inexperienced. But the kids thing? This was new territory for him.

He heard Tanner's voice in his head. *Think about whether you're ready for all that, all at once.* He shrugged it off.

Angelo laughed. "Not yet. You think I would, working with students all day." He hit a button to slow the treadmill to a walking pace, grabbing a towel off the machine to wipe his face.

Gavin did the same. "So you don't know what the protocol is for this, then?"

"Nope."

Damn. He exhaled, wrapping the towel around his neck.

Angelo stepped off the machine, motioning him to follow as they wound around the gym equipment towards the locker room.

"So do you like her?" Angelo asked.

Gavin felt a rush of energy fill him that only partly had to do with his workout. "Yeah," he said. "I really like her."

Angelo shrugged. "Well. Okay then."

Gavin raised his eyebrows. "Okay?"

The therapist nodded. "Okay."

"It's that easy?" Gavin asked.

"Isn't it?" Angelo replied.

THEIR FOURTH DATE was that Saturday. They'd gotten coffees and then parked by the dark expanse of the county park—the closest he'd managed to approach a night picnic.

They were holding hands when he finally got up the nerve to broach it.

"What if," he began, "I met your kids?"

Josephine's eyes sharpened. "Like came over?"

"Yeah." He watched her face as he took a sip. "What do you think? Not to invite myself over, but if you wanted me to do that, I'd be open to it. I'm housebroken."

"I guess you know Jackson," she said slowly.

"Yeah."

She pursed her lips. "And you've seen Kayla at least."

"But I haven't exactly met her."

"Nope…"

He snagged on something in her tone. "Does she know about me?"

Jo took a sip of coffee, her expression darkening. "Uh-huh."

"Uh-oh." He remembered the teen's insolent look at her mother across the parking lot. That one looked like a handful. Like mother, like daughter.

"Yeah…" Jo exhaled.

He arched an eyebrow. "Did she ground you?"

"Worse." Jo laughed harshly. "She judged me for dating

someone who works for the school district. Someone 'way younger' than me. Also she has issues with me dating period, for some reason. Wants me to go hang out with other moms at Applebee's or something."

"We could go to Applebee's." At Jo's doubtful look, he added, "Eventually." He shifted in his seat. "I could at least come over. Your place isn't public. And we could have more time to, you know, do this." He gestured between them.

"This?" The corner of her mouth lifted and she tilted her head, a teasing note entering her voice. "Or... this?" She walked her fingers up his arm until her hand reached his jaw. They both shivered with pleasure as her palm made contact with his skin and bristly five o'clock shadow.

"That." He leaned closer to her, close enough to feel her body heat. Their lips not yet touching, he added, "Definitely this, too." Before they kissed, she murmured, "Let me think on it."

# CHAPTER 26

The next Wednesday was Halloween. Jo's stomach was stuffed with mini chocolate bars, her hands were full of Jackson's costume, and her head was occupied by Gavin's question.

The sun had set, and she was helping Jackson into his Batman costume so they could go trick or treating. Jackson was stretching his legs into Batman's blue spandex outfit as Kayla strolled into the room wearing a slinky black dress, bright green tights, and black thigh-high boots. Jo looked to see if she was wearing a hat, correctly guessing that this sexy witch, or whatever she was, didn't want to get hat hair. Chuck, his black fur poofed out, was batting at Batman's eye mask on the ground, assuming it was a toy they'd brought him.

Jo knelt on the floor in front of Jackson, keeping his costume untangled as Kayla fussed with her hair and said casually, "So a group of us are going to watch horror movies at Misty's tonight."

Jo looked up, her mouth opening in surprise. "You're not going trick or treating with us?" She couldn't disguise the hurt in her voice. She knew Kayla was hanging out with friends more and more, but they'd always gone trick or treating together, even after Kayla had stopped wanting to get her own candy.

"Trick or treating," Jackson repeated. "Candy trick or treating."

"That's right, Jackson," Kayla said, adding to Jo, "I'm coming out for a little bit. Misty said they'd come by and pick me." She paused, catching her mother's eye. "Can I go?"

Jo didn't have a legitimate reason to refuse, other than wanting to spend the time after Jackson fell asleep with Kayla all to herself, eating Crunch bars and watching their own scary movies. "Sure." She sighed. "You can go."

"Trick or treat!" Jackson jumped up and down in the Batman costume, the material whispering with the movement.

They hadn't been able to take him trick or treating every year. Sometimes they'd only been able to go to a door or two before he'd become confused and upset, wondering why they were going to houses but not going inside. (The candy was a temporary balm.) But whenever he had gone, he was usually a superhero. The stretchy costumes were comfortable enough without a lot of appendages that would irritate him, and when he inevitably whipped off a mask or helmet, he remained in character, the hero's insignia blazing from his chest. To Jo, it was more than fitting.

Donning jackets, the three of them headed outside. Jackson's bright orange plastic pumpkin was in his hand, ready to receive its bounty. The night was blue-black, and a curl of fog drifted around the corner at the end of the block, illuminated under a streetlight.

After they'd gone to the first house, they spied Holly with Abby and Sean one house over. Grabbing Jackson's left hand, Jo made her way towards them.

"Happy Halloween!" Abby shouted as they neared. The four-teen-year-old's enthusiasm for the holiday hadn't dimmed through the years, and Jo grinned at her costume this year: a sparkly pink and blue fairy costume, the red hair she shared with her mother and brother piled high on her head with a crown balanced on top.

"Happy Halloween," Jo said as she reached them.

"Is it time to eat the kids' candy yet?" Holly winked at her and grinned.

"I wish."

"Happy Halloween, Kayla!" Abby said, beaming at her. With being two years younger and carrying a diagnosis of Down's, Abby wasn't in the same classes at the high school as Kayla, but she had a special fondness for her.

"Happy Halloween." Kayla leaned forward to hug the girl and whisper something in her ear. Despite the shouts and squeals of children down the street and the breeze rustling the trees, it was quiet enough to hear Kayla say, "You look beautiful, Abby."

Abby's expression was incandescent, and Holly tilted her head and smiled. Sean was positively beaming at her, his chest rising and falling with some emotion he was trying to check because it probably wasn't in a teenage boy's playbook.

Jackson wrung his hands, moving from side to side. "Trick or treat," he said, growing agitated.

"Okay, Jackson," Jo said. "I think Jackson wants to go to the next house."

"Understandable." Holly turned to her son, "Sean, can you help Kayla take Jackson and Abby to the next house? I have to talk to Jo about something. We'll be behind you all."

"Sure." The nineteen-year-old looked over at Kayla and smiled as they grabbed their siblings' hands and strode down the sidewalk to the next house that had its porchlight on.

To Jo's confusion, Holly grabbed her arm to slow her pace as they hung back until they were out of earshot. Then Holly turned to her.

"Okay, so who is he?"

Jo opened her mouth, thinking she'd play dumb, but stopped herself. Here was another reason why Gavin's suggestion that he come over was a good one. Holly had been generous enough to watch Jackson during a couple of their dates, but after last Saturday evening's "appointment," she could tell her friend was getting suspicious.

"He's..." Jo's face crumpled a little, anticipating the reaction from a fellow special needs mom. "Okay, so he's Jackson's coordinator at school."

Holly's southern accent grew thick. "Oh my God."

"It was unexpected. On both ends," she rushed to add.

"Oh. My. God."

"We're keeping it a secret until we know what's happening." Her eyes drifted to her kids. They were at the door of an elderly neighbor, shouting a chorus of "Happy Halloween!" Sean and Kayla hung slightly behind, laughing.

Jo looked back to see Holly's hands covering her mouth, and for a moment Jo feared she was so appalled she couldn't speak. But then Holly started clapping her fingers. "You're dating someone!"

It was Jo's turn to look shocked. "Did you not hear the awkward, ethical dilemma part?"

"I heard you were dating someone! It's the suit, isn't it? The suit!" She grabbed Jo's arm and whispered in her ear as they walked slowly towards the kids. "So how did this happen? Spare no details. Was it the cookies?"

Jo snorted. "Definitely not the cookies."

"So how?" Having got their candy, their kids walked back to the street and turned on the sidewalk. At Holly's high pitch, Kayla cast a questioning glance back at Jo.

Jo waited until they were out of earshot again before speaking. "We just started, you know, hashing out the IEP and then it turned sort of, I don't know, flirtatious?"

Holly put a hand to her chest. "At the IEP?"

"No. After."

A little boy in a werewolf costume barreled past them, his tired-looking father chasing him.

"Happy Halloween!" Holly lowered her voice. "Well, it's the least they can do to flirt with you. That entire process is usually so awful. That's why some parents take a slug of alcohol before they go into meetings."

Jo's jaw fell. "That's a thing? I thought Jackie at support group was just joking."

"Yeah, it's a thing. You know, to fortify yourself."

"Oh, okay. I get that." Jo smiled. "You know what else? Jackson really seems to like him. He doesn't usually respond to men that way."

Gavin's suggestion of coming to her place, never far from her mind these past few days, poked at her again. It wasn't as if the possibility hadn't occurred to her. Forty-year-old bodies weren't meant to spend so much time cramped inside cars. And yet Jo hadn't figured out when, or how, to bring him into her home life.

Maybe it could be okay if he came over. For dinner, for drinks after Jackson went to bed and Kayla retreated to her room and her boyfriend's terrible music. As she explained to Holly in more detail, Jackson liked him, and from years of having therapists and social workers come in and out of their house, he wouldn't be weird about seeing Gavin in a different context. At least, not as much as he would protest not being able to eat yogurt with a fork.

If she were honest, she'd been expecting to want to end this because of Gavin's involvement in her son's education—and not, at present, in a positive way. Yet it'd never come. If anything, the secret thrill tickled her insides. If you would've asked her a year ago, she would've claimed she'd long since aged past keeping secrets and entertaining scandals.

And Gavin was so kind and funny, so flirtatious and handsome, so willing to learn about her and let her set the pace. It made her stomach drop to realize it, but she was falling for him, and she hadn't fallen for anyone in twenty years. Not since she and Neil had first met.

Still trailing the kids, Holly slung an arm around her shoulder and squeezed. "Well, I'm happy for you. If anyone deserves this, it's you."

"Thanks." They both sighed happily and watched the kids twenty feet ahead of them. Abby's crown had gone askew, but she was turning her head from side to side, smiling wide. Jackson was bouncing on his toes and shaking his orange plastic pumpkin full of candy. The white clothing hanger he often carried was poking out of it, like he'd tossed it in, which Jo took to mean he was having such a good time he didn't need it.

Jo felt a lump in her throat. Despite all the dreams she had for her son—that he would talk more or read, or be able to hold a job someday, or find a friend his own age—what she wished for almost the most was this sweet, fleeting thing in front of her: a childhood.

Kayla and Sean were walking on either side of the kids, Sean's tall form towering over the rest. He said something and Kayla giggled. It wasn't her laugh that caught Jo's attention—she laughed often, after all, except when she was pissed at her mother—but Sean's gloriously happy look in return.

Holly must have caught it, too. "Speaking of romance," she whispered conspiratorially, "I think Sean has a little crush on Kayla."

Jo nodded, watching him watch Kayla. "I think you're right."

"Remember how they used to play together when they were little and I was working with Jackson at your house?" Holly smiled. "They were so cute."

"They were," Jo murmured. "I think he used to let her win at Checkers." She remembered small, six-year-old Kayla bossing around Sean, who must've been eight or nine at the time. She recalled his messy red hair and the endless patience he'd had with Kayla. He must have inherited that from his mom.

"Anyway," Holly continued. "He seemed so eager to go pick up the baking supplies I'd lent you. And then I remembered him staring at her at our Labor Day barbecue."

"Kind of like he's looking at her now?"

"Uh-huh." Holly's voice was honey, a mixture of pleasure, humor, and bless-his-heart pity. "Just the same."

Jo sighed. "Well, he's a sweet kid, but she's still in high school, so nothing's going to happen."

Holly spoke carefully. "I think it would be okay if they hung out as friends, though—I mean, if that's alright with you. They have a lot in common, growing up with special needs siblings. It could be good for them to talk."

As they strolled down the sidewalk, a car pulled up beside the kids. The passenger side window rolled down and music poured out. Jo didn't have to see the teens in the car to know it was Misty and Kayla's other friends, come to collect her.

Kayla stopped and turned around, tugging Jackson to a stop. "Mom, Misty's here. I'm going, okay?"

"Ok-ay," Jo forced herself to say. They were close enough now she could see Misty behind the wheel and Austin in the passenger seat, checking out her daughter's slinky black dress and giving Sean some serious side-eye.

Sean looked confused, but at something Kayla said, he nodded and took Jackson's hand, waiting for Jo and Holly to reach them. He looked so dejected, it was as if the sad Snoopy tune was playing in the background.

As Kayla climbed into the backseat of the car and rode off, Jo scrunched her nose and said, "No, I don't think I'm ready for my daughter to hang out with college boys just yet. I've had about all I can take this year."

"If it makes you feel better," Holly whispered, "Sean is technically a college dropout."

Jo said, "Oddly, that doesn't make me feel better."

AFTER JACKSON FINISHED trick or treating and went to bed, Jo held her phone in her lap, ready to make a decision.

There was a third reason why she wanted to invite Gavin over, beyond the cramped car and the babysitting issue. They'd been making out like crazy in his Prius, but it was tricky to go further without a place to be horizontal. Her body was clamoring for that more and more. Dread and desire of getting intimate with Gavin had been playing a game of tug-of-war, but desire was currently winning. She thought of the kisses they'd shared last weekend, the way they'd ended with resting their foreheads together. She had felt his smile without opening her eyes. They were both dizzy with what they had, but they wanted more.

And her home was the one without the special ed teacher nearby—or a curfew.

Finally, she sent him a text.

*How about you come over this weekend?*

# CHAPTER 27

*H*umming The Cars under his breath, Gavin knocked on the Palladinos' door Sunday evening. He'd dressed down, in jeans and a dark blue Henley under his coat. In one hand he held a bouquet of white roses, and, in the other, a carton of ice cream. If Jackson and Kayla were anything like their mom, he figured the smoothest path to their good sides was paved with sugar.

The door opened to a teenage girl scowling at him.

Even if he hadn't caught a glimpse of her before, Gavin could have identified Kayla as Jo's daughter in a lineup. Except in Kayla's case, her dark, curly hair was streaked with blue dye and she was wearing skinny jeans. And the annoyed scowl.

"Hi," he said. "You must be Kayla."

"And you are?" she asked, raising an eyebrow.

Ah, this was definitely going to be the tough one.

He stuck the ice cream under his elbow. "Gavin Steinberg." He put out his hand.

Reluctantly, she reached out to shake it.

"So you're the guy," she said, and he felt relieved Jo had at least explained they were dating.

"I'm the guy." He smiled.

"The guy who's trying to put my brother in the wrong classroom."

His smile fell. "Well, that's not entirely accurate—and anyway, somebody else is handling that now."

She propped a hand up on the doorframe. "Handling your job as the crusher of hope?"

"Wow, you're a tough crowd," Gavin said. "I actually prefer the phrase 'destroyer of dreams.'"

She tapped her fingernails on the frame. "Your hand is cold and clammy."

"It's the ice cream." He attempted another smile and showed her the carton. "I brought ice cream."

"I don't take sweets from strangers," she said, but left the door open as she walked inside.

Exhaling, he stepped over the threshold and into the house as Kayla called, "Mom, your destroyer of dreams is here," and turned down a hallway and out of sight.

"What?" Jo peeked her head out from behind a wall, saw him, and smiled. "Oh. Hi, Gavin."

Even at a casual glance, she was more comfortable than he'd seen her. He was already glad they'd done this, even with the frosty welcome.

Also, she looked hot in a pair of worn jeans and a fitted black shirt.

He let the door shut behind him and set the flowers and ice cream down on a nearby table, suddenly unable to take his eyes off her. They walked to meet in the middle, a sloppy grin spreading over his face. Every time he saw her, it just got worse.

"Hi," he said, clasping her hands.

"Hi." She looked like she was about to kiss him, but then she glanced to her side and took a step back.

Jackson was sitting on the couch in an alcove to his left, his head bowed over an iPad.

Gavin squeezed her hands and released them. "Hi, Jackson," he said, walking over to him.

The kid looked at him briefly, then back at his device. "Hi, Jackson," he repeated. Then he did a double-take, jumping to his feet and hopping on his toes. He wore jeans and a light blue Captain America t-shirt, a cowlick of brown hair swaying with his movements. "Hand! Hi. Hi."

"Yeah, you traced my hand, that's right." Gavin laughed. "Next time, I'm requesting you answer the door."

"Did Kayla let you in?" Jo asked.

"That was your daughter?" he asked. "I assumed it was your dad. She gave me quite the interrogation."

Josephine grimaced and put a hand on her hip. "She's being weird. I think it's going to take some time."

"I get it. She's protective." He smiled back at Jackson, noticing that along with Jo's green eyes, he had her grin, too. The kid grabbed his hand and pulled him deeper into the house.

"Where are we going?"

Jackson didn't respond, but he led him to a fish tank against a wall beside the kitchen.

"Those are Pickles and Prometheus," Jo called behind them. "They're Jackson's pets."

He patted the boy on the shoulder. "Cool fish. They look well-fed."

"I'm just frying up some burgers," Jo said. "But it kind of smells like they're burning, so maybe I should…"

"Go ahead," he said. "Just tell me you didn't make cookies."

Their eyes met, and she gave him a saucy smirk.

Grinning, he turned back to see Jackson shifting the lid of the aquarium to one side.

"Are Pickles and Prometheus going to come out to play?" Gavin asked, wondering what he was about to do.

His face serious, Jackson didn't respond. He just gave him a momentary glance that Gavin could've sworn looked a little judgmental.

The aquarium lid ajar, Jackson grabbed a small plastic canister, twisted off the lid, and very gently pinched some fish food between his thumb and forefinger. Then, biting his bottom lip, he carefully sprinkled it on the surface of the water.

As Gavin watched, the fish swam up, gobbling the food flakes with their tiny mouths. "Cool," he said. He looked back at Jackson to see him watching him, his face a mixture of happiness and satisfaction. *Pride*, Gavin thought. *He's proud he can do this.*

"That's a good job, Jackson," he said. "These little guys really depend on you, huh?"

Making a grunting noise, the kid pushed the aquarium lid back as a jolt of awareness spread through Gavin. In all the paperwork he'd read about Jackson, all the goals and charts and reports of aggressive behavior, none of them had managed to capture this: that he cared for his pets, and that he drew such pleasure and purpose from it.

"I think these burgers are done," Jo called. "Or done-ish."

Feeling amused apprehension, Gavin helped her set the table, and a few minutes later they sat down to very well-done hamburgers, potato chips, and ice waters. Jackson bounded to a seat beside Gavin as Jo added pickles, onions, tomatoes, and a variety of condiments to the table.

Jackson's speech device sat near him, the one Jeannie said he hadn't been using, but at the sight of the yellow bottle being set on the table, he said, "Mustard," and then found the corresponding button on his device, pushing it repeatedly.

A robotic voice filled the room. "Mustard. Mustard mustard mustard."

Jo laughed and passed him the yellow bottle. "Mustard is its own food group here, right Jax?" She turned to Gavin. "The other day I caught him squirting a bowl full of the stuff and just digging in with a spoon."

He laughed and leaned towards the boy. "Better not feed that to the fish, buddy."

Jackson was busy squirting a large pile of mustard into the middle of his plate as Jo said, "Don't give him any ideas."

Kayla emerged and joined them at the table, pointedly ignoring Gavin. But he wasn't going down without a fight.

"So, Kayla, your mom says you're a big music fan."

Still not looking at him, she threw a tomato slice on her plate. "Yup."

"Who are your favorite bands?"

The teen rattled off a dozen band names, half of which he was pretty sure weren't actually real—either that, or he was more out of touch than he suspected.

He latched onto one of the names he did recognize. "Jack White is great."

The girl shrugged.

"Kayla, Gavin's really into music, too," Jo said as she smeared ketchup on a bun.

The teenager looked up. "Really." She narrowed her eyes at him. "Let me guess who you're into: Justin Timberlake. Or Green Day. Maybe some Coldplay. The stuff we call 'oldies music' at school."

"Ouch," Gavin said. "That hurts my soul."

"Or, no, wait," Kayla continued. "I bet you are the kind of guy who grew up secretly listening to boy bands when no one was around."

"Man." Gavin glanced at Jo. "She's almost as judgmental as you are." He turned back to Kayla. "Look, the 2000s were a hard time to grow up. All those girls crushing on O-Town and 98 Degrees. You had to listen to them to figure out what the deal was."

The girl smirked, ready to throw more shade at him, but Jo

piped in. "Kayla, you're not one to talk. You were obsessed with the Jonas Brothers when you were little."

"Aha!" Gavin said. "We all have secrets. Nice to meet you, pot. My name's kettle." He started humming Jonas Brothers' "Burnin' Up," though felt a stab of regret as Kayla's face turned as red as the tomato on her plate.

He stopped humming, but then Jackson took over where he left off, mumbling an approximation of the rest of the verse.

Jo laughed. "Jackson doesn't have any secrets when it comes to music. He's loud and proud when he loves a song."

"My kind of man." He raised a palm for the kid to high-five.

After they'd finished their burgers, Gavin remembered the ice cream.

"I think it's time for dessert." He got up and fished the dessert from where Jo had stashed it in the freezer. She got out bowls and spoons, and as she scooped the ice cream, he slung an arm around her waist.

"Is this okay?" he whispered in her ear.

In response, she gave him a coy smile and sucked a drop of ice cream off her finger in a way that made him wonder when the kids would go to bed.

"Who wants ice cream?" she called.

"Ice cream!" Jackson shouted, his voice cracking. He was all out of mustard and ready for something more.

Leaning back in her seat and fiddling on her phone, Kayla asked, "What flavor is it?"

"Neapolitan," Gavin said proudly. "Something for everyone."

She looked up with a sweetly evil grin on her face and nodded at her mother. "She doesn't like Neapolitan. Do you, Mom?"

"Kayla, it's fine," Jo said hurriedly.

"You always say it's ice cream for people who have commitment issues."

Gavin looked at Jo. "Wow, that's a lot to put on someone for an ice cream choice. What would you have said if I'd brought rocky road?" he teased her.

Kayla sighed from the kitchen table. "Mom, Misty and I are going out. We have a thing."

Jo frowned. "What thing?"

"It's a thing. It's just at her house. I'll be home by twelve."

"Eleven."

"Eleven-thirty."

Jo put a hand on her hip. "This isn't an auction, Kayla." Then, glancing at Gavin, she realized the same thing that he was thinking, that the teenager staying out later meant more time for them alone. "Okay. Eleven forty-five."

"Bye." The girl sashayed off, and a few minutes later they heard a car pull up and the door slam.

"Sorry about that," Jo said. "She's sixteen. Did I mention she's sixteen?"

"It's fine," he said. "I'm just going to make my ice cream a wine float, if that's okay."

Jo laughed and they joined Jackson at the table for dessert. Afterward, she cleared the dishes as Gavin turned to Jackson. "Can we help your mom wipe the table?"

She tossed them a couple of rags. Gavin smiled as Jackson took a rag from him, swiping with, if not thorough strokes, at least enthusiasm. Between swipes, he made loud noises and flicked his hands in the air, but he managed to wipe a section of the table.

Jo's eyes were wide. "Wow. You're hired. I can't even get Kayla to do that most days."

He helped her start the dishwasher, and the three of them settled down to watch music videos for an hour—Jackson hanging upside-down on the couch as the pop stars danced.

"Music," Jackson called out.

"Yeah, that's right, this is music," Gavin said.

"Music," Jackson repeated, his voice insistent.

"OKGo," Jo said, then explained, "He likes for you to name the artist. Even if he knows it. He likes to hear who's singing."

"Cool." Gavin nodded. Then he took the remote and chose a round of videos he thought Jackson might like, identifying the artist each time he said "Music." This hadn't come up in the paperwork on him, either. Maybe there'd been a sentence in there about enjoying music, but who didn't? It hardly did justice to the way he saw the boy's eyes light up now, and his fascination with the musicians who made sounds come together in a way that, even as an adult, Gavin couldn't help but consider magical.

Finally, when Jackson's eyelids started drooping, Josephine ushered him to bed.

Gavin was toeing off his shoes and lining them up by the door when she reappeared, flipping off the hallway light. She gave him a shy smile.

"Hope you don't mind," he said, nodding at his feet.

"I don't mind," she said softly, moving to dim the dining room light next.

She padded over to the couch and sat next to him, curling her legs underneath her. "Jackson conked out pretty fast. I'm surprised—usually he's keyed up when someone new is over. Not that I'm going to look this gift horse in the mouth..."

She put her hand close to his, hesitantly, trailing one finger over his thumb, gentle enough to be tender and light enough to tease him.

He laced their fingers together. "This is nice," he said. "You, me. Enjoying a meal together without the smell of leather upholstery in the background. The gear shift not cockblocking me."

She laughed, but then blushed, pulling away and standing. "I need some wine," she said quickly. "Do you need some wine?"

"All I need is you."

"Well, I need some wine," she called over her shoulder. "'Uptown Funk,' remember?"

Right. It had been a while since she'd been alone with a man. That anxiety was still there.

Gavin was nervous, too. But mostly he had plans for Josephine and this couch—if she was willing, of course. More than anything, he didn't want to push her too far.

So when she brought back two half-filled glasses of red wine, he sat up and tried to steer the conversation into more comfortable territory.

"So," he started, "does Jackson have any talents or..."

"Special powers?" Jo smiled and took a sip of wine. "Yes, he does. He's the most loveable boy on the face of the planet."

Gavin smiled back, a little sheepish.

"If you're asking if he has any savant skills, I haven't seen any," Jo said. "Some autistic kids have those, I know. A friend's kid could read at age two, and another one has perfect pitch."

"It must've been hard," he said. "Navigating all this on your own." In the months he'd worked for the district, he'd seen how harried and discouraged some parents could get with their kids' progress. There were triumphs and good days, sure, but he'd learned enough to know that raising a child with special needs could be challenging. And Jo had been doing it on her own.

She shrugged and took another sip of wine. "I used to have friends with typical kids say to me, 'I couldn't do it,' and I just wanted to say to them, 'You don't get a choice.' Not that I would've chosen differently if I could—I love my son—but they wouldn't have, either. What's the alternative? Just get the diagnosis, throw up your hands, and say, 'Sorry, I'm out.'" She let out a wry laugh. "Well, I guess that's what Neil did."

"He's an asshole," Gavin said before he could stop himself.

"Hmm." She looked down at her wine glass, tipping the drink back and forth. "I'm not supposed to say that about my children's father."

"Then let me," Gavin said. "He's an asshole for leaving the kids, and he's an idiot for leaving you. I mean, *look* at you."

He gestured to her body with his free hand, but then he couldn't help but take his own good advice. She had one leg curled underneath her, and one sleeve of her tight black top was pushed slightly off her shoulder, revealing a black bra strap. He wanted to stick a finger underneath it and trace it to its source. Instead, he leaned forward and kissed her.

Her lips were sweet and tart, and they parted for him immediately, their tongues touching. There was a looseness, a receptiveness, to her mouth that hadn't been there before. It could've been the wine, but Gavin suspected it was the way she'd opened up to him.

They deepened the kiss, Jo's head tilting. Her curls grazed his collar.

The wine glasses were still in their hands, and, without opening his eyes, he collected them both between his fingers. Reluctantly, he pulled away to stash them on the floor at the other side of the couch. Then he lifted Josephine up to straddle him where he sat.

"This is crazy," she whispered. Her breath was wine-drenched, her curls spilling over his arms as he placed his hands on either side of her face.

"Crazy good," he countered. His voice had gone husky.

"Josephine," he breathed, grabbing her hips to press their bodies together.

But then came a shout and a loud thump.

Josephine pulled away and gasped. "Jackson."

Gavin heard him, too. The boy was awake, and he was screaming.

She scrambled off him, darting for the bedroom.

Gavin stood and followed her.

"Jax," she said as she opened the door. "It's okay, Jax. What's wrong?"

Gavin stood outside the door as Jo paused inside the room. "Oh, no," she moaned. "Oh, shoot."

Gavin stepped inside the darkened room, alarmed. "What is it?" Then the smell hit him. The room reeked of feces.

Rustling noises came from the other side of the room before Jo stepped into the light with her arm guiding a sobbing Jackson. From the stain on his pajama pants, he'd had an accident, but as they came closer, Gavin saw it was on his hands, too. Instinctively, he took a step back, away from them.

Jo took Jackson into the bathroom. "Let's get in the shower, honey." She led her son to the tub, opening the shower curtain and ushering the boy inside, fully clothed. Gavin could see why; he was covered in crap, and from the lingering smell in the hall, the bedroom hadn't fared better.

"Is he sick?" he asked Jo.

She glanced at him briefly. "No, probably not. This just… happens sometimes."

"Why is it on his hands?"

She had her back to him, whispering to Jax and pulling off his clothes. "He doesn't have the same feelings you and I do about it. Sometimes he smears it around." She balled up the clothes and turned on the shower, pulling the curtain shut around him.

She still hadn't looked at Gavin, but she held the pile of soiled clothing in front of her and walked to the entrance of the bathroom. She flicked her eyes to him. The irises were flat. "It's probably best if you just leave," she said. "It's going to take a while to clean up Jax. And the room. And…"

He swallowed. "Okay. Are you sure?"

"Yes."

He took a breath. "I'll call you tomorrow. Okay?"

"Sure." She turned away, pulling soap out of a drawer.

Gavin was ashamed of it, but he wanted away from the smell. He'd always been a neat freak, and he wondered whether

Jackson had tracked some of the poop into the hall and whether he himself had then stepped in it.

But the guilt hit him before he reached the front door. He had his coat in his hand, but he just stood there.

Josephine told him he should go, but did she really want him to? If he didn't go, would he be acting against her wishes? If he didn't stay, would he be proving himself to be the guy who wasn't cut out for this relationship, not long-term, because he couldn't handle this?

Because he didn't want to be that guy.

He dropped his coat on the couch and walked back down the hallway.

Under the shower spray, Josephine whispered softly to Jackson as his cries calmed.

Gavin popped his head around the corner, careful to leave the boy some privacy.

"I'm sorry," he said. "I just need to ask you one more time."

She turned around, startled. Her eyes were rimmed in pink, like she'd been holding back tears. "What?" she asked in a hoarse voice.

"You told me to go, and I'll do that if it's what you want. But from where I'm standing, the skills this situation needs are the ability to do laundry and pour more wine. And I'm pretty excellent at both of those."

She sniffed and hiccupped a laugh.

"Okay," she said.

He leaned against the doorframe. "Okay as in you agree that I'm excellent at pouring wine, or that I should stay?"

"Yes. Both." She took a deep breath. "Thank you."

He turned and walked into Jackson's bedroom, flipping on the overhead light. The bed had poop on it. A lot. He fought the urge to just ask Jo if they could set fire to the bed and start over. Instead, he tugged the fitted sheet loose, then wrapped it around the rest of the dirty blankets and pillow, creating a bundle. He heaved it all up and staggered to the washer and dryer. After squishing it all into the washing machine, he located a bottle of detergent and poured a generous amount in, then added some more for good measure. He then walked back into Jackson's room to assess the rest.

He was wiping at the few smears on the walls with paper towels when the shower turned off and Jo prompted Jackson to dry himself off. After they'd gotten him back to bed, Gavin would offer her not only another glass of wine, but a massage. This woman needed a massage. Whatever happened after that was up to her, but he wanted to do something to take care of her.

She walked into the room with a clean Jackson in fresh pajamas. The kid grinned at Gavin and bounced around like it wasn't two hours past his bedtime. Even as messy as he'd been, Gavin couldn't help but laugh and hold his hands as he jumped on the mattress.

Sighing, Jo grabbed some clean sheets, a waterproof mattress cover, and blankets from a nearby linen closet and remade the bed.

Gavin stepped out while she tucked him back in, the soft sounds of her singing reaching his ears where he sat in the living room. While he waited, a scruffy black cat hopped up on his lap.

"What's your name?" he asked. "I hope the fish don't know about you. Or maybe vice versa."

The cat didn't respond, but did start kneading his legs and purring loudly.

Finally, Josephine walked out.

"He's down again," she said. She brushed her hair out of her eyes with the back of her hand.

"Good." He gingerly moved the cat to a nearby chair and patted the spot next to him on the couch. "Come here."

She took a deep breath. Even with him staying, she was avoiding eye contact for some reason.

"I'm really tired now," she said. "I just want to take a shower and crash. Is that okay?"

"Are you sure?"

She nodded, not quite meeting his eyes. "For real this time. I just feel gross and wiped." She spared him a brief glance. "Thank you for your help tonight."

"No problem." He was confused but he stood, putting on his jacket, giving her a quick kiss, and walking to the door. He moved slowly, in case she changed her mind.

But she didn't, and Gavin couldn't shake the feeling that he'd done something wrong.

# CHAPTER 28

*I*t had to happen sooner or later. She'd known it, hadn't she? She and Gavin had been having fun together, but there was eventually going to be that time when he got close enough to see what her life was really like.

She sighed as she sat at the kitchen table the following Monday morning, finalizing the details of a sisters' trip to Mexico City's Isle of the Dolls, and allowed herself a moment of pity.

Most people saw only the outer world of special needs families. The odd boy in their kid's class who always wore a hat. The heartwarming greeting card scene of a mother hugging her daughter with Down Syndrome. Maybe, if they looked close enough, the lines of worry and exhaustion around those parents' eyes.

But they didn't often see this reality. The epic meltdowns, the aggression, the heart-pounding anxiety, the tendency of some kids to not understand what was socially acceptable and what wasn't, to smear their waste or nosebleeds on the walls. Did that happen with other three-year-olds? Sure. But thirteen-year-olds? Thirty-year-olds? There was a line between typical and special needs families, and sometimes it had less to do with *what* than *how much* or *how long*.

Or how short, in the case of the length of any relationship Jo was bound to have. If she were honest with herself, those failed dates years ago hadn't just been about incompatibility. They had been about avoiding letting anyone into their lives, of realizing that what she ultimately wanted just wouldn't mesh with reality. When she'd gone on those dates years ago, Jackson had been a preschooler fighting fits of rage, and she'd frequently had bruises from his pinching and scratching up and down her arms. She'd hid under long-sleeved shirts on those outings, even in the summer. Because what would someone think who didn't live her life?

She swallowed, her throat raw with unshed tears. Gavin was a sweet guy. He'd been thoughtful enough to help the previous night. When the time to break up with her came, he'd let her down easy. Probably she wouldn't hear from him for a couple days, while he warred with his guilt, but he'd eventually end whatever was between them. Maybe he'd take her on a couple more dates, just to pretend like this hadn't been the dealbreaker for him. It was a lot to take in, especially for a younger single guy without kids. Whatever Hollywood said, relationships weren't just two people; you were dating much more than the person you were with.

As she hit send on the email to the clients, a knock came.

She glanced up. Gavin's silhouette appeared in the frosted glass window to the side of the front door.

She closed her laptop and rolled her shoulders back. So this was it. Not even a few courtesy dates to ease out of the relationship. He hadn't even needed to war with his guilt that long.

At least she hadn't slept with him. That would've made all of this so much harder.

She walked to the door and opened it.

Gavin stood in the doorway in his suit and tie, one hand

braced on the frame and a somber look on his face. Despite the cold November wind, he wasn't wearing a jacket.

"Hi," he said.

"Hi," she said. "On your lunch break?"

"No. I told work I had a dentist appointment."

"You lied?"

He shook his head. "No, I did have a dentist appointment. I just canceled it on the way here."

"Oh." She shifted her weight, unsure what to say next.

His eyes roamed her face. "Can I come in?"

"S-sure." Jo almost cringed at how hesitant she sounded. She needed to be a grownup. Breakups happened. It wasn't like they'd been married. She opened the door wider and stepped to the side so he could enter. "Come on in."

"Thanks."

He walked in, but didn't take a seat. He looked around the room and then at her. He was nervous.

So it was going to be quick and dirty, then.

"It's okay, Gavin," she said. "I get it."

"Get what?"

"Why you're here."

A line appeared between his eyebrows. "You do?"

"Look, last night must've been intense for you." She crossed her arms over her chest, but kept her voice reasonable. "Intense and eye-opening. But for me, it was just, like, Sunday night. You don't have to apologize. I knew this was coming." She sounded so calm, she was almost consoling herself. Almost.

"What was coming?"

Was he going to make her be the one to say it? "Us having... this talk."

His mouth opened and closed as his eyebrows drew together. "Which is...?"

She exhaled, uncrossing her arms. She'd gotten dressed that morning in yoga pants and a large, ratty gray shirt. She wished

Gavin's last experience of her didn't include her looking so slovenly. Would that she had ended this before it began, before he'd kissed her in the hallway at the fundraiser, when he could've remembered her untouched in a beautiful blue dress.

"I know this is too much for you," she said. "You're young, you haven't been married or had any kids. We probably jumped into this too fast, especially given the circumstances. But I've had fun with you, and I'm grateful for that. I don't go out much, and I'd forgotten how... restorative it can be." She gave him a weak smile. Her throat had gone raw again, but maybe if she said it, he'd leave sooner and she could be alone when she cried. "I'm trying to say thank you and that it's fine if you want to end things."

"Wait." Gavin shook his head. "You think I'm... *trying to break up with you?*"

"It's okay," she said, trying to keep her voice light. "I understand."

"Well, it's not okay with me." He swallowed. "I mean...Is this what you want?"

"I think it's what makes the most sense," she said.

"That's not what I asked." He took a step closer, staring intensely into her eyes. "Is this what you *want?*"

They stared at each other.

His voice was soft, but his jaw was rigid. The conversation had edged into confusion and desperation, something larger and more emotional than she expected. The tension between them coiled tight.

A shiver of anticipation ran the length of her body. One more word from him, one slight touch, and she'd be undone.

Couldn't he see she didn't want to be undone?

She couldn't seem to remember what she should have been saying, not with him looking at her like that with a gaze blistering with need. Which left only the truth.

"No," she whispered. "I want you."

He traversed the last foot of space, took her face in his hands, and kissed her. Kissed her hard and unapologetically, in a way that left no room for argument. She knew; she would've tried. He'd pulled her so close she lifted up on her tiptoes, her neck craned so their lips could meet. Kissed her until she was out of breath and certainly out of excuses.

He broke the connection to put his mouth to her ear, whispering furiously as he gripped her tight against him. "Jo, can't you see I'm just a schmuck who's trying to deserve you?"

She hadn't seen, but she felt it now, how desperate he was for her. For all Gavin's sweetness and humor, he'd been holding back.

Whimpering, she ran her fingers through his hair and brought his head down to hers again. All that flirtation, those car rides, the night before on the couch—they had generated a heat between them that hadn't been released, and now it was boiling over.

She broke the kiss. "My bedroom," she gasped.

"Yeah." He nodded rapidly. "Yeah. Like right now."

Panting, he started to untuck his shirt, but she made a noise of frustration and grabbed him by the waistband, pulling him down the hall to the master bedroom.

Ever since her kids had come out of her body, Jo had learned to deny its desires. For years she'd put her own hunger, sleep, and even bladder after her kids' needs. So she was surprised at how much her body screamed for Gavin at that moment. The urge was strong and undeniable, an almost painful ache.

Yet when they reached the foot of her bed, she was shaking with not only excitement, but anxiety. She hadn't slept with anyone in almost a decade. She hadn't let a man even see her naked in all that time. Her body was more than ready, but her mind began flapping its hands in warning. She hadn't shaved her legs that morning. When she'd imagined this happening, she'd pictured herself wearing a lace chemise, not ratty clothes and cotton underwear.

Gavin was kicking off his shoes, unbuttoning his cuffs, looking at her like she was dinner. "Come here," he said, one hand bringing her face to his to kiss again, the other making quick work of unbuttoning his dress shirt. Of their own accord, her fingers reached up to help him fumble with the buttons.

The shirt loose, he pulled it off his arms, tossing it on the floor.

"*Oh.*" Even with her worry about what was going to happen, she couldn't help but run her hands over this newly exposed skin, his strong shoulders and arms.

He groaned. "There you go with your *oh* again."

"It was a good one."

"It better be."

Her fingers trembling but curious, she continued her perusal, exploring the taut, slightly ridged flesh of his stomach. His muscles flinched with ticklishness, but she guessed he didn't mind so much.

Or did he? "Jo, you're driving me crazy," he growled. He reached around her body, his hands sliding underneath her top to lift it.

"I'm taking your shirt off," he said. "I'm not asking."

Good thing too, because if he'd asked, she wouldn't have known quite how to answer. *No* because he'd never been with a woman her age, and he had no idea, and the c-section scar would just confuse him. *No* because he'd notice the way her breasts had finally accepted gravity or the faint white stretch marks low on her hips. *Maybe* because they could probably do this with her shirt still on, but it would be more fun if they didn't. *Yes* because there would be no substitute for his warmth against her bare skin, and even though it'd been years, she wanted this, she wanted it so bad.

She lifted her arms obediently, and he pulled the shirt over her head.

The air against her naked flesh made her shiver, but he pulled her to him, releasing her shirt and wrapping his arms around her.

He felt warm and strong as he kissed her throat, sending tingles of pleasure down her body. His fingers brushed the edges of her bra.

She pulled away, her hand reaching up to cover his eyes. "Don't look, I'm not…" *Perfect? Young?* Her heart hammered in her chest.

He removed her hand and paused, their eyes meeting. "Tell me to slow down," he said, his voice rough with restraint, "and I'll do it. But only if it's because you don't want this. You're beautiful, Josephine. Inside and out."

She didn't want him to slow down. Not even a little bit.

# CHAPTER 29

*G*avin wanted everyone to know. He couldn't be with her, not like that, and then feel anything but wrong about telling a lie of omission. Josephine deserved better.

It was getting harder to keep a secret, anyway. They'd each told a friend, his parents knew something was up, he'd formally met her kids. Something could slip from any of those sources, a cat thudding out of the bag to claw his face.

But even if it would be possible to keep their relationship a secret, he didn't want to. He wanted to tell everyone about her —what she was like, how happy she made him.

He'd visited her at home again on his lunch hour Wednesday, and they'd ended up on the couch, having a repeat of Monday.

Afterwards, both of them trying to catch their breath, he kissed her cheek and cupped her face, pushing it back slightly so he could look into her eyes.

"I want to tell Charlene," he said.

"Are you sure?" Josephine said breathlessly.

He nodded.

"Won't this endanger your job?"

"Maybe," he admitted.

All at once, this thing between them had turned serious. They weren't just flirting in cars, they were becoming part of each other's lives. He'd wanted her from the start, but the past couple days, he couldn't get enough of her—her laugh, her body, her pleasure. It was complex, sure, and he didn't know what would happen once Jackson's evaluation came through in a couple weeks.

But he was done hiding it. He wanted everyone to know. Today.

Wednesday afternoon, after he returned to work, he knocked on Charlene's door.

"Come in."

She'd just ended a phone call, but she waved him in and gestured to the seat in front of her desk. Gavin knew that, even though she was director, the school district probably hadn't provided the elegant upholstered chairs in her office. He'd suspected she'd gotten them herself, to convey the respect of her position and because she liked fine things. It didn't escape him that she could've probably succeeded at any number of careers that would have netted her a salary four or more times what she made working in special education.

"Hi," he said. "How are you?"

"Fine." Charlene crossed her legs. "What's going on?"

He took a deep breath. "You remember Josephine Palladino? The one working with Carrie?"

"Mmm-hmm."

"Well, as it turns out…" He chuckled nervously. "I have a conflict of interest with continuing to work as her coordinator."

Charlene lifted an eyebrow. "Oh?"

"The thing is, I've developed feelings for her."

She stared at him.

"Man-woman feelings," he added.

She raised her hand. "I got it." Still staring at him, she exhaled, her cheeks puffing out with air. "Is she aware?"

"Yes, she's aware." He resisted the image of Josephine laying across her bed.

"Hmm." Her dark brown eyes narrowed slightly, and Gavin suspected she could see his dirty innermost thoughts.

He bit down on the side of his cheek to focus. "I'm sorry," he said. "I should've brought this to you sooner. This isn't something I intended to happen—it's never happened to me before, I mean, with someone so connected to my job." He cleared his throat. "I understand if I need to step down."

Charlene exhaled again, uncrossing her legs and leaning towards him. "You're a good coordinator, Gavin. You're organized, you're efficient, most of the parents seem to like you." She smiled wryly. "I thought Josephine Palladino wasn't one of those parents, but apparently I was wrong."

He tensed, unsure how to react. Was he supposed to laugh at that? Was Charlene making a joke?

She pushed back in her seat. "I'm not going to fire you," she said. "I understand that life is messy—believe me, I do. But we will need to establish some clear boundaries."

His body relaxed. He'd expected her to toss him, and the fact that he wasn't going to lose his job was an enormous relief.

"Of course," he said. "Anything."

"I'll take over for you once the evaluation is complete later this month. I would have anyway, since our friend Carrie Stiepler is involved." She gave a tight smile. "When the evaluation is completed, you can send an email to Ms. Palladino transferring the coordination to me."

"Okay, sure."

"But," she added, "I need to have your word that anything you may hear from this office related to Jackson Palladino's placement should in no circumstances be discussed with his mother. Do you understand?"

"Yes," he said. "I think that's more than fair." With an advocate on her side, Josephine would probably get what she wanted in terms of Jackson's placement, anyway. Though what that looked like with the shuffling of classrooms, he didn't know. He felt sure she could take care of herself, especially with Annie Oakley by her side. He only had to send her one email when the evaluation completed, and it would be a simple one. Otherwise, he'd stepped aside.

"Good," Charlene said. "Then that's that."

After work, Gavin drove to his parents' for dinner.

He found his mother hunting for matches in the kitchen and muttering prayers—or maybe those were curses—under her breath.

"I put them right here," she said.

"No, you didn't," his dad said. "You put them in the silverware drawer."

"Why would I do that?"

"I don't know."

Gavin located the matches on top of the fridge, and the three of them set the table. Even though it wasn't Shabbat, as the sky outside darkened, his mother lit candles and they sat to eat.

But to make room for the meatloaf they were serving, he had to get rid of the butterflies in his stomach. "So... I wanted to tell you about the woman I've been seeing," he started.

Dina dropped her fork, her attention riveted.

He took a deep breath. "This woman I've been seeing, her name is Josephine. Josephine Palladino."

Dina shifted in her seat. "Palladino. Is she Italian?"

"A few generations back, I think."

"Jewish?"

His gut twisted. "No."

The two of them exchanged a look.

Nobody said a word for a few long, torturous seconds.

Finally, sensing the need to lighten the mood, his dad piped in. "Is she a redhead?"

Letting out a breath he hadn't realized he'd been holding, Gavin smiled. "Brunette. Dark curly hair. Green eyes."

His mother picked up her fork and knife and started dissecting her meatloaf into small, neat bites. "So tell us more," she finally asked. "What's she like?"

"Well, she's really kind and funny. She works as a travel agent." He watched his mom carefully. She wasn't happy about this, he could tell. And he wasn't even through with telling them the pertinent details about Jo.

Dina suddenly put her utensils down with a clank and looked up at him, her voice prim. "When can we meet her?"

He was taken aback. He expected disapproval, but his mom had switched to an offensive maneuver for some reason. "Um, I'd have to check."

"Check? What for? Let's find a time." Dina's loud tone struck a false note of cheer. Yes, she was unnerved by this. But she also wanted to meet Josephine, too.

"Her life's pretty busy, Mom," Gavin said. "It's got a lot of moving parts. Her job and—and her family." He waited for it to sink in.

But Dina didn't catch his meaning. "Her family? Everybody's got one of those."

"Not everybody, Mom. And not like hers." He paused, trying to get the message across as indirectly as possible. To point it out seemed to be marking it as a problem. And it wasn't. Not in his book, anyway. "They're great, but they keep her on her toes."

"You've met her family already?" His mom's voice was wounded. "How come we're just learning about her?"

"I met her *kids*," he clarified. "Her parents live in another area of the country."

His parents exchanged a stunned look.

Gavin cleared his throat. "She has two. Kayla is sixteen, and Jackson is thirteen."

Dina's eyes widened.

His dad froze with a piece of meatloaf halfway to his mouth. "How old is she?" he asked.

"Forty-one," Gavin said.

"Huh." Ray set his fork down, then picked it back up. "Did her husband die?"

"No. Divorced." Gavin gritted his teeth, thinking of what he knew of her ex. "He's not in the area."

"How many times?" his father asked.

"What?"

Ray gestured with his fork. "How many times has she been divorced?"

"Just the one," Gavin said. "I think that was enough."

His mother hadn't said a word since he'd mentioned the kids, and her face looked pinched.

"Mom?" he said. "You need to take a drink?"

Dina shook her head, flustered. "Forty-one is considerably older than you. It's older than both your sisters."

"It's younger than you," he said.

"Oh, stop." She swatted like there was a fly in her face. "How did you meet this woman?"

"Well, that's kind of a funny story," Gavin said, looking around and rubbing the back of his neck. "She's a parent of one of the special ed kids I work with."

His mother stilled. "He has a diagnosis?"

"Autism," Gavin said smoothly. "And intellectual disability. He's a great kid. He loves music, likes to trace hands."

"Isn't that against the rules at your job?" his dad asked.

Gavin sighed. "It's not a great idea. I didn't exactly plan it. But I told my boss today, and we've agreed to take me out of the picture."

His dad paused again, this time a glass of wine halfway to his mouth. "You got fired?"

"No, no. I just won't be on Jackson's case."

The two exchanged a look again, their faces trying—and failing—to give nothing away. They hadn't expected this, the possibility of him dating an older woman with kids. Who wasn't Jewish. Who wasn't someone like Ellie.

The mood at the table had grown heavy, so he tried to inject some positivity into his speech. "It'll be fine," he said. "She's great. You're both going to love her."

"Fine," Dina said crisply. "Then let's schedule a time for us to meet her."

# CHAPTER 30

*Hey, there. How's travel agent-ing today? (Can I use that as a verb?)*

*You can with me. And fine. I'm booking some winery tours.*

*Lucky you.*

*Not for myself, this group of women. Somebody's thirtieth birthday. How's your day going?*

*Good. Been thinking about you all morning at work. Specifically that thing we did last night. We should do that again. Soon. Maybe this time with the lights on.*

*\*blush\* Can't we keep a little mystery?*

*Naw. You're a woman of many sides and I'd like to see them all. Especially your back side.*

*!!!!*

*What? Too honest? \*evil grin\**

*So I probably should've asked you this three weeks ago, but what's it like being a travel agent?*

*A lot of details. It is rewarding to see people take that trip they've always dreamed of.*

*Did you travel much BK? (I learned in a meeting this morning that among parents that means "Before Kids.")*

*Glad you're staying hip at the job. And I traveled some, not much. I don't like to travel.*

*But you're a travel agent.*

*I don't like to travel.*

*And you have this job because...?*

*I didn't say I didn't like* others *to travel. I like being home. In a warm house, in a place I'm familiar with. With my kids.*

*Really? Not even a big beach with white sand where it's somebody's job to bring you cocktails all day long?*

*Nope. Just so you know, this isn't going to end with you convincing me I need to take a dream trip. I'm almost forty-two. I know who I am.*

*Noted. \*writes it down on sticky note, puts it on corner of computer screen\* You know where I'd like to travel to right now?*

*Where?*

*Your bedroom.*

*Should've seen that one coming.*

*There are other places on my list after that. Want to learn about them?*

*I have a feeling I'm about to.*

*Okay, first I'd like to start off the trip with a quick stop at that spot between your ear and your shoulder. You know the place? Do you think you can reserve me a spot?*

*I think that can be arranged.*

*Then I'd like to take a long, leisurely tour down the rest of your body. I want to make sure I see all the sights. Really take my time there.*

*That's going to cost you.*

*How much?*

*I'll put it on your tab.*

*Oh, shoot, we're going to have to pause building this itinerary. This IEP meeting is about to start.*

*You're at an IEP right now??*

*I will be in two minutes. We're all just sitting around the table right now. You know how boring these things are. It's like the only thing you can do is sext your girlfriend.*

*That's true. See you today for lunch? Your trip isn't going to plan itself, you know.*

*I'm counting on it. Book me a reservation.*

# CHAPTER 31

*J*o pulled into the parking lot of Carrie Stiepler's office after school that Thursday afternoon.

"Twenty minutes," she said to Kayla next to her and Jackson in the back seat. "I have to go over some details with her, and then we'll grab some dinner on the way home. Gavin's coming over."

"Hand!" Jackson called from the backseat. He rocked back and forth, but unlike the agitated rocking he'd done when she picked him up from school—it'd been another hard day, the teacher had said—this time he was excited.

"*Gavin*," Jo corrected, but the boy just shouted "Hand!" again. She smiled. "Yes, Hand." Apparently Jo wasn't the only one taken with him. And she was really, really taken with him.

"He's coming over again?" Kayla asked, her voice rife with irritation. "Why?"

"Because we need to eat, he needs to eat, and we kind of like each other." Jo sighed. "Please try to be less rude to him this time."

"It seemed like he could take it." Kayla crossed her legs and jiggled one foot. "Plus, I don't need to be there."

Jo shook her head, at a loss for words. She'd never guessed Kayla would be this weird about her dating, and she didn't fully understand why.

"What?" Kayla said, her posture defensive. "You're the one who invited him over. Everyone knows you're not supposed to have someone you're dating meet your kids this soon." Her voice took on a lecturing tone that sounded an awful lot like Jo's own mom voice.

Jo stifled another sigh. She was really growing tired of this teenager thing. "Beyond your being rude to him the other night, it went fine. More or less," she added, remembering Jackson's accident. "Anyway, Jackson likes him. Right, Jackson?"

Jackson was swaying back and forth in the middle of the backseat, but at his name his green eyes met Jo's. "Right Jackson."

"Great," Kayla said dryly. "So it'll be that much worse when he inevitably bails."

Jo's jaw dropped. She didn't even know where to begin with that, between Kayla's assumption Gavin wouldn't stick around to the larger belief it implied, that maybe no man ever did. Was this because of how Neil had left? Or had Jo herself somehow been broadcasting her own secret fears? Either way, damn Neil. Damn him to hell. She shut her mouth and pressed her lips together until she could speak calmly.

"Kayla, retract your claws," she finally said. Opening the car door, she added, "Come on, Carrie's waiting."

They entered the immaculate office, where Kayla chose to hang out in the waiting room with Jackson, probably so she could text Austin.

Still irritated at her, Jo spoke sternly. "Keep an eye on Jax."

"I will," Kayla replied, her eyes already locked on the phone screen.

Carrie sat behind her desk, giving her a smile as she entered. "Josephine. Good to see you. Have a seat."

"Thanks, you too." Jo sat down in front of the advocate's large mahogany desk. The air smelled like crisp paper and furniture oil.

Carrie was dressed in a white blouse, her eyes focused behind her glasses. She opened a folder of paperwork in front of her. Underneath her expensive clothes and no-nonsense demeanor, Jo could see she was much younger than herself—at least Gavin's age, if not in her late twenties.

"So the school district has about two weeks left in the evaluation period," Carrie said. "I've taken the liberty of asking an independent evaluator to visit Jackson in his current classroom as well."

"Good," Jo said. "He's still been struggling a lot. His teacher said he struck her this morning while transitioning back from lunch."

"Because they don't know what they're doing," Carrie said. "Any progress notes you receive, any type of communication, keep for documentation."

"I have been."

"Good," Carrie folded her hands together. "So have you looked into private schools in the area?"

"Some," Jo said, but then shook her head. "Not enough. I'm still not sure that's what Jackson needs."

"You need to seriously consider it." Carrie looked down for a moment before meeting her eyes. "I wouldn't say this to the school district, but most kids, including autistic kids, do well in public school. The teachers are well-educated and trained, and most kids are able to adapt to the classroom environment with behavior plans and modifications, and occasionally aides. But other students need a different environment—and, though I don't know Jackson, his uptick in behaviors may indicate he needs something this classroom can't give him. You'd be smart to think outside the box."

Jo paused, considering the advocate's words. She remembered sitting with a social worker when Jackson was first diagnosed with autism and answering dozens of questions so that he would get the resources and services he needed. In the middle of asking about her son's symptoms, the social worker had asked, "He probably does the sniffing thing, right?"

"What?" Jo had asked.

"You know, like he smells everything? These kids often do the sniffing thing."

Jo knew what she meant—autistic people were often more sensitive to sensory input, from sounds to smells. But Jackson had never done "the sniffing thing," and something about the question disturbed Jo in a way she couldn't articulate.

She knew now what it was: With that little question, whether she realized it or not, the social worker acted like because she knew Jackson was autistic, she knew who he was—his behaviors and tendencies, maybe even his personality. But she didn't. Jax was an individual, not someone who could be put in a box.

Maybe it was time Jo opened herself up to the possibility that she needed to think more creatively about where he would best learn.

She nodded to Carrie. "You're right. Can you send me names of some of the private schools in the area you'd recommend?"

The advocate smiled. "Sure, I'll send you a few of the more established ones. Though of course there are smaller schools popping up all the time."

With that decided, Jo moved to the edge of her seat, her insides twisting. "Look, I have an update on this end."

"Oh?" Carrie reached for her pen.

Jo had hemmed and hawed about delivering this news, but she figured if Gavin was coming clean, she should too.

"I'm, um…" Jo tucked her hair behind her ears. "Do you remember Gavin Steinberg, Jackson's coordinator?"

"Of course." Carrie nodded. "What's he said? He's a newbie.

If he's said anything he shouldn't, we can use that in our case."
She looked eager.

"It's not that." After a pause, she forced the words out. "I'm actually dating him now."

Carrie's jaw dropped. "What?"

"We're dating," Jo said. "It just sort of happened." Her stomach fluttered at the thought of Gavin—from having this conversation with Carrie, yes, but also just the thought of him. In the past week, they'd been talking every day and seeing each other as much as possible. They were weaving their lives together, and quicker than either of them expected. Her hours felt empty without hearing his voice or seeing his name pop up in her text messages, and her body craved his like it hadn't craved another man before. *Dating* felt like too simple of a word.

"It's complicated, I know," Jo added, but then she couldn't keep the smile off her face. "But it's happening."

"You shouldn't do that," Carrie said automatically.

The smile fell off her face. "What?"

"It's a huge conflict of interest." Carrie shifted in her seat, agitated. "*Giant.* He's working for the school district. He's not working for your son."

"I know," Jo said quickly. "But we also know that with you in the picture, Charlene Matthews and the lawyers will probably be the ones involved in any negotiations. He said he just needs to send an email to let me know when the evaluation is completed, handing it off to Charlene. So he's not really part of the situation anymore, not exactly."

"But he is," Carrie said. "He works for *them.* And they're not on your side. Does Charlene know about this?"

"Yes."

Carrie's eyes widened. "And she didn't fire him?"

Jo blinked. "No."

"I would've fired him."

Jo felt a wave of defensiveness rise up. "Charlene trusts him."

Carrie pointed a finger at her. "And that's why you shouldn't."

Jo straightened in her seat, her surprise heating into anger. "Look, I'm not paying you the equivalent of three mortgage payments for relationship advice."

Jo respected the advocate's work—clearly she got kids what they needed in the school district—but the woman seemed unable to fathom the complexities of this situation. Well, life was messy.

Carrie pressed her lips together and looked down, bracing her hands on the desk for a moment. Then she looked back up at Jo, calming her voice. "I'm sorry. I just want for this situation to resolve itself in Jackson's best interest. That's what's important, what we need to keep in mind."

Jo nodded and exhaled, trying to let her anger go. "I know. It *is* what I'm keeping in mind."

"Good." Switching into business mode, obviously her most comfortable setting, Carrie pushed her glasses up her nose and started running down the details of what the independent evaluation would cover. Jo took notes on what she was saying, but as the advocate spoke, her mind kept drifting to what she'd said about Gavin.

Jo knew Gavin meant well. He liked Jackson, he liked kids, he believed in his job. They had bumped heads before, but it was to be expected. With him stepping out of the picture, it wouldn't be an issue anymore. She'd be arguing with Charlene at the table now—or Carrie would. She might even be able to vent to Gavin about his boss. Carrie just had a legal brain and a black-and-white mindset; she couldn't see the nuances here, couldn't understand how strong both their feelings were, how much Jo wanted him in her life so badly, how long she'd waited for this without even realizing it. And anyway, she was paying the woman to fight on her son's behalf, not be her life coach. Her opinion didn't matter.

It was going to be fine.

Still, Jo was restless as she left the advocate's office.

Kayla barely acknowledged her presence, but Jackson walked over and flung his arms around her, saying, "Mom mom mom" and squeezing her tight like she'd been gone the entire weekend, not just half an hour. Jackson had his moments, but at least he wasn't so far gone into the teenage years that he didn't need his mom occasionally. Unlike Kayla...

Over his head, Jo said to her, "You're having dinner with us, Kayla."

The girl rolled her eyes but didn't talk back.

Jo squeezed Jackson, kissing him on the head and ruffling his brown hair. "Thanks for the hug, buddy. I needed that."

They headed home, Jackson making them identify the artist of every song on the radio. Jo still couldn't shake Carrie's words. Had the advocate had some experience that made her think dating Gavin would end horribly? Had this happened with another parent and led to some disaster? Or was it just the advocate's prejudice against the school district?

Well, whatever anyone else thought, Jo knew she could trust Gavin. She really could. Couldn't she?

# CHAPTER 32

*A* day later, Gavin stood in front of Josephine's and knocked to the tune of Wilson Phillips' "Impulsive," their secret sign.

She opened before he finished the chorus.

"You again?" Jo leaned a hip against the doorframe and arched an eyebrow. It was early afternoon and she wore a pair of dark jeans and a plain white tee, but the way his body responded, it was as if she was standing there stark naked smirking at him.

He wanted her. So much he'd played hooky again from work.

He took a step closer to her, close enough that their toes touched. She smelled of coffee and shampoo. "Me again."

She craned her neck to look up at him, a knowing smile on her face. "Another dentist appointment?"

"Yeah." He put his hands on her waist and pushed her backwards until they were both inside, kicking the door shut with his foot. Then he pinned her against the wall by the door and kissed her until her hands fluttered up to encircle his neck.

"I've got really bad teeth," he added, running his lips over that soft, sensitive spot underneath her ear.

"You'd better be careful," Josephine said, her breath catching, "or this talk is going to dive into non-sexy territory."

"I don't think that's possible." His hands roamed underneath her white shirt, teasing her warm skin. "Being near you is never not sexy."

It took them five minutes to reach the bedroom, given the need to make out against the walls on the way there. Gavin lost his dress shirt in the living room and his belt down the hall before they made it into the master bedroom and onto the bed.

"You're so warm," he marveled. "How do you get so warm?"

She rolled over and straddled him. She was getting more comfortable with him—with this. She already dominated his thoughts, and she was rapidly learning how to torture him in other ways. It wasn't fair.

It wasn't fair, but it felt damn good.

Then they both heard it: the opening and closing of the door.

They froze.

A frown line formed between her eyebrows. "Honey?" Josephine called.

In response came soft sobbing.

Josephine's eyes widened. "Kayla," she whispered, scrambling off him.

"Go," he whispered back, already buttoning up his pants.

Jo nodded, smoothing down her hair as she darted out of the room.

It was too early for the high school to let out, so something must've been wrong with Jo's daughter. Gavin felt momentary disappointment as he realized this wasn't going to be the afternoon tryst he'd been expecting, but it was soon replaced with concern—and the need to figure out where he'd shed his clothes.

From the front room came the sound of Kayla sobbing louder, great big gulps, while Josephine questioned her in a low, soothing voice.

"Something at school?"

Her daughter's answer was indecipherable to Gavin as he crept down the hall, quietly picking up his belt and looping it back into his pants. Something about a boy who was *an asshole* —correction, *such an asshole*—and *my locker* and *stupid guitar* and *everyone saw.*

Where was his shirt? Ah, there behind where Josephine stood. Unfortunately, that meant walking out into the living room where the two of them were speaking.

Kayla must've caught sight of the shirt just as he did. She stopped crying. "Whose is that?" Though only Josephine was within view, Gavin saw Kayla's finger pointing to the ground where it lay as Chuck the cat came over to sniff it.

"Um, it's... Gavin's," Josephine answered. With her toe, she slid it towards the hallway within reach of his grateful hands. He picked it up and began buttoning rapidly.

"He's here?" Kayla squeaked.

"He's just here for a visit."

There was a beat before Kayla spoke. "Eww."

Gavin stepped into the living room, fully dressed.

"Hi, Kayla." He cleared his throat. "I'm sorry about..."

The girl's pretty face was blotchy and swollen from crying, and at his words, she started sobbing again.

Josephine gathered her up in a hug, meeting his gaze over her daughter's shoulder.

*Sorry*, she mouthed.

*It's okay*, he mouthed back, but then said out loud, "I should probably..."

She nodded, but then her phone rang loudly from her pocket, startling all three of them. Sighing, Josephine pulled it out, saying, "Let me just turn this off, Kayla," before stopping at the name of the caller.

She immediately put the phone to her ear. "Hello?"

Josephine's face grew tight, her eyes narrowing. "Are you sure? He isn't—Well, why don't—Okay... Okay." She ended the call.

"Honey," she started, reaching out to her daughter—but Kayla pulled away.

"It's Jackson, isn't it?" the teen asked, her arms folded across her chest.

Josephine sighed. "Yes, something happened at school. He banged his fist into a wall—hard enough to break the skin. He's fine now, but they want me to come get him. I'm sorry, honey. It can't wait."

She sniffed and looked away. "It can never wait, can it?"

Josephine squeezed her eyes shut and took a breath. Gavin could feel the guilt radiating from her in waves.

"I'll be fifteen minutes. I promise." She opened her eyes and looked at Gavin. "Can you stay?"

Kayla startled and uncrossed her arms. "What?"

"He can stay with you, Kayla," she said softly. "While I run to get Jackson."

The girl raised her voice. "I don't need him to *babysit* me."

"It's no problem," Gavin said smoothly. "At the job they think I'm having dental work. I have the rest of the afternoon off."

Kayla mumbled something else, which Josephine cut off. "You're upset, Kayla. I want to make sure there's someone here with you."

She grimaced, but didn't say another word as Josephine ran to get her keys, coat, and purse.

"I'll be back soon," she called as she rushed out the door. "Fifteen minutes."

Kayla threw her hands up dramatically and trudged over to the loveseat, collapsing into it with her back to Gavin. She twisted her dark, curly hair back with a band and started sniffling.

"Hey." Gavin walked over to the couch perpendicular to the loveseat and sat. He leaned forward with his elbows on his knees. He was in over his head here. The last time he'd hung with teenagers, he'd been a teenager himself. But he didn't want to let Jo down—or get even more on Kayla's bad side. "I'm sorry about what happened." He cleared his throat. "It sounds rough."

"You don't even know what happened," Kayla snapped, wiping her eyes.

Gavin tried to recall what he'd overheard and what it meant. Boy troubles. Right. "I know whoever did this to you, he's such an asshole," he said, repeating her own phrase.

Kayla grunted, but then responded in the affirmative. "Such an asshole."

"Bad breakup?" he ventured.

"Yes." Still not looking at him, Kayla swiped a box of tissues from the coffee table and nested it in her lap.

What should he say next? Maybe he should just keep apologizing. "I'm sorry."

"He said he was falling for me," Kayla told the wall, tears in her voice.

He paused. "He probably wasn't ready."

Kayla shot him a brief glare. Gavin couldn't decide if it was progress or not.

An analogy burst into his mind, and, before he could help it, it spilled out. "I mean, he was a Padawan, and you need a Jedi," he started.

"What the hell is *that* supposed to mean?" Kayla said, looking over at him.

God, he used to be cool. He was still within kicking distance of his twenties. When did he lose the ability to talk to a teenager?

"It's just, uh, he's still a boy," Gavin said, stumbling through what he meant. "He doesn't realize a good thing when he finds it. He'll learn. We all do." That was true enough.

She was looking at him like he was a smashed cockroach, so Gavin tried a more traditional approach. "You know what men are like?"

"Buses," Kayla said automatically. "You miss one, another will come around in a few minutes." She rolled her eyes. "I've heard that like forty times already. God, you suck at this."

He exhaled. "I'm sorry," he said, and then admitted, "The last time I was with a high school girl upset over a breakup, it was because I was breaking up with her."

She looked aghast. "That's terrible."

"I know." He hooked a thumb at himself. "Padawan."

"My mom's dating a *Padawan?*" She still sounded irritated, but he could swear there was amusement buried somewhere in there.

"I'd like to think I've advanced a little since then," he said. "Now I'm maybe like one of those mid-competent Jedis that gets slaughtered when a more powerful Jedi turns evil."

Kayla rolled her eyes again. "You're really weird."

Another flash of inspiration struck him. "You know what else guys are like?"

"What?" she said, like she could care less.

"IEP meetings."

"Oh, God." She closed her eyes and put her face into a couch cushion.

"No, no, hear me out." Gavin raised his hands. "You never know what you're going to get with an IEP meeting. It could be terrible, it could last three hours, you could get spit on—"

"*What?*" Kayla mumbled into the couch.

"—but sometimes it could be really great and lead to better things. Or at least bad cookies and a good woman. And also," Gavin added, really getting into this, "you have a right to call an IEP meeting whenever you want. Just like you, Kayla, could probably just walk down the hallway of the high school tomorrow, getting another guy just like that." He snapped. "One that probably plays the guitar better."

Her face still buried in the couch, Kayla snorted. "Okay, that was marginally better than the bus thing."

Gavin shifted in his seat, an actual good idea coming to mind. "You know what you need?"

She raised her face. At least she wasn't crying anymore. "Ice cream?"

"No. I mean, yeah, probably eventually. But..." He stood and grabbed the remote off the coffee table. "You need some angry female singer-songwriters."

She gave a dramatic sigh, but she didn't protest as he turned on the television and pulled up the app for YouTube.

"Since you've got your mother's DNA, we'll start with Alanis and work our way forward," he said.

"Doing what?"

"Singing," he said, like it was obvious. "Angry singing. Or screaming if you prefer."

Kayla looked at him like he was nuts. "No."

"Try it."

"No way." She shook her head.

"Come on," Gavin said. "Just one song. Unless you want me to start talking about Jedis again?"

It took three songs, and Gavin demonstrating how to sing to angry music by using the broom as a pretend microphone and singing incredibly off-key. But eventually, in the middle of him shouting along to Ani Difranco's swear-laden "Untouchable Face," Kayla scowled, stood up, and ripped the faux mic from his hands, like she would show him how it was done.

She started off tentative, like she was simply trying to show him that it was possible not to butcher the song. But soon she grew more fervent in singing along with the chorus, growing louder and mad as hell.

"That's what I'm talking about!" Gavin shouted, and they hit repeat on the song.

Ten minutes and three more angry songs later, shuffles came from the front. The door creaked open.

"We're back." Jo's voice was laced with worry, but after taking in the scene of music videos and her daughter yell-singing with a broom in front of the television, her jaw dropped.

"What's going on?"

"We're going full emo here, Jo," Gavin said, his voice raised to be heard over the music. "With help from our friends Alanis, Ani, and Tori. I think you remember them?"

"Um…" She dropped her bag on the floor as the door shut behind them. "What?"

Jackson stood behind his mother, a bandage wrapped around his hand. Despite Jo's confusion, Gavin could see the kid got what was going on. Taking in the scene of his sister swaying and singing to music, his eyes lit up and he joined her, jumping and pacing in front of the TV. Music was its own language, and it was one Jax spoke fluently.

Jo was a little slower. "Huh?"

Gavin laughed. "What did you do when you had a breakup back in the '90s?"

"Are you holding some kind of party here at my house?" Jo asked. "Is there beer involved? Are cops going to show up at our door?"

"*What did you do when you had a breakup back in the '90s?*" he repeated. "Honest question."

She paused, then looked at the music video, and Kayla, and back at him. A slow smile crept over her face.

"Exactly." He nodded. "Come join us."

They let Kayla pick the songs, but soon they were all singing. First it was just lyrics and Jackson bouncing alongside on the trampoline, but then Josephine pulled the boy down to twirl him, and Gavin grabbed Jo to dip her, and Jackson put his hand over his sister's throat to feel the vibrations of her voice. Soon they were singing loudly to happier songs, spinning and clutching and swaying and rocking. Kayla had stopped crying and Jo was laughing so hard she'd started, and Jackson's green eyes were so bright you would've thought the kid was at an amusement park. Gavin's face already hurt from smiling, and as they linked arms while singing along to a show tune, a thought drifted up into his mind: *So this is family.*

Then there came a loud knock at the door.

# CHAPTER 33

"*J*ust a minute!" Jo scrambled for the remote to turn down the volume. "Crap, maybe the cops *are* going to come," she whispered furiously to Gavin.

"Don't worry, we'll give them a turn with the broom," Gavin whispered back.

Jo snorted and opened the door.

On the stoop, wearing dirty jeans with his hands shoved deep in the pockets, stood Austin.

Jo gritted her teeth. She hadn't been able to decipher the full story from Kayla, but she'd gotten that it'd somehow involved another girl giving Austin back his guitar, like he'd left it at her house doing God knows what, and that this was a very bad thing, and that the display had been painfully public for Kayla.

Jo gave him a glare that could've incinerated a snow cone stand. "Can I help you?"

His face sullen, the boy asked, "Is Kayla here?"

Behind her, the house had fallen into silence.

"She is," Jo said, "but I don't think she wants to talk to you. Neither do I, so…" She moved to shut the door in his face, when Kayla grabbed it and held it open.

"Mom," she said, catching Jo's eye, "can you give us a minute?"

Jo pressed her lips together, but she nodded. Moving away from the door, she gestured Gavin towards the kitchen. She glanced at Jackson, but he was on the couch, rocking out to the music still playing softly and seemingly unaware of their unwelcome visitor. She saw Austin glance at him, a perplexed look on his face, before he turned to Kayla and started whispering furiously to her.

She and Gavin turned the corner into the kitchen, but they stayed near the doorway to listen—and to interfere if need be.

Gavin came up behind her, putting his arms around her. "She's going to be okay," he whispered. "She can handle herself. Did you hear her rocking out to Tori?"

Jo chuckled lightly. "That's my daughter out there."

Gavin paused for a moment. "I've been wanting to bring this up, and maybe this is not the best time," he said, "but my parents want to meet you."

She twisted her neck to look at him. "Really?"

"Really." His blue eyes were hard to read.

"Wow." Jo looked away. "Meet the parents? That sounds really... official. Is that something you have to do when you're over forty?"

"I'm afraid so." He added, "I mean, if you want."

They were getting so close, so fast. Yet as nervous as she was to meet his family, and to have them meet her, she also knew that it was only fair she was introduced to his life the way she'd introduced him to hers. Plus, she wanted to know more about Gavin—how he'd grown up, what he'd been like at six and sixteen, whom he'd inherited that incredible smile from.

She turned in his arms and gave him a quick kiss on the nose. "Okay."

His eyes widened in surprise. "Really?"

"Yeah."

Gavin gave her a smile that was half relief, half anxious. "Good. Because we have a lunch date with them on Tuesday."

She started. "That was fast."

The corner of his mouth turned up, his voice wry. "My mother doesn't mess around."

"Obviously."

Suddenly worn out from the music and dancing, Jo rested her head against her chest as they embraced.

Coming home with Jackson earlier, she couldn't have been more surprised at the scene she'd walked into. Her daughter and Gavin standing together singing '90s music? She'd almost had to check if she'd walked into the right house.

She'd expected a night of tears and ice cream and *Law and Order* with Kayla as she grieved her first big breakup. And maybe that would come, but what they'd had in the past hour had been something different, something joyful and unexpectedly magical. A year ago, five, she wouldn't have dared to dream that someone new could come into their lives, that a fourth person could fit into the complicated Jenga tower that was their reality without making it crash down. Yet the feeling of rightness she'd briefly felt at the fundraiser was back with her, stronger than ever. *This* was right. Gavin in her house, as part of her family.

Out near the front door, Austin was speaking low to Kayla, but as their voices grew agitated, words reached the kitchen.

"It wasn't a big deal, me and Nikki," Austin was saying. "We just hung out."

"Sure," Kayla hissed back. "With your tongue down her throat."

"It's not like that," he retorted. "She's going through some stuff."

"Sure she is," Kayla snapped. "Everyone saw you touching."

"Nothing happened!" Austin said, dropping the whisper.

Jo stepped out of Gavin's arms to peek around the corner. Austin was gesturing expansively, but Kayla held her own, her arms crossed and posture firm.

Jo glanced to make sure Jackson was still on the couch before turning back to Gavin.

"Can I kick him out now?" she whispered.

"From the sounds of her voice, I think she's about to do it for you," he said. "Let her have the satisfaction."

Kayla said something that Jo didn't catch, but then Austin exploded.

"Bullshit!" he shouted. "I can't even believe that—"

Before Jo could come into the room to intervene—and she was about to—there came a smack and a yelp.

"What the hell!" Austin shouted, his voice going high pitched.

Jo rounded the corner to see not just Kayla and Austin by the front entryway, but Jackson between them, holding Austin to the wall with one hand, his bandaged fist raised with the other.

"Jax!" Jo shouted.

"He just came up to him!" Kayla cried. "I didn't see him."

"He head-butted me!" Austin cried.

"Jackson, let him go," Jo said. She froze, afraid that if she did anything, he'd let his fist fly. Jackson was shaking, his eyes maintaining the eye contact with Austin he usually struggled with. It wasn't until Gavin stepped up to him and put his hand on the boy's raised fist that he lowered it.

"You need to leave," Jo told Austin. "Now."

"We were just having a conversation!" Austin said to Kayla, ignoring Jo. "Before your freak of a brother here smashed his head into my face."

Jo gasped. Jackson sank to the floor, curling his knees towards his chest and rocking. "*Face, face, face...*"

Jo lowered down behind him, hugging him from behind.

Gavin stepped in front of Austin, his voice deep. "Go. Now."

Austin looked between Jackson and Kayla, his face confused. "What? What's wrong? Is something wrong with him?" At Kayla's face, his own contorted. "Shit, Kayla, I didn't know anything was wrong—"

"Get out," Kayla said through her teeth. Her fists clenched as she glared at him, but her voice trembled.

The boy drew a quick breath, his words catching up with him. "I'm sorry, K, I didn't mean—"

"You said it," she hissed. "You said it because you were thinking it. Get out of here. Don't ever talk to me again."

Without another word, Austin walked out the door.

"Kayla." From her vantage on the floor, Jo could see the side of her daughter's face as her boyfriend, and maybe the boy she'd given her virginity to, walked away from her as an enemy. She would run to her room and sob for the next couple hours, probably while blaring loud, angry music in her earbuds, and she wouldn't open the door for anybody.

But Kayla proved her wrong. As the door clicked shut, Kayla turned to her brother and knelt on the floor in front of him, wrapping her arms around him.

"I'm sorry, Jax," she whispered. "I'm so sorry."

LATER THAT NIGHT, after Gavin left and Jackson had fallen asleep, Jo crept into Kayla's room. By the sounds of sniffles and tinny music from the other side of the door, she knew she was still awake.

Padding across the floor, she climbed under Kayla's comforter and lay on her side, facing her.

Kayla was on her back with her earbuds in, but she pulled one out at Jo's arrival.

"Who are you listening to?" Jo whispered.

"This new singer I just discovered." Kayla sniffed. "Austin said her music was crap. But actually it's amazing. I'm never giving up a musician for a boy again."

"Smart girl." Jo patted her arm.

They both lay there for a couple minutes, listening to the soft, melodic sounds of the music over a quiet night.

"I didn't tell him," Kayla finally said, rolling over on her side to face her mother.

"What?"

"Austin." She sniffed. "I didn't tell him I had an autistic brother or any of the other stuff. That's why he acted that way."

Jo assumed as much. "Why didn't you tell him?"

"I don't know." Kayla pulled the other earbud out and untangled it from her hair. "I guess I wanted something different, someone who didn't know about it and wouldn't ask. A chance to pretend like I had this normal life for a while."

Jo's heart squeezed. "Oh, Kayla."

Squishing the pillow underneath her head, Jo moved closer, wrapping an arm around her daughter.

"It's okay, honey," she said. "You'll get that chance."

"I'm not in denial, you know," Kayla said, her breath hot against Jo's neck. "I know someday you'll be gone, and I'll be all he has. I'll be the one to take care of him."

Jo bit her lip hard enough to draw blood. As difficult as her life could be, this was the thing she couldn't bear to acknowledge. She was shocked that Kayla not only was aware of it, but brave enough to say it aloud. It was clear now that out of the two of them, Jo was the one more in denial about the future. She couldn't stand the thought that someday she wouldn't be there to take care of Jackson—to take care of either of them.

So she tried to lightly laugh it off, stroking Kayla's soft curls. "No way. You've got one of those immortal moms."

Kayla sniffled into her chest a couple more minutes, Jo's pajama shirt growing damp from her tears. As painful as it was to see her daughter sad, there was a sweetness to the moment. They hadn't been this close in months.

Kayla pulled slightly away. "Just so you know, I didn't sleep with him."

*Good*, Jo thought, but said, "Okay."

"I know you hated him."

"He wasn't the one," Jo said, trying to stay diplomatic. "There'll be other ones."

Kayla paused. "That's what Gavin said."

Jo smiled. Gavin had been so sweet, comforting Kayla when she'd had to rush out and then, after Austin left, ordering pizza and taking Jackson for a walk around the block.

Pulling farther away from Jo so she could breathe, Kayla suddenly said, "I don't think guys can hack it."

Jo blinked. Her smile faded. "What?"

"The special needs stuff," Kayla explained in a hard voice. "If I'd told Austin, he probably wouldn't have been able to deal. And God knows Dad can't."

Jo exhaled. She guessed this belief was behind much of her daughter's attitude and behavior towards Gavin, but Jo regretted it. As disappointed as she was with Neil, she didn't want Kayla to feel the way Jo herself often had. She took a deep breath, trying to be the bigger person. "Your dad loves you, Kayla. He loves Jackson, too. He just kind of sucks at it a lot of the time."

They cuddled a few minutes longer, until Kayla's breath deepened with sleep. As exhausted as she was, Jo remained wide-awake, staring at the dark ceiling.

A thought kept coming at her like a mosquito she couldn't swat away from her face.

It was irrational to think so. Totally irrational. He'd proven time and time again he wanted to stick around, despite her life and all its complications.

But what if Gavin ultimately decided he couldn't hack it either?

# CHAPTER 34

*G*avin had picked a local deli for his parents to meet Josephine for the first time, and when they all sat down at the table and both his mother and Jo ordered grilled chicken sandwiches, it was like kismet.

As they sipped iced teas and waited for their orders, his dad spoke to Josephine with the tone he'd used for acquaintances since Gavin was a kid. His Jersey accent was polite and breezy, giving nothing away. Gavin came by his charm honest.

"So," Ray began, "Gavin tells us you've got kids."

"Yes." Jo smiled. She wore the black dress she'd put on for the third IEP meeting they'd had, and Gavin tried to not observe her too closely lest he got an urge to ask for the check. "Kayla is sixteen, and Jackson is thirteen."

"And he told me Jackson is…" His dad waved his hand in a circle, trying to find the word.

"Autistic," Josephine supplied. "Also a Pisces." She flashed a quick smile in Gavin's direction and he warmed.

"We watch that show sometimes, with the doctor? You know the one?" Ray asked. "Is he kind of like that?"

"No," she said. "Jackson has very limited language, and also some cognitive challenges. I've never seen him perform heart surgery on anyone."

"Oh." Ray paused, at a loss for what to say next.

Gavin smiled sheepishly, feeling a bit embarrassed by his dad's naïve questions, but grateful Josephine was handling them so gracefully. "He's a great kid," he added. "You should hear him hum Taylor Swift."

Dina leaned forward and addressed Josephine. "So your daughter must be a junior in high school."

"Yes." Josephine took a sip of her tea and nodded.

"Which colleges are you looking at?"

"Um." Jo picked up her straw wrapper. "We're not at the point of narrowing them down yet."

"Well, you might want to get there," Dina said, her tone verging on lecturing. "I work at a local university, and we have juniors coming for campus tours all the time. The junior year is very important."

Jo looked uncomfortable. "It is?"

"Yes." Dina sat back, unfolding her napkin and placing it on her lap. "She'll want to start narrowing down schools to decide which places she wants to visit this summer, if not sooner."

Josephine was still fiddling with her wrapper. "But the summer's still so far off. Right?"

Dina raised an eyebrow. "It'll come quicker than you know," she said. "And you'll want to be prepared. There'll be visits, and then she'll need to start getting her applications ready next fall. Does she want to stay local or go to a university in a different area of the country?"

"Probably local," Jo said, but Gavin could tell she was making it up. He couldn't remember Jo ever bringing up college and Kayla, now that he thought of it. It looked like she didn't want it brought up now, either.

"I know some kids want to spread their wings," Dina continued. "My two eldest certainly did. Does your daughter want that?"

"I don't know." Jo looked faintly nauseous, so Gavin changed the subject.

Injecting humor into his voice, like he was starting to tell a joke, he said, "Josephine is a travel agent, but she hates to travel."

"Hates to travel?" his dad asked. "Who hates to travel?"

"Apparently travel agents," Gavin laughed, relieved he'd managed to change the subject.

"*Hate* is probably too strong a word," Jo said, tossing him a grateful look. "I'm just not crazy about it. I'm a homebody. And, even if I liked it, it would be too difficult to leave Jackson."

"What about your ex-husband?" Dina asked, and the table fell silent.

"What?"

"The children's father," Dina said. "Couldn't he watch them if you took a trip?"

Josephine shook her head and colored slightly. "Oh, no. No, no." She took a long sip of iced tea. "He hasn't seen Kayla since his wedding two years ago. And with Jackson it's been four years. If I had him come here to watch his son, it'd basically be Kayla in charge with her father just standing around." She let out a short laugh, even though it wasn't funny.

His parents exchanged a look.

Anger burned in Gavin's belly, like it usually did, when he was reminded of Jo's ex. Though some of the irritation was reserved for his mother, who seemed like she was deliberately trying to pry his new girlfriend open with a letter opener.

"Anyway," Jo said, twining the straw wrapper around her finger, "finding someone to watch a person with special needs is difficult, especially as the kid gets older. Jackson's my height now, and strong as an ox. It'd be tricky to find a babysitter who could watch him for days at a time. Which is fine." She put down the wrapper. "Like I said, I don't like to travel."

The food came, and, thankfully, they launched into more comfortable topics—which movies they loved, what Gavin had been like as a kid, if it was going to snow on Thanksgiving next week and, if so, how much.

Near the end of the meal, Jo excused herself to return to work. Gavin walked her to her car.

"Sorry about the third degree," he whispered.

"They're your parents, I get it," Jo said, but her posture looked stiff.

As they reached her car, he leaned over and gave her a quick kiss on the lips. "I'll call you later."

She smiled.

Gavin returned to where his parents sat polishing off their drinks. He was anxious after that tense first part of the lunch, but cautiously optimistic. After all, who wouldn't love Jo?

He sat down across from them. "So what'd you think? She's great, right?"

Dina poked at her iced tea with a straw. "She's lovely."

"Seems like she's got a good head on her shoulders," Ray added.

Dina nodded, not meeting his eyes. "Very smart. Pretty, too."

"*Beautiful,*" Gavin clarified.

"She seemed like she was funny," his dad said, tilting his head and looking at him. "Is she funny?"

Gavin grinned. "Very funny."

Ray pointed his finger at him and wagged it. "I've always said you need a funny woman."

Gavin felt like jumping for joy. "I knew you'd both love her."

"We like her." Dina paused, glancing up. "I'm just not sure she's right for you."

His heart plummeted. "What?"

His mother took her fork and picked at the remains of her sandwich. "She's in a different place in her life, Gavin."

He leaned back in his chair and sighed. "And which place is that, Mom?"

She fixed him with a stare. "Don't take a tone. You asked for my opinion, and I'm giving it."

Irritated, he gestured for her to continue.

"She's an older woman," she started, then catching Gavin's eyes, added, "*Older*. I didn't say old. She's just got different things on the horizon than you do. She has two teenagers. Her son has a lot of needs. Her daughter will be on her way to college soon, as much as she seems to be in denial about that."

"She's got a lot going on right now," Gavin said protectively.

"Her future isn't the same as the one you've envisioned," Dina said.

Gavin stifled a groan. His mother sounded a lot like Tanner had. "How do you know what I have envisioned?"

With a clank, his mother set down her fork and leaned back. "She's got older kids, Gavin. She probably doesn't want to have more. Are you willing to accept you'd never have children of your own? Setting aside the fact that she's not even Jewish…"

Gavin blanched. He'd been waiting for her to bring up the Jewish thing, but still it stung. It had happened to work out when Ellie turned out to be Jewish, but then he and Ellie hadn't worked out. Ideally, he had always imagined himself marrying a Jewish woman and having his own kids, to help pass down his culture and its traditions to the next generation. But then he'd pictured himself staying in sales, too. In a single year, he'd gone from heading in one direction to not being sure at all what he wanted. And then this amazing woman walked into his life.

Still, even though he wasn't as observant as his parents, his religion and background were important to him. But so was Josephine, increasingly so.

Gavin cleared his throat, lowering his voice as he addressed his mother. "Whatever our faiths are or become—and the kids thing—that's between the two of us."

Dina reached an arm across the table towards him, gentling her voice. "You've always been a kind, loving person, and I worry that you'd rush in to save someone. If you ever thought about getting serious with this woman—"

"I am serious," Gavin said quietly.

His mother paused. "I'm not saying you should stop seeing her—"

His jaw tightened. "That's good. Because I'm not going to."

"—just that maybe you should pump the brakes a little," Dina continued. "Take your time. Find out if this is really what you want. For both of you."

Gavin put his napkin on the table and pushed back his seat. He was through with this conversation. "You already decided what you thought before you met her, didn't you? Took the facts you knew and decided you didn't want your son dating a divorced, forty-year-old, non-Jewish woman with kids." He looked between them both. "I can't believe you guys."

"Calm down." Dina raised her palm. "I'm not judging her, son. I'm also putting myself in her shoes. I'm afraid that maybe someday you'll be the one getting hurt. I saw the way you were looking at her."

"You were *mooning* over her," Ray added.

"I wasn't mooning," Gavin said irritably, glancing away.

"There was definitely some mooning," he argued.

"I'm not a kid." Gavin exhaled, trying not to act like one. "I know what I'm doing."

"I know you're not a child," Dina said. "But you're not a parent, either. A woman thinks of her children above all else—especially when they're struggling."

He waved his hand. "I know."

"You don't," Dina said. "I say these things to you because *I* know. Because I worry for you. If things become too complicated for her, if she sees you as coming between her and her kids, she'll choose them."

Aggravated at them both, Gavin stood. "I've got to get back to work."

"Gavin…" his mother said.

Without meeting their eyes, he said, "I'll call you later."

"Will we see you at Shabbat Friday?" Ray asked. A rare note of raw vulnerability was in his father's voice, enough that Gavin looked into his lined face, which was drawn in worry. He loved both his parents, but he wasn't always sure they had his best interests in mind.

"I guess," he finally said, shrugging.

"*Gavin.*" Dina's voice was high. Hurt.

"Yes." He met his mother's eyes briefly, unwilling to let her down, even in his anger. "I'll be there."

Walking out of the restaurant into the brisk November day, Gavin groaned and shook his head. Family was family, even when you wanted to vote them off the island.

He knew his mother would be weird about this, what with her tendency to pair him with twentysomething daughters of her Jewish friends. But he didn't expect her to be so forthright. Forthright and calm in a way that unnerved him. He was used to her being the one overacting, and him being the one who made sense.

His phone beeped with an incoming text. It was Angelo.

*Want to hit the gym after work?* the text said. *I could use it.*

*HELL YES*, Gavin replied.

AT THE GYM, he and Angelo worked on the weight machines. They rotated through the machines together, as Angelo advised him on his technique and they both blew off steam.

After Gavin ranted about his parents, he turned to Angelo. "So what happened to you today? Difficult speech therapy session? Disappointed parent?"

"Nothing," Angelo said.

"No?"

Angelo scanned the crowd at the gym before turning back to Gavin. "Look, man, I heard something. Something I probably shouldn't tell you. Something you can't tell anybody I told you."

Gavin froze. "What?"

The therapist lowered his voice and leaned closer to Gavin. "That Palladino kid, the one whose mom you've been seeing?"

"Yeah?"

"They've got the data."

Gavin's stomach twisted. "What?"

"They've got data showing he's not progressing in his current class, and that he can make progress in the new one. The evaluation isn't totally over, but the other teacher, she's taken him out to her class a few times, worked with him. And he's learning. He's still having behavior issues, but he's progressing in some of his academic goals. The mom probably doesn't know."

"No," Gavin said, a spot above his right eye starting to throb. "She doesn't."

"Carrie Stiepler will probably put up a fight," Angelo continued, "but it'll be a hard one. Probably take a while, too."

Gavin collapsed on a nearby bench, leaning his elbows on his knees and dropping his head. "Shit."

"I know." Angelo plopped down beside him. "I'm guessing they didn't tell you. Conflict of interest and all."

Maybe Charlene didn't trust him with the information—or maybe she hadn't wanted to put him in the position he was now in. After risking his job to date Josephine, he'd made a promise to his boss that he wouldn't share district information with her. He was bound to that promise, and now he was also bound to keep Angelo's confidence.

Josephine wanted what was best for her son, and she thought that new class wasn't. But, if Angelo was right, the district had data to prove she was wrong.

She wouldn't win this fight.

# CHAPTER 35

*G*avin couldn't tell Josephine what he knew. He just couldn't. But maybe he could get her used to the idea that change might be good for Jackson. That he was growing up. That maybe even though she was an incredible mom, if she let go and trusted the process on occasion, everything would be okay.

"Didn't you tell me he picked out a completely new pair of shoes?" he asked her the following evening as they cuddled on the couch, her head tucked under his chin.

"Yeah," she said. "Orange Chucks. So weird."

"Maybe he's trying to tell you that he's ready for a change."

She turned in his arms and raised an eyebrow at him. "I'm not a fan of changes."

"So I've gathered."

Kayla drifted out of her room, looking morose. Jo told him that since the breakup last Friday, she had spent every evening at home, which Jo felt guilty about enjoying so much.

"She's not happy, though," Jo had said. "Maybe one of these days, we'll play hooky on a weekday and go see some cheesy holiday movie."

Now, a moment of inspiration striking him, Gavin took Jo's hands. "What if," he said, "you and Kayla go to the movies tonight, and I take Jackson somewhere? Like to play basketball maybe?"

Jo frowned. "Basketball?"

"I don't know, just... something. A guy thing. Give you a break." It was true her love for her son was admirable, but he'd also seen Jackson bristle under her helicoptering. He got that; God knows he had his own mother hovering a bit too closely at times. Some guy time might do Jax some good—and show Jo that she didn't have to be in charge all the time.

She was still frowning. "A guy thing?"

He squeezed her hands. "Let's just try it. Just an hour or two."

She thought for a moment, and then she exhaled. "Okay."

He grinned. "That's the spirit."

"You need to make sure you hold his hand when you're out in public," she said. "He's been known to run in the street or grab things he shouldn't."

He arched an eyebrow. "I've also been known to grab things I shouldn't."

She rolled her eyes. "I'll just take Kayla out for pie and coffee. That way if you need to reach me, I'll hear the phone and be able to answer right away."

"I won't need to reach you," he said. "We're just going to shoot hoops, not launch a dangerous military campaign."

"Well, leave your ringer on anyway, in case I want to check in."

After further back-and-forth, several instructions, and additional reminders to check his phone periodically, Gavin was given leave to take Jackson out.

When he strolled into the kid's room, Jackson seemed unsure at the mention of "hoops," but grew eager once Gavin told him to put on his orange shoes. Above his oversized orange and black Philadelphia Flyers jersey, his green eyes were large, his brown hair bouncing with his movements. After putting on their winter coats, they piled into the car.

"We're having some guy time," Gavin explained on the drive over. "Just us men."

"Just us men," Jackson repeated as he rocked in the back seat, twisting the plastic clothing hanger he liked to hold.

"That's right," Gavin said, smiling.

"Hand. Jackson. Just us men."

Gavin did a double-take, staring wide-eyed in his rear-view mirror. "That's right, Jackson! Good talking." He hadn't heard him say that much all at once before. Of course, he was still calling Gavin "Hand" instead of his name, but after a few corrections, they'd all just accepted it. The four of them knew who he was talking about, anyway.

The outdoor court was illuminated by bright white lights in the dark evening. They had the court to themselves, though some teenagers loitered at the adjacent park. Shrugging off their coats—Gavin knew that despite the cold, they'd warm up quick enough with the exercise—he showed Jackson how to throw the basketball so it was more likely to hit the net. The kid had probably experienced basketball in gym class, but Gavin couldn't imagine they'd had the staffing to give him as much one-on-one time.

Jackson laughed when the ball flew in the air, whether it landed back at his feet or bounced off the rim and sent them chasing down the shadowy court. Gavin laughed, too. The past couple days had been stressful. He'd felt torn between his duty to keep his professional life separate from this personal one he'd been building with Josephine. He knew a promise was a promise, but guilt cramped his gut when he wondered what would happen when the evaluation period was up next week.

All these weeks they'd been seeing each other, Josephine hadn't once asked him what was happening on her case from the district's end. He knew she was meeting with her advocate, but she didn't discuss the details with him. She'd kept the boundaries up, same as he. Maybe his guilt was for nothing. After all, their feelings had still grown at the beginning when they were duking it out at the meeting.

Anyway, maybe once the numbers were in front of her, Jo would accept the new placement for her son. She wanted data, hadn't she? Something to show where he belonged?

After an hour, Jackson grew tired of shooting and dribbling and chasing, so they put back on their coats, gathered up the ball, and headed for the car.

There hadn't been that many baskets made that day, but under their clothes they were both sweaty and satisfied. Slinging an arm around the kid, Gavin walked alongside him.

Nodding at his jersey, Gavin said, "Maybe we should go to a Flyers game sometime, buddy." His dad had taken him to a hockey game or two as a kid, and though he hadn't been able to follow it, it'd been fun to be among the raucous crowd and watch the players skate furiously down the rink. He wondered if Jax would enjoy all that fast action and movement, the puck speeding along the ice.

"Oh!" Jackson shouted, and because Gavin didn't know how to respond, he repeated the sentiment. "Oh!"

"Oh!" Jackson said, bobbing his head.

A gaggle of girls was sitting on one of the park benches. As the two of them passed by, they giggled and turned away.

"You'll get that," Gavin said sagely. "Sometimes they're just as haughty when they're older, too."

"Girls." Jackson turned to look at them. "Girls, girls."

Gavin grinned.

"Girls haughty," Jackson said loudly.

"Yeah," Gavin said. "That's the God's honest truth."

They got in the car, and on the way home, Gavin put on the radio and Jackson rocked against the backseat in time with the music.

"Music," the boy said, and this time Gavin knew what that meant.

"Maroon 5."

A few minutes later: "Music."

"Still Maroon 5. I'm playing you the whole album, buddy. Don't tell your sister."

Truth be told, Gavin didn't know how he would do in the new class. None of them did. But if Jackson couldn't tell them, they had to follow the data, didn't they? What else could they go on?

# CHAPTER 36

*J*o had to admit Gavin was right. Taking Kayla out, just the two of them, was what Kayla needed—what both of them needed.

At a local coffee shop that served rich, sugar coma-inducing desserts, they ordered two slices of thick pumpkin pie drizzled in caramel along with hot teas.

After they'd each taken a bite of pie and moaned over how good it was, Jo said, "I have a confession to make."

Kayla paused with another bite en route to her mouth. "What?"

Jo was sheepish. "I've liked having you home these past few days. I don't like the reason why, but… I've missed you, honey. *Law and Order* isn't the same without you."

The corner of Kayla's mouth turned up. "They still catch the bad guys."

"Yeah, but it's not as satisfying." She leaned forward to rest her chin in her hand as she studied her daughter. "You know, Kayla, you're really a beautiful young woman."

"*Mom,*" Kayla protested, but by her blush and the smile she tried to hide, Jo knew she didn't mind hearing it. Even in worn jeans and a black shirt with some unidentifiable band on it, Kayla was gorgeous—and, of course, way too good for what's-his-name.

"I say young *woman* because I know you're growing up," Jo continued. "As much as it pains me to admit sometimes."

Kayla's forehead crinkled. "Are we about to have a sex talk?"

"God, no," Jo said quickly, then added more carefully, "But I think we should have the college talk."

Kayla was taken aback. "Really?"

Jo nodded. "I think it might be time to unearth that box of brochures from the cabinet and start looking through them."

Kayla's jaw dropped. "But the stuff with Jackson isn't settled."

"I know." Jo took a sip of hot tea. She was anxious to learn the results of the evaluation next week and finally settle on a placement for her son, whose troubled behavior wasn't improving. In addition to the aggression he was displaying at school and occasionally at home, he'd taken to biting his own arm when he was upset—hard enough to leave teeth marks, and sometimes even breaking through the skin.

Jo thought of Sadie Yates at last Sunday's support group meeting. Her teenage son, Toby, was now in a temporary residential program. His aggression and self-injurious behavior had gotten to the point where they were unable to manage him at home, for both the safety of his siblings and himself. It was not uncommon with kids or adults in the autistic community, where mood swings, impulsivity, misunderstanding, and the environment sometimes mixed to ill effect. Still, Sadie was a black hole of guilt and despair, as Jo imagined she herself would be. And more and more she was imagining it, as Jackson grew bigger and stronger and more hormonal with puberty. If they couldn't find the right environment where he could thrive during the day, chances were more likely that he would lash out at someone else or himself, to a frequency or intensity she wouldn't be able to manage.

But Kayla had been right when they'd argued before: there would always be something. That box of college brochures was growing, and Gavin's mother's warning about junior year had galvanized her. "We should at least set a date to open it and start looking through them," Jo said to Kayla across the table. "Maybe after Thanksgiving week? Of course, I don't have to help, if you'd rather look through them yourself and—"

"No," Kayla said quickly. "I want your help."

Jo smiled, full of sweet pie and a hot drink and such love for her daughter. She pulled out her phone. "I'm putting it on the calendar for the Saturday after Thanksgiving. Box Day." She was pleased to see no messages from Gavin, and proud that, despite her nerves at Jackson being out with him alone, this was the first time she'd checked her phone. Well, there was a time in the parking lot, too.

As Jo pocketed her phone, Kayla said, "I have a confession to make, too."

Jo looked up. "Oh?"

"Yes." A smile played on Kayla's lips. "I maybe don't think your boyfriend is the worst person I've ever met."

Jo laughed. "Can I tell him you said so?"

"Noo..." Kayla shook her head vehemently. "I don't want him getting a swelled head."

"Good point," Jo said.

WHEN THEY PULLED into the driveway back home, Gavin and Jackson were sitting on the porch step, listening to music on Gavin's phone, Gavin bouncing his leg and her son swaying side-to-side and wringing his hands in delight.

Both their faces were damp with exertion, but Jackson looked satisfied. Most importantly, he was still in one piece.

"Okay, you were right," she admitted after they'd all gone inside and taken off their coats, and the kids had dispersed to their respective corners of the house. "That was good to do."

Gavin smiled and kissed her on the nose. "You're cute when you're admitting I was right."

She narrowed her eyes at him. "Don't push it."

It'd grown late, so they ate sandwiches for dinner. Kayla's friend Misty invited her over, and Jo shooed her out the door, thinking it'd help her mood even more.

"Tell Fiona thank you for all the happy hour invites," Jo told Kayla. "Tell her I'll come out... eventually." She probably wouldn't—what would they talk about?—but she was grateful for the other mom including her anyway.

It was still a half-hour before Jackson's bedtime, but his eyelids had grown heavy, his posture droopy. Playing basketball had worn him out. Jo guided him to a quick shower while Gavin cleaned up the kitchen table.

As she tucked the boy in, he was already falling asleep. She shut off the light and closed the door, making her way to the master bedroom, where she heard Gavin rustling around.

Though her bathroom had a toilet stashed to one side behind a door, the room itself was wide and open, without any separation from the bedroom. Through the archway she could see Gavin standing at the sink, splashing water on his face.

"Do you mind if I grab a shower here?" he asked. "I got pretty sweaty when we were out."

"Sure."

In the master bathroom, the counter held his-and-her sinks with a wide space between. At the sink Jo didn't use, Gavin had begun stashing a few items—a comb, a toothbrush, an extra tie. He hadn't stayed overnight yet, but he was at her place frequently enough he'd started to make himself at home in small ways.

His taking out Jackson—that had been a large way. No man had taken out Jackson like that since he was a toddler, and as much as she'd worried about it, she was grateful—not just for the alone time with Kayla, but for what it meant to her son.

"Thank you for what you did today," she said as Gavin walked to the shower stall and turned on the water.

"No problem." He ran his fingers under the spray, testing the temperature. "I'd love to do it again. I had fun."

She smiled. "So did he. I can tell."

"You know," Gavin said, adjusting the water, "I know you said to hold his hand, but we walked to the court side-by-side and he did fine."

She started. "What?"

"I don't think he needs the hand-holding," Gavin said. "He's thirteen."

Jo's eyebrows drew together. "I specifically asked you to hold his hand."

He glanced over at her. "It was fine, Jo. He didn't run off."

She exhaled, exasperated. "Gavin, you need to hold his hand while you're out. I know you said he did fine, but it could've just as easily gone the other way. And if you'd been near a busy street…"

"We weren't." He shrugged. "And he seemed like he knew to stay with me."

"You don't know that."

"And you don't know it's not true," he retorted, sounding almost as patronizing as he sometimes had at those IEP meetings.

She glared at him as he pulled off his sweaty shirt and tossed it to the floor.

"Look," Gavin said, softening his voice. "I'm just saying that maybe you could give him some space from time to time, some room to try new things and prove you wrong."

Jo crossed her arms. "Are you trying to tell me how to parent my kid?"

"No," Gavin said. She knew that he knew she was annoyed, but he pressed on. "You're an awesome parent, nobody doubts that. But I'm saying it's okay for Superwoman to hang up her cape from time to time."

She rolled her eyes and shook her head. "What does that even mean?"

Gavin unbuttoned his jeans, pushing them off to puddle on the floor and stepping out of them. "It means that you're not always great at letting other people try new things with him."

Jo opened her mouth to retort, but then her gaze dropped to Gavin's muscled legs. Standing there in navy boxer briefs, the shower steam building behind him, he was like some fantasy she'd had back when she thought her dating days were done. But he was here, in the flesh.

"God!" she exclaimed.

Startled, he looked over. "What?"

She bit her lip. "Could you just… put your clothes back on or something?"

His eyes widened. "Why? Do I smell bad? Are you kicking me out?"

"No. It's just that I'm trying to make a point about you not telling me what to do, and I can't do that when I'm thinking about…" She flushed.

After a beat, he grinned. Which was unforgivable.

He shook his head, chuckling lightly. "Naw, I think I'm going to leave my clothes off."

"You're a jerk," she said. "I knew it from the start. Could you at least be less attractive when you're annoying?"

Ignoring the shower—which still ran, steam gathering in the room—he walked a few paces to where she stood by the sink.

He was slow enough to seem casual, but with all the nonchalance of a stalking lion.

"Josephine…"

"Hmm?"

"You seem overdressed, all of a sudden."

She folded her arms tightly against herself. "Well, what would you suggest? Since you seem to have all the answers tonight."

"I would suggest you take off your clothes. Right now."

Despite his younger age, he had a way of bossing her around that belied his years.

"Fine," she snapped.

"Fine," he echoed, laughter dancing in his voice.

As his arms encircled her, she said, "I just want you to know that—that you drive me crazy."

He chuckled low. "The feeling is mutual."

So this was opening her life to a man. The chafing opinions and the friction between their bodies. The heated arguments and the hotter nights. The intrusions, the passion that made her clutch his shoulders as steam filled the room and their mouths met. She had to hold on to something when she was with Gavin, always, because he took her to a place no one had reached, not for a long time.

AFTERWARDS, they lay in bed holding each other.

Jo had her head against his chest, lightly stroking his skin. "I know you're right about Jackson," she said. "In *some* ways. Maybe not the hand-holding, but he's changing. He's growing up. It's just that I don't think you get how much advice I've gotten since he was small. I've had to harden myself to it."

"Okay." He brushed her hair off her forehead and tucked a curl behind her ear. "I'm sure it can be overwhelming. But I think most people—like most of the people at the district—have Jackson's best interest in mind. There are people with degrees in this stuff." He paused. "I'm just trying to help."

"Well, get in line." She exhaled. "I mean, I know we need some assistance, I do, but... It's like nobody agrees why Jackson is so different or how I should feel about it." She tugged a sheet over herself and turned to her side.

"When he was young," she started, "I was supposed to get on the floor with him and act natural. Then I was supposed to do flashcards with him or give him candy when he got a word right. We got into school, and his therapist said he didn't need a speech device because he had some words—but then two months later another one's telling me he needs one to communicate more fully, he's frustrated, that's why he hits me sometimes and why couldn't I see that?" She pushed her hair off her face. "And then all the health stuff... I was supposed to give him pure oxygen or fish or vitamins with names I couldn't pronounce. But no yogurt because it had dairy—which, by the way, was the only food he ate from the age of four to about six."

"Okay," he said, but she was on a roll.

"And meanwhile everybody was telling me that their cousin's babysitter's sister is on the spectrum, and do I want them to email me more advice? And people are telling me they're sorry, like he just got diagnosed with a terminal illness, and others are saying I'm a special person, and God only gives you what you can handle. And so by implication I should be able to handle this. But here I am barely showering, and eating all my meals in the car to and from appointments, when I remember to eat..." She swallowed over the rawness in her throat. "And all through this, this person whose life is making ours so much more confusing and challenging and stressful and weird, he just wants to be a kid. And I love him so much I'd walk into a burning volcano for him, and I don't tell any of the other parents or therapists or well-meaning others to screw off, even though I want to a lot of the time."

He exhaled. "I'm sorry, Jo."

"Sometimes I don't need any more advice," she said, meeting his eyes. "It's why my confidence as a parent is so riddled with bullet holes. Sometimes I just want someone to watch my kid for an hour so I can wash my hair or do some work or watch something terrible on Netflix. Do you get that?"

His voice was low. "I get that." He added, "I mean, as much as I can."

She sighed and rested her head back on his chest, suddenly exhausted.

"One question," he said. "Would it be sexist if I said Jackson could stand to hang out with another guy more?"

"Yes."

"Then I'll just say I think Jackson could stand to hang out with someone cooler than his mom occasionally. Someone like me."

She smacked the back of her hand on his arm, but his reflexes were too quick; he grabbed her hand and held it, intertwining her fingers with his.

"Was that foreplay?" he asked. "Are we going to have round two of hate sex? Because I've got to say, I'm up for it if you are."

"In your dreams," she shot back. But then she wriggled closer to him.

# CHAPTER 37

*G*avin knew his parents had reservations about his relationship, but he intended to get them used to Josephine and her family. He was Dina Steinberg's son, after all; he knew how to wear people down.

That Thursday, he strategized his plan of attack with Liz and Ben over the phone.

"Just announce you're inviting her over to their place," Liz suggested. "Don't let Mom get a word in."

"Obviously," Gavin said. "I plan on launching a surprise offensive. What else?"

"Invite the kids, too," Ben said. Liz had put her husband on speaker so he could participate. "It'll put them on their best behavior."

"You mean remind us all to act like adults." Gavin smiled. "Good thinking. Have I told you lately that you're my favorite brother-in-law?"

Ben was Jewish like the Steinbergs, so their parents hadn't protested his sister getting serious with him. But Liz and Ben were sympathetic to Gavin's plight of falling for someone who wasn't from their faith. Moreover, Liz knew the ins and outs of his mother's psychology as well as he did.

"Why don't you invite them to—" she started before Gavin finished the sentence with her. "—Shabbat."

"It's brilliant," he added. "She'll be too guilty to say no."

Straight from work, he went to their place without calling first.

He knocked and opened their front door to his dad vacuuming and his mom sorting the mail.

They both looked up at him. His dad killed the vacuum.

"I want you to invite Josephine and her kids to Shabbat dinner this Friday," he said without preamble.

His mother paused, a stack of mail in her hand. "*This* Friday? As in tomorrow?"

"Yes."

The two glanced at each other.

"You don't need to silently confer about this," Gavin said, exasperated. "It's *Shabbat*. Let's be welcoming."

Dina gave her husband a small nod before meeting Gavin's eyes. "Okay."

"Good." He pulled a folded piece of paper out of his pocket and handed it over. "Here's her number. Call her tonight and invite them. I'll tell her to expect your call."

"Do they like challah?" his dad asked.

"Everyone likes challah," Gavin said.

Ray shrugged and nodded, agreeing.

*Victory is mine*, Gavin texted Liz and Ben as he left their house.

When Dina called, Josephine accepted the invitation, and late Friday afternoon Gavin arrived with the three of them for Shabbat. He hadn't told Josephine about his parents' reaction to their relationship, and he didn't intend to. She would just be uncomfortable—or, worse, fear that they were right, since she'd shared some of the same reservations herself. His parents would get over it. They were being stubborn. It ran in the family.

His mom opened the door. "Welcome." She'd dressed nicer than usual for Friday night dinner, wearing a burgundy blouse and black skirt, and even a few pieces of gold jewelry.

"Hi," Josephine said. "Thanks so much for having us."

"Come in, come in," she said warmly.

His dad stood behind her, similarly dressed up in slacks and a tucked-in shirt.

"So this is the crew," he said, taking in the kids. Gavin was glad his parents were making an effort to not only be presentable, but friendly.

"This is Kayla," Josephine said, gesturing to the teenager, who stepped forward with a shy smile and shook Ray's hand.

Dina put a hand to her own cheek. "My, you are gorgeous."

Kayla blushed and smiled sweetly. "Thanks."

Ignoring Kayla's outstretched hand, Dina pulled her in for a hug.

Gavin put an arm around Jackson and stepped forward. "And this is Jackson."

"Oh." Dina smiled and said, a little loudly, "Hello there." She looked between Gavin and Josephine. "Does he—does he say hello?"

"Hello there," Jackson repeated.

Josephine laughed. "He does. Sometimes it just takes a few extra seconds to process. Right, Jackson?"

"Right, Jackson." The kid wore a dark turquoise Philadelphia Eagles hoodie, one end of the drawstring frayed from being chewed on during the drive over. His green eyes were large as he looked around the unfamiliar home. In his hand, the clothing hanger he gripped for security rotated in his grasp.

His father grabbed Jackson's hand and pumped it up and down. "Cute kids," he said to Josephine. "Very cute kids."

Gavin felt a weight lift off his chest. This was going to work.

After a few minutes of small talk, where Kayla stood awkwardly and Jackson flicked the mirror in the entryway, Dina ushered them into the dining room.

"Has the sun set yet?" she said hurriedly.

"Not yet," Ray answered.

The dining room was filled with the warm, buttery scent of his father's freshly-baked challah. The table was also dressed with lemon chicken, julienned vegetables, garlic mashed potatoes, and a small bowl of cranberry dressing. Plates of his mother's best china were laid out, with goblets at each seat. A couple bottles of good wine sat on the sideboard. Gavin had to hand it to his parents; they'd gone all out. Guilt was a powerful sous-chef.

Turning off the lights, his dad lit the candles while his mother sang the blessing over them.

*"Baruch atah, Adonai Eloheinu, Melech haolam, asher kid'shanu b'mitzvotav, v'tzivanu l'hadlik ner shel Shabbat..."*

They fell into silence after the blessing. Then Ray gestured to the spread. "Let's eat. I know we've got starving kids here." He winked at Gavin.

They all dug in. Jackson was skeptical of the dishes, but he took seconds, then thirds, of the challah.

Josephine had brought his speech device, and it sat beside him at the table.

"Bread," the device chanted. "Bread, bread, bread."

Gavin's dad sat to one side of Jackson. He nodded appreciatively at the machine. "I could use one of those here," he said. "Maybe it would help me get a word in with Dina."

"I heard that, Ray Steinberg." Dina turned to Kayla. "Your mom tells me you're a junior in high school."

The girl swallowed a bit of chicken. "Yes."

"Have you thought about colleges yet?"

"We're starting to," Kayla said.

"Well, there's still time." Dina smiled at Josephine before

looking back at the girl. "But if you'd like to come visit the university one day, I'd be happy to show you around campus. I'm not sure if your mother told you, but I work for the dean."

Kayla looked to her mother, who gave an almost imperceptible nod.

"Thanks," Kayla said. "I'd like that."

Jo smiled. "Thank you. That's a very nice offer." She turned to give Gavin a warm look. He smiled back. She was very pretty in a white blouse that draped in front and a black pencil skirt, which she claimed was too tight but he thought hugged her just fine.

"So you met our son at work," Gavin's dad said to Josephine.

"Yes." She laughed and took a sip of wine. "Never expected that to happen."

"He's a good worker, Gavin," Ray said.

Gavin leaned over to Josephine. "He has to say that. I paid him."

"No, but it's true!" Ray gestured with his fork. "So does he still need to send you work emails? Does he sign them 'xoxo'?"

The two of them exchanged embarrassed smiles.

"Not really," Josephine said to Ray. "We're actually nearing the end of the school's evaluation of Jackson. When it's through, Gavin will notify me. I'll meet with my advocate and the district again, but not with your son."

"And what happens then?" Ray asked.

"They'll decide the most appropriate class for him," Josephine said.

Gavin's gut twisted. He set down his fork.

"But what if there's not a class for him there?" his dad pressed.

Josephine's gaze flicked to Gavin before she answered. "Then we'll ask the district to pay for private school."

This was the first Gavin had heard of this. Did she really think the public school couldn't meet Jackson's needs?

"I'm sure there's a class in the district for him," he said. "There are a lot of really talented, highly-trained teachers who know what these kids need."

Jo looked at him, a slight frown tugging at her lips as he realized, too late, that his voice had slipped into that calm, assured tone he used with parents at meetings.

"Maybe," she said, and took a sip of wine.

# CHAPTER 38

$\mathcal{O}$n Monday afternoon, Jo was researching Gnome Countryside in Pennsylvania for a client when someone knocked on the door.

Jo answered it to find Holly at her doorstep.

"I need an intervention," Holly said as she entered.

"Oh?"

"It's that song!" Holly threw up her arms. "The one on the game Sean and Paul and Abby have been playing? The one that's driving me crazy?"

Jo laughed and closed the door. "You want me to stage an intervention for your family?"

"No." Holly shook her head. "Worse. I need you to stage it for me."

"What?"

Holly wrinkled her nose. "It drove me crazy for weeks, with them playing the game and humming it all the time. But now it's like... I think I like it?"

Jo laughed again, walking over to move couch cushions so they could both sit down.

"It's like it's brought us all together," Holly said as she

collapsed onto the couch. "One of us will hum part of it, then another will finish. It's sick. Now instead of them annoying me, we're just annoying everyone else around us."

Jo shook her head, curling her legs underneath her. "No, I don't think I'm going to stage an intervention. That sounds kind of cute."

Jo had been in a good mood since Shabbat on Friday. She'd been surprised at how well it'd gone, between the kids and Gavin's parents. Nothing had broken, the Steinbergs enjoyed meeting Kayla and Jackson, the bread was excellent. She could tell Gavin was surprised, too.

There was that moment when Gavin had sounded like a mouthpiece for the school district, but Jo reasoned he had to say things like that at his job so much, it was a knee-jerk reaction. He didn't mean to lecture her.

Holly was humming the song to her, Jo still laughing, when her phone rang.

"Just a second." She stood up and stepped a few feet away, thinking it was a client, before she saw the caller.

It was Jackson's school.

She answered quickly. "Hello?"

"Ms. Palladino?" a female voice said.

"Yes."

"This is Jen at the nurse's office."

Jo tensed. "Yes?"

"I'm afraid there's been an accident."

Jo's heart leapt into her throat. "What do you mean?"

"It's Jackson. It's—"

"Is he okay?" she blurted. "Where is he?"

The nurse paused. "He's okay, it's just... He broke his arm."

"Oh God." The blood drained from Jo's face and her heart started to hammer.

"There was an incident in the class," the nurse continued.

"Jackson got frustrated and he punched a wall before his aide or the teacher could intervene. That's when it happened."

"Oh my God." Her heartbeat pounded in her ears. "Where is he?"

"He's on an ambulance on his way to the hospital. They'll be waiting for you there."

Jo ended the call. Raced to slip on shoes. Choked back tears.

Holly was standing by the door, her face concerned. "What happened?"

"It's Jackson." Jo grabbed her purse and spun to the door. "He's hurt."

"I'll drive you," Holly said.

ON THE WAY to the hospital, Jo tried to remain calm and breathe, but her hands trembled. To imagine the pain Jackson must be in —and the fear he might be feeling riding in that ambulance...

"It's going to be okay, Jo," Holly said. "It's just a broken arm, not a broken—"

"Back? Head? Not this time." Jo sucked back a sob.

Before finding a parking spot, Holly dropped her at the emergency room entrance and Jo sprinted inside.

After interrupting a nurse at the front desk, she was led into a back room—though she could've found the way without medical staff. Jackson's keening could be heard all over the unit.

"Where is he? Where's my son?" Jo darted past the nurse, following her son's voice.

Jackson sat on an exam table, surrounded by four medical personnel and his teacher, Jeannie. His face was red and perspiring, so much that his brown hair was damp around the edges. His expression contorted as he hollered and wrung his hands. Or one of his hands. The other arm hung limply at his side.

"We can't get him to calm down to treat him," a nurse shouted over the noise. "Can we give him something?"

"Yes. Please." Tears stung Jo's eyes. She ran over to Jackson and hugged him from behind to hold him. Squeezing her arms tight around him, she whispered into his ear, "It's going to be okay, honey. Mama's here."

It took a few tries, but they eventually got him to swallow a small cup with medicine. A few minutes later, his cries grew less frequent. He leaned back against Jo, his head lolling on her shoulder. He smelled like sweat mixed with the scent of whatever grape-flavored medicine they'd given him. Underneath, of course, was that hospital scent, like plastic curtains and band-aids. Together it could've made a signature cologne. Eau de emergency children's hospital visit.

The shock of the situation was making Jo's brain off-kilter.

"Hey, Jax," she mumbled into his ear, stroking his good arm. "Everything's going to be okay."

In response, he turned his head and gave her an expression that looked slightly loopy as medical professionals moved around the room, preparing their equipment.

"I rode with him in the ambulance," Jeannie said.

Jo looked over. The fair-headed teacher stood in the corner, her face pale and her arms crossed, like she was holding herself together.

A flare of anger ignited inside Jo. This had happened at school. This woman's class. How could she have let this happen? Somebody wasn't doing their job, and now her son had a broken limb.

"I didn't want him to ride alone," Jeannie continued. "Especially with his communication challenges. Ms. Palladino, I'm so sorry. He's so quick and—"

"At least you did something right," Jo snapped. "Because you sure as hell aren't doing anything right in that classroom."

The woman looked ashen. "We tried to tell you. He gets frustrated."

Jo closed her eyes and forced herself to take deep breaths in and out. She didn't want to see anyone from the school district now. Her protectiveness over Jackson felt so large and difficult to contain, it was almost feral. "Please leave," she said without opening her eyes.

"I'm sorry, Ms. Palladino," the woman whispered. But when Jo opened her eyes, she was gone. There came a pinch of guilt, but then Jackson put his hand to her cheek.

"Music," he said.

Jo was confused for a second, then realized there was music playing from somewhere, softly. Christmas music, even though it wasn't even Thanksgiving until later that week.

"Bing Crosby."

She took his hand from her cheek and pressed her lips to his palm. "My sweet boy…"

Jackson had grown much calmer, lethargic with a goofy grin on his face. Jo helped the nurse coax him to a reclined position so they could set the bone.

"He'll be in a cast for some weeks," the doctor, a young man with spiky black hair, explained during the procedure. "It'll be itchy and uncomfortable. But the good news is it's a simple break. He should heal nicely."

Jo nodded. Forced herself to breathe. Asked all the questions she could think of and wrote the doctor's answers in a little notebook in her purse.

Holly must've let Kayla know, because she showed up a while later. Jo didn't know how long they'd been there; time was moving strangely.

Jackson was put in a cast, and the doctor called in pain medication for them to pick up on the way home. She and Kayla stood on either side of Jackson, their arms around his waist, as they walked out of the hospital. Though the boy was sluggish, he could walk fine. But Jo wasn't ready to let go.

Holly was waiting out front to drive them home. As they walked together to her car, the full fury hit Jo's system. The school was going to pay for this.

"Josephine!"

In a daze, Jo looked across the lot to see Gavin jogging towards them. He was dressed for work, in a tie and slacks. His face was pinched with worry.

Holly took Jo's place helping Jackson inside the car while Jo stood ten feet away, waiting for him.

"Hey," he said as he reached her. "I came as soon as I heard. Is Jackson okay?"

"No." Her voice shook. "His arm is broken."

"Oh, God, Jo. I'm so sorry." He cast a look at the backseat of the car, where Jackson pressed his face to the glass. "What happened?"

"He put his fist into a wall." She sniffed. "I'm going to tell Carrie Stiepler about this, and I'm going to give them hell. How dare they let this happen to my son? How *dare* they."

"Jo…" Gavin swallowed and looked at the gray sky above, then back down at her. "They have the data."

"What?"

"They have the data showing that Jackson would be better suited for that other classroom."

Jo flinched like she'd been slapped. "You knew about this?"

"I heard through the grapevine," he said. "But when I came clean about us, Charlene made me promise not to share any district information with you, because of the conflict of interest."

She stepped back. "How could you not tell me this?"

He reached a hand to her arm, but she pulled out of his grasp. *How could he?*

His eyebrows drew together. "I wanted to tell you. I felt

guilty about it. But I gave her my word at work. You didn't seem to want to discuss the details with me. And you have Carrie…" He shook his head. "I'm sorry, I should have. That class he's in is ending, anyway. They've got to do some reshuffling due to budget cuts."

Jo's heart thudded in her head, a fury so great it threatened to burst out of her ears like some cartoon animal. "*What?*"

"That class is over," he said, paling as he saw the anger on her face. "It was always going to end. We knew it from the start."

He tried to move closer, tried to take her arm again, but she shook him off. Hard.

"No." Moisture stung her eyes. "All this time, all this energy and money I've poured into trying to figure out where Jackson belongs, and it never mattered. You just decide where the kids go, don't you?" This entire fall, there'd been greater forces at work that limited their options. And they hadn't told her. *He* hadn't told her.

"Not me," he said quickly. "Jo, not me."

"But it is you!" she shouted. "You work for them, you would've placed Jackson in that new class if I'd said yes that first meeting, even if it'd been the wrong choice."

"I'm just trying to do my job," he said quietly. "I didn't mean for this to happen."

He'd kept something from her—for his job, sure. But kept it from her all the same. She loved her kids more than anything, and now Jackson was hurt through the district's negligence. If she had known that class was going to end, she would've made a different choice.

Jo remembered something—Gavin's words the other night at Shabbat, and then the weekend before, when they'd been in her bathroom.

Rage stung like bile at the back of her throat.

"*Maybe he's trying to tell you that he's ready for a change,*" Jo said, echoing his words. "*You're not always great at letting other people try new things with him.* What was that, Gavin? You trying to prepare me? Convince me you and the district still know best?' God." She dropped her head back and uttered a harsh laugh.

"That wasn't it, Jo." He shuffled his feet. "Okay, I might've been trying to prepare you, yes. But I believe what I said."

"I'm sure you do." She looked back at him. "I thought you cared about him. About me."

He winced. "I do."

"Obviously not."

"Bullshit, Jo. You know I do." He raised his voice. "Doesn't the fact that I risked my job to be with you mean anything?"

"Hardly. Especially since I'm realizing you weren't all that off the job when you were with me."

"That's ridiculous!" He paused and took a deep breath. "Look, I know you're upset Jackson got hurt. That must've freaked you out. It would've freaked me out. It *did* freak me out. Let's get him home, and then we can talk about this later."

Jo shook her head. "You're not going home with us."

"Jo…"

"Oh, am I not being calm or rational enough for you, Mr. Steinberg?"

Jo watched his face tighten as he moved from frustrated to nearly as angry as she was.

Good. Because she was as mad as hell.

"This, this right here?" Gavin moved a finger between the two of them. "This doesn't have to do with Jackson. Not entirely. You've been looking for a reason to prove to yourself that I'm not committed to this when I've shown you time and time again I am. What's it got to take to prove it to you?"

She huffed. "To be on our side for once. To care about me enough to put my kid above your job."

"I do care about you," he said. "Both of you. Very much."

"Well, Jackson's got a broken bone that tells a different story."

Gavin's mouth opened, but no words came out.

Jo pivoted on her feet and walked to the car.

"Wait…" he finally called.

Jo had only one thing left to say to him.

"My son is everything to me," she said. "You were just a mistake."

# CHAPTER 39

Gavin tried to call Josephine later Monday night, then again on Tuesday and Wednesday. He sent her a couple texts, too.

She didn't return any of his messages.

He didn't know what to do. She was so angry. So angry she probably thought he couldn't tell she was terrified, but he knew. Gavin never wanted Jackson hurt like that, he sure as hell didn't, and hearing the news had sent him flying to the hospital. But Gavin's own fear had given him clarity. He couldn't keep what he knew about the data from Jo. He'd planned on telling her before he even saw her, his job be damned.

But then once she knew, she didn't want to talk to him again. Her son's broken bone would set and heal, but their relationship felt damaged by multiple fractures.

By Thanksgiving, there was still no word. After the success of last week's Shabbat, his parents had invited the Palladinos to come over for the holiday meal, along with a neighbor couple and one of Gavin's cousins who lived locally.

But he went to his parents' alone, and his stomach dropped when his mother glanced behind him.

"Where is...?" She trailed off.

"They're not coming." Gavin swallowed. "Jo and I... I'm not sure we're seeing each other anymore."

He felt a sharp pain behind his ribs at having to admit it, and, as if intuiting this, Dina's hand flew to her own chest. "What happened?"

"We had a fight." He shrugged his jacket off, hanging it up in the coat closet by the door. He heard the sounds of laughter from the guests gathered in the dining room. He couldn't remember ever feeling this emotionally wrung out. If it weren't Thanksgiving, he wouldn't have even come. "Jackson hurt his arm at school, and it came out that I knew some information about his placement that I'd been told not to share with her."

Dina's voice was low. "Oh, my. I'm sorry to hear that."

His dad appeared beside her, his grave face showing he'd overheard. "Did you send her flowers? Women love roses."

"I'm not going to send her roses, Dad." A shiver of irritation coursed through him. "If she doesn't want to hear my apology, it's not going to help if I say it with flowers." There was a thin line between being persistent about making amends and borderline harassment. As much as he felt panicked at the thought of losing Josephine—never teasing her, never kissing her, never holding her again—he wanted to respect that line.

"Is Jackson okay?" his mom asked.

"I think so."

"She loves that boy."

"I know she does." Gavin felt a dull ache then he didn't expect. Along with the panicky feeling of his relationship slipping away, there was a secondary pain. He'd grown close to Jackson, and even Kayla recently. If he and Jo were breaking up, would he be able to see and talk to them again?

His friend Tanner's voice echoed in his mind. "...a woman with kids is a package deal. Think about whether you're ready for all that, all at once."

At something in his face, his mother reached out and squeezed his arm. "Don't worry, honey. She'll call. Give her time."

LATE THAT NIGHT, as he lay in bed, his sister Liz texted him.

*Mom told me what happened. You know our family is like a sewing circle. I'm sorry. I know you cared for her. I've never heard you talk about a woman that way, actually.*

He read the text and deleted it. Not that he was mad at Liz, but he didn't want to have to read that last sentence again. Because it was the truth, and it hurt like hell.

He closed his eyes and rolled over in bed.

FRIDAY MORNING, when the rest of the world was out shopping Black Friday deals or sleeping off their Thanksgiving meal, he met Angelo at the gym.

Gavin chose the chest press to start his workout. As he got into position, Angelo added the usual amount of weight to his barbell. But it wasn't enough.

"Put more weight on," Gavin told him.

"You sure?"

"Yeah." He wanted to feel something. With a shrug, Angelo added another twenty-five pounds to the barbell."So Carrie's going after the district about the Palladino kid getting hurt. In case you hadn't heard."

"I hadn't heard." He'd mentioned to Angelo that he and Jo weren't speaking, but only because he didn't want to be asked about her. He still didn't.

His sweaty hands gripping the bar, he grunted and pushed

up, his muscles hardening and straining under the weight. Then he lowered the bar, his arms shaking.

How could he be so stupid to keep this from her, to jeopardize what they had? Liz was right; he'd never felt what he had experienced with Josephine. What he wouldn't give for a chance to start over with her.

Angelo sat on his own bench. "Carrie's a pitbull. She'll get the kid whatever they want. Private school, even."

Not looking at him, Gavin asked, "Can you add more weight?"

"You're already doing more than usual. Let's take it easy."

"I can do it."

Angelo didn't move, so Gavin looked over to find his friend squinting at him. Exhaling, Angelo stood and walked over to the barbell.

"Anyway, I know how Carrie operates. We went to high school together. Even tried to go out with her—*tried* being the accurate word." He laughed. "She'll get them what they need. You know, in case you were concerned."

Gavin didn't respond. He'd figured as much, but it hurt to be reminded of Jo, even alongside what would normally be the amusing notion of Angelo and Carrie Stiepler in the same room, let alone a romantic scenario.

Angelo started adding extra weight, the metal clanking on the barbell. "You're not going to be able to lift your arms to use a phone tomorrow."

Gavin gritted his teeth, squeezing the barbell in anticipation and thinking of all the unanswered messages he'd left. "That's fine by me."

Angelo stopped. "No."

"What?"

He slid the extra weight he'd added back off the barbell. "You're doing this to punish yourself. Like some kind of penance. I don't want any part of this, man." He put the weight away.

Gavin grunted. "Just add more weight, Angelo."

Angelo sat on the bench beside him and leaned forward, resting his elbows on his knees. "I know you're going through some stuff. I know you're waiting for her to call." He raised his eyebrows, waiting for Gavin's slight nod.

Gavin looked away. Focused on the barbell in his grip.

"You need to get out of here," Angelo continued. "Cool off. Go home and look at pictures of puppies on the internet. Shit, even llamas."

Gavin's voice was hard. "I'm fine."

"You're not."

But he knew just how right Angelo was when his phone pinged from his pocket and he released the barbell, springing up.

His heart hammering, he prayed to God it was Josephine. Even just a short text to say she was okay or to call him a jerk. Anything.

But it was an email. A work email.

Jackson Palladino's evaluation was complete.

# CHAPTER 40

*From: Gavin Steinberg <gsteinberg@psd41.org>*
*To: Josephine Palladino <momof2masterofnone@hmail.com>*
*CC: Charlene Matthews; Carrie Stiepler*
*Date: Saturday, November 25, 4:13 a.m.*
*Subject: Meeting to go over Jackson's evaluation*

*Josephine,*

*I just wanted to let you know that the district has concluded its evalua-tion of Jackson. As you know, Charlene Matthews will be meeting with you on behalf of the district at a time that's convenient for both of you. I'm copying both her and your advocate, Carrie Stiepler, on this email. Please let Charlene know a time that works for you and Carrie.*

*Charlene will be your point of contact moving forward, but know that if you have any questions or concerns, you can reach me at any time.*

*I would very much like to hear from you.*

*Gavin*

*From: Josephine Palladino <momof2masterofnone@hmail.com>*
*To: Gavin Steinberg <gsteinberg@psd41.org>*
*CC: Charlene Matthews; Carrie Stiepler*
*Date: Saturday, November 25, 8:31 a.m.*
*Subject: Re: Meeting to go over Jackson's evaluation*

*Mr. Steinberg,*

*I understand the evaluation has been completed. I will contact Char-*
*lene about a time to meet.*

*In the future, please send any information you have for me directly to*
*Carrie Stiepler.*

*Josephine Palladino*

# CHAPTER 41

*G*avin's hand was on her fridge.

Jo tried to ignore it at first. It was a tracing that Jackson had done weeks ago, one of the first ones of Gavin's hand that had come home in his folder from school. Jackson himself had placed it on the fridge, between a tracing of Kayla's hand, the school lunch calendar, and a coupon for a local Chinese restaurant. It'd been easy enough to deny its existence —and those messages he'd sent, which she'd deleted without listening to or reading—as she tended to Jackson those first few days, giving him pain meds and encouraging him to rest as she worked and ate quick snacks to keep her energy up.

On Thursday, they'd picked up a premade Thanksgiving meal from the grocery store, and Jo had tried to put on a not-depressed face for the kids as they had a quiet dinner at home. Mostly she had ended up eating her feelings smothered in gravy and cranberry sauce.

But when she'd gotten that school email from Gavin, she strode to the fridge, ripped the hand tracing off, and shoved it in the recycling bin.

There. She'd recycle her experience with him, too. Take it

and transform it into a life lesson. Don't fall for men who are in positions to screw over your child. Maybe don't fall for men, period.

But by Saturday afternoon, the tracing appeared back on the fridge.

Jo looked around, but Jackson was on the couch, watching television. Had he done this? Either that, or they had a poltergeist. Kayla was gone at the movies with Misty, and Jo wasn't that sleep-deprived to move objects unconsciously, was she?

Sighing, she pulled the paper down and quietly slipped it into the recycling bin again.

She'd been working on her laptop at the table for twenty minutes when Jackson wandered in.

"Do you need something, honey?"

Rocking on his feet, he looked around the kitchen. He'd gotten more used to the cast, and even started to feel proud of it, especially once Kayla had drawn a couple designs on it.

His gaze landed on the fridge.

"Hand," he said. "Hand."

Pretending like she didn't know what he meant, Jo walked to the fridge and pulled it open. "Do you want a yogurt? Or maybe an apple. We also have juice boxes. What about a juice box?"

Jackson walked over, but instead of peeking into the fridge, he put his hand on the empty spot on the fridge door. Then he looked at her, his voice intent. *"Hand."*

Jo swallowed, knowing at some point she'd have to explain this in a way her son could understand. That time had just come a lot sooner than she'd anticipated.

She touched Jackson's shoulder and looked into his eyes. "We're not going to be seeing Gavin much anymore," she said. "We had fun with him, but he's busy with work now, and he won't—" She bit her lip as a sob threatened to spill out. She'd been having those lately, little hiccup sobs, bright bursts of emotion she had to fight to keep in.

Jackson moved away from her, walked to the recycling bin, and fished in it until he found the tracing. It was wrinkled and might've smelled, but he carried it back to the fridge.

"Hand," he said, and stuck it under a magnet.

Jo pressed her fist to her mouth, struggling not to cry. It was hard enough to process her own loss, but now she would have to carry Jax's, too. They'd seen so many people come and go through their lives—therapists, teachers, Neil—and it never got any easier. Her heart broke a tiny bit at each goodbye, not knowing if Jackson fully understood that this might be the last time he'd see someone he'd come to depend on each day. The weight of having to process that sadness for him was heavy on her heart.

And now Gavin…

What was she thinking, pretending like she could bring a man home and it wouldn't ultimately harm her kids?

She heard the door open as she made her voice more firm.

"Jackson," she said, pointing to the god-awful hand on her fridge. "He's not our friend."

His brow lowered. "*Hand.*" It was as if she'd turned off one of his favorite Taylor Swift songs mid-chorus, the amount of betrayal he'd packed into that single syllable.

Jo snapped. "Jackson, for the love of God, get that off our fridge!"

Footsteps thudded as Kayla ran in.

"Mom?"

Jo breathed hard, staring at her son. But he didn't relent. Worse, he put a hand over Gavin's hand, as if to protect it.

"Jackson!" she yelled.

"Mom!" Kayla said. "You need to go take a nap."

"I don't need a nap."

"Take one anyway."

~

THAT NIGHT, Jo lay awake, quietly sobbing into her comforter. Her thoughts grew morose and then philosophical as the night waned, finally settling on inconsequential and strange.

Was she still within her rights to deem this a rebound relationship, eight years in the making? And if so, was she strong enough to call it that so casually in conversation with others, like Gavin hadn't been a life raft to her?

At midnight, the door softly squeaked open. Footsteps padded across the carpet, and the mattress trembled as someone climbed up beside her.

"Hey," she whispered.

"Hey," Kayla said.

Jo was both grateful Kayla had come and sad and ashamed she needed her own daughter's comfort. This wasn't a teenage breakup. She was an adult. She would get over it.

Kayla curled up on her side, burying her face in the crook of Jo's elbow, like she was the one who needed comforting. A minute later, Chuck jumped up on the bed too, curling into a fluffy ball behind Jo's knees before Kayla finally spoke.

"Remember when we went out for frozen yogurt that one time, after Jackson got the intellectual disability diagnosis?" she mumbled into Jo's elbow, making the spot warm and moist.

"Sure." Jo sniffed. "You said you were surprised Jax hadn't been diagnosed as cute, too. You were a smart little eight-year-old."

"And you said his cuteness would be chronic. You explained that meant he'd probably carry that diagnosis all his life," Kayla added. "You were right."

"I know," Jo said. "Some things you don't need a crystal ball for."

"He is still cute," Kayla said. "Even when he's annoying."

Jo sighed, thinking of the fridge. "But he can be as stubborn as anything."

Kayla paused. "You can cry in front of me, you know. It won't make you seem less mom-like."

"Good to know." Jo wasn't about to start crying in front of her daughter. There was a reason snails and clams had shells. She didn't want to become all soft and slimy. She might never go back.

"Do you think we could find *Law and Order* on some channel right now?" Jo mused.

"Of course," Kayla said. "It's magical like that." She reached over Jo to find the remote for the TV on the bedroom wall. "I'll find it."

As Kayla surfed the channels, the volume turned low to not wake Jackson, Jo grew philosophical again.

"Maybe you were right," she said. "About men not being able to handle this special needs stuff and eventually bailing. Gavin certainly couldn't handle it."

Her eyes focused on the TV, Kayla said, "He didn't leave."

"What?"

"He didn't leave," she said. "You told him to go."

# CHAPTER 42

*G*avin would go through the stages of grief. It wasn't like this was his first breakup, as much as it hurt like hell. He'd pedal across denial, burn with anger at himself and the situation, breathe through the suffocation of sadness. But Jo had left her mark in places he didn't expect.

She was the most real woman he'd ever been with—so forthright and funny, honest and caring, beautiful and accepting of the messier parts of life. It was going to make dating anyone new difficult; there was no way any woman could compete. And it was soon making his position with the district impossible.

Because even before the breakup, he'd found himself slipping into the terms and tone of his sales job. After all, he was trying to calm parents, assure them that their children were in good hands—and most of the time, they were.

When he knocked on Charlene's door the Wednesday after Thanksgiving, he could tell she knew it was coming. It was written all over her face.

"Sit down, Gavin."

"After you hear what I'm about to say, you may not want me to," he said.

"Sit down anyway."

He collapsed into the chair in front of her desk. Unlike the time he'd come here to admit his feelings for Josephine, he wasn't nervous. He wasn't anything.

Defeated, maybe.

He exhaled. "I sucked at this job."

Charlene lifted one shoulder, let it drop. "You didn't. You were organized, on time, polite, and efficient." She leaned forward. "You helped these kids, Gavin. Those IEP meetings weren't all discouraging. Some of those kids are speaking more, or reading, or learning to love school. You helped make that happen." She paused. "Remember how I told you when you started that this was like putting together a giant jigsaw?"

"And all the pieces have to fit together?"

"Yes." Charlene sighed and leaned back. "I lied. It's more like putting together one of those do-it-yourself bookshelves. Except you're missing half the instructions." She tapped her desk with her fingernails. "We're here to help these kids. You know that. We both could be making more money doing something else. But we're here. And sometimes we nail it. But sometimes..."

"I know." A weight pressed down on his chest. "It's those sometimes."

He thought of Josephine's face. Of Jackson's. What could he have done differently to prevent that boy from getting hurt? From not breaking his mom's heart?

Because he knew their relationship hadn't been one-sided. And if Josephine was hurting half as much as he was...

He shook his head. "I think I'll be better suited for something else."

"I think so, too," Charlene said. "I hope you find it."

"I'll give you as much notice as you need," he said.

"Luckily we've been trying to hire another coordinator. So I have lots of resumes. We'll be able to get someone new in here soon."

"Good." He shifted awkwardly. "I'm sorry about this."

She shrugged and gave him a small smile.

He swallowed. The thing he wanted to ask was something Charlene probably shouldn't answer, especially for the reasons he was asking. But he couldn't help himself.

"Have you, um, heard from Josephine Palladino?"

"We've been in touch," Charlene said. "We're giving her whatever she wants. The district can't afford to open itself up to litigation, and the fact of the matter is that Jackson's arm was broken while he was here at school."

"What does she want?"

"Private school."

He thought as much. "Do you know which one?"

She shook her head. "I think they're in the process of figuring that out."

FEELING ADRIFT, he drove to a nearby park after work, where he sat on a bench in the bitter cold.

Despite the temperature, there was an older woman there with a young boy. The boy looked about five, and both he and the woman, whose bearing seemed almost too classy for the park, had on winter coats, hats, and scarves dripping down to the ground. He watched them for a moment, noticing with a start that the boy spun in place while flicking his hands at the gray sky like he was on the spectrum.

After a few minutes of spinning, the kid started running towards him. Gavin sat up, assuming the child was going to launch into his lap. Instead, he reached a hand out to Gavin's chest and tugged on his tie.

Gavin laughed and looked down, realizing he hadn't

buttoned his coat, and the bright red tie had caught the boy's eye.

"I'm so sorry," the woman said as she reached the bench, out of breath from giving chase.

Gavin chuckled as the kid tugged once, then again, on the tie, his gaze fixed on it. "It's no problem at all."

"He loves red," the woman explained, and he was struck again by how elegant she seemed. She held herself like one of the department store ladies at the places his mom used to shop when he was a kid.

"Ethan," the woman chided gently as the tugging continued. "Remember what Grandma said about personal space."

Gavin looked down at the tie, then the boy, then the tie again. "You know," he said, taking his index finger and unknotting it. "He can have it." At the woman's surprised expression, he added, "I quit my job today."

"Oh. Well, I'm terribly sorry about that."

He draped the red tie around the kid's neck and watched his face light up. It made him happier than anything had in days.

"I'm not sure I'm sorry," Gavin said. "I don't know if I was any good at it. I worked with kids like..." He nodded to the boy, and waited for the woman's eyes to dawn with understanding. "But I couldn't always do everything I could for them, not like I wanted to." Thinking of how much success he'd had at his soul-sucking sales job before, he laughed harshly. "Thirty-two years old, and the one job I've actually been good at is parting people from their wallets." He sighed. "But I will miss the kids." One in particular.

Without speaking, the woman sat down on the bench beside him, carefully arranging herself. The boy was in front of them, the red tie twirling around as he spun in circles again. Gavin watched him, smiling sadly.

"You know," the woman started. "I work in a boutique clothing store. Sometimes people walk in, not knowing what they want. And, it may sound strange to you, but I've developed a sense of sometimes knowing just the thing they need."

He looked over at her and their eyes met.

"I think you need to work for these kids. I feel it in my bones." She paused, then reached into her pocketbook, where she extracted a small square of paper and a pen. "My niece teaches at a private school for special needs children. It's called Arietta Academy. They're looking for a development officer. If you believe in these kids, and you're as good at parting people from their wallets as you say you are, maybe they're looking for you."

# CHAPTER 43

$\mathcal{T}$he next time Jo was able to attend support group, everything had changed—not just for her, but for other members of the group.

Now that it was December, everyone was in the Christmas spirit. Especially Jackson, whom Jo had kept home since the accident and wanted Christmas music to be played constantly throughout the day. He was bored and restless, only satisfied by Bing Crosby, but Jo couldn't bear the thought of him returning to that classroom. In the meantime, Carrie and Charlene Matthews were communicating by phone and email. The three of them were scheduled to meet later that week.

It had been almost two weeks since she and Gavin had broken up, and she sat quietly in the circle at support group, hoping no one would notice her dour mood and ask her to talk.

Sadie and Tom Yates, on the other hand, were doing better than she'd seen them in months.

"Fill us in," Holly said as she, too, noticed the couple holding each other's hands and smiling tentatively.

"Well, Toby's been in this residential program," Sadie began. "And it's been hard—it killed us to send him there, even though he's been going to the day program and we knew the staff were skilled and loving." She waved her hand. "But, anyway, it's been a couple weeks and Toby has been doing so much better. They've got him on a routine, and they're helping him learn to manage his behaviors." She sniffed as tears filled her eyes, which she wiped away with her fingertips. "I'm sorry, I cry at everything. Anyway, the rest of us have been in therapy, and taking some much-needed time for ourselves. We visit Toby as much as they let us, and it's been—it's been so good." She smiled through her tears. "The staff thinks that at the rate he's going, we'll be able to bring home soon, definitely by Christmas." She looked over at Tom. "I know it won't be easy—it's never easy—but that will be the best gift ever, having our boy back home with us for the holiday."

"That's awesome," Dirk said. "I'm happy for you all."

"Wonderful," Jackie agreed.

Jo smiled, feeling the Yateses' joy spread around the room. "We need a toast," she said. "Where are the brownies?"

"Way ahead of you," Holly said, bringing the plate of treats over. They each took one and raised them to the air, toasting to Toby.

"Well, Maisie and I have been making little Christmas ornaments together," Jackie said. "Little knit stockings and things like that. We've been selling them at a few church bazaars."

"Fun," Holly said. "I bet Maisie loves that."

"She does. She's a very crafty girl, that one." Jackie pumped her eyebrows. "In more ways than one." They laughed, and she added, "The only other thing that's going on is I've become addicted to Dirk's YouTube channel."

"YouTube?" Tom asked. "What channel?"

Dirk hung his head, smiling sheepishly. "So I just started doing videos where I share stuff that's going on with Deenie and our family. Just funny things, like the super creative way she lines up her toys, or stuff we're working on." He shrugged. "It's been a great way to process what we're going through, celebrate her successes, and connect with others."

"He's gotten a lot of subscribers already," Jackie said. "We can say we knew him when."

"Send us the link, Dirk," Holly said over a big bite of brownie in her mouth. "We all want to see."

"Okay, sure."

Their eyes drifted to Jo then, as if following a beacon. She realized with a start that as much as she was trying to pretend like everything was okay, they saw through her defenses.

She took a deep breath, figuring she had to let out a little truth, at least so they'd stop looking at her like that. "It's been a hard couple weeks," she began. "I started a new relationship after not dating for, you know, *ages*. But it ended up not working out." She paused. Swallowed. "But I'm trying to see the positive in it, what lessons the situation brought me. This person, he told me that I wasn't always great at letting people in or welcoming change. And I know it's probably about the divorce, about my ex-husband... having that person who I relied on the most leave. But, what this person said, it's true. It's all true. I was so mad at him, but I—I realize those *are* things I need to work on."

"You can say his name, Jo," Holly said softly.

But she couldn't. She really couldn't. It was still an open wound, not yet scarred over.

"And there's this other thing," she continued. "About taking care of myself. Because I wasn't, before all this. Not really. Part of me wants to let that slide again, because, really, didn't this whole experience show me that maybe it's still not a good idea to let people in or try new things?" Her voice shook. "But there's a reason I don't want to forget, and that's my daughter. I don't want her making the same mistakes."

Jo stopped, took a deep breath, and waved her hands in front of her face. "Anyway, I'm not a public crier, so I'm going to stop talking now. I'm fine. Really."

Jackie reached over and squeezed her shoulder, but Jo studiously avoided looking into anyone's eyes, afraid doing so would release the floodgates she'd been working day and night to construct. Instead her eyes landed on the hands of Sadie and Tom Yates. Their palms were clasped together, a union through good times and bad.

Jo knew there was a truth she would never admit aloud. In her entire adulthood, there'd only been one Gavin—one person who'd made love and made her laugh the way he did, a connection that made the other men, even the father of her children, fade into bland memory. What were the chances she'd ever find that again?

If she were honest, he had probably been it for her.

# CHAPTER 44

The day after Gavin quit his job and met the woman and her grandson at the park, he called Arietta Academy. They were indeed looking for a development officer, and with Gavin's experience in sales and education, would he be interested in coming for an interview?

The following Wednesday he found himself on Arietta Academy's small campus, a collection of wood cabins set back in a forested area on the edge of the western Philadelphia suburbs.

They'd had the season's first snow the evening before, and the trees surrounding the school were dusted lightly with snowflakes.

His tour guides included the school's director, Donna, an older Italian-American woman, and Steve, a younger white guy who was the senior development officer at school. The school was expanding, so they'd opened up a second position to raise money among donors in the community.

Donna and Steve took him around the grounds to get a feel for the place. He liked it immediately—the trees; the open, natural atmosphere—but once they were inside the buildings, he became aware of how special it was.

They strolled by a class of elementary-age kids in a circle. At quick glance, he could tell that some of the kids were autistic, but there were other disabilities and learning differences in the classroom as well. As Gavin watched, a girl in a wheelchair pounded on a drum while a boy across from her sat cross-legged on the floor, playing a keyboard.

"Is this music class?" Gavin asked.

"Not exactly," Donna said in her accented voice. "At Arietta, we like to incorporate music in all we do. We find that the children love it and are more eager to learn. We're able to teach them to expand their language through songs, or count using drum beats. We've even used musicals to teach them American history."

"That's awesome," Gavin said. "I can totally see that. Everybody loves music. I knew this kid who..." He stopped at the twinge of pain that came whenever he thought of the Palladinos. He started again. "This boy I worked with before, he's thirteen, and he loves music. Taylor Swift, Maroon 5, whatever. He struggles in school, but it's like music is his happy place."

Steve nodded. "We've got some kids like that."

They showed him a couple more classrooms, including some with older kids. Gavin couldn't help but picture Jackson in a school like this, holding a triangle or singing along to a math song.

"This is amazing," he said.

Donna and Steve exchanged a smile.

"More people should know about this place," Gavin continued. "I mean, it looks like you're really reaching some kids."

"We like to think so," Donna said.

"If I was here, I'd shout about it from the rooftops," Gavin said. "Or sing I guess. I bet if more people in the community knew about this, they'd want to support it, too. I mean, you could have these kids do concerts, maybe videos online..." He shook his head in amazement. "I've met parents who are at the end of their rope, who've tried everything, but their kid still isn't learning. Or he's acting out at school. And it's so frustrating. It's like the parents are angry and scared and don't know what to do—and neither, by the way, does the school system sometimes—and the kid can't always tell them." He thought of Josephine's face. "To think there's a place like this…"

The two exchanged another look Gavin almost missed in his wonder. He'd been a music fan all his life, and working in special education had shown him how many kids needed help. Maybe this could be a place where he could finally be real— where he could strip away some of the bullshit that'd clouded his professional life. Sure, he'd have to shake hands and sweet talk donors, but here was something he could be passionate about. Shoot, he already *was*.

Did Josephine know about this place? Had she been here and seen what he was seeing?

"Mr. Steinberg," Donna said. "I've got a very good feeling about you. But what about you—Do you have any more questions for us?"

"Just one," he said. "Can you give me a brochure? I know a family that needs to know about this school."

# CHAPTER 45

That Thursday, Jo went to Jackson's school to sign the paperwork accepting the district's proposal to pay for her son to attend private school.

The idea had been growing on her, slowly, that this might be what Jackson needed, even if it meant a big change. Jackson could get more individualized attention, a radically different approach, an alternative atmosphere. After he'd broken his arm, the possibility had sunk its teeth in and held fast.

The meeting was just a formality, of course—Carrie and Charlene had hashed out the agreement that first week when she was home with Jackson—but Jo's hands shook as she entered the school building and walked to that room where she'd met with Gavin those three earlier meetings. Holiday decorations and kids' artwork festooned the walls, but she hardly noticed them.

Would he be at the meeting? And if he wasn't, would she pass him in the hall?

She didn't know what she would say if she saw him. *I miss you* were the first words that came to mind, along with three other words she only admitted late at night, when her pillow was cold with tears.

Her anger had dulled in the weeks since the hospital. She'd realized she'd been as angry at herself as anybody and blamed him for things that couldn't have been his fault. But still it would never work. It was a conflict of interest, same as it'd always been. Letting him into their lives had been a mistake and an emotional clusterfuck. She was still feeling the reverberations.

In the room, there were only Charlene and Carrie, a few handouts, and a couple blue pens. With trembling fingers, Jo signed the final paperwork.

"The district is always here if you want to look at more options," Charlene said. "We don't turn our back on any kid."

Carrie stood, put a copy of Jackson's paperwork in a folder, winked at Charlene, and said, "Neither do I."

They all shook hands, and Jo walked to the exit, waiting for elation to fill her. They hadn't chosen a private school yet, but chances were she wouldn't have to step into this school again. They were free to find a place where her son would thrive. Yet regret washed up around her heart.

There would never be any more meetings here with Gavin. Or conversations in this parking lot she now walked across—the spot where she'd first seen him as someone other than a suit, and where he'd made her feel more like a woman, like herself, than she had in years.

"Ms. Palladino!"

She looked over her shoulder. There across the lot was Jeannie, Jackson's old teacher. She wore a thick red-and-white holiday sweater and slacks, her kitten heels crunching on the gravel of the lot. She clutched something in her hand.

Jo felt a stab of regret. She'd treated the teacher unfairly at the hospital, too.

Jeannie reached her, giving her a tentative smile. "I heard

you were meeting with Charlene. I wanted to say goodbye. And to give you something."

"Thanks." Jo pressed her lips together. "Listen, that day at the hospital, I was mean to you. I know I shouldn't have been. I was upset and lashing out. But I know you're trying your best, and I appreciate that you stayed with Jackson in the ambulance."

"I know." Jeannie nodded. "I have a daughter, I understand."

"Good."

Jeannie paused. "For what it's worth, I did enjoy having Jackson in my class. He can be such a loving boy."

Jo smiled.

"Sometimes kids just need—a break," Jeannie continued. "Most of our kids do well in the district, but I know there are exceptions." She lowered her voice. "Not that you heard that from me."

"I didn't hear a word," Jo said, her smile deepening.

"Anyway," Jeannie said. "I also came to give you this." She handed Jo a brochure. Black with white music notes, the words *Arietta Academy* were written across the front in gold cursive script. "Have you heard of this school?"

Jo opened the brochure. It wasn't one of the names Carrie had given her on the list of schools. Maybe it was one of the newer, smaller schools the advocate had mentioned. "I'm not sure I've heard of it."

"You should go there and take a tour," Jeannie said, tapping the brochure. "They use a lot of music in their program."

"Oh?" Jo scanned the information. "Well, in that case, we will check it out. Thank you for this." She looked up. "How did you hear about this school?"

Jeannie colored. "Oh, someone gave me the brochure, and he —I thought it might be a place Jackson would fit in."

# CHAPTER 46

*G*avin arrived that Saturday of Hanukkah with a bottle of champagne in his hands, feeling more hopeful than he had in weeks.

He strode into the kitchen, where his mother was setting a salad on the table. "Put away the plastic cups and get out the wine glasses, Mom. We're celebrating."

The salad bowl clattered on the table as Dina took in her son's smile and her hands flew to her mouth. "Oh, I knew it! I knew she'd—"

The grin fell off Gavin's face.

Dina froze. "I mean, I... What are we toasting?"

"I got the job at Arietta Academy." He thudded the bottle on the table, his spirits falling. "It seemed like good news...at the time."

Dina stirred to life. "Oh, it is, it is!" she said in an overly high voice. She grasped her son and hugged him tight, the scent of her vanilla perfume a small comfort at least. "I'm so proud of you, Gavin. Your father's upstairs sick with a cold, but I know he's proud of you, too."

"You thought Jo had taken me back, didn't you?"

Still squeezing him, she said, "Hmm?"

He pulled back. "You thought this was about Jo."

She was sheepish. "You just seemed so happy."

"I am." He sighed. "About this. I feel like I've finally found the right job." He rubbed a hand down his face. "Look, give me a couple months, and you can set me up with any of your friends' daughters you want. I'm sure I'll find some woman I like enough to marry and procreate with eventually."

For a moment, Dina was silent. She turned her back to him, moving to silently whisper prayers and light the menorah before walking to the cupboard by the table to get the good wine goblets. Finally, she said, "I'm not setting you up anymore."

This was a surprise. "No?"

"No," she said firmly.

His eyebrows drew together. "Why not?"

"Because you're capable of finding a woman all on your own." She said the words slowly, like the notion was new to her.

He pulled out a chair and collapsed into it. "I don't know about that."

"I do."

They fell into silence again as Dina located the corkscrew, opened the bottle, and poured him a big glass of bubbly champagne. Then she sat across the table from him, her eyes meeting his.

"I've always said I wanted you to find someone who makes you happy. Preferably Jewish. And smart. And who doesn't wear shirts with fashionable holes in them. Could I find that woman? Sure. But I saw the way you were with Jo. With her kids. I never would've predicted that." Her smile was bittersweet. "It's taken me some time to acknowledge it, but maybe this isn't a choice a mother should make. Maybe only you can find a woman you'll love."

He grabbed the glass of champagne, downing half in a gulp

that fizzed down his throat, mingling with the knots in his stomach.

"I never told you I loved her."

"Oh, Gavin," she said. "You never needed to."

THE NEXT DAY, he met Tanner for brunch in downtown Philadelphia. Gavin reasoned that he should try to make an effort to go out and see people, even friends from his old job.

Over omelets, coffee, and orange juices, they blew through their usual points of small talk—football, the old company, new restaurants in town—before Tanner asked, "So what's new with you?"

Gavin considered not mentioning the breakup, but he didn't want to experience that moment where Tanner asked him about the woman he was dating. So he buried the news.

"Oh, I stopped seeing the woman I told you about," he said quickly, "but I just landed this really great job."

Tanner paused a fraction of a second, his coffee cup on its way to his lips. After taking a neat sip, he said, "Sorry about the woman thing," offhandedly, like he was apologizing for spilling salt on the table, before he raised his voice and asked, "So what's this big new job?"

Gavin smiled, grateful to talk about something that made him hopeful. "It's at a school called Arietta Academy," he explained. "They're out west, sort of back in the woods. It's a school for special needs kids, and they hired me as their development officer."

"Hmm." Tanner took another sip of his coffee, his expression blank.

"I'm actually starting soon," Gavin added. "Really looking forward to the change." For many reasons.

Tanner set his mug down and looked away. "That's interesting. I always thought you'd go back to sales." He looked at Gavin, his eyes a little hard. "I didn't even know you were looking. I would've helped hook you up with something better. Something with more money, at least."

Gavin laughed, trying to brush the money comment aside. "I wasn't looking long. I got a lead on this job, and I kind of just leapt for it."

Tanner's brows drew together. "You've been doing that a lot. Just leaping. That's kind of your thing this year, huh?" He chuckled, but it sounded harsh to Gavin's ears.

"Yeah, I guess I have," Gavin said slowly, wondering why Tanner seemed so bent out of shape all of a sudden. He knew his old buddy was gunning for him to return to his former position, but he didn't really expect Gavin to get back on that train, did he? There was a reason he'd quit. There were always reasons people quit jobs, and they didn't usually cease to exist down the line.

"Whatever, man," Tanner said, waving his hand like he was erasing Gavin's news. "I guess it's your life and you don't need anybody's advice."

Gavin shouldn't have asked, he really shouldn't have, but they'd already talked about football and the words just came out. "So what would've been your advice, Tanner?" He gave a short laugh, like the conversation was playful, and picked up his orange juice to take a long drink.

Tanner leaned back, hooking an elbow over the back of his chair, while he fixed his eyes on Gavin, appraising him. "It just seems like you've been so lost, man. Working at some random school and seeing some divorced woman with kids? And then you switch jobs, but just to another one of these schools?" He shook his head. "Come on, Gavin. You're better than some shitty nonprofit job and another man's sloppy seconds."

Gavin gripped his juice glass so hard, the pads of his fingers turned white. Carefully and ever so slowly, he set the glass down on the table. The alternative was smashing it so hard against the wood it shattered. Anger ran through him white-hot.

"Tanner," he began, his voice tight, "I don't know if you're unhappy with your own life choices, or you're so happy you think everyone should do what you've done, but these choices I've made? They're the ones I wanted to make. I hated working in sales. Hated it. I was just so good at it, it took me a while to realize it. If you like it, that's great, but it's not for me."

Tanner cleared his throat and put out a hand. "I'm just saying—"

"No, I think you've said enough." Gavin reached back and pulled out his wallet, extracting a ten and twenty. "I love working with special needs kids. They're some of the best people to be around, and, trust me, I've been around some real assholes."

He arched an eyebrow, waiting for the meaning to hit Tanner. Two seconds later, the man's jaw dropped.

Gavin stood and added, "And that woman I was dating? The one you called, what was it? *Another man's sloppy seconds*? I'm in love with her. I'd still be with her now, if she hadn't told me to get lost." He tossed the bills onto the table and turned. "See you around, Tanner."

They both knew he wouldn't.

Gavin pushed open the diner's exit door with force. Yet once the cold December air hit him, his anger dissipated with the cloud of his breath.

He was surprised that it'd taken him so long to realize Tanner was such a toxic asshole. He'd left his job almost a year ago, but meeting up with his old sales buddy had still kept one of Gavin's feet in that world—with its values and priorities, ones he no longer shared. Cutting loose his friendship with Tanner felt freeing, like now he could start over completely.

It wasn't as if he regretted working at his former job. The

sales experience had shown him what he was good at, and he'd built up skills he could now use at a position he found more worthwhile. It had all led him to this place.

Feeling too wired to get back in his car and drive home, Gavin walked the snow-crusted Philadelphia streets, taking in the holiday displays. With just a couple weeks until Christmas, the city was at peak festivity. Lit Christmas trees and leaping reindeer, jingling bells, giant curving candy cane archways, shops advertising golden boxes of chocolates or teddy bears adorned in red ribbon. The parallels between last year's December and this one came so easily that Gavin wasn't surprised when his feet led him to that storefront with the Christmas village, the one that last holiday season had spelled the end of his sales career and relationship with Ellie.

The tiny village was there again. A mother and her young daughter stood by the display, oohing and aahing, as Gavin paused to stare. Sure enough, the small train still circled the village with its little chugs and whistles. Santa in his red suit was on the same rooftop, delivering presents on his sleigh. The skaters still traversed the rink, impervious to the cold.

Gavin waited to be disturbed by the vision again, all those automated movements and frozen people. But instead, a grin tugged at his lips.

It was just a toy. A delightful one, even. Ellie had been right; it was cute.

It was the exact same Christmas village he'd seen last year. The difference was *he* was different. He no longer felt controlled by some timer or mechanized track. So much of what he'd done this past year had been his own choice, regardless of what anyone else had planned for him. Quitting his job, going to work at the school district, dating Josephine Palladino. He'd followed his gut, and that had led him down incredible paths he never expected. Especially with Josephine.

Despite his broken heart, she was still the best mistake he'd made when he went off the rails.

# CHAPTER 47

*J*o stood in the kitchen Thursday evening, tapping her fingernail against the fish tank. She watched Pickles and Prometheus swim contentedly in the water, living a peaceful existence free from goals and data, dating and heartbreak.

In those first few months after the divorce, while Kayla was at school, she'd put Jackson in the stroller and taken him to their local pet store. There was something soothing about that shop with its chirping birds, softly bubbling fish tanks, and faint smell of straw and seed. And Jackson had been so fascinated with the aquariums—that electric blue water where fish swam, their fins gracefully waving in the water, the miniscule bubbles they emitted filling him with such delight.

Years later, when Jackson was in school himself, Jo had brought home two little guys in an aquarium. She'd taught him how to gently shake just a few flakes of food into the tank—not too much; they were on their third Pickles—and push the lid back in place so Chuck didn't get any ideas. It was different keeping fish as pets versus just ogling them in a pet store. Yet the tank served as a reminder to Jo not only of her son's joy, but the knowledge that even in hard times, she could find peace in small moments.

The past two weeks had been full of research, phone calls, and tours to private schools in the area. She'd found a handful that would be appropriate for Jackson, and they'd visited classrooms to meet with the teachers and see how he responded to each environment.

It had actually been at Arietta Academy, the school Jeannie had mentioned to her, where Jackson seemed to belong the most. He loved the music, of course, and Jo saw an ease to him there she hadn't ever experienced. It was hard to predict the best environment for any nonverbal autistic kid, but one look at her son's face while sitting and singing with an Arietta teacher was enough to convince Jo to at least try it out.

Earlier that day, they had received the official letter of acceptance, and tomorrow she'd go to the academy to sign paperwork—there was always paperwork—and Jackson would be set to start the following Monday.

Despite what she'd said at support group, these past couple weeks she'd slipped back into her old habits of falling asleep in Jackson's paperwork. It was a necessary thing with this big step in their lives, but still she was more aware of her weariness now. In so many ways, being with Gavin had brought her back to herself—her body, her interests, her desires—and along with missing him so strongly it sometimes hurt to breathe, she was aware of a hollowness inside her, a place she needed to fill.

Calling Gavin was out of the question. She'd thought of it, of course, again and again. But he still worked for the school district and she was still a mom; the roles that had made their relationship come pre-baked with conflict were still there. And anyway she'd jumped into it all too quickly without thinking, like a toddler touching a hot stove. She doubted she'd ever find someone new, but if she did, she'd move more slowly, carefully, so she wouldn't have to feel this heartache again. She didn't need another catastrophe.

Yet she needed to take care of herself—if not for her own sanity, then for her kids. Tapping on the aquarium glass one last time, she made a quick decision and texted Holly. Then she walked to where Kayla was sitting on the couch with Jackson, the girl's cell between them and an earbud in one of each of their ears.

"I'm expanding Jackson's musical taste," Kayla explained. "I think he's ready."

"Okay," Jo said. "But you and I are going out tonight. To support group."

Kayla wrinkled her nose. "Support group?"

"Our personal support group, just the two of us. Wear something comfortable."

Kayla's mouth opened to respond, but owing to Jo's heartbreak, she didn't talk back.

Jo wondered how long that would last.

After Holly arrived, they donned coats and climbed into the car. The night was dark and bitterly cold, but inside the vehicle they were toasty.

"So what's our support group going to be like?" Kayla asked. "Is it going to be all like, here's how autism affects me, here's this weird thing my kid or brother did, here's how much of a jerk the rest of the world is?"

Jo smiled. "Something like that."

They drove west, past the brilliant twinkle of red, white, green, and gold holiday lights, until houses and businesses grew few and far between and the dark night opened up above their heads, brilliant stars dotting the sky.

They played music while they drove—Taylor and Adele and some of Jo's old '90s music, too. A blend of women singing and screaming and whispering about yearning and heartbreak, hurts and triumph.

Jo couldn't help but think of Gavin again. About how he was the reason she was doing this. It might not have worked between them, but he'd shown her something those weeks they'd been together. She meant to not forget it.

"Are we taking the long way there?" Kayla asked after half an hour. "Where are we going, anyway?"

"We're already there."

"Huh?" Kayla looked over at her.

"We're playing hooky," Jo explained.

"From what?"

"From life."

Kayla's eyes narrowed. "Is this because of the thing I said about you not having a life?"

"No, it's because you were right. Well, half right," Jo added. "You were right about the need to do something else from time to time. To blast music and just shut it all out for a while. So that's what we're doing."

"Okay," Kayla said. "I approve."

They drove on, music blaring and their cares blowing back.

"Kayla..." Jo started.

"Hmm?"

"Now that we're getting Jackson settled into a new school, we should probably figure out when we're going on those college visits." Despite the breakup, true to her word they'd opened up the box of brochures the weekend after Thanksgiving and had started slowly narrowing down schools. Jo bit her lip. "And, if I didn't say this before, it's okay if one of those schools—a place you want to go—isn't around here." She glanced over to see Kayla's eyes grow wide. "We'd be okay, if you, you know, wanted to go away for school."

"Okay." Kayla's voice was small, like she was close to tears. But then she sniffed. "I don't know if I do, though. I mean, somebody has to get Jackson off all that pop music."

Jo laughed. "Just think about it."

They fell into silence.

The ache came again. Jo knew it would, driving around like this. She remembered that first date when Gavin gave her flowers stored in the cup holder of his car. Driving around and learning about each other's lives. Kissing him in that dark carwash, the rest of the world washing away.

She missed him. So badly.

But she could do this—take care of her needs, play hooky from life. Tonight, in the future. She could do this with Kayla, probably with Holly, too. She could even do this alone. When she needed it—when she could slip out—the wind, the music, and the night would be there.

It wouldn't always hurt this bad. She hoped.

# CHAPTER 48

*G*avin was acclimating to Arietta Academy. It was his third day there, and he'd already gotten the rundown from Steve on the major donors to the school, met most of the staff, and danced with a nine-year-old girl to a Justin Timberlake song. So not his worst week.

It was Friday, and Steve was helping him gather supplies for his office from various nooks and crannies around the administrative cabin. Later, they had a dinner meeting with one of the founders of the school who wanted to meet Gavin.

"I think there's an extra printer stashed in the meeting room," Steve said.

They walked down a narrow hallway that smelled sharply of pine, Gavin a few steps behind the senior development officer. Artwork from the kids hung crookedly on the walls, interspersed with framed quotes on music or education.

"There's a parent registering her kid in there," Steve added, "but they won't mind if we just pop in."

Gavin was learning that Arietta was a place where nobody minded if you just popped in, and assumed you didn't mind, either. It was quite the adjustment from the school district, with its rigid rules and boundaries. He was starting to enjoy this new relaxed atmosphere. All the same, he was glad the individual bathroom stalls had locks.

Light filtered down the hallway from around the half-ajar meeting room door, and murmurs of two women conversing reached his ears—one voice clearly Donna, the director, with her heavily-accented English.

Steve reached the door first and gave a quick warning knock before pushing the door wide open in the midst of their conversation.

The corner of Gavin's mouth turned up. If this parent hadn't yet been introduced to Arietta's Pop In, this would be their first of many.

"Don't mind us," Steve said. "We're just popping in to find a printer."

Gavin reached the door as his co-worker was squeezing around the big meeting room table. Donna stood to one side, dressed in an elegant tan caftan and smiling and nodding at someone across the room.

Gavin turned to offer an apology to the new parent.

He froze.

It was Josephine.

She let out a small gasp, her green eyes growing large.

"Hey." He forced himself to breathe.

*She was here?* She was here.

Of course she was here. The brochure he'd taken and given to Jeannie to pass along, without saying it was from him. Because she'd hated him at the time. Maybe still did.

"Are you alright?" Donna asked her.

Gavin tried to swallow, but his mouth had gone dry. "We're just surprised. I used to work with Jo—Josephine's son."

"That's right." Donna nodded. "You're both from the same

area. Well, you can help Jackson and her feel even more welcome!" She turned to Jo. "Josephine, Gavin is our new development officer."

Jo took a deep breath. Attempted to smile. "Oh. Wow."

Gavin's gut clenched. What an idiot he was. He'd caught her off guard, but he shouldn't have been that surprised. He'd given Jeannie the brochure to give to her, after all. He knew there was a chance she'd check it out. He just hadn't known for sure if they'd even visit, and if they did, if their paths would cross.

Maybe he hadn't dared to hope.

So much for staying on the non-creepy side of making amends. *Way to go, Steinberg.*

"I gave Jeannie the Arietta brochure," he blurted, adding to Donna and Steve, "Jackson's old teacher. I just didn't know if it'd be a good fit." He paused and stared at Jo. "I hope that was okay."

She was still a moment, her lips pressed together and two spots of color in her cheeks that matched the thin, holiday-red sweater she wore. Then she smiled again, this time genuinely, her eyes warming. "Thank you."

His own mouth broke into a grin. "You're welcome." He still stood in the doorway, because if he moved any closer to her, he was afraid he'd grab her face and kiss her.

God, she looked so good. Her curly brown hair was longer than he remembered, and her face was more pale with the season, making the freckles across her nose stand out.

He'd missed her like hell.

He cleared his throat. "So how is Jackson?"

"He's good." She smiled more and nodded, even giving a nervous laugh. "Kayla's helping him expand his musical repertoire. On a related note, they're both now way too cool for me."

He laughed. "That sounds about right." He shifted his weight. "And how are you?"

Her smile dimmed. "I'm okay."

He didn't trust himself to speak, so he just nodded.

"So how are you liking Arietta?" she asked, her voice sounding breathless.

"Great," he said. "The school, the staff, the students—they're all pretty amazing. Definitely a more relaxed atmosphere."

Her eyes twinkled. "But not relaxed enough to keep you from wearing that tie?"

He looked down and laughed, shaking his head. "Nope. Not yet."

Jo opened her mouth, like she was about to say something else, but instead she bit her lip. "I should go. The kids…"

"Sure. I'd walk you out, but Steve and I have a meeting in a few minutes." He mentally kicked himself. Old habits died hard, but Jo had given him no indication she would've wanted him to walk her to her car. She didn't seem angry like before, but if she wanted to pick up where they'd left off, she would've called him during the past month.

"That's fine. I'll just…" She grabbed her purse and smiled at Donna and Steve before moving to the door without another word.

He stepped to the side as she brushed past him on her way out of the room, making the mistake of inhaling her floral amber scent as she passed.

As if shot by a stun gun, he watched her retreating form as she walked down the hallway and exited the building.

Somewhere in there, Donna and Steve started talking to one another, but he was only vaguely aware of it as he heard the sounds of Jo's car starting and pulling out of the lot until it finally disappeared into the cold night.

"Oh," Donna said, "Josephine left her coat. She will be freezing!"

Gavin turned around to see the director pluck the purple

winter jacket from a chair. "I'll ask Jackson's teacher to put it in his school bag on Monday afternoon, yeah?"

Steve nodded.

"Don't bother." Gavin held out his hand. "I know where she lives. I'll bring it by her place tomorrow."

# CHAPTER 49

"*Oh my God.*"

Jo had repeated those words five dozen times since she'd gotten into her car at Arietta Academy. She was in no condition to drive home. She was close to vomiting. Or fainting. And she didn't keep smelling salts in the car.

Gavin didn't work at the school district anymore? And he worked there? At Arietta? Where they were going to be?

This was… God, she didn't know.

She'd spent the past month thinking that even if she'd come to forgive Gavin and see his side in what had happened at the district, he still worked for them and there was still a conflict of interest. But now that wasn't the case. It made her feel like what she believed had all been an excuse.

*An excuse?*

Of course, he worked at Arietta now, but in a different capacity, not with students. He had no say or power over her son's education, only how much the school raised.

And he looked really good. As cute and clean-cut as ever. Knee-knockingly so. Even with the tie. Maybe especially with the tie. How had she ever hated the tie?

She needed to talk to someone. Figure this out.

She called Kayla, who answered on the second ring. "Yup."

"Honey, can you watch Jackson for a while more? There's somewhere I want to go."

"Sure. Where are you going?"

She couldn't believe she was doing this. "Do you know if Misty's mom is at happy hour tonight?"

Kayla paused. "I think so…"

"Good. So… I think I'm going to do that."

"O-kay…" Kayla sounded unsure, but then added, "Have a margarita."

Maybe she would and maybe she wouldn't, but one thing was for sure: she'd be talking about her old boyfriend. That is, if she could figure out how.

She gave Fiona a quick call. The fellow mom was surprised to hear from her, but happy that she wanted to come out for drinks with her and her friend Patricia. They were already on their way over, and Jo would meet them there.

At the restaurant, Jo stepped out of the car, only realizing when she felt the winter chill that she'd left her coat back at Arietta. Still, she strode into the place, where among a few couples, some loud Christmas decorations, and terrible pop holiday songs playing, she spotted Fiona's magenta-streaked hair. Obviously between the margaritas and hair dye, Fiona was winning the cool mom contest.

"Hi," she said.

"Hey there!" Fiona slid off one of the tall chairs surrounding their table and gave Jo a hug. "It's so great you could finally come!"

"Yes, well… thanks." Jo found a seat, a little embarrassed.

Across the table was an Asian-American woman with a ready smile.

"I'm Patricia," she said. "I'm so glad to meet you. My Devon is in your Kayla's math class."

"Oh, Devon." Jo recalled the name. "That's right."

Fiona leaned forward. "I told Misty to tell Kayla you are always welcome at happy hour. I just didn't want to put pressure on you—you know, because of the situation with your son."

Jo inwardly cringed at Jax being referred to by his "situation," but then Fiona waved a server over. "Do you want a drink? I think you need a drink. We're having peach mojitos."

Her mouth watered. "Sure, a peach mojito sounds great." She might've needed something stronger, but she didn't want to become a suburban mishap, the middle-aged mom who couldn't handle her liquor and also men.

"So how is Kayla?" Fiona asked. "Is she driving you crazy? Because Misty is driving me *crazy*." She elongated the word so it was at least four syllables, and Jo wondered if the peach drink on the table was her first.

"We were just talking about how cute our girls were when they were little." Patricia shook her head wistfully. "And how sweet. Nowadays, Devon acts like she can barely stand me."

Jo laughed. "So it's not just me, then? Though it's been better with Kayla since she broke up with this boy…"

Fiona clucked her tongue. "Oh, that boy was bad news."

"We heard all about that," Patricia added. "Just because our girls hate us, doesn't mean we don't occasionally get the hot gossip."

Jo laughed again. She really should have done this sooner.

"So," Fiona said, picking up her drink, "aside from the teenager stuff, how are you?"

"I'm…" An image of Gavin popped into Jo's head. She struggled to find the words—it was all so complicated—but then she realized it was actually pretty simple. "I'm weird. I just saw my ex."

At the same time Patricia asked, "Your ex-husband?" Fiona said, "Kayla's dad?"

"No, no, he's in Arizona," Jo said. "I just ran into the man I dated this fall—did Kayla mention him?"

Fiona looked embarrassed. "I might've overheard something while snooping on the girls one time. He worked with your son?"

"Sort of. It's just, it was a complex situation and he's younger and never had kids and I'm divorced and I wasn't sure—I'm not sure—if there's still something there or if I'm even ready again for...for..." She trailed off as the women leaned forward, latching onto one thing only.

"He's younger?"

"How young?"

"Not too young," Jo said, exhaling. "Thirty-two."

"That's kind of young," Patricia said, and Fiona playfully smacked her arm.

"No, hear me out," the woman said. "If forty is the new thirty —and I think that's something we've established in conversations here at happy hour many times—he's only really, what? Twenty-two?"

"It's not *that* much," Fiona argued, swirling a straw in her mojito. "It's more like seven years. So really this thirty-two-year-old is like twenty-five."

"And twenty-somethings are not ready to settle down and be responsible," Patricia finished. "Did he scram when things got too serious?"

"Not exactly." Jo had been the one to tell him to go, as Kayla pointed out. Although maybe he would've left her eventually; Neil certainly had. Maybe her breaking up with him was pre-emptive, a prophylactic sort of ditching.

"I bet he couldn't deal with the kid thing," Fiona said. "Not long-term at least. Maybe he'd toss around a ball with them, but he wasn't really there when you needed him."

Jo remembered the night Gavin had been over and Jackson

had the accident. The way he'd stayed and cleaned up, even though he might've been uncomfortable.

Her heart was beating loud, like something was banging to get out. At some point, a mojito appeared in front of her and she took a long drag of the chilled peach concoction. "I think he was... there when I needed him."

*Jo, can't you see I'm just a schmuck who's trying to deserve you?*

Fiona and Patricia were staring at her. "So what was wrong with him?"

"His job made our relationship weird," she said. "But he has a new job now." Boy did he ever. "But also—also he had opinions about my son, about how I should let him do this or that and be more independent. We argued about it."

The other women paused, then Patricia said, "Yeah, you'll get that."

"My husband does that *all the time*," Fiona said. "All this mansplaining. It drives me crazy."

Jo took another drink, guzzling the cold cocktail so fast it gave her a headache. She pinched the bridge of her nose as she asked, "So that was normal?" Not something to ditch someone over?

"Totally normal."

"Annoyingly so."

Jo felt a rush of something. Relief, maybe. Or confusion. Gratitude? "I'm sorry it's taken me this long to meet you guys," she said. "I don't know why I didn't earlier." She did, sort of. She'd thought as the only special needs mom, she wouldn't relate, that isolating herself from others outside her community was a necessary protection against thoughtless comments and pain. Maybe it had protected her at times. But she had vastly underestimated the satisfaction of having other women complain about men and teenage girls with.

Fiona rested her forearms on the table, her bracelets

clanking together. "So this thirty-two slash twenty-five-year-old... Was he good in bed?"

The mojito must've gone straight to her head, because as Jo lowered her hand from her face, she couldn't keep from smiling.

The women burst out laughing.

"He was good in bed," Patricia said, nodding and laughing.

# CHAPTER 50

The next day, Gavin knocked on the Palladinos' door. He had Josephine's coat over one arm. He was praying. Hard.

The door opened.

It was Kayla.

At the sight of him, her eyes widened.

Gavin waited for her to sneer and say something mean. Maybe to tell him to get off her lawn.

Instead the teenager exhaled a long, relieved breath.

"It took you long enough," she said.

"I'm sorry. It wasn't for lack of trying." He paused. "Is she home?"

"She's out buying clothes with Jackson," Kayla said. "But they should be home soon. He was on his speech device this morning and kept typing 'orange shirt,' so she took him shopping. She's going to let him pick out his own clothes, even if they're all that god-awful orange color. Her words."

Gavin smiled. "I'm glad."

Kayla's eyes narrowed slightly. "You better be here to try to get her back."

"I am."

"Then you can come in and wait."

He followed her inside, closing the door behind him.

# CHAPTER 51

*T*hey were leaving the store with two orange shirts, orange socks, and, amazingly, even a pack of orange underwear.

"At least you'll always be able to spot him," the clerk at the checkout said.

Jo laughed. "That's true."

It wasn't even Christmas yet, but already it felt like the new year. Her insides fluttered with fresh excitement when she recalled seeing Gavin the day before—and what she was going to do about *that*, she hadn't yet decided. But it was also the adventure of starting a new school, because Jax seemed to feel it, too.

As she watched him choose the items, she mused about how much he'd grown. Jackson was a different kid than he'd been in elementary school. He was her height, and soon he'd be taller. He had hair in places he didn't have six months ago. His moods and tastes were changing. She couldn't keep up, and he couldn't always tell her. But she was trying to be better about listening.

They drove home, Jax requesting music with the new buttons they'd added to his speech device.

She pulled the car up to the house, got out, and walked to the door with Jackson trailing her. The street was full of parked cars; the neighbors must be having a holiday party.

She was anticipating Kayla's laughter when they showed her the orange clothes as she unlocked the door. But as she nudged open the door with her elbow, she froze.

A man was standing in her living room.

Gavin Steinberg was standing in her living room.

Her jaw dropped.

"Hi," he said.

From behind her, Jackson caught sight of him. "Hand!"

The boy pushed Jo aside and ran to him in his orange shoes and new orange shirt and threw his arms around him. "Hand!"

Gavin grunted at the impact, but then put his own arms around the kid and gave him a squeeze. "I missed you too, buddy."

Jo burst into tears.

She couldn't have prevented it. The sob was from a place deeper than one of her little hiccup-cries, and it had the force of a gale wind.

"Jo..." Gavin started.

She put the sleeve of her sweater to her face to staunch the flow. But it was no use.

Kayla, who stood to Gavin's side, stirred. "Come on, Jackson." She walked over and took her brother's arm, gently extricating him from the man's body. "Let's go for a walk."

Reluctantly, the boy let go of Gavin.

"I'll be here, buddy," he said, looking at Jo's face for confirmation that he could stay at least a few minutes.

Still crying, she bobbed her head in something that approximated a nod.

Kayla cast her a hard-to-read glance as she grabbed her coat and her brother's hand and ushered him outside.

At the slamming of the door, they were alone.

Jo swallowed back a sob. Then she just looked at him.

Unlike the suit and tie from the other day, he wore athletic pants like he had that time at the grocery store months ago. Underneath a dark wool jacket, a blue waffle knit long-sleeved shirt matched his eyes perfectly. He swayed on his feet, like he didn't know what to do, whether it was okay to comfort her. Slung over his arm was her deep purple coat.

"Oh," she said.

"You left it at the school," he said. "I told them I'd bring it to you. Since we live in the same area and all. Didn't want you freezing to death over the weekend."

"Oh." She blinked and found his eyes again. "Thank you."

He set the coat gently on the back of her couch.

Was this why he was here? To just bring her her coat? And here she was, bawling like he'd been the one to end things.

Or was there more? Gavin stood still, his eyes locked on hers. There was a fluttering in her belly. Did he—

"I'm sorry I gave Jeannie the Arietta brochure to give to you," he said. "When I toured the school during my interview, I just couldn't help but think how much Jackson would love it. And maybe do well there. So I slipped her the information, just to make sure you knew about it."

Her voice shook. "You were right."

"I didn't know for sure, of course, but I knew you'd be able to figure it out. You always do." His voice deepened. "I'm sorry if I ever acted like you didn't."

Jo wondered if *this* was why he was there. To bring her coat, but also to put the past between them to rest, especially now that they'd be sharing the same school community. She'd had her chance with him, after all, and she'd let him slip away.

"Oh, and there's this." He shifted and pulled something out of his pocket, giving a nervous laugh. He handed over a pamphlet with a bright yellow school bus on the front, the material crinkling as it exchanged hands.

Their fingers brushed, and a shiver of excitement ran the length of her arm.

"It's the number for the transportation service the school uses," he explained. "They wanted you to have it, in case the driver gets lost on Monday." He dove his hands into his pockets. "I wouldn't want to pass Jackson on my drive to work and see him out there hitch-hiking."

Jo sniffed back a laugh and bit her lip. "No, he'd probably get in the car with whoever was playing Taylor Swift."

They shared a smile that was so much like before that it made Jo's heart ache. She could tell he was torn about whether he should come to her—but whether that was about desire or just old habit, she didn't know.

Like a timer winding down, she felt their conversation coming to a close. He'd given her the two things he'd come for, he'd apologized. Soon he'd shift his weight, jiggle the keys in his pocket, and make his way to the door.

Unless she did something.

"Arietta is a great school," he said. "I hope he's as happy there as I've been—"

"Gavin." She took two steps closer to him, her heartbeat echoing in every molecule of her body.

"Y-yes?"

She didn't know if there was a fourth reason he was there—beyond the coat and the brochure and the closure—but she hoped. She hoped with every pounding of her heartbeat.

"Gavin, I'm sorry," she whispered. "I'm sorry for yelling at you in the hospital parking lot—you were right, I was so scared —and I'm sorry for pushing you away."

He stood stock-still, his face revealing nothing.

"It's hard for me to let anyone into our life here," she continued. "Our very complicated, messy life. I've been doing it on my own for so long... It's hard for me to admit I need anyone's help. Or want it." Her voice cracked. "It's hard for me to admit I need you. But I—I do. You brought me such joy and laughter and passion, I'd forgotten how good that could feel." She swallowed. "I need you and I want you and I love you. I don't know if you just came here to give me the coat—"

"No."

"—but I wanted you to know that if..." His reply caught up with her. She took a deep breath. "It wasn't just the coat?"

"No." He shook his head once, and in two long strides, he had his arms around her, pulling her close. His hands found her waist and pressed her against him as her own arms encircled his neck.

She tilted her face to look up at him, feeling his chest rise and fall with deep breaths, his heart hammering against her own.

It was like they were dancing again in that darkened hallway at the high school, but everything was much more complicated and much more simple.

His face was more serious than she'd seen, his voice husky with need. "I love you, Josephine Palladino. I'm not going anywhere."

He kissed her then, long and slow—a kiss salty from her tears, and one that was like a chorus, solid and true, pointing them back to where they belonged.

When they parted, they were both smiling.

She held onto the collar of his jacket. "Full disclosure: when we had that first IEP meeting, I had fantasies about ripping off your tie and shoving it down your throat."

"Kinky." His grin spread. "Full disclosure: I've had a lot of fantasies about you, too. When we had that first IEP meeting, you bent over and I saw your bra."

Her jaw fell open. "Nuh-uh."

He laughed. "Yeah."

"Really?" That red bra, the one she thought was well hidden under her shirt. Not so much, apparently.

"Uh-huh." His eyes twinkled devilishly.

"Is that why you—"

He shook his head. "No. But I'd be lying if I didn't admit that it got my brain going in that direction. That was some bra."

She pushed his jacket off his shoulders. He slipped it off and tossed it on top of hers on the couch.

"Can you stay?" she asked.

"Oh yeah." He gathered her to him again. When he kissed her, it left no question in her mind how much he'd missed her.

"What time do your kids go to bed again?" he asked.

She laughed. "Not early enough."

His mouth found her neck. "I want to hang out with the kids," he said. "And you. I want us all to spend the rest of the day together. But when night comes, we'll put them in their rooms and stick earphones in their ears if we have to," he said. "Because I've got big plans for us to do that thing. And then the other thing."

Jo squirmed closer. "I like that thing."

"I know you do. Trust me, we're doing the thing. All night long."

# EPILOGUE

## KAYLA

*S*ix months later, the month after she turned seventeen, Kayla's mom's boyfriend moved in with them.

She knew it was going to happen, but they'd wanted to wait until Jackson had settled in at Arietta Academy. He had loved it when he visited, but still it took some time to adjust to a new school, new routine, new teachers—the usual autism stuff.

Jackson had been riding to school with the aforementioned boyfriend, Gavin, where he'd been forced to listen to terrible oldies music like Train and Savage Garden. At least, it would've been torture to Kayla.

Gavin was a development officer at Arietta, which meant he hit rich people and companies up for money. They'd already had one or two fancy fundraisers for the school where her mom had gone as his date. But really Kayla thought it was just an excuse to dress up and make out somewhere that wasn't their couch at home.

Kayla had to admit that she didn't like Gavin at first. But he grew on her, like a bad pop song. When he came over to try to woo her mom back after their breakup, she might not have let him in if she didn't know that her brother loved and missed him almost as much as her mother did. Which, judging by the angsty music she played those couple of weeks, was a lot.

That weekend after Gavin moved in, they had a barbecue to celebrate. Kayla's friend Misty and her mom came over, and some of her mother's support group friends were there with their kids. Gavin's friend Angelo had come—Misty thought he was kind of hot—and Gavin's family of course, including his sister Liz and her family since they were in town.

They stood around the backyard, the June sun beating down. Dirk from support group had come with his daughter, Deenie, who stared fascinated at Gavin's one-year-old niece as she took tottering steps on the grass. Over by the grill, which Holly's husband was manning, that older woman Jackie was standing around with Angelo, drinking beers and laughing while Misty and Misty's mom sat on a bench nearby, both drooling over his biceps. Holly was there with Sean and Abby, of course. Abby sat on a picnic bench by Toby Yates, staring at the dark-haired teen like she was getting a crush on him. If she was, he'd better treat her right. Kayla liked all of their neighbors pretty well, but Abby was her favorite.

Gavin, her mom, and Gavin's parents stood in a circle drinking iced teas. Her mom had become interested in the Jewish stuff, and Dina was giving her tips on how to approach their rabbi.

"Our people don't proselytize," Dina was saying. "You'll need to be really persistent until he gives you what you want."

Gavin laughed. "I think Jo can be pretty persistent and stubborn when she wants something."

Her mouth falling open, Mom smacked him playfully. Still laughing, Gavin dodged the smack and put his arms around her from behind, which he did a lot and was sort of cute bordering on gross. Mom seemed to like it, though.

Before they started kissing, Kayla stepped away to fish a cold water out of the cooler stashed by the house. It was finally starting to get hot. Sean appeared by her side a minute later, so he probably had the same idea.

"Hey," he said. "Pretty warm out here, yeah?"

"Yeah, it is." His shirt was sticking to him, but it wasn't as gross as it seemed. Kayla kind of got why Misty called him "Thor" when she saw him around.

"I think we're almost out of drinks," he said. "Maybe you and I can run and get some more?"

"Sure."

He looked at something over her shoulder, then quickly added, "As a friend, I mean. Because I respect you as a woman."

What? Sean could be so weird. "O-kay…"

She turned around to see what he'd been staring at, but there was just her mother and Gavin, giving her funny smiles like they were trying not to laugh.

Whatever.

"Let me just go splash my face," Sean said, darting inside. It was probably a good idea. He'd turned really red from the heat.

"I like him better than the other one," Gavin stage-whispered to Mom, but she could hear him perfectly well across the ten feet of grass between them. Maybe he'd suffered hearing loss from all the Coldplay.

"Shh," her mom said, swatting him.

Kayla hated to do it, but she walked a few steps towards them and took the bait. "What are you talking about?"

Gavin's parents, Dina and Ray, were now sitting on lawn chairs nearby with Jackson between them, talking on his speech device. Sometimes Kayla thought they liked to talk with it more than he did.

But as she heard their words, Dina leaned forward in her seat and called, "What's this about?"

"Sean likes her," Gavin said. "It's obvious."

God, could they not keep their voices down? Her face flushed.

"Are you looking for a boyfriend, Kayla?" Dina asked. "Because I know some nice boys at—"

"No," Gavin said. "No, Mom."

Kayla hadn't been dating—not since Austin the douchebag. It might've had something to do with her brother's reputation as her personal bodyguard, with a tendency to put a hurt on any guys who pissed her off.

She might've had something to do with spreading that rumor.

"Shh," she hissed, annoyed with them all. "Sean can probably hear you from inside. Plus he doesn't like me. We're just friends."

She and Sean had known each other since they were kids, ever since his mom had been Jackson's speech therapist and he'd played Legos with her while they worked. And Checkers, which he'd been terrible at. He probably didn't like her like that. That would be weird.

Right?

Mom sighed. "At least he's one of the nicer ones," she said. There was a twinkle in her eye.

"Oh. My. God." To get them to shut up and drown out their voices, she went to the music Gavin had on shuffle and chose Pharrell Williams' "Happy."

Proving he was her number-one guy, Jackson jumped up and started dancing, because, true to its title, the song put some pep in his step. Pretty soon, Abby, Toby, Deenie, and the other kids joined in.

Gavin started singing along, and then Mom. Angelo began bopping his head with Jackie as they downed their beers. Dina and Ray stood and sort of shuffled and swayed to the music.

When Sean came out of the bathroom, he started laughing. She hoped he hadn't heard what they'd said. But then, surprising her, he started rocking out too.

Kayla just stared at all of them, amused and faintly horrified, when Sean came up and grabbed her by the waist, spinning her around.

It was just once, just a brief touch, but it was enough that a single, strange thought popped into her head.

*Maybe.*

# BOOK DISCUSSION QUESTIONS

- If you've attended a school meeting (on either side of the table), can you relate to the tension Jo experiences before and during the special education meetings she attends?
- Near the beginning of the story, Kayla tells her mom she needs to "get a life" because she spends all her time on Jackson's needs. Do you think this is a fair criticism? How do you achieve balance in your life?
- When Jo takes Jackson to the grocery store, they experience a range of responses from the people around them. If you have a loved one in your life who's disabled and/or neurotypical, how do people respond when you're out in public? How do you respond to others who are different in your community?
- Jo delays helping Kayla explore colleges because she's so focused on Jackson. If you're a parent of multiple kids, how do you balance their needs?
- Why do you think Jo is attracted to Gavin?

- What do you make of the ethical dilemma in the relationship between Gavin and Jo? Do you feel they make the right decisions throughout the story? Why or why not?
- After Gavin comes over to their home, Jo reflects that most people do not see the messier reality of special needs families. Do you think this is true?
- Gavin's mom tells him, "A woman thinks of her children above all else—especially when they're struggling." Does this match your experience? Why or why not?
- How do the characters of Josephine and Gavin evolve throughout the novel? What about Jackson, Kayla, and Gavin's mom?

# ABOUT GINA ANDREW

A writer of women's fiction, Gina Andrew is fueled by hot tea and good music. She lives outside Houston, Texas, with her husband and two sons, both of whom are autistic and intellectually disabled and provide her with challenges, joy, and laughter each and every day.

She also writes romance as G.G. Andrew. In both genres, she loves to play with words, write her way through challenging plots, and watch her characters develop unexpected connections in love and friendship.

When she's not penning fiction, Gina is a freelance writer for BookBub who also enjoys yoga, cooking, thrift shopping, genealogy, all things Halloween, and that popcorn smell at the movie theater.

Find out more or join her mailing list at https://ggandrew. com/.

# ALSO BY THIS AUTHOR

## GINA ANDREW/G.G. ANDREW

*Graffiti in Love*

*Stolen in Love*

*Girl Meets Grammarian*

*Crazy, Sexy, Ghoulish*

*Scary, Lovesick, Foolish*

*Jaded, Bearded, Wolfish*

*Geeky, Freaky, Clueless*

*Ghost Fire*

*Somewhere Warm*

*Someplace Secret*